# KENTISH CRIME SERIES

# OMNIBUS EDITION

# VOLUME ONE

# INDEX

# IN THE PAST

**Praise for In The Past**

*'An excellent summer read. I'm a fan of Agatha Christie and Dick Francis. Once I started I found it really difficult to put down. The story kept me guessing right up to the very end. I would definitely recommend it as an excellent summer garden read. I enjoyed it so much I've ordered the next one.'*

*'Engaging and gripping. Would love to read more from E M Elliot.'*

*'A really enjoyable and page turning read from start to finish. Looking forward to the next one please!'*

**Praise for Opportunity for Death**

*'A must for mystery addicts! Read it!'- Dorothy Simpson*

*'Superb read. A classic whodunit brought up to date.'*

*'Start to finish in an evening, not able to put down.*

*'Intriguing and totally absorbing. A wonderful and fascinating tale of the intrigues of English village life... beautifully written and well told, a brilliant book to disappear into.'*

# IN THE PAST

# BY

# E M ELLIOT

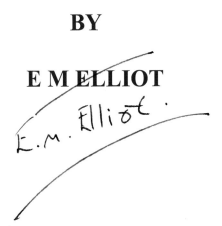

For Allan

who has always believed in me

# Chapter One

Katherine Muier gazed at the wreck in front of her and, not for the first time, wondered whether she had done the right thing. Wynenden Farm was a traditional Kentish Farmhouse which consisted of a brick base, white weatherboarding and a Kent Peg Tile roof. Currently covered in brambles and ivy which had cunningly, and sneakily, weaved their way through any little cracks they could find, searching for ways into the house. Persistence had paid off, ivy had crept in so successfully that it had created a wallpaper effect in parts of the interior; an absolute nightmare for any house as it eroded brickwork, and set about its domination determinedly. That, along with the leaking roof, collapsed ceiling in parts of the house, rustic wiring and atrocious plumbing, meant that the house was in need of some serious TLC.

Katherine had purchased the house from the Wynenden Park Estate owned by Sir Geoffrey Percevall-Sharparrow. It had been empty for more than thirty years, Katherine had stumbled across it, and its five acres, when out for a walk one bright spring day. Now, a surprisingly swift six months later, she had just completed on the property and the reality of what she had done hit her like a slap in the face. She leant back against the rickety gate, only to stagger backwards when its rotten timbers gave way. Composing herself, she gingerly picked her way through the long grass, keeping as much to the path trodden down by her surveyor, architect and builder on their numerous visits, as possible.

Pushing aside her panic attack of fears, she did her best to immerse herself in her usual positive, bright and cheery self, and retrieved the cumbersome iron key to the front door from her rucksack. Fiddling around to get it into just the right position to open the door, she smiled with satisfaction as it gave a heavy clunk into place, and turned the key creakily in the lock. As quickly as the wave of panic had hit her moments before, a frisson of excitement buzzed inside her. This was it, this was hers, she almost couldn't believe it. She shoved the door with her shoulder to open it, swollen by years of neglect and the dampness of the autumn season, even the warmth of the October day failing to have any effect. As usual, she was hit by the damp, mushroomy smell, which escaped in a rush each time the door was open. Her tall, skinny figure stooped slightly under the door frame to enter in. She stopped and listened, silence, and then faintly, the drip, drip, drip of one of the many leaks.

'Hi Kitty,' called a cheery voice from behind her, making her jump. It was Dougie Brown her builder who, like many, automatically called her Kitty, rather than Katherine, she could never fathom out why some people she met called her by her school nickname from the offset. He was a short, round, jolly fellow in his mid-fifties, with a huge smile that filled his chubby face, and a messy mop of grey hair. Her 5'9" towered over his 5'5", but what he lacked in height, he made up for in personality. She'd never seen him grumpy, but a cynical part of her thought that perhaps this was due to the huge profit he would be making out of the restoration of her house, if the figures he'd presented her with were anything to go by.

'Hi Dougie, how are you?'

'Grand, just grand.' He smiled, rubbing his hands together. 'So, where do you want to start?' He was here to go through, one final time, the schedule of works, before they started on site the following week.

'Page one and work our way through I suppose.'

They progressed their way through the two reception rooms, the jumble of smaller rooms at the back, which would be knocked into one large kitchen/breakfast room, and were upstairs going through the four bedrooms, other rooms which would become two bathrooms, and the loft area, when they were interrupted by the one voice which set Katherine's heckles rising – Andrew Battle.

'Kitty, looking as lovely as ever,' he oozed giving her, what he thought, was his most seductive, and winning smile.

'Andrew.' She pulled a taught smile in response. Her gold-flecked brown eyes narrowed suspiciously at him. She knew what was coming, and wished he'd leave her alone. Dougie stood behind her, his arms crossed firmly across his chest, and scowled at Andrew. He too knew what Andrew was after.

Andrew continued, seemingly oblivious to the hostility facing him. 'Just picked the keys up then?'

'Yes.'

'Complete wreck, isn't it? Far too much to do. You really don't want to be worrying your pretty little head about something like this. An enchanting woman like you must be far too busy to bother with this sort of project?' He tilted his head slightly to one side, and gave her a knowing look with his piercing blue eyes.

I think I want to slap him, thought Katherine, and I do wish he'd stop calling me Kitty, far too over familiar for a Lothario like him. 'Actually, Andrew, it's exactly what I need, and what I have spent my whole life looking forward to, taking on a project like this.' All 47 years of them she thought to herself.

'OK. OK. Tell you what. I will add another ten percent to my offer price, how about that? Can't say fairer than that. I'll take it off your hands. Won't take my solicitor long to get the paperwork sorted. How about it?' His smile seemed pleasant, but Katherine could see the hardness in his eyes.

She sighed, and was glad that Dougie was beside her, coiled like a stubby spring ready to pounce and remove the irritation from her house. 'Andrew.' He smiled encouragingly back at her. 'Let me make this absolutely clear one last time. I do *not*, and *never will*, want to sell this house. And if, in many years to come, I should change my mind and want to sell it, I will never. Do you hear? NEVER. Sell the house to you. Do I make myself absolutely clear?' she glared at him.

He stared deeply at her, the air bristling with animosity from him. Quietly, almost imperceptibly, he replied. 'You're making a mistake Kitty, a *big* mistake. I will get this house, whether you like it or not.' He swung round, and strode arrogantly out of the room. His back stiff in his tailored shirt, the diamonds on his watch flashing furiously. They listened in silence, until they heard the roar of one of his many high performance cars, screech off up the lane.

Katherine shivered. 'Did he just threaten me?'

'Pay no attention to him. The house is legally yours, there's nothing he can do. He likes to throw his weight around, expects to get his own way, and throws his toys out of his pram if he doesn't. Now, let's get on shall we?'

# Chapter Two

With her old house, ten miles away, sold and having rented a small, modern, terraced house in the village of Wynenden, to be near to her new house, and to enable her to start integrating into village life. Katherine took the few days, before the work was due to start on Wynenden Farm, to continue to familiarise herself with the area on foot. Wynenden Village was not one she knew particularly well. Her work as an administrator at a Preparatory School, fifteen miles away, kept her busy during the week. Prior to her springtime walk, which had resulted in the discovery of Wynenden Farm, she had tended to visit villages around where her previous house was located, in the opposite direction to Wynenden.

She saw it as fate that she had been sent up to Wynenden School, an Independent Mixed School for children aged 3 to 18, to deliver some urgent paperwork and have a look around, because prior to a meeting the system at her school had crashed, and there was no chance of e-mailing the necessary paperwork to them. She was taken by the prettiness of the village, driving through that day. It had a main road running though it, this being the link between two main roads which both led down to the coast, but the heart of it was set just off this. The large village green, which played host to village events in the summer. A narrow lane looped round the green in an arch, which took you up first to the village primary school and a play area, and also playing fields, on the left hand side. Beyond them further up round the green, was the village hall followed by the Church. The remainder of the green, from the Church back down the other side of the arch, to the main road was filled with an eclectic mix of houses, built during different periods from Tudor to Victorian, all fairly substantial properties, and all originally owned as part of the Wynenden Park Estate, until death duties got in the way, and necessitated the sale of assets from time to time, to assist with the payment of these duties.

Opposite the green, along the far side of the main road was the public house – The Speckled Goose - a post office cum stores, a small Michelin Star Restaurant, a butchers, a terrace of Edwardian houses, a doctors surgery, a veterinary surgery and a garage, which was purely there for mechanical purposes rather than for the sale of new, or second-hand cars or fuel. Whilst the main road took away some of the rural character of the village, it ensured that there was enough passing trade to boost the resident businesses, and ensure their continued place within the village - a rare occurrence - with so many villages now without shops, pubs or any such kind of local business.

Further up the road from the public house, in the opposite direction to the shops, was a housing estate built in the 1970's. Perhaps innovative in their time, but now very dated, and rather an eyesore, in an otherwise picturesque village. But this was where Katherine had managed to rent her temporary house, so she couldn't complain too much.

Katherine had deliberately organised for completion on the houses, and the building works to start, during the time she had off for the two week October half term. Ignoring the piles of boxes, which ought to be unpacked, Katherine shrugged on her pink gilet, zipped some cash into her inside pocket, grabbed her keys and phone, and set off for a walk around the village.

Coming out of the housing estate, she turned right and walked along the pavement to the post office and stores and entered.

'Good Morning,' came a cheerful voice from behind the stores counter.

'Oh. Hello.'

'Nice Morning out there, lovely and crisp.'

'Mmm, yes, it is.' Katherine looked round for the newspapers, and spied them over by the window, pondering whether to go for intelligence and get something like The Times, or get something less highbrow. In the end she opted for The Times, and perused the magazines impressed by the range available, she picked up a copy of Hello! Magazine for some light reading, and took them to the till. 'Are you open on a Sunday?' she asked.

The older woman, with tightly permed, grey hair, who, Katherine estimated, was in her early sixties, clicked her tongue in disapproval, making Katherine feel as though she had committed a major faux pas. 'I'm afraid we are. I don't believe in it myself, but it's not me who owns this place. But I told them right from the start that I wasn't going to work on a Sunday. It's a day of rest and I'm in Church every Sunday morning.'

'Oh, OK. I just wanted to know if I'd be able to get a Sunday paper here?' She placed her paper and magazine on the counter.

The woman's eyes lit up. 'New to the village are you?' Katherine nodded. 'Which house have you moved to?'

Well, they're not backwards in coming forwards round here, thought Katherine, mildly irritated, and not wanting to proffer the information. 'It's just on the outskirts of the village.' She replied, hoping her vagueness would be enough. She ought to have known better.

'Really? Which one? Do you mean on the estate?' The woman's brow wrinkled in thought.

'Um, well I'm living there at the moment.' Perhaps ambiguity would halt the questions.

'At the moment, does that mean temporarily?'

I'll give her that, she's sharp thought Katherine. 'Er, yes. Just while I have work done on the house I've bought.'

'You must be Kitty!' exclaimed the woman. 'You've just bought Wynenden Farm haven't you? I'm Betty by the way.' She offered her hand, along with a beaming smile.

How on earth does she know who I am? Let alone which house I've bought? Privacy was the one thing which Katherine treasured the most. She liked to keep things to herself, having seen the way that gossip can be produced out of thin air, by parents at the Prep School, and experience from living in her previous village. Gingerly she took the woman's hand, and shook it.

'We've all been expecting you. You've caused great excitement in the village! Sir Geoffrey is very territorial about his Estate. We couldn't believe it when we heard that he had sold off Wynenden Farm! We'd never have believed it! Of course, that Andy Battle has been trying to get his hands on it for years, and Sir Geoffrey has refused to sell it to him. Some even said that he offered Sir Geoffrey two million pounds!' Betty paused for breath.

Katherine was startled by this news. No wonder Andrew - or Andy as he seemed to be known - was so furious that she had bought the house. But why on earth could he be so desperate to buy it? Granted, it was a lovely house, in a stunning position, with loads of potential, but even done up it probably wouldn't be worth half of what he had offered for it. And why had Sir Geoffrey sold it to her at below market price? When she had approached him, or rather his Estate Manager, Ted, about possibly purchasing the house, a price had been offered to her. She knew from having researched the local property market, that it was below market value, and despite her raising this point, -which some thought she was mad to do but her conscience told her to - with Ted, the price was not adjusted. Most would think her a fool for even suggesting that the price was too low, but she was honest, and she wanted to buy the house at a fair price. Properties like Wynenden Farm were like gold dust, most having already been snatched up, done up, and sold on at a huge profit.

'So, how did you manage to get Sir Geoffrey to sell you the house? We've all been speculating.' She looked eagerly at Katherine, not able to believe her luck at being one of the first to set eyes on her.

There's no way I'm giving her any information, thought Katherine. 'You appear to know a lot about me. How is that so?' She tried not to sound terse, but felt ridiculously violated.

'Oh, Dougie was overheard in the pub talking to one of his builders about the job, and Hetty who works there is such a gossip, she told anyone who would listen.'

Not the only one who likes to gossip, thought Katherine whilst making a mental note to ask Dougie not to discuss the house, or her, anywhere in public. She absolutely did not want her day to day life broadcast across the village. 'It seems that you are very well informed. I don't think I can really add to what you know.' And there's no way I'm answering your last question, she thought. She offered the money for the paper and magazine to Betty, and smiled as sweetly as she could, realising - perhaps a little late - that if she were grumpy, it would be all round the village in a flash, but the "grumpy" would evolve into "stuck up", "arrogant" or worse.

Sensing defeat, Betty took the money, and proffered the change, disappointed that she had not found out more, but still quietly delighted, that she had been the first to encounter the most talked about woman in the village. 'Lovely to meet you Kitty. Anything you want to know about the village, just pop in and ask. I'm always willing to help.'

'Thank you Betty, I will remember that.' And with a smile still fixed on her face, Katherine strolled to the door, doing her best not to bolt for it and run. Just as she pulled the door closed behind her, she heard Betty dialling a number, and start gossiping to someone about her down the telephone. She rolled her eyes, and sighed, hoping that tomorrow, she would be old news. She continued up the road, pausing to read the simple menu at the village's Michelin Star pride and joy – The Restaurant at Wynenden – it sounded delectable, seasonal, not overly fussy, and rel-

atively reasonably priced. Perhaps she should have a cele-
bratory meal there with some friends? She pondered. Her
pondering's took her on to Wynenden Butchers where,
bracing herself for another interrogation, she joined the
queue in the tiny shop. Murmurs of "Good Morning" were
made and to avoid any further interaction, Katherine studiously studied the interesting array of products available
in the chilled display unit, until it was her turn.

She smiled at the short, rotund, bald figure, behind the
counter. 'Please could I have a couple of the lamb chops,
and a couple of the lamb, mint and apple sausages?'

'Of course.' He silently went about his work. 'That'll
be £6.70 thank you.' He smiled at her.

'Thanks,' she replied, handing over £20, relieved that
the butcher was not as inquisitive as Betty.

'Don't look so worried,' he chortled, handing her the
change, 'we're not all as forward as Betty.'

Katherine felt her body relax, unaware that she had been
holding her breath. She smiled, and said diplomatically
'Well, she appears to be very friendly.' Suspecting that it
was the butcher, Betty had phoned when she had left the
shop.

'Aye, that she is. She means well, and she's got a heart
of gold, but working in that shop doesn't really get her out
into the real world, if you know what I mean. Most people
don't want to chat for hours these days, they just want to
rush in and straight out again. I think she gets a bit lonely
in there sometimes. A bit starved of real conversation.
Anyway, I'm Bob, Bob Bond, pleased to meet you Kitty.'
He offered a clean hand, which had just been washed under
steaming hot water.

'Pleased to meet you too Bob.' She responded, taking his hand, and thinking that she would forever be known as Kitty in the village, and not Katherine. Was there any point in correcting them?

'Welcome to the village. You'll get used to us!' He was interrupted by the tinkle of the bell over the door as it opened. 'Morning Mrs Bush.' He waved at the sparrow like figure hurrying into the shop.

'Bye,' called Katherine making a speedy exit, in case Mrs Bush turned out to be working undercover for Betty.

The remainder of her stroll was, fortunately, uneventful and upon returning home Katherine settled down with the house plans, the kitchen plans, and the piles of catalogues and samples she had gathered. Now the fun would really begin, as she buried herself excitedly in the many decisions which still had to be made.

# Chapter Three

A couple of days later, Katherine was up early so that she could get to the farmhouse before the builders arrived for Day One, of the restoration. She pulled her eight year old, bright red, VW Golf into the drive, and parked it on some flattened rough grass. She got out, grabbed her trusty rucksack - which was packed with plans and a flask of coffee - from the back seat, locked up, and walked silently over the dew drenched drive. Barely recognizable as a drive, because it was so overgrown, the odd bald patch where gravel or some other kind of unrecognizable surface had been, indicated that it was not part of the garden.

She stopped, and drank in the glorious silence, the odd tweet from a bird awakening, and nothing else. From a distance, the house looked like it had some kind of fuzzy hairdo. A couple of windows peeped out from the mass of brambles and ivy, which covered the house from ground to roof. Again, she trod her way carefully to the front door, and opened up. Quietly she walked around, absorbing all the decay and neglect, drinking it in to store away as memories, so that she would remember how much the house had changed in years to come, feeling that photos alone would not do it justice. She shivered slightly, and momentarily felt an unsettling eeriness. She shook her head to clear it, and moved away into another room.

The silence was broken shortly afterwards by the distant rumble of vehicles, as they made their way cautiously up the narrow lane. It was as though someone had said "lights, camera, action!". In an instant, the drive was full of cars and vans, and there were two lorries piled high with scaffolding poles and other building equipment, queuing and blocking the narrow lane.

Katherine ran cautiously down the stairs and out through the front door. 'Morning Dougie!' she grinned.

'You ready for us?' he laughed.

'As I'll ever be! Bring it on!'

Men swarmed all over the site in purposeful mode. Several were set to clear the site immediately surrounding the house, to enable ease of access and the building of the small garden room extension, and to enable the scaffolding to go up securely. Katherine went over a couple of points with Dougie, and then retreated to her car. Taking out the flask off coffee and sipping the hot liquid, she wrinkled her nose up at the slightly plasticky taste, which was always the unfortunate consequence of drinking a hot liquid out of plastic - particularly a flask lid - and wished she'd brought a china mug to drink from. She made a mental note to do so next time.

As far as she was concerned, watching the workmen working, and her house begin to emerge from its Sleeping Beautyesque slumber, was more exciting than going to the cinema. It was incredible how much had been cleared by the time they stopped two hours later, for a coffee break. There were beeping of horns in the lane as another lorry, delivering a portaloo for the workmen, tried to get the scaffolding lorries to move. With a bit of negotiation, the builders carried the portaloo off the lorry themselves, and let the driver have the fun task of reversing back up the single track lane. With the drive blocked there was nowhere for him to turn.

Unable to get her car out, and with no desire to get in the way of the workmen, Katherine took a stroll up the lane to stretch her legs and warm up, as the chill in the air had settled on her whilst sitting for so long in the car without her engine running. Upon her return she gasped at the sight of her house, now externally free from its fuzzy hair.

'Looks a bit different, doesn't it?' grinned Dougie.

'You can say that again! It looks huge! So much bigger than I thought it would be, it's amazing!

'It certainly is a lovely example of a Tudor house. Once we get the ivy off the inside, you will be able to see so many more beams. There are some pretty chunky ones there.'

'Great! I can't wait.' She studied the building. 'I never knew there were two fireplaces. How come I missed them? There's a chimney at that end, as well as the large one in the centre. Where's the other fireplace?'

'Bricked up I suppose, we can have a look when we've cleared the ivy off. Maybe it's just covered in that pesky stuff?' He looked thoughtful.

'OK. So when's the scaffolding going up?'

'As soon as. I would hope they'll make a start by mid afternoon. They'll keep going as long as it's light, but it should all be up by the end of tomorrow.'

'And it's definitely being covered?'

'Oh yes, don't you worry. That house will be more water tight than it has been in years.'

It had, perhaps, been a little extravagant of Katherine to insist on the scaffolding being covered in thick plastic, to protect the house from rain. But she didn't want anything to slow the build down. With winter approaching, she didn't want to get caught out and for the house to end up filled with rain or snow, because the roof was off. It was hoped that the majority of the roof timbers were going to stay, but if more needed to be replaced it would delay the re-roofing, which in turn would have a knock on effect to the rest of the build. And it would be typical that the bright, sunny, autumnal days would instantly change into wet, hideous, weather.

Satisfied that there were going to be no further dramatic changes to the house that day, Katherine negotiated her car out into the lane, and drove home to spend more time poring over the brochures, narrowing down the choice of fixtures and fittings, the radiators and the million and one other things she needed to make decisions on, so that products could be ordered and not delay the works.

By the end of the week the scaffolding was up, the brambles and ivy had been ripped away - both internally and externally - and work was starting on stripping the roof and the internal walls - those with Listed Building Consent to remove - were starting to come down. The builders bucked the trend and turned up prior to their 8 a.m. start time, worked hard, took the same breaks at the same time each day, and finished at 4 p.m.

Katherine lay in bed and stretched, it was Friday morning and she was aware that next week she would be back at work, and unable to be on site every day. Fortunately, she had managed to persuade the school to let her start an hour earlier each day for the next few months, and have Wednesday afternoon off for the remainder of the Michaelmas Term and also the Lent Term. Though not ideal, this at least ensured that she would be on site once a week, and if anything urgent cropped up she'd just have to deal with it. When the evenings became lighter, she would be able to go to the house after work each day, until then, she would have to make do.

As she dressed and breakfasted, she thought smugly that the weasel-faced, rat of an ex-husband of hers, was missing out big time. Married for twenty years, relatively blissfully she had thought, she and Rex had been desperate for a family from day one of getting married when she was twenty-three. Sadly, despite operation after operation, and treatment after treatment, nothing happened until, suddenly, at the age of forty-three she became pregnant. Assuming that it was an early start to the menopause, she had gone to her G.P. only to discover that she was pregnant. They had, she thought, been thrilled at the prospect of finally fulfilling their dream of parenthood, after such a struggle. Rex had become more attentive than he had for a long time; they excitedly read the books, the magazines, surfed the net, and drenched themselves in the forthcoming joy. Tragically, at sixteen weeks, and totally out of the blue, Katherine miscarried. She was devastated at having come so close to such joy, and having it so cruelly snatched away. She thought that Rex felt the same, but just when she felt nothing worse could possibly happen, and in the depths of deep despair, he left her.

Still numb from the shock of losing the baby, his callousness was uncomprehending to her. Blocking it out for several weeks, hoping he was going to walk back through the door as though nothing had happened. When the reality finally hit that he wasn't going to, it was the last straw and pushed her into a deep depression which was, over time, overcome with the help of medication, counselling and the support, care, consideration, love and kindness of her closest friends and her parents. In the cold light of day she had wondered, and still wondered, whether she ever knew him. How could someone who was supposed to be your life partner treat you like that? How on earth could there have been, in her view, no indication that something was wrong in their marriage? In time she came to believe that he was having a midlife crisis. He'd left her a week after her miscarriage, for a much younger woman. He never told her, and she never wanted to know, how long it had been going on, because that would mean that the special few weeks she had experienced of being pregnant would be devalued and, worse, the thought that maybe he had not even wanted their precious baby.

Now, four years later, he was forty-eight and had had a string of girlfriends, each younger than the last, and in amongst these he had tried to come back to Katherine. He begged, pleaded, promised, but she could no longer trust him and no longer loved him. She felt that she would just be a stop gap until some flighty young thing came along and took his fancy. Realizing he had burnt his bridges, he'd tried to get more than his fair share of their marital home, but by then Katherine was stronger and the fight kicked in. Why should she move? Why should he get more than he deserved after the way he had treated her? There were times when she felt he didn't deserve a penny. Yes, they may have made money on their house, but why should he get any of it? Fortunately the Judge presiding over the case was fair and split everything equally, and also ruled that Katherine should have the option to stay in the house. She re-mortgaged, gave her ex his share of the profit, and washed her hands of him. The struggle to pay the large mortgage each month was worth being free of him. From time to time she saw him, strutting around, dressing too young for is age, acting eighteen not forty-eight, and she felt sorry for him. He was all about appearance now, and she'd heard on the grapevine that he'd blown his share of the house on a flash car and splurging on girlfriends, and now lived in a pokey one bedroom rented flat in a less than desirable area.

But, here she was now, having moved on and glad that she was no longer with him, but mourned the loss of a close relationship, someone to talk to, to share experiences with, someone to comfort her in a way that best friends couldn't when both her parents had died in a car crash eighteen months ago. As their only child she had inherited their mortgage free house, savings, pensions and other assets. Leaving her, after inheritance tax, with a considerable lump sum, enabling her to buy Wynenden Farmhouse outright, pay for the renovation and, combined with her profit from her marital home, a nest egg for her future. Pushing these now melancholy thoughts away, she made herself reflect on how lucky she was, packed her rucksack for the day and set off to the farmhouse.

'Morning.' She smiled cheerfully to the builders as they all started for the day.

'Do you want to have a look at this fireplace then?' asked Dougie.

'Great! You've cleared the ivy then?' He nodded. 'Is it an open fireplace?'

'Not at the moment, it looks like it has been bricked up at some point. We'll have to pull some bricks away to see what's behind.'

'You sure that's ok? Do we need permission or anything?' Katherine had played it very much above board. Sir Geoffrey had been happy for her to have meetings with the local Conservation Officer, Planning Officer and Architect to discuss what may, or may not be, carried out and make the relevant applications, before exchange and completion as the house was Grade II Listed and the primary concern was to protect the house from inappropriate work or changes, and preserve its character and history.

'I had a word with the Conservation chap yesterday and he's happy for us to investigate, he'll probably pop out sometime today to see what we're up to anyway.'

'OK, that's fine then. Let's go. It'd be so exciting if there's another inglenook fireplace there!'

She and Dougie watched as Pete, one of Dougie's workers, started carefully tapping away at a brick. After a while they turned away and poured over plans whilst the banging and crashing echoed through the house all around them and the more refined tap, tap, tapping from Pete carried on.

'Bloody Hell!' shouted Pete, jumping back.

Katherine and Dougie started in surprise. 'What's up?' asked Dougie.

Pete's normally tanned and rosy face, had gone a peculiar shade of white. He pointed at the small opening he had made, about six bricks square.

Dougie strode over and peered into the dark recess. 'Shit!' he swore, leaping back. 'Sorry Katherine.'

Puzzled, Katherine couldn't work out what would freak two grown men out. 'What is it? Let me have a look.' She moved forward.

'I don't think you should,' said Dougie.

'Why ever not? It can't be that bad?' She looked from one to the other.

They glanced at one another, then Dougie spoke. 'There's ... There's a skeleton in there.'

'You're joking?' She paused, 'you *are* joking aren't you?' She looked nervously at them, and realized that they weren't. Her stomach bottomed out, and she felt a wave of nausea.

# Chapter Four

A swarm of police vehicles arrived a while later. After calling the police, Katherine and the builders left the building and stayed in their vehicles to await further instructions, nothing was to be disturbed. Katherine sat alone in her car shaking, clutching her coffee to her in an attempt to calm and warm her. Surely it must be a joke or something? It had been the grim realization that, apart from being virtually impossible, no one in their right mind would have bricked themselves up into a fireplace and, if they hadn't, then someone else had, and in that case the person must have been dead before they were bricked in. In other words it must have been murder. She trembled at the thought, the thought that something so awful had happened to someone, but not just that, that it had happened in her house, her dream house. She rested her cold, clammy, head on the steering wheel. A knock on the window made her start. She looked up to see a tall man using his fingers to indicate for her to put her window down. She fumbled with the keys and pressed the down button.

'Mrs Muier?' he asked.

'Yes.'

'I'm Detective Inspector Allix. I'd like to ask you a couple of questions if that's alright?' He looked questioningly at her. His face was kind but serious, with crinkles around his eyes from days off from his job when he could relax and smile. Katherine noticed a tiny scar on his chin, a result of his occupation or some other accident she wondered? She got out of the car and realized then how tall he was, at least 6' 2" she thought.

'I'm not sure that I can help you really,' she replied.

'Perhaps you could just tell me in your own words what happened this morning?' He looked kindly at her.

She did her best to recount what had happened, all the while D.I. Allix listened patiently, whilst slightly off to one side a non-uniformed woman made notes.

'And how long have you owned the house?'

'I completed last week. Tell me, what happened to whoever it was? Why are they there?'

'I don't really know any more than you have told me at the moment Mrs Muier. It will be sometime until I do. I'm afraid I'm going to have to ask you and your builders to leave the site.'

'How long for? They've only just started!'

'I'm not sure. Forensics will be here for some time. We are treating this as a suspicious death, and until such a time as we know more, and are satisfied that we have obtained all the evidence we require from this site, it will remain cordoned off. I'm sorry.'

Katherine felt irrationally ambivalent. On the one hand she was horrified that someone had seemingly come to an unpleasant end, but on the other hand she was desperate for the work to carry on at the house, and was irritated that they had to stop for an unknown period of time. The momentum which had begun was halted, and she worried that it may never get back to the way that it had been. She was aware of the D.I. talking, and shook her head to clear it. 'Sorry, what did you say? I guess I'm a bit shaken up.'

'That's understandable. I was just saying if you could give your details to my colleague, Detective Sergeant Windsor.' He indicated to the woman standing near him who had been taking notes. 'So that we can contact you when necessary, then you can go home. Would you like someone to accompany you?'

'No, no that's fine, thanks. I'll just speak to Dougie, my builder' She pointed to him, it looked like his details were already being taken.

'Fine. Thank you for your cooperation. We'll be in touch.' Katherine watched his tall, suited, figure stride off towards her house and speak to the uniformed policeman who was standing guard outside the front door. A few words and a nod and he disappeared inside.

There was a knock on the door, making Katherine start. She'd been curled up on the sofa with a cup of tea, brooding over the events of the day. Stiffly, she uncurled, feeling every one of her forty-seven years and more, and padded to the door. Cautiously she peered round it. It was Dougie. She smiled at the familiar face.

'Hi, come in. I was just having a cuppa, fancy one?' She led him through to the small, insipid, kitchen and flicked the switch on the kettle.

'I just thought I'd pop in to see how you are? You know, after this morning?' His worried face searched hers for an indication of how she was bearing up.

'Oh, I'm fine,' she sighed. 'I'll be back to myself by tomorrow. It's my own stupid fault. I shouldn't have taken a look. You know the saying "curiosity killed the cat" well I should have known better. I can't get rid of the image of that hideous grimace on the skull. Maybe they all look gruesome and I'm letting my imagination run away with me, but it really looked as though - whoever it was - was screaming, and doing so right up until the moment of death.' She shivered again at the memory.

'I know what you mean,' replied Dougie, 'best not to dwell on it.'

'Do you think it had been there for a while? I mean, do you think it could be really old, like hundreds of years?' she looked hopefully at him.

'Hmm, not sure, unlikely though. The fireplace would have been in use for many, many years. I can't believe it would have been bricked up for that long.'

'What about the bricks? Surely you could tell? I mean, if they are old, then the skeleton would be old?'

'Not necessarily. Reclaimed bricks could have been used. Doesn't necessarily mean anything.'

'So, what happens now?'

Dougie looked glum. This was the perfect job to keep them going through the winter. The last thing he wanted was a delay, which would mean a delay in payments be-cause the work was behind, and he had no other job lined up for his team until the spring, having put all his eggs in one basket. 'We have no choice. We have to wait until they have finished investigating the site, but I can't see us being back there on Monday.' He followed her with his mug of tea into the sitting room, and lowered his plump frame into a squashy chair.

'It'd be nice to know what was going on. They said they'd let me know. I guess they'll have police outside the house twenty-four hours a day until they have finished, won't they?'

'I would have thought so, but not got a clue really. Once word gets out they'll be a handful of ghoulish people who'll want to poke around.'

'Damn! That's the last thing I want, people poking around. I was hoping the work could carry on in quiet oblivion, the more people who know about this, the more they'll be nosing around. And what about the security risk once the police have gone? Do you think there'll be people snooping about on site after dark? What about the materials? There'll be a higher risk of them getting stolen, particularly those old, reclaimed, Kent Peg Tiles.'

'I know, they're twice the price of new ones. I suppose I'll have to get some kind of security up there initially. Just until the fuss has died down.'

'Oh, great, more cost. Sorry Dougie, I didn't mean it like that, I'm just hacked off that something I was so excited about has come crashing down, and to add insult to injury, it's going to cost me more.'

'That's ok Kitty. I'm as annoyed as you are. Still, I can't sit around here all afternoon, I'd best get back and do some paperwork whilst I have the time. Thanks for the tea.'

'No problem. If I hear anything, I'll let you know, but perhaps we can keep a lid on this as much as possible?' she looked at him questioningly.

'My lips are sealed. Though I think once it's got out, it'll be hard to stop the floodgate of rumours.'

Katherine sighed again, let him out, and went back to brooding on the sofa with her, now cold, cup of tea. Barely had she had a good wallow in her misery, when there was another knock at the door. This time it was D.I. Allix, accompanied by D.S.Windsor. Her offer of tea was refused, and she ushered them into the sitting room.

D.I. Allix waited until Katherine had settled herself, before he spoke. 'How are you?' he enquired.

'Oh, fine, you know, bit spooked, but ok thanks.' She glanced at D.S. Windsor who was sitting there poised, ready, and alert, in a black trouser suit and cream blouse buttoned to a respectfully high level, and low-healed, black lace up, shoes. Dull but practical. Her hair was a sort of mid-brown-cum-mousy mix, of collar length, tucked firmly behind her ears, making her look slightly fierce. Katherine glanced back to D.I. Allix, who looked a lot less fierce than his colleague.

'The skeleton has been removed now, but we will of course need access to the house for a while longer. Please be assured that we will hand it back to you as soon as it is possible.'

'Thanks. Can you tell me anything more about the ..., well...?' Her voice trailed off, and she shrugged and fiddled with her hands, not willing to say the "skeleton" word.

'Not a great deal at this moment, but I have been told that the skeleton is female, and younger, rather than older. Obviously, when I have further information, I, or one of my colleagues, will update you.'

He rose to go. Katherine got up to show them out, then made herself a replacement cup of hot tea, flopped down on the sofa again, and flicked the television on to watch the local news. She'd just missed the headlines, and the presenters went straight into their lead story, the discovery of remains at a house in Wynenden. Oh no! thought Katherine. The whole world is going to know now! It felt like the situation was a train careering out of control, and there was nothing she could do to stop it. She felt any chance of peacefully doing up her house, was now blown out of the water. Everyone in the village is going to be trying to track me down to get the latest, I'll never have any peace, she thought agitatedly. Barely had the story finished, when the phone started ringing. She hesitated, wondering whether she ought to answer it. But what if it's a friend who knows nothing about it? Cautiously, she picked up the phone and said hesitantly 'hello?'

'Kitty?'

She relaxed, it was Libby, her best friend. 'Libs, how are you?' she replied, delighted to hear a friendly voice, 'I was going to call you later.'

'I've saved you the trouble. What's up? You sounded rather guarded when you answered the phone?'

'You can say that again! You are never going to believe what happened today…!' She proceeded to tell her best friend in great detail, the events of the day. '... so you see I wasn't quite sure who was going to be on the other end, when I picked up the phone!' she finished.

'Honestly! I can't leave you alone for a minute without you causing trouble!' she laughed. 'Want me to come over? I can ditch dinner with James and be over for 8 o'clock.'

'Thanks, but I'll be fine, and there's no way I'm going to be responsible for you and James missing out on your date night. I don't think James would ever forgive me! Really, I'm fine, I'll catch up with you soon.'

'That's what I was phoning for, to get a date out of you. When are you free?'

'How about next Wednesday afternoon? I can't see the builders being allowed back on site by then, why don't you come and have a sarni with me here. Say about 1.30?'

'Great! I'll see you then.'

'Have a nice evening!'

'Don't worry, I will! Bye.'

Katherine smiled to herself, she could always rely on her best mate to perk her up. The phone rang again. 'OK, so what did you forget?' she laughed.

'Oh, er…,' said a male voice.

'Oh! Sorry, I thought you were someone else.' She paused. She recognized the voice, but her brain was grappling to identify the name.

'Oh, right,' came the voice. 'Katherine?'

'Yes?'

'It's Ted. Ted Armstrong.'

'Hi Ted. How are you?' Ted, being Sir Geoffrey's Estate Manager.

'I'm fine thanks. I've heard about what happened today at the farmhouse. Are you ok?' His voice was soft and gentle.

'I'm fine, thanks for asking. Bit of a shock that's for sure.' She liked Ted, he was always kind and courteous towards her and, she suspected, to everyone he dealt with. Some might class him as old fashioned in his manner, by the way he stood up when a woman entered the room, held the door open for them and was generally very polite. Pity more people weren't like that in this me, me, me, culture of today Katherine had often mused.

'Good. Um ...,' he hesitated again.

'Was there something else?'

'Sir Geoffrey has asked me, to ask you, what you know about the remains which were found? He thought you might know more than had been presented on the news.'

'No, I'm afraid I don't. There's very little to tell, and what there is to know, has already been on the news. We're not allowed near the house until the police tell us the builders can start again.'

He sighed. She had ascertained from her own encounters with Sir Geoffrey, that he was a man who always expected - and got - his own way, which made for uncomfortable situations at times with his staff, and guessed that Ted would be grilled again, and again, and demands as to why he didn't know more, would be repeated. 'Ok. Well if you do happen to hear any more, could you possibly give me a ring? I know Sir Geoffrey is keen to find out as much as possible.'

'Of course I will, no problem. Thanks for ringing.'

'Thanks,' he hesitated again and Katherine got the impression there was something else on his mind, 'bye then.' The phone clicked dead, and Katherine looked at it, puzzled.

# Chapter Five

Katherine spent the weekend hidden away, only slipping out in her car, to avoid the curiosity of those in the village which, she was in no doubt, was reaching fever pitch. A little extreme perhaps, to get in her car to drive to another village to buy the weekend newspapers, when the shop was a few minutes walk away, and stocked the very papers she wanted. But she wasn't going to take the risk, and justified it by convincing herself that it was only for this weekend.

Monday came with the start of children freshly back from their two week break. Getting to work an hour earlier, and starting at 7.30 a.m. rather than 8.30 a.m, meant that Katherine was able to plough through a large pile of paperwork with no interruptions. Far more than she would normally be able to get through in a morning, simply because the phone wasn't ringing, and there wasn't constant interruptions as parents, prospective parents, children, teachers, delivery drivers and the like, flowed in and out of the office, in the normal wave of activities. 8.30 a.m. brought in the rest of the office staff. The prep school was large, with 700 pupils, but it was divided into three separate areas; kindergarten and pre-prep were in one building in an area of the school grounds, prep which was Years 3 to

6 were in another building also in a different area of the school grounds, and finally, the seniors in Years 7 and 8 -which took them to the age of 13 - was in yet another building, one which adjoined the administrative offices and Headmasters' office. They all shared the same facilities i.e. sports fields, music rooms, sports/assembly hall, refectory and all had plenty of opportunities to come together as one whole school.

All the office staff, including the Headmasters' Secretary/Personal Assistant, shared a large, open plan, office, off a welcoming entrance hall in the new wing of the school. It was light and airy and a pleasurable environment in which to work. In the entrance area were a couple of sofas and a coffee table, with a neat arrangement of school brochures and magazines for visitors to peruse, whilst waiting for their appointments. The walls were filled with photographs, paintings and works of art, created by the children. All ages from the school equally represented, a good advertisement for the school.

'Morning Katherine,' called Liz, coming through the entrance door and making a "would you like a cup of coffee sign" as she headed off to the small kitchen located off the left hand side of the entrance. Having made an affirmative sign, Katherine ploughed on until Liz placed a mug of freshly brewed coffee on her desk. She'd been followed in by Jane and Mary, who was the Heads' secretary.

'Well?' asked Liz expectantly. Her eyes sparkling through her round, gold-rimmed, spectacles.

'Well what?' smiled Katherine back, knowing fully what Liz meant.

'The house on the news? It is yours isn't it? It's got to be. How many houses can there be in Wynenden, that are

41

complete wrecks and where building work has just started?'

'OK, you've got me there! But just keep it to yourselves, I don't want to be the main topic of gossip for the school. I think I've got enough of that in the village.'

'Goes without saying,' she replied. Jane and Mary who were listening, whilst taking off their coats and setting up for the day, nodded too.

'Well, there's not a lot to tell, other than what was on the news. I've not been told any more by the police, and we're not allowed at the house until they've finished with it, and I've no idea how long that will be.'

'What a pain! The builders have only just started,' remarked Jane. 'But were you there when they found it? Did you see it? What was it like?'

'Don't be such a ghoul Jane!' reprimanded Mary.

'Oh, come on! You can't say you're not interested?' she retorted.

'Interested, but I don't need the gory details!'

'Yes, I was there, and yes I did see it. But no, I don't have a clue about anything else, how's that?' She was silenced by the school bell ringing outside the office, calling the children to assembly. 'Anyway, if I have any more to tell, I will tell you. Don't worry!' With that, they all settled down to the hustle and bustle of the days' work.

Monday evening came and went. Tuesday past by and Katherine was wondering if she would ever hear from the police. Surely it couldn't take them that long to search the house? She'd just finished washing up her supper dishes when there was a knock at the door. Katherine frowned. She wasn't expecting anyone. She put the chain on the front door and opened it. It was D.I. Allix. 'Hold on a moment.' She indicated to the chain, closed the door, slid the chain back and opened the door fully. He was accompanied again by D.I. Windsor.

'Could we come in please Mrs Muier?' he asked politely.

'Please.' She indicated the way through to the sitting room and offered them tea, which was again turned down. Sitting in identical places to their previous visit, Katherine got a sense of déjà vu. She noticed that he looked a little more tired and drawn than his last visit, like he'd not slept for the past four nights. However D.S. Windsor looked as fresh as a daisy, as though nothing ever got to her, it was just a job, and it all washed off the hard exterior.

He cleared his throat. 'I wanted to keep you in the picture Mrs Muier,'

'Does that mean we can start building works again?' she interrupted.

'No. I'm afraid not. We need a little longer. I have more information I can give you about whose remains were discovered, dental records were checked and her parents have been informed.' She looked questioningly at him. 'I'm afraid it was a local girl who went missing ten years ago. Her name was Cecilia Stillingfleet. She was sixteen when she went missing, which we believe was when she was killed. There is no doubt that she was murdered.'

Katherine felt the bile rising in her throat and let out a sob. 'Poor girl. But who would have done such a thing? I mean, a young girl. Why?'

'That's what we have got to find out. Did you know the girl? Know anything about her?'

She shook her head. 'No, I didn't, sorry. I only moved here a couple of weeks ago, before that I lived about fifteen miles away. I don't really know anything about the village, or the people in it, though I vaguely remember hearing about her going missing from the news back then.'

'That's OK, I needed to ask.'

'If she was local, do you mean she lived in this village?'

'Yes, and her parents still do.'

'Oh no! The poor things! They must be beside themselves.'

'They are very distraught, naturally, but they have had ten years of not knowing whether their daughter was dead or alive. Whilst they have always clung onto the hope that she was alive, they do at least now know, which is small consolation. Every time there was the hint of a sighting, or potential new evidence as to her whereabouts, their hopes were raised.'

They sat in silence for a few moments. 'I guess, if she was a local girl, then a lot of people in the village knew her?'

'Yes. When she went missing, the whole village pulled together in an effort to find her. As time has gone by people have apparently come to their own conclusions about whether she was dead or alive, but nothing really prepares one for the stark reality of death.'

He looked sad, she thought, surprised that he would feel anything for someone he did not know. Another body. Another day. It must be part of his regular routine.

'Anyway, if you hear of anything that may be of help to us, please call on the numbers I gave you. Anything, no matter how insignificant.' He rose to go.

'Of course. Anything I can do to help, I will.'

'Thanks. We'll be in touch. Goodnight.'

'Night,' she replied absent mindedly as she closed the door behind them. Not a great drinker, she did, however, feel in need of something to fortify her and rummaged through some boxes in the hall until she found the bottle of brandy she used to "feed" her Christmas cake each year, and poured a generous glug into a tumbler from the kitchen.

She sank down into the sofa and clutched the brandy to her, sipping it from time to time, feeling the liquid burn its way down into her stomach, warming her from the inside, but not enough to take away the shaking that had started and the clamminess of her hands as the reality set in. A young girl, barely a woman, murdered and bricked up in her house. The hideousness of it was hard to comprehend. How could a person take another's life? And how evil must you be to go that step further and take a young person, or child's, life? She reached for the phone and dialled Libby.

After an agonizing few rings Libby answered. 'Hello?'

'Libs, it's me,' she sniffed.

'Kitty, what's wrong? You sound dreadful,' said Libby slightly alarmed.

'The police have just been, they know who the, who the ...' she couldn't say it. She paused to compose herself. 'It was a girl. A local girl. She was only sixteen, Libs. Sixteen and somebody snatched her life away. How could they do that?'

'Oh, Kitty. How awful. Poor child. Do the police know any more? Have a motive?'

'No. Apparently she's been missing for ten years, they think she died then. She lived in the village, her parents still live here. Apparently they kept hoping she was alive and would turn up one day.'

'How terrible for them, utterly ghastly.' Libby closed her eyes as she pushed away the nightmare thoughts of how she would feel if one of her two darling children disappeared, to have that daily struggle, not knowing, imagining what horrific things could be happening to them. The agony of not being able to help or to protect. 'Shall I come round? James is not back yet, but I could get my neighbour to pop in, to look after the children, until he does.'

'No, I'll be fine Libby. Really, it's just the shock and it's not even my own child. I can't imagine how completely devastated, and bereft, her parents must be feeling. Really, I'll be fine.' She continued as Libby protested. 'I just needed to hear a friendly voice, to tell someone. But please, don't say anything to anyone. I don't know who else knows.'

'Of course I won't Kitty. Call me anytime if you need me, and I do mean anytime. I'll see you tomorrow for lunch anyway. Go and have a hot bath and curl up, try to get some sleep.'

'I think I will. See you tomorrow. Bye.' She'd momentarily forgotten that she was seeing her friend the next day and, comforted by that thought, and having just spoken to her, she slowly sipped the remainder of her brandy, calming herself down. She closed her eyes for a few moments and opened them suddenly, having remembered that she'd promised to phone Ted if there were any developments. Should I? But if I don't and it's on the news, I'll have let him down, she mused. Reluctantly, she decided she ought to tell him. After all, it had happened whilst Sir Geoffrey still owned the house, and she vaguely thought that Ted had told her he had worked at the Estate for ten, or eleven years, so maybe he and Sir Geoffrey could help the police?

She found his number in her phone and dialled it.

'Hello?'

'Ted? It's Katherine.'

'Katherine. Hi, how are you?' His voice change from businesslike, to soft, when he realized who it was.

'I'm fine thanks,' she replied automatically. 'You asked me to keep you updated about what was happening at the farmhouse.'

'Yes. Any news?'

'The police have been this evening. The remains were of a girl, a local girl, Cecilia Stillingfleet. Apparently she went missing about ten years ago.'

'No! Really? Gosh, that's awful. I remember the up-roar when she went missing. To start with nobody believed her parents. She was a bit of a wild thing, by all accounts, but once the village realized it was serious, and the police were involved, everyone turned out to help. Searching the village, the Estate, everywhere they could think of. It was shortly after I arrived here, not a very pleasant thing to happen, and in an unspoken kind of way, it has always hung over the village.'

'I thought you should know, but I don't know how many others do. Her parents know, but it might be an idea to keep this to yourself. Though I guess you will have to tell Sir Geoffrey?'

'He and Lady Susan ought to be told. Particularly as it occurred at one of their properties. This is dreadful. I suppose I ought to go and tell them now.'

'I would imagine the police are going to want to speak to them, and you and anyone else who works, or worked, on the Estate at that time. Sorry to be the bearer of such grim news.'

'Please don't worry. Thank you for telling me. I'd best get off and break the news to them. Thanks. Bye.'

Katherine decided she'd had enough of the day and ran herself a long, hot, bath, adding some comforting lavender bath oil to sooth her. After half an hour she was visibly relaxing, and took herself off to bed to read for a while to wind down. Reaching for the bedside lamp to switch it off, having calmed and settled herself, she jumped in alarm as the phone rang. Who on earth is phoning at this time of night? It was 11 p.m.

'Hello?' she answered cautiously.

'Katherine, I'm so sorry to disturb you.' It was Ted. 'But Sir Geoffrey is absolutely insistent that I phone you, he needs to see you.'

'What? Now?!'

'He wanted to, but I've calmed him down and persuaded him that it's not a good idea, that a few hours won't make a difference.' He sounded incredibly apologetic and had hated having to phone her at that time of night, but when his boss became insistent about something, there was no other choice. 'Could you come up to the house tomorrow morning?'

'No. Sorry, I'm working and there is no way I can get out of it,' she said firmly. 'I could be up there for three o'clock,' she conceded reluctantly.

'Is that the earliest? Are you sure?' Sir Geoffrey was not going to be happy about it.

'I'm afraid so. Tell him I will be there at 3 o'clock. Now, I have work tomorrow and I need my sleep, good night.' She put the receiver down feeling decidedly grumpy and wide awake, which made her feel even grumpier.

Ted looked at his phone, his heart sinking. Not only had he managed to upset Katherine, but he knew it was going to take all his tact and diplomacy to restrain Sir Geoffrey from going round to see her in the middle of the night, to demand information.

By 1 a.m. Katherine was still awake. The more she stayed awake, the more agitated she became, which made her more awake. It was a vicious circle. She reluctantly got up and made herself a cup of camomile tea, and took it to bed to sip and read her book, making a concerted effort to push away her anger and focus on the book. At 2 a.m. she switched the light off, snuggled down and hoped for the best. She did drift off, but it was an uncomfortable, nightmare-ridden sleep, tossing and turning. She awoke exhausted, and not in the least prepared for a morning at the office. At least, she thought, there was the blessing that it was just the morning she had to get through, and not a whole day.

# Chapter Six

The morning had had to be caffeine filled to keep her alert and on top of her job and, having had a light lunch and a good chat with Libby, Katherine just wanted to curl up and go to sleep on the sofa. Instead, she found herself driving up to the stunning stone mansion, which was Wynenden Park, set in 2000 acres of rolling countryside and farmland. Normally a drive up to the "big house" as it was known in the village, filled her with excitement. As an enthusiastic member of the National Trust, she adored looking round large country piles, absorbing the history, and imagining what life must have been like in years gone by. But this afternoon she felt tired and lethargic, and not in the best of moods to face the grilling she was expecting from Sir Geoffrey. Her few dealings with him had been pleasant. He had always been respectful and a perfect gentleman, not living up to the reputation he seemed to have as a tyrant. But if what Ted had said last night was true, and he was on a mission to grill her, then their encounter may not be so civil.

She pulled up to a halt in front of the imposing stone steps, and looked at the forlorn façade. It was a house which had seen better days, days when money was no object and staff were abundant. Unfortunately, dwindling fortunes had resulted in the house gradually falling into a decline, with only the bare minimum of maintenance being able to be funded. It was a sad state of affairs, but not one that was unusual in this day and age. She got out of the car into the fine, misting, drizzle, which had started, and reluctantly walked up the steps, ringing the push bell to the right of the door. She thought she heard it vaguely ring in the distance, but wasn't sure. After what seemed like a lifetime she eventually heard a posse of dogs barking and yapping, and a motley crew of ageing Labradors, terriers and several unidentified mixes, bounced towards the half glass door to greet her. Following in their wake was Ted, his face alight with a smile when he saw her.

'Hi, come in. Sorry it took so long, we were right at the top inspecting another leak.' He ushered her through, shushing the dogs, and shooing them away to stop them jumping up at her.

'That's OK. Once I heard the dogs, I knew someone would come eventually!' She smiled back at him, feeling a little brighter.

'Lady Susan is waiting for you in the yellow drawing room, Sir Geoffrey went to join her. Do come through.'

She nervously followed him, he appeared to be in a good mood, which she hoped indicated that Sir Geoffrey was in a good mood too. They seemed to walk through corridor, after corridor, all the while Ted chatting amiably, and Katherine following his mixed blue, green and almond coloured, tweed jacket clad back, beneath which was a country check shirt, a green wool tie and a paler green jumper. He was shod in his usual brogue footwear, above which were his honey coloured cords. He stopped briefly as he came to an imposing pair of double doors, turned and smiled at her. 'Don't look so worried, you'll be fine.' So why did she feel she was about to face a very tricky interview? He opened one door and stood back to allow her to walk past him and into the room.

'Katherine, lovely to see you again,' smiled Sir Geoffrey, rising to shake her hand and kiss her lightly on the cheek.

'It's nice to see you again too,' she replied cautiously, 'and you too Lady Susan.' She always felt like she should curtsey when she met Lady Susan who was an imposing figure, brimming with confidence. Slightly shorter than Katherine, she was well padded, with stout legs which protruded from her below-the-knee skirt. Lady Susan always wore a skirt, no matter what, never "slacks" as she referred to trousers. She'd been brought up in an aristocratic family, sent to finishing school and, after a stint doing The Season, had moved swiftly on to marrying Geoffrey, for he was not a Baronet until his father died. She was not the type who was willowy, graceful and doe like, but of the more stocky, jolly hockey sticks collective, a no nonsense character, who always wore her straight, grey, hair at just above the shoulder, pushed back by a black velvet Alice band. Skirts were always the same length and invariably of wool with some kind of check, and a cashmere twin set which coordinated with one or other of the colour's in her skirt, along with the obligatory pearl necklace and earrings. On her wedding finger was a slim gold band and an enormous sapphire surrounded by substantial diamonds, an engagement ring passed down through the generations on Sir Geoffrey's side. This was a formidable woman, who took no nonsense from anyone, including her husband.

Lady Susan smiled graciously at Katherine. 'Please do, sit.' She indicated to an ancient settee which, Katherine discovered, was even more uncomfortable than it looked. 'Tea?' Enquired Lady Susan lifting the fine, bone china tea pot.

'Yes please, that would be lovely, thank you.' There was silence whilst Lady Susan poured milk into the delicate, rosebud painted cups and poured the tea through a strainer. Ted perched next to her and whilst they waited, continued to discuss the latest leak, discovered in the house with Sir Geoffrey. Katherine observed Sir Geoffrey, who was animated when the conversation turned to anything about the Estate. He was not much taller than his wife and barely an inch taller than Katherine. He was slim built, erring on the thin side, with thinning short, grey, hair and a pristinely brushed, bristly little grey moustache above his lip. It stuck straight out on each side and Katherine wondered how long it took him to groom it to stay in place. He had been brought up in the "stiff upper lip" generation, not showing his emotions or affections, always wore a jacket, shirt and tie, never ever just an open neck shirt. His clothes were well cut, excellently tailored but slightly jaded after many decades of use. Despite his brusqueness with his wife, Katherine liked to think that underneath he had a real affection for his wife.

'So, Katherine, Ted tells me that the police have kept you up to date about this jolly awful show at the farmhouse. Jolly bad luck that, eh?'

'Well, er, yes.' She wasn't quite sure she would call the death of someone "jolly bad luck" but having met Sir Geoffrey several times, she got the gist of his use of the English Language.

'Tell me then, Katherine, what do you know?' he peered intently at her with his slightly faded green eyes.

'I don't know if there is anything else I can tell you. I've told Ted what the police have told me and I've not heard anything further from them.'

'Well, where exactly were the remains found?' Lady Susan's cup rattled as her hand trembled when her husband said this.

'It was in the fireplace, the one that's at the end of the house, not the central fireplace. It had been bricked up. It was only when all the brambles and ivy had been pulled away that we realized there was another fireplace there. It had been impossible to see. I was hoping that there might be another nice inglenook fireplace and it could be opened up. Only a few bricks were taken out so that we could have a look, of course we got more than we bargained for when we did peer through the gap.'

He looked thoughtful before speaking again. 'What did you see when you looked through the gap in the bricks?'

'Um, well I only glanced, it was a skeleton, you know, a skull, that was all I saw. We called the police immediately. I've not been allowed back into the house since.'

'But,' interrupted Lady Susan, 'was there anything else there?'

Katherine looked confused. 'Sorry? I don't understand, like what?'

Momentarily Lady Susan looked flustered before regaining her composure. 'Anything, really, anything at all.'

'I didn't see anything else. The best people to ask are the police. I would imagine they will come and see you as you owned the property at the time the murder was committed.'

'Yes, yes, quite right, they're coming later this afternoon. Some detective chappy telephoned.' They lapsed into silence again. Katherine sipping her tea cautiously, trying her hardest not to make a slurping sound or show herself up in any way.

'Right, well, if you don't know anything more then so be it. Might come and have a look round when the builders start up again.' The assumption was there that Katherine would be agreeable to this and she wasn't about to upset the man who had just sold her, what had been and she hoped still would be, her dream home.

Taking this as her cue to depart, she thanked them for the cup of tea and followed Ted back to the front door.

'So,' he said, his hand on the front door handle. He smiled and hesitated. Yet again Katherine got the impression there was something he wanted to say, but couldn't bring himself to do so. 'Well, thanks for coming and I'll no doubt see you in the village sometime.'

'Quite possibly, thanks.' He held the door open for her. 'Bye,' she called as she went down the steps.

'Goodbye,' he replied, watching her get into her car and drive off.

She saw him in her mirror, standing, staring after her as she drove off and puzzled about what he hadn't said. When she reached the end of the long and winding drive she paused, then decisively turned left rather than right which would take her directly back into the village bringing her out into a lane close to the green. Instead she'd decided to drive past her farmhouse, after a short distance she turned left again into the single track lane, round a few bends and then saw the rickety entrance gate and moments later glimpsed her house, not busy with builders restoring it but people dressed in white, alien looking suits, coming and going in and around the house, forensics she guessed, though she wondered why they were back there again. She pulled up slowly and stopped by the entrance to the drive and observed a man and a woman who were gesticulating wildly at a uniformed policeman, who appeared to not be giving them the answers they were after. She didn't see the other policeman until he tapped on her window. She put it down a fraction.

'Sorry Madam, but I must ask you to move on. You are not allowed to stop here.'

'Yes, I will, I know, I mean I own the house.'

The policeman stared intently at her. She could almost hear him thinking "yeah and I've heard that one before" but instead he simple said 'Really?'

Katherine felt a frisson of irritation. It was her house, he could at least believe her. 'Yes. I'm Katherine Muier. I know I can't stop here, but I just wanted to see my house. If you don't believe me, check with D.I. Allix,' she said truculently.

'Ah, yes, sorry Mrs Muier, but we have had quite a few people turning up and claiming they own the house and they just need to pop inside. It's incredible the lengths people will go to.'

Katherine felt outraged. How dare other people try and gain access to her house and how dare they claim that it is their's! In amongst her indignation she felt slightly guilty for having been so brusque with the officer, as he was only doing his job and was ultimately protecting her property. She changed the subject slightly. 'Who are those people over there?' she asked indicating to the couple who were still giving the other police officer a hard time and, now that she had the window open could hear raised voices.

'That's Mr & Mrs Stillingfleet.'

'Oh! The girl's parents.' She could understand why they were so het up. 'Poor things.' The officer said nothing. 'I'd better go, thanks.' He gave a brief nod and said goodbye. She drove off, her heart aching for the distraught parents, imagining how she would feel if it were her daughter who had been murdered, perhaps a minuscule blessing of not being able to have children meant that she would never run the risk of ever knowing.

# Chapter Seven

Two more work days passed and nothing further from the police. As a pale golden sun shone weakly through on the Saturday morning Katherine felt out of sorts, she couldn't settle to any particular task, she was too restless. Eventually she decided that she had to go out, she couldn't stand being stuck inside any longer and thought that now was the time to face the inevitable, get it over and done with rather than having it hanging over her like a black cloud. She'd been aware of a certain amount of curtain twitching every time she came and went at her rented terrace, it was time to face the music and let the gossips do their worst. She picked up her phone, purse, keys and a jute bag and headed into the village to the Farmer's Market which was held every Saturday morning in the village hall.

Feeling a little as though she was throwing herself into the lion's den, she felt in some masochistic way she was almost looking forward to it. She enjoyed living on her own, having given such a large chunk of her life from a relatively young age to looking after her husband and worrying about his needs, but from time to time she felt incredibly lonely and isolated and when it overwhelmed her she had a desperate need to be with others. Katherine knew she could always rely on her friends, but felt acutely that at weekends it was family time, a time for families to catch up together and she didn't want to intrude.

Katherine felt self-conscious walking through the estate to the main road, feeling as though all eyes were on her, when in fact she knew they probably weren't. She continued along the footpath and just before the post office crossed the road, walked across the grass and joined the road which went all around the perimeter of the green, the green being on her right and the primary school and playing fields on her left, a few steps later and she was at the village hall. A steady stream of people seemed to be coming and going and there was a large sign outside to match the one at the bottom of the green, by the main road, which announced "Farmer's Market Today 10 a.m. to 12 noon." She smiled nervously at the people who walked past her in the opposite direction, they smiled back but there was no hint of recognition. She began to realize how stupid she had been. Why on earth would anyone know who she was? How vain of me to even think that I would be the talk of the village, she felt foolish and ashamed.

There was a buzz of activity inside the hall, which was relatively modern having been built only five years previously to replace the rotting old building which had sufficed as a village hall prior to that. From what she could see there were about twenty or thirty stalls selling different produce and products, all seemingly local. The stall with the longest queue was the bread stall, everyone was standing patiently, chatting to one another and whilst she hated queues she was curious to discover what was so magical about this particular range of bread which made people queue so harmoniously? It also occurred to her that if she delayed joining the queue, the bread may have run out.

She stood quietly in line, listening in to the idle chit chat which was carrying on around her. Nobody seemed particularly curious or interested in her and she felt herself relax, she didn't feel like she was going to face the Spanish Inquisition after all. She tried to peer round those in front of her to see the different types of bread on display, they did look good, a large variety of flours were used to produce interesting looking and tantalizingly tasty bread. Not just your standard brown or white. There was rye flour bread, spicy bread, oat bread, a mix of different flour bread, bread with cheese and onion in it, olive bread, caraway seeded bread and many more, the selection was impressive and in addition to them, there was also a delectable array of mouthwatering cakes and pastries on offer. With a limited selection left by the time she reached the head of the queue, she settled for an oat mix bread, a 'meaty' looking croissant and an unadventurous doughnut. Katherine then decided to have a cup of coffee as refreshments were being served at one end of the light and airy hall. She was impressed that it was freshly brewed coffee and not out of a jar. She took her cup and sat at the only free table left, there was a buzz of conversation around her. Katherine sat and observed the ebb and flow of the market and sipped the piping hot coffee.

Behind her, several tables had been put together and a posse of people had gathered, regulars, she assumed by the way they greeted each other. She caught snatches of their conversation, though she wasn't really listening. Katherine finished her coffee and took it to the counter for washing up, it was only when she turned around that she came face to face with Betty, her heart sank.

'Kitty!' Betty eyed her with delight. 'How lovely to see you, I haven't seen you round the village, but I suppose that's understandable what with all that's been going on up at your house. Let me get you another cup of coffee.' Katherine tried to protest but found she was fighting a losing battle, before she knew it the coffee had been ordered and she had been propelled to the long table. The mix of older men and women sitting there eyed the interloper with suspicion. 'This is Kitty,' introduced Betty, 'she owns Wynenden Farmhouse.' She announced this triumphantly, as though holding up a gold medal at the Olympics. There was a collective inward gasp, followed by a babble of "oh, do come and sit here dear, come on make space," as they jostled amongst one another to get the top prize of sitting next to her.

Katherine looked round wildly, desperately hoping for some form of escape, but there was none forthcoming. Just as a black widow spider entices its partner back into its web, only for it to eat her mate, so she felt she was being irreversibly drawn into theirs. They crowded round her. 'So,' said Betty when she was settled, 'tell us exactly what has been happening at the farmhouse?'

About fifteen eager faces were focused on her. 'Well, um, I would imagine you know what I know,' she stuttered.

Betty clicked her tongue in a disapproval. 'Come on, I'm sure you know far more than we do! It is your house. Did you find the remains? Where was it? What did it look like?'

If ever there were a freak show, this was it and Katherine felt like she was the freak. 'I … Well … It was scary,' she was frantically trying to think of as many words and phrases as she could, which would make them believe she was telling them something important, but without actually divulging anything. There was a collective "ooh" at this. 'Yes. It was terrifying.' This produced lots of nodding and patting of her hands. 'We had to call the police right away.'

'Oh, course, of course,' muttered one.

'Absolutely, very wise,' murmured another.

'They were very quick.' She glanced around at them realizing that if she paused after each small statement, it appeared to have a more dramatic effect on them. 'They were very efficient.' Pause. 'There were detectives and uniformed policemen and suited forensics people.' She gave another pause. 'They're very busy.' She stopped. They looked at her eagerly. She suddenly had an idea. 'Tell me,' she said to her captive audience. 'What happened ten years ago? Were you all here? Did you help with the search?' She hoped that by deflecting back on to them, she would take the pressure off herself. It seemed to work, they all started talking at once, but Betty, having brought the prize to the table, seemed to be unofficially in charge.

Happy to be in the spot light, she started. 'We were all here. It was dreadful. Well, in fact to start with, we didn't believe Cecilia's parents. They said she'd gone missing, but she was a bit of a wild thing.'

'You can say that again,' interrupted her neighbour.

'And she'd been away you see. No one saw her from Easter until October. Of course they said she'd gone on an educational trip to stay with a relative in France.' Betty glanced round and, as if on cue, there was a lot of rolling of the eyes and muttering.

'You don't think she did then?' asked Katherine, intrigued.

'Who knows? There were rumours.' She paused as though contemplating what to say next. 'But no one really knew. Then she was back, we only saw her for a few days and then she disappeared. Of course we all thought she'd been sent away again. That's why no one believed her parents when they said she had gone missing. And also, she had been known to just disappear for a day or two previously, and back she'd come as though nothing had happened. So it was a good week or so before any of us took them seriously. Once the police got involved and started asking questions we realized maybe there *was* something wrong.'

'So what happened next?' prompted Katherine.

'Well, we did what all villages do in a time of crisis, we pulled together. We had search parties out all over the village and surrounding fields and woodland. Sir Geoffrey got Ted, who was his new Estate Manager then, to coordinate searches on the Estate, he was most insistent that we keep going. Even when we had searched and searched, he made the staff up at the Estate keep searching. Day after day, from dawn 'til dusk, for two whole weeks.'

'Really?' Katherine was surprised.

'Yes. He just wouldn't give up. As time went on we began to wonder if something awful had really happened to her. There was just no sign of her. After several months, when there was still no sign of her, we all concluded that maybe something horrid had happened to her. No matter what a person is like, they don't deserve to be murdered.' She shook her head sadly as others agreed with her.

They lapsed into silence, which was eventually broken by a rotund, elderly woman with a tight blue-rinse perm, wearing a synthetic red jumper and a rather large mole on her right cheek which sprouted numerous thick dark hairs. 'She was a bit of a madam though.' There was a silence, before there were quiet murmurings of "true, true". 'She gave her parents the right run-around and with her having gone to that posh school up the road too!'

'What? Wynenden School?' Katherine was suddenly alert. That was where Libby's children were, at the Prep School.

'Yes, that's the one. Right snobby lot up there. Flashing their money around, driving round in their four wheel drives like they own the place.'

Katherine felt herself bristle with anger. It always irritated her when people made stereotypical judgements of the children at private schools and their parents who sent them there. It was assumed that, if the parents sent their children to such a school, they were snobby and full of themselves and loaded in cash. In fact, from Katherine's experience - though it varied from school to school - the majority were far from that. She knew some parents worked two jobs, just so that their child/children could attend such a school, wanting to give their child or children the best education they could. Many sacrificed going out, holidays, new cars, new clothes, in order to give them a private education. In some cases, grandparents paid for their grandchildren to attend such schools. Whilst there always would be an element of overtly wealthy parents, this did not automatically make them snobby, rude or arrogant. Katherine knew that you got that in all walks of life, whether you sent your child to a private school or a state school. The selfish attitude seen today in many an adult, and inevitably their offspring, was a symptom of the me, me, me society in which they now lived.

Seemingly unaware of the effect her comments on Katherine had had, the woman continued to prattle on, gaining confidence as her audience listened. 'Her parents have got a lot to answer for. They think they own this village from the way they behave. They live in their average detached house behind their silly electric gates. No manners, not like Sir Geoffrey and his wife, now they've got true breeding,' she sat back smugly.

Katherine didn't want to listen to any more of this. It was spiteful and hurtful and probably not true. She didn't know the Stillingfleet's, but no matter what they were like as individuals, they should still be shown compassion at a time like this.

'Well, thanks for the coffee,' she said doing her utmost not to appear rude, 'but I would really like to have a look at the stalls before they pack up, it's 11.30 already.' She forced a smile on her face and thanked them again. There was a cheery goodbye from them all, but Katherine was sure that, as soon as she was out of earshot, she would be subject to a discussion. What was her fate to be? Liked or reviled? She wasn't sure if she really cared.

The stalls turned out to be an interesting mix. Katherine bought cheese and milk from a local farmer, ham and chicken breasts from another, honey from a local apiarist, vegetables from an elderly couple who grew the produce themselves, apple juice from another and, finally, a delectable looking lemon cupcake, with perfect lemon butter icing, sprinkled with glitter, from a young mum trying to earn a little money whilst being a full time mum to a toddler, Saturday being one of the morning's when she could leave the toddler with her husband. Laden with her goodies Katherine weaved her way purposefully towards the door, endeavouring not to glance in the direction of the group she had been sitting with. Glimpsing down for a moment, she bumped into someone. 'Oh, sorry!' She exclaimed, looking up, only to see that it was Ted smiling down at her.

'Hi! How are you? You look like you've been busy single-handedly keeping the market in business!'

'Thought I'd do my bit! I have to say, I'm very impressed. I was expecting a couple of stalls with a few moulding vegetables on them and nothing else.'

'We're lucky, it is a good one, some of the others round here don't have as many stalls and are not doing so well. It's a vicious circle, stall holders are there to earn a living and need people to come in to buy, if the markets don't get the stallholders, people don't continue to visit and of course if there aren't interesting stalls selling good produce and products, people won't come. Fortunately, the one here is thriving. It's been going for about five years now.'

'I'll certainly be back. There are a few stalls I didn't get to, lots of people gathering round them and I'm a bit laden down, besides I didn't want to get caught again.'

'Caught?' he looked quizzically at her, his head cocked to one side.

'They're only being friendly. Betty from the post office and some other people from the village.'

'Sitting on the long table at the back,' he grinned.

'Yes. How did you know?'

'They're always there. Woe betide anyone who tries to sit at their table uninvited! I guess they mean well. I think some of them are lonely and this is the highlight of their week.'

Katherine felt a twinge, she knew what loneliness was like, that's what had propelled her to the market in the first place. Her face must have flickered with something which Ted saw and recognized in himself. A bachelor himself, having never married, he'd broken up with his long term girlfriend over a year ago. She'd wanted commitment, he was happy as they were and whilst, in hindsight, it had been the right decision to part company - for he could see that his reluctance to commit was down to his lack of strong feelings for her - he had times when he too felt lonely. All his friends were married, some divorced and on their second marriage, it was an isolating world being older and single sometimes.

Impulsively he spoke. 'I don't suppose, if you are free tonight, you'd fancy meeting for a drink would you?' he blushed a bit as he asked.

Caught off guard, it had been a long time since someone had asked her out on a date and not something she had been actively searching for. She blushed a little too. ' Oh. Um...'

'Sorry. It's presumptuous of me, you must be busy, forget I asked,' he blustered on.

'No. No I am not actually. That would be nice, I don't really know any of the pubs round here. Though perhaps we could give The Speckled Goose a miss, bit too local for me at the moment!' She gave a slight smile.

His face lit up. 'Of course! I'll have a think. Would you like to meet at the pub or can I pick you up?' He didn't want to be too forward, quite ridiculous he thought, for a man of forty-two in this day and age of internet dating and the apparent easy come and easy go attitude to dating and sex.

'Um.' She hesitated again, weighing up the pros and cons of being picked up, verses meeting there. The advantage of meeting there being she could leave when she wanted to, if the evening went pear shaped. But on the other hand she knew Ted, he wasn't someone she'd picked off a dating site, and he was perfectly pleasant and a gentleman, so she should be able to trust him. 'If you could pick me up, that would be lovely, thank you. Say about 8 p.m.?'

'Great! I'll see you then.' They bade farewell until later and Katherine walked home feeling slightly lighter and with a grin on her face. She was impressed that at forty-seven, she still got asked out and by a younger man too!

Of course, as the evening drew nearer, Katherine began to feel apprehensive about what lay ahead. After all, the last time she had been asked out, was thirty years ago when Rex had first asked her out on a date. And look what a disaster that eventually turned out to be, she muttered to herself. Her friends had all tried to fix her up on blind dates, which she had refused. She would rather stay at home and stick pins in her eyes, than go out on a blind date. They'd also done the usual trick of holding a dinner party and seating her next to the only single male at the dinner. Each occasion turned out to be unique and not always in a positive way. Eventually her friends got the message to leave her to her own devices and she had settled into her single life, on the whole quite contentedly. What was the protocol these days? Society seemed so promiscuous, she sincerely hoped that she wasn't expected to leap into bed on the first date with any man who happened to ask her out. Maybe she should have met him there? Several times she came close to picking up the phone and arranging to meet him at whichever pub they were going to, but chickened out each time.

By 7.30 p.m. she was ready. She'd settled on a pair of sage coloured, slim fitting, needle cord trousers (in case he had wandering hands, a skirt may be too inviting), a cotton scoop neck, slim fitting, thin double-layer top in damson with a stripy green and damson under-layer, along with a damson coloured cashmere cardigan, and her feet were shod with a pair of low heeled, dark tan, slim fitting, riding style boots. She wore simple diamond stud earrings and a white gold pendant with a tiny diamond in it. She thought she looked smart, rather than scruffy. Not overdressed, nor underdressed, for the evening, though worried that possibly she was being a bit safe and dull, in her bid to avoid being overtly sexy.

8 p.m. prompt brought his knock on the door. She opened it and smiled. 'Hi.'

'You ready?' he asked, eyeing her appreciatively.

'Absolutely.' She slipped on her navy pea coat, scooped her glossy chestnut hair, from under the collar, and closed the door behind her, all the while admiring the jeans, casual shirt and plain jacket he was wearing. She caught a waft of something lovely and citrusy and spicy.

He held the door of his freshly washed green Land Rover Discovery, closed it behind her and walked round to the driver's side. 'I thought we'd go to The Grouse & Peacock. It's about 3 miles away in the Cranbrook direction. Should be far enough away from the locals, though anywhere round here you're likely to bump into someone you know.'

'Sounds fine. Not been there before.' They lapsed into silence, interspersed with the odd polite comment regarding the weather or the countryside they were passing. The Grouse & Peacock turned out to be in the middle of nowhere, down several little lanes. But despite this, the car park was packed. It was an old sixteenth century building, with low beams and a couple of log fires burning merrily away. Not for the first time, Katherine was glad that smoking had been banned. It made for a far more pleasant experience in her opinion. She didn't have to choke on hideous cigarette smoke all evening and come home with her clothes and hair stinking of it.

'It looks lovely,' she commented as they weaved their way through the throng towards the bar. Ted spotted a tiny table with two chairs unoccupied near one of the fires.

'Here. Have a seat,' he said pulling the chair out for her. 'What would you like to drink?'

'A glass of white wine please. Something like a sauvignon blanc if they have it.' He disappeared off to the bar leaving Katherine to observe the clientele in the pub. There seemed to be a whole mix of ages, from those who seemed too young - in her eyes - to even be in a pub, all the way up through the middle aged, like herself, and on to the elderly. Quite a few seemed to know Ted and he appeared to be chatting amiably to them whilst waiting his turn at the bar.

'Sorry about that, bit too busy tonight. Not usually quite this hectic on a Saturday night.' He sat down. 'Cheers!' He said raising his glass of ginger beer.

'Cheers!' she responded, taking a sip of her wine. It was fresh, delicious, citrusy, zingy, just the way she liked it. 'You not even having one drink?' She'd assumed he would have had one alcoholic drink, even though he was driving. Personally, she never had an alcoholic drink if she were driving, but was realistic about other people having a different opinion on this matter.

'No. Don't drink. Never have done.'

'Really?' she was surprised 'Why?'

He shrugged. 'Seeing most of my mates getting plastered from a young age, acting like idiots, throwing up and generally being complete morons, kind of put me off.' He grinned.

'Ah, well. Don't worry, I'm not going to get like that!' She now felt rather self-conscious sipping her wine.

His face fell. 'Oh! I didn't mean anything by it really!' He said hastily. 'It's a free country and everyone's entitled to do what they want.'

She relaxed a little. 'I don't drink if I'm driving, never have done, never will. I think one alcoholic drink is too many when driving. Of course, most people don't see it like that and are happy to drink and drive.'

Ted grimaced. 'I know what you mean. They just don't see what the consequences can be...,' his voice trailed off.

They sat awkwardly in silence for a few moments. 'So,' said Katherine breaking the silence, 'what made you become a Land Agent?'

'Easy,' he smiled. 'I've loved being outside since I was tiny. I grew up on a farm surrounded by countryside, loved it. The rolling hills, the fresh air, changing seasons, could never imagine working in an office 24/7, I'd feel too cooped up. With this job there is such variety, there's always something different going on, problems to solve.' He looked contented.

'If you grew up on a farm, did you not want to be a farmer? Take over the family farm or something?'

'No. I loved the farm, but I knew I didn't want to be a farmer. It's relentless and I also knew that my elder brother would always take over the family farm. I'm still involved in farming because of the farm on the Estate, but it's not the day in, day out, farming that the farmer has to deal with. I don't think I'm explaining myself very well?' He raised an eyebrow in question at her.

'I think you are. I suppose there's the farm, the house, the properties, managing the budgets and all that sort of thing, which your job entails?'

'Pretty much. Coming up with new and innovative ways to increase income just to maintain the main house, is constant. You've seen it. It needs major work on it. You'd need several million, just to do the basics at the moment, as soon as we plug one problem, another occurs. Bit like trying to stop a sieve from leaking,' he grinned ruefully.

'There must be loads of different ways to raise money? It's such a beautiful house. Can't it be opened to the public?'

Ted rolled his eyes. 'Don't start! I agree with you, but it's not my house, if you know what I mean. Oh no!' he groaned.

'What? What is it?'

'Don't look round.'

Of course, the instant he said this, she wanted to. 'Why not?'

'Andrew Battle's just walked in. If we keep a low profile, he might not see us.'

'Oh no.' She echoed his earlier sentiment. 'He's the last person I want to see. Did I tell you he came over to the farmhouse again? Shortly before the works began. He was, yet again, trying to persuade me to sell up. Being all smarmy, saying things like "you really don't want to be worrying your pretty little head about something like this" and "an enchanting woman like you must be far too busy to bother with such a big project," it was hideous.'

'I can imagine.' He grimaced in sympathy.

'I don't understand why he's so desperate for me to sell? He even added a further ten percent on top of the ridiculous sum he'd previously offered me.'

'You didn't accept did you?' he asked sharply.

Surprised by his tone, she bristled. 'No! Of course I didn't! I would never sell to him and besides, as you are well aware, I agreed as part of the terms of my purchasing the farmhouse, never to sell to him and I won't. I told him as much too.'

'Sorry. I didn't mean to be brusque. It's just I know how strongly Sir Geoffrey feels about that man. He absolutely loathes him. It would probably kill him if it ended up in Andrew's hands.'

'I know he's an unpleasant man. But why does Sir Geoffrey feel so strongly?'

Ted Shrugged. 'No idea.'

'Ah! What do we have here?' They winced as Andrew's foghorn voice boomed at them. 'Having a lovely drink together. Plotting some plan together? Is that how you got the house Kitty? Did you do favours?' He leered at her.

'How dare you!' shouted Ted, leaping up in her defence. 'Just because you are such a low life, doesn't mean that everyone else is. Don't judge people by your own standards.' He was quite red in the face with fury and the pub had fallen silent. Ted sat down as quickly as he had leapt up, embarrassed at drawing attention to himself.

'Touched a sore spot have I? Didn't come up with the goods? Never mind, better luck next time. My offer still stands Kitty, despite the gruesome goings on up there.' With that he sauntered off in a cloud of cloying aftershave to a young woman in a short skirt, low top and surgically enhanced breasts.

'Don't,' she whispered to Ted. Grabbing his arm before he could leap up and punch him. 'He's not worth it. If he can't get his own way, he'll do everything to rile the other person. Leave it. He's really not worth it,' she reiterated.

Ted scowled at him. 'Sorry.'

'What for? You were my knight in shining armour! Thanks. Made a change for someone else to step in for me. He's an awful, awful man. Come on, let's not allow him to spoil our evening. I'll get some drinks. Another ginger beer or do you want to throw caution to the wind and have a sparkling mineral water?' she grinned at him.

He laughed. 'Surprise me!' he replied.

## Chapter Eight

The phone rang persistently, interrupting Katherine's delicious sleep. She fumbled for the handset. Picked it up and mumbled into the receiver. 'Hello?'

'Oh, sorry Kitty. Did I wake you?' It was Libby.

Katherine yawned and glanced at the clock – 8.00 a.m. Why was it, that people with children just assumed that everyone else was up at the crack of dawn at the weekend? 'S'OK, what's up?'

'I thought you might like to come to lunch today? We didn't get much of a chance to catch up last Wednesday and the children would love to see you.'

'That'd be nice. Thanks.'

'Great! 12 o'clock do? Do you think you'll have been able to drag yourself out of bed by then?' she giggled.

'Hah, hah. You know I don't often have a lie in and it is only 8 o'clock and it is Sunday!'

'Just joking. Jealousy really. Never get to have a lie in these days. Anyway, see you later. Bye.' The phone clicked and Katherine flopped back down onto her pillow, pulled the duvet up and snuggled back down for a bit more kip.

Katherine beetled through the countryside later that morning, having thoroughly enjoyed a luxuriant lie in and a lazy breakfast. She reflected on the previous evening, which had made a pleasant change. Ted was good company. Fun, witty and relaxed, once Andrew had left the pub half an hour after his little performance. She scowled as she remembered him. Pesky man, she thought. Ted had filled her in a bit, on Andrew's background. Born and bred locally, he grew up on a local council estate with his mother and sisters, his abusive father having left when he was five years old. He'd left school with no qualifications and had started doing odd jobs and a bit of wheeler dealing from a young age. If there was a scam going on, he was usually behind it. Somehow, he had then managed to find enough money to buy a wreck of a terrace. Did it up and sold it on for a substantial profit. Then he did another and then another and another. Next he started doing the properties up, keeping them, and then renting them. After that, he moved into commercial property to diversify, and in conjunction with this were his sidelines. Basically, anything he could make money out of. Apparently this was all common knowledge and was what Andrew constantly bragged about. It would appear that he had done very well for himself. He'd bought a scrappy, derelict, bungalow in 7 acres on the edge of the village. Got planning permission, knocked it down and built a huge, flash new house with several garages, where he kept his collection of expensive cars. He worked hard and he played hard. Whilst Katherine respected and applauded hard work, she was not sure how ethically he worked, nor how legally, but that was pure speculation on her part.

She arrived at Libby's house and pulled up in front of the magnificent Tudor house, surrounded by its manicured lawns. Libby had worked for years in the city. Long hours, good pay and substantial bonuses. Unlike her colleagues, who blew their bonuses on flash cars and fast living, she had saved her bonuses. And by the time she eventually met her future husband, James, had a tidy sum tucked away to ensure - if she were wise and not extravagant with it - she need never work again. James too worked in the city, with good pay but not quite the astronomical level of bonuses which Libby had received. After a swift courtship they were married, and this was quickly followed by the arrival of Henry, now eight, and subsequently Alice, now 6. In ten years, her life had changed from work obsessed single woman who, at 36, felt she would never marry and have children, to domesticated wife and mother, living in the country, yet another huge change to the London life she had lived for so long. For Katherine it was wonderful that her best friend from school had moved out from London and was living so close and now, having moved to Wynenden, Katherine found herself only seven miles away from her friend. But despite their wealth and their comfortable lifestyle, Libby did not take it foregranted. Her parents had had a constant struggle with money, often going without, so that Libby could have extra lessons to help her academically, and even more so when she went on to university. She had done the comprehensive school she attended - and her parents - proud by getting into Oxford University and Katherine had been so very proud of her best friend's achievements.

'Kitty!' Two small figures ran out of the front door and flung themselves at her, their blond heads burying themselves into her.

She squeezed them tightly to her and kissed their heads. Hi, you two! It's so lovely to see you. Let me have a look at you. She held them away from her, squinted at them closely. 'Yup, I'm absolutely sure! You've most definitely grown since I last saw you!' - which had only been three weeks previously. The children swelled with pride at the complement.

'Come on.' They dragged her by her hands. 'Can you come and play with us?' they pleaded.

'Let poor Kitty get her coat off first!' reprimanded their father good naturedly as he kissed her on both cheeks.

'Good to see you Kitty. You're looking well.' He peeled the children away from her, who then ran ahead yelling to their mother that Kitty had arrived.

'They are such lovely children.' She gazed after them fondly. She adored seeing her Godchildren, they brought such joy and, in some small way, helped fill a tiny corner of the empty feeling she had, from not being able to have had children.

'Hmm,' replied James, 'they have their moments!'

She laughed. Looking into his good natured face, bags under his eyes from overwork, but crinkles round them from laughter. His short blond hair was tousled and slightly wild.

'Kitty!' Libby came out of the kitchen, wiping her hands on a tea towel. She kissed and hugged her friend. 'I'm afraid you are not going to get any peace until you play with them!'

'I know. Don't worry! I don't mind crawling around on the floor and playing whatever it is they want to.'

Libby eyed the knee length, suede, skirt Katherine was wearing. 'In that? Are you sure?'

Katherine laughed. 'I'll manage somehow. Don't worry!' She headed off to the playroom. It was a ritual which she enjoyed. As soon as she arrived, she dived off to play with the children. This kept the children happy and prevented the constant nagging of "will you play with me?" for the rest of the afternoon, which drove their parents mad. Katherine didn't mind. After all, she wasn't with them twenty-four hours a day, seven days a week.

A few moments later James wandered in carrying a mug of coffee. 'Thought you might need this.' He raised the mug at her and put it down onto a mat on the windowsill.

'Thanks,' she replied, delving deep and swishing around in a large box of Lego. He left them to it and went to help his wife with the lunch.

An hour later, they were all seated round the large kitchen table, enjoying a full Sunday roast lunch. The works, with roast beef, Yorkshire Pudding, numerous vegetables and gravy, to be followed by homemade apple pie and custard. The children munched happily having had an hour with their favourite adult (after their parents of course) and her undivided attention. They were eager to get back and finish the challenge which Katherine had set them – to build the largest castle they possibly could, with stables, barns and anything else she could think of to keep them busy – and had to be chided by their parents to not gobble their food down. The conversation flowed easily between the five of them and, with apple pie finished, the children raced off to continue with their Lego and Libby and Katherine abandoned James to do the clearing and washing up and settled themselves by the fire in the sitting room with their mugs of coffee.

'So, tell me, what's the latest?' asked Libby.

Succinctly, Katherine brought her up to speed ending with the information that Cecilia had been a pupil at Wynenden School.

'No! Really? Gosh!' Libby was rather at a loss for words.

'I don't suppose you'd heard anything about her had you?'

'No. There's no reason why I should have.'

'I know, but I just wondered? You know how people gossip and this is a pretty hot topic. There must be a few people up there who knew her, maybe even teachers who taught her?'

'I suppose, but they would be at the Senior School.'

'Hmm.'

'Hmm, what?' asked Libby.

'Oh, I don't know. I guess I'm curious. I can't get my head around the fact that somebody would murder a six-teen year old child, I mean I know she wasn't strictly a child, but she was barely an adult. How could anybody do such a thing?'

Libby shook her head and shivered. 'I don't know. It's too horrible to think about. Do you know anything about her?'

'Not really, only what those women were gossiping about. But it just seems, so, so ..., so local I suppose. That sounds stupid, but I can't help feeling that whoever killed her, must be close by. I mean, that house hadn't been lived in for a good twenty years or so when she was murdered.

And it's not exactly in a location where you would just happen to pass by, it's so tucked away. Whoever killed her *must* have known the area. Wouldn't you think?'

'Yes. I think they must have. It seems unlikely they would happen across the house by chance, but I suppose you never know.'

'And to have gone to such lengths to brick her body up in an old fireplace. You must be talking pre-meditated, wouldn't you think?'

'I don't know.'

'Well, the average person doesn't just happen to have bricks and mortar and everything you need to murder and then brick up a body on them, do they?' Libby shook her head in response.

'Any more coffee?' enquired James carrying a tray with his mug, milk, a cafetiere and a box of chocolate truffles on it.

'Please.' They both replied.

'You two look deep in thought,' he commented, flopping down onto one of the sofas and stretching his legs out. 'What are you talking about?'

'The girl. You know the one who was found?' replied his wife as she endeavoured to choose a truffle. Absentmindedly they munched on them and brought him up to speed.

'You on a mission Kitty?' She looked questioningly at him. 'Too find out who did it? You becoming the new Miss Marple?' he smiled.

She snorted in laughter. 'You've got to be kidding haven't you?! I'm just curious. When something like that turns up in your house, you're bound to be. Don't you think?'

'True. So why do you think that house was chosen? You know, for the body?'

'Remote I guess. You're not going to be disturbed by anyone. Which brings me back to thinking it must be someone local. Someone who knew of the house, knew it was empty. It had to be.'

'What a horrible thought,' shivered Libby. 'To think that someone you may have passed in the street, did it.' She wriggled her shoulders in disgust.

'Horrible. Really horrible. But does that person still live around here? Or would they have scarpered soon after the murder?'

'Possibly. But if they thought they had got away with it, then there would be no reason to leave would there?' reasoned James.

'If that's the case, then what will they do now that she's been found? Is he, or she, a threat now?'

'What a hideous thought,' replied Libby. 'Whoever it is must be feeling vulnerable. I mean, it's amazing what the police can discover these days. Even the tiniest speck of something or other can lead to the discovery of the killer.'

'So says the expert.' James smiled indulgently at his wife. 'I think you've been watching too many crime drama's on TV.'

She threw a cushion at him. 'Don't be mean! And besides, Mr Great Authority On Such Things, how would you know?'

'Touché!'

'It's true though. There may be a clue there. Something the police find, I mean that's why they're ripping the house to bits.'

'They're not are they?' asked Libby tucking into another truffle.

'Well, I don't know. Who knows what they are doing. I can't get in there. The saving grace is that the house was being ripped to bits anyway, so hopefully they won't be doing anything the builders wouldn't have been doing.'

'The question you have to ask,' James' mind was whirring away now, 'is why? Why was she killed?'

'Good point, darling'

'Yes. Why indeed?' Thoughtfully Katherine twiddled some of her hair round and round her fingers. 'If you have the motive, then maybe you will find the murderer?'

'Definitely think you have been watching the same programs as Libby, Kitty! It might have been totally random, maybe some paedophile or something.'

'Oh, don't say that James! I hate even hearing mention of such sicko's. It fills me with dread and makes me want to surround the children in cotton wool and never let them go out.'

'I know. I feel the same,' he replied, 'but it is a possibility.'

'The only personality trait those women really came up with, was that Cecilia was a bit "wild". But I suppose it depends what their definition of wild is? Do they mean someone who doesn't always say "please" or "thank you" or do they mean someone who's off partying every night and joy riding around the village?'

'Hmm. I'm sure that Betty woman at your village shop would know more. You could always ask her and I could subtly ask around at school. Normally I try to keep out of the gossip loop, but there might be something useful there.'

'That's the problem, how do you know what's gossip and what's not?'

'The only people who can answer that, are those who are being gossiped about,' interjected James. 'And they may not even be aware that they are being gossiped about and if they are, they may see no reason to set people straight. Anyway, apart from the obvious Kitty, how is life treating you at the moment?'

Kitty smirked to herself, but not before Libby - who had known her for far too - long had noticed.

'Kitty,' she said slowly as though talking to a naughty two year old, 'what aren't you telling me?' She narrowed her eyes and peered at her friend. 'Come on. Out with it! Something's up. What is it?'

'Nothing!' she denied vehemently.

'Don't give me that! I know there's something,' she paused and then gasped as a thought struck her, 'it's a man isn't it!'

Katherine felt a slow, creeping, blush rise up her chest, neck and finally her face. Why on earth was she blushing? She wasn't dating anyone, she'd just happened to go out for a drink with a friend. Totally casual. Nothing to it. Or so she liked to convince herself. 'It's nothing, really, I just went out for a drink last night.'

'A drink? With whom?'

'Oh, no one really. Just a friend, no big deal.'

'If it was no big deal, why are you blushing?'

'Come on Libby. Give her a break. She doesn't have to tell you and besides who wouldn't blush with you interrogating them so ferociously?'

Katherine shot him a grateful glance.

'Hmm. I'm suspicious.'

'Well there's nothing to tell. I went out for a very casual drink. Had a pleasant evening, apart from that pest Andrew Battle making a nuisance of himself, and that was it. End of. Nothing to tell.'

Reluctantly, Libby decided not to pursue the line of questioning any further. There'd be time enough when she got Kitty on her own, without James sitting there giving her piercing glares to drop it.

Much to Katherine's relief, they changed the subject and spent the rest of the afternoon chatting about the children, work, the house and admiring the Lego structures the children had created.

# Chapter Nine

Having refused offers of supper, Katherine had left Libby and James to calm their over excited children down and prepare them for a good night's sleep before school the next day. Feeling joyously happy for some reason, Katherine drove home humming to herself and parked up on the narrow driveway in front of her rented terrace. She eyed all the packed boxes, neatly lined up in the hallway and kitchen, and knew she had to get round to unpacking them, but really she couldn't be bothered. Why spoil a lovely relaxing day, she thought, and flung her coat on top of a pile in an attempt to hide them. Out of sight, out of mind, she told herself. Instead, she made a camomile tea, flopped down onto a sofa and switched the television on. Barely had she flicked through a couple of channels, when there was a loud and determined knock at the door. Who on earth was that? She groaned, reluctantly getting out of her comfy spot to answer it.

Standing on her doorstep were a couple who looked vaguely familiar, but whom she could not place. The man was tall, with a paunch, short grey hair and a pair of black rimmed glasses perched on his bulbous, porous, nose, which indicated - along with his ruddy complexion and broken capillaries - that he was a heavy drinker. Next to him stood a woman who looked a bit like mutton dressed as lamb. Her hair was heavily highlighted blonde and straightened to within an inch of its life, to below ear length, along with a sharp fringe and her clothes were tight and short, with high heels which seemed to make her wobble in the cool evening air.

'Can I help you?' enquired Katherine cautiously.

'I'm hoping you can,' replied the man in a gravelly voice, which also hinted that he was a smoker. This was backed up by a burst of phlegmy coughing. Katherine looked questioningly at him, waiting for him to stop. 'I'm Rupert Stillingfleet and this is my wife Audrey. We're Cecilia's parents.'

Now she knew why they looked vaguely familiar, this was the couple she had seen having a heated discussion with one of the policemen at her farmhouse. She hesitated, not keen to invite them in. 'What is it I can help you with?'

The couple looked at one another. 'Could we come in please?' asked Rupert.

Reluctantly, Katherine stepped back and showed them through to the sitting room. 'Please, take a seat.' She indicated to a sofa and then sat opposite them. 'I'm very sorry about your daughter.'

A slight sob came from Audrey, who pulled herself together, but sat there with the slight all-over tremble of a small dog. 'Thank you,' replied Rupert.
There was an awkward silence. 'So what is it I can do for you?'

'We really want to know more about what happened when our daughter was found? You were there I believe?' he looked questioningly at her.

Katherine squirmed uncomfortably. 'Yes I was, but there isn't really much to tell. I mean, the police must have told you everything?' She looked queryingly from one to the other, observing Audrey wringing her fingers.

'Of course they have. But please, go through, step by step, what happened. What you saw?' His brown eyes pleaded with her through his thick rimmed glasses and she caught an unpleasant waft of stale smoke and alcohol.

'Well. I was talking to my builder and one of the men was carefully removing bricks, from what we hoped would turn out to be a bricked up fireplace. When a few had been removed, he peered inside and then discovered, well discovered ...,' she struggled to find the right words, 'discovered your daughter. The police were called and we left the house until they arrived. That's it.'

'But what did you see?'

Katherine looked confused. 'What do you mean?'

'You looked. So what did you see?' he persisted.

'I um ... Um. Saw your daughter. Briefly. Very briefly. That was it.'

'Was that all? Nothing else?'

'Nothing else, no.' She was puzzled and not sure where his line of questioning was going.

'Are you absolutely sure?' he said forcefully.

'Yes. Quite sure. Now if there's nothing else...' she tailed off hopefully.

Audrey Stillingfleet spoke for the first time, her voice was high and squeaky. 'She had a necklace. We gave it to her for her sixteenth birthday. It was gold with a gold butterfly on the chain, about the size of a fifty-pence piece. Was she wearing it?' Her green eyes were filled with so much pain and desperation that it made Katherine want to cry to look at her.

'I don't really know,' she said softly, 'I don't think there was anything like that. But the police might have found it, have you asked them?'

'Yes,' she whispered hoarsely, trying desperately not to cry again.

'If they've not found it, then it's probably not there. They're certainly doing a thorough search of the house.'

'Please,' she pleaded, 'please look for it.'

'I will ask the builders to keep an eye open for it. If they should find it, I will let you know, but I will have to let the police know first,' she replied kindly, knowing full well that if the police hadn't found it, there was no chance that she, or the builders, would.

'And you're quite sure there was nothing else?' interjected Rupert, staring so intently at her that Katherine felt like a criminal.

'No,' she replied firmly, standing up to indicate that she expected them to go.

They took the hint and got up too, on their way out Audrey's thin bony fingers grasped Katherine's. Desperately she looked at her. 'You'll let me know if you find it then?'

'Of course,' she replied.

Katherine shut the door behind them and closed her eyes. That was awful, she thought, and what on earth was Rupert going on about? Was he talking about the necklace? Whatever it was he gave her the creeps, she shivered to get rid of the picture of him in her mind and dropped herself down onto the sofa, feeling disgruntled. Why oh why had it had to happen at all? And why at the house she had just bought? Why couldn't life be straightforward sometimes? She belatedly realized she had missed an opportunity to ask them about their daughter. About what she had been like, she was sure it would have been a very different picture to the one which had already been painted to her. Feeling totally out of sorts, she took herself off for a nice relaxing bath and an early night.

Katherine immersed herself in work and did her best to forget about the murder investigation, but despite doing her utmost not to think about it, it kept popping in to her head. She couldn't get over her thought that Cecilia had been murdered by someone local, it had to be, she was convinced of it. It kept niggling away at her. If only the girl hadn't been found at the farmhouse, been found somewhere else, then she would barely have given it a second thought. But Cecilia hadn't. She had been found at her farmhouse and there was no getting away from it. Nipping in to the village shop to pick up a pint of milk on the way back from work one evening, she was caught by Betty.

'Kitty, how are you?' she enquired pleasantly.

'Oh, fine thanks and you?' Inside she was wrestling with her conscience. Should she ask Betty about Cecilia and risk being a gossip or should she just keep out of it, mind her own business and stop playing detective?

'Any news?' asked Betty hopefully.

'No, nothing, but I'm not likely to hear anything. I won't be told anything about the case. There's no reason I will be, only about when the builders can get back on site.'

Betty made her little tutting sound. 'It must be so frustrating for you to not be able to get on,' she paused.

Katherine took the opportunity and dived in. 'How about you? Have you heard anything? After all, you are at the centre of the village.' She smiled encouragingly at Betty.

'Well,' she paused looking round in the kind of "walls have ears" way, 'I don't like to speak ill of the dead...'

Katherine held her breath and continued to smile pleasantly.

'But there's a lot of talk around the village.'

'Really? Like what?' Katherine opened her eyes wide in innocence.

'About what Cecilia had been up to during those months when she had supposedly been in France with relatives.' Betty leaned forward towards Katherine and lowered her voice. 'They say that she was pregnant and was sent away to have an abortion and to get her away from her boyfriend.'

Katherine was shocked. 'Really? Gosh! So who was her boyfriend? Was he someone local?'

Betty nodded. 'Lovely boy, an absolute gem, soft as anything, but her parents didn't approve. They had high hopes for their daughter and didn't want her being led astray by a local lad. Didn't even try to get to know him. Just did all they could to keep them apart, but they seemed besotted with one another. Well he certainly did, she might have been going out with him to deliberately spite her parents,' she paused thoughtfully, 'he was devastated. Absolutely devastated when she went away. You should have seen how thrilled and happy he was when she came back, couldn't stop grinning, he was like the Cheshire Cat. Then, of course, when she went missing, he was beside himself. For years he kept hoping she would come back. Sad, really sad, but now he seems happy enough. Got married two years ago to a local lass and they've got a six month old baby boy now,' she smiled at the thought of them.

'So, this local lad. Who is he? Does he still live in the village?'

'Oh yes, he owns the garage just up the road. There's a certain irony to the situation, he was always mad for cars and spent hours tinkering away with them. Because he lived in, what her parents called, a "rough part" of the village and went to the local comprehensive, they deemed him unsuitable. But he went on to do an apprenticeship and study mechanics at college and got a job at the small garage up the road. Just the two of them, when the owner retired he gave first offer to Tom, who managed to persuade his bank to lend him the money and here he is, at the age of twenty-seven, running his own business and doing quite well by all accounts. Her parents thought he'd be a deadbeat who would come to nothing and sponge off benefits for the whole of his life.'

'So this Tom, he's nice then?'

'Lovely. Goes that extra mile for you, so kind and caring, does a lot round the village. If ever you need your car fixing, or servicing or an MOT done, he's your man. Fullwood Garage. He changed the name once he bought it so that it has his surname.'

'Great. Well thanks.' Katherine handed the money over to Betty. 'I shall bear that in mind.'

'No problem. Have a nice evening.'

'You too, thanks. Bye.' Katherine hurried out to her car to get out of the rain as quickly as possible and mulled over what she'd just been told. Had this Tom person had anything to do with Cecilia's death? Was she really pregnant? Could he have been furious that she had had an abortion and in the heat of the moment killed her? Was Wynenden Farmhouse their secret meeting place? As if by some telepathic sense that she had acquired something relevant to the case, she arrived home to see DI Allix pull up near her house.

'Hello,' he called pleasantly, pulling the collar of his raincoat up round his neck to stop the torrential rain going down inside it.

'Hi,' she replied, racing up to the front door to open it as quickly as possible. 'Come in,' she called breathlessly. She shook her coat off and wiped the damp hair away from her face. 'Yuck! It's horrible out there tonight.'

'Not very pleasant, I must agree,' replied DI Allix removing his soaking coat hanging it over the banister, where Katherine had indicated that he should do so.

'I don't know about you, but I'm in desperate need of a cup of tea. Would you like one?'

'Thanks. That would be most welcome.'

They made idle chit chat about the weather whilst she made the tea, then took it through to the sitting room. She switched on a couple of lamps and drew the curtains to block out the miserable night. 'So,' she said once settled, 'what can I do for you?'

'I just wanted to let you know that your builders will be able to get back on site towards the end of the week, hopefully Thursday.'

Katherine's face lit up. 'Really? That's great!' She paused for a moment then asked. 'But you could have told me that over the telephone and saved yourself a soaking. Was there something else?'

He smiled. 'You're right, I could have done so, but I wanted to speak to you to find out if you had heard anything. I gather that you have had a visit from Mr & Mrs Stillingfleet?'

'Mmm, yes I did. Did they tell you?' He shook his head. 'Well I don't know who told you, but they did visit me. A week last Sunday. I couldn't really help them. They wanted to know if I'd found anything else.'

'Anything else?' he frowned, 'like what?'

She shrugged. 'That's it. I don't really know, Rupert Stillingfleet was most insistent, but wouldn't say what it was I was supposed to have found. Audrey Stillingfleet did mention a necklace, but I got the feeling that that wasn't what Rupert was referring to. You haven't found a necklace have you? She said it was gold with a gold butterfly on it. I think she said she had mentioned it to the police, but I'm not sure.'

'No. Nothing like that has been found and we've given the house a good going over. Your builders couldn't have taken it could they?'

She shook her head. 'No. I was there when she was found. There was no way that either of them could have taken a necklace, even if they had the inclination to do so. We all left at the same time and that was after we had made sure all the other builders had left the house.'

He looked thoughtful. 'Okay, well we're there for a couple more days to go over the site yet again. I wonder what was so special about the necklace that they would come and ask you?'

'Something about it being a sixteenth birthday present, but I really don't think that was what Rupert was getting at. I just don't know what he wanted?'

'OK. Well, if you have any other visits, or come across any other information which you think would be of use, please do let me know.'

'Mmm,' Katherine hesitated not sure whether to pass on what Betty had just told her. He looked at her questioningly. 'I. Well ... I was just chatting to the woman who works in the shop. I don't like to gossip...' She felt guilty about deliberately doing so in the shop. 'But Betty asked me if I knew anything, which I don't. And I asked her if she knew anything,' she flushed in embarrassment, 'um, and she told me about Cecilia's boyfriend. Tom.'

He nodded encouragingly. 'Tom Fullwood.'

'Yes, that's him.'

'Yes, poor lad was distraught when she went missing. Phoned us regularly to see what we were doing about finding her, did that for years. Eventually, I think he realized it was time to move on.'

She felt relief that he knew about Tom and that she wasn't entering totally unchartered territories. 'Well apparently, they were inseparable. But what Betty said, and I think this is pure speculation and gossip but her parents will know, is that Cecilia was pregnant and was sent away to have an abortion and to keep her apart from Tom. Now whether that's true or not I don't know. If she was pregnant maybe Tom didn't know about it. And if he did, how did he feel about having his baby aborted? Apparently when she returned, he was over the moon that she was back, though I guess her parents wouldn't have been keen on them starting up where they had left off?'

'Hmm. Interesting. I knew she had gone to France and the relatives she stayed with were contacted, but if she were pregnant and she was made to have an abortion that could be relevant.'

'I hope I haven't made things worse for her parents. I don't want to distress them any further, particularly if it is pure speculation and gossip.'

'Don't worry. This information will be handled sensitively and ultimately, at the end of the day, they want whoever murdered their daughter to be found and brought to justice.' He rose to go. 'Thanks for your help and the tea.' He shrugged himself into his still soggy coat and disappeared off into the wet evening.

Hurrah! thought Katherine hurrying to the phone to call Dougie. 'Dougie? It's Katherine.'

'Hi, how are you? Any news?'

'Yup. I just had DI Allix here. You should be able to be back on site by Thursday.'

'Great! Thank goodness for that. I've found someone to stay on site overnight for the next few weeks. I've got a mate who's just been made redundant from his warehouse job, not good timing with Christmas approaching. Anyway, he's got a caravan and two big dogs - Alsatians - for £50 a night he's going to turn up at 4 p.m. before we go and stay until we get there at 7.30/8 a.m. I hope that's OK? I know we discussed getting some kind of security in, but it's so expensive. I know you want to keep costs down and I can trust him. He's a great big burly man, so combine that with his two dogs and I think it should put people off!'

'That's fine, thanks for arranging it. I think it's just one of those things I'm going to have to grin and bear. Not really fair though,' she moaned, 'after all, I didn't ask for a body to be found there.'

'I understand. But apart from anything, with those roof tiles worth thousands, they're a prime target for someone to steal and though I've got insurance, it would be a real problem to have to source such a huge number of old Kent Peg Tiles. It could potentially cause a major delay on the build.'

'Yeah, I know. Still, hopefully it won't be for too long. Once the novelty factor for the ghoulish day trippers has gone and the roof is on and firmly fixed, then maybe it won't be necessary to have someone on site every night?'

Doubtful about this, Dougie thought it wise to say nothing. 'So we'll be on site bright and early on Thursday, unless you hear otherwise and let me know. And whilst this mild weather is still around, I'll see if I can get the lads to work over the weekend. Get the foundations and brickwork done for the Garden Room before the frosts start coming in.'

'That'd be great! I'll come down on Saturday then and have a look. See you then. Bye.'

## Chapter Ten

True to his word, the police confirmed on Wednesday afternoon that the builders could resume work the following day. Delighted, Katherine eagerly awaited for Saturday morning to arrive, so that she could head over and have a look around her farmhouse. The weather was on their side as it remained dry and above freezing at night, no ground frost and with the forecast predicting the same for at least the next ten days - unusual for November.

Excitedly, she got to the farmhouse for eight o'clock, eager to see what had been done in two days. 'Hi!' she called out as she entered the house, which was already filled with a cacophony of noise.

'Hi Kitty. You need one of these.' He tapped his hard hat and pointed to one sitting on the window sill waiting for her, it was bright pink. 'Thought you might like your own and you know that none of the lads are going to wear that!' he laughed.

How stereotypical she thought, couldn't have bought a red one, but she smiled, he was right, none of the others would dare to wear it.

'Where do you want to start?' he asked.

She glanced nervously towards the room where Cecilia had been discovered. 'I suppose in there. May as well get it over and done with.' She followed him in.

'Mind yourself,' he said indicating to where floorboards had been taken up.

'Wow!' For some reason, despite her logic that the police would have opened up the fireplace, she expected the fireplace to be as it was when she last saw it, bricked up with a small gap. Instead she saw in front of her a magnificent inglenook fireplace with a huge thick oak Bressemer beam above it. 'That's amazing! What a fantastic fireplace!'

'It is isn't it. If we get the beam sandblasted to get all the rubbish off it, it'll look really good.'

'Mmm, certainly will.' She sighed, envisioning the poor girl being stuffed in there and bricked up. What had pre-empted it? Why had she had the life so cruelly taken out of her? Had she died in this room? Or had she been dragged in here?'

'Try not to think about it too much,' said Dougie gently, reading her thoughts.

'I know. I can't help it though, it's so unfair, so unjust, no matter what she was like, she didn't deserve to have her life end that way.'

'No.'

'Any luck with the necklace?'

'Nope. If the police couldn't find it, then it's highly unlikely we will.'

'True. Right, let's get down to business then.' She pulled out the plans and she and Dougie went round the house methodically. The roof was stripped and timbers were being inspected to decide whether they needed replacing or treatment. The foundations had been dug for the Garden Room and the concrete was being poured. Katherine was impressed at how much had been done in such a short period of time.

'Here Dougie, found this when we were digging,' said one of his men, handing over a tightly wrapped plastic bag.

Katherine took it and unwrapped it. Inside was a diary, damp but readable. She looked at Dougie who was thinking the same as she. Was it Cecilia's? Carefully Katherine turned back the cover and there in faded and slightly smudged writing was the name. Cecilia Stillingfleet. Katherine gulped. 'I think perhaps I'd better phone DI Allix,' she said.

'Where exactly did you find this?' asked Dougie. An area where the concrete was being poured was indicated. Inwardly he groaned. Surely this wasn't going to halt the build again?

With the phone call made, Katherine had discovered that DI Allix was already on his way to the house anyway. She couldn't resist having a peak at the diary whilst waiting for him. Her fingerprints were on it anyway, so a few more wouldn't matter, she reasoned, her curiosity getting the better of her. She half expected a grand revelation from the diary, but flicking through it; it seemed like a typical teenager's diary full of scribbled notes and coded words and initials. There were several entries for "extra English!" along with a lot of entries "TF@WF", with a jolt she realized that could be Tom Fullwood at Wynenden Farm. Were they using her farmhouse for secret liaisons? And if so, did anyone else know? She went to the end of the diary and worked back to where her last entry had been made. All it simply said was "Payday!". What she meant by that was anybody's guess, thought Katherine. Suddenly remembering about France, she flicked back. Just as she had found the first entry for her mysterious trip away, DI Allix startled her.

'Hello,' he said.

Guiltily she looked up. 'Oh, hello, that was quick.'

'I was on my way anyway,' he glanced down at the diary in her hands.

She blushed. 'I have to confess, I did have a peek, sorry. I suppose I shouldn't have.'

He smiled back at her. 'No harm done on this occasion. But if there is a next time, please leave well alone for us to deal with. Did you come across anything of interest?'

'I don't know. Inner angst of a teenage girl. I didn't really see much. I was just going to read about her visit to France or whatever it was.'

'Ahh.'

She looked at him questioningly. 'Or was it not a trip to France? Did you speak to her parents?'

'Yes and yes.'

'Sorry. I suppose I shouldn't ask questions and you can't tell me anything anyway, I'm sure.'

He smiled. 'Don't keep apologizing, there's no need. I did speak to her parents and they confirm that the plan was for Cecilia to have an abortion and stay with relatives in France, to try and help her forget about Tom, or as they put it to "get over her silly infatuation with him".'

'Oh.'

'I'm sure you can keep this to yourself though, there's enough gossip going around. The Stillingfleet's have enough to cope with at the moment, without fuel being added to the fire.'

'Of course. My lips are sealed. Oh no!' she groaned.

'What is it, Mrs Muier?' he looked quizzically at her.

'Andrew Battle, that's what and please call me Katherine, Mrs Muier is too formal and always reminds me of my ex-husband,' she paused, 'long story, very boring,' she added.

'And Andrew Battle?' He turned round to see the aforementioned opening the door of his new Range Rover, at that split second he glanced up, realized it was DI Allix, hastily got back into his car and roared off up the lane.

'Now, why would he do that?' said Katherine puzzled.

'I think I may have put him off,' grinned DI Allix.

'Thank goodness! But why would you have put him off?'

'Let's just say, he and I have crossed paths many a time over the years, he's one who likes to walk a fine line with his business interests.'

'That doesn't surprise me, not after what I've heard.'

'Really?'

'Oh, I'm sure it's nothing you've not heard before, particularly if you've had dealings with him.'

'Why was he here anyway?'

'It certainly wasn't planned. I suspect he was coming to hassle me again,' she sighed.

'What's he been hassling you about?' His eyes had narrowed and brow was furrowed.

'Oh, he wants to buy this place. Sir Geoffrey refused to sell it to him despite his persistence over the years, apparently Sir Geoffrey can't stand him. In fact, I had to agree never to sell this house to him, as a condition of my being allowed to buy this house. I don't know what's gone on with them but there's no love lost there. Anyway, Andrew keeps turning up like a bad penny. Keeps upping his offer. I'll never sell to him, even if I hadn't agreed that I wouldn't, I never would. He's such a horrible man. He makes my skin crawl every time I see him and I've got no idea why he's so desperate to get his hands on this place. By all accounts he's got enough money to buy whatever he likes, he doesn't need to rely on doing up houses and selling them on to make money any more. It's a real mystery.'

'Well, if he's being a nuisance, I could always pull him in for a little chat.' Something DI Alix felt he would secretly enjoy.

'Oh no! I don't want him to get into any trouble because of me. I just want him to leave me alone.'

'OK. But if he doesn't get the message, give me a call and I will have a quiet word with him.'

'Thanks.' As though reading his mind, she thought that DI Allix would like a legitimate reason to pull Andrew in for questioning. 'Anyway, would you like to see where this was found?'

'Yes please.'

They walked round the side of the house to the back where the Garden Room was being built and would eventually be attached to the main house. Dougie had halted work on the area and sent the lads off to do some clearing in the main house itself. After much deliberation DI Allix gave them the all clear to continue with the work on the Garden Room.

'Really? I thought you'd probably want forensics out again' said Katherine.

'I don't think so, they've gone over this place several times with a fine tooth-comb. Unless we physically dig up every inch of the five acres and take every single tile and brick down from the house, I don't think we'd find any more evidence than we have and we don't have the resources to spend more time here. If she used this place regularly as a meeting place, she perhaps thought it safer to bury her diary in a secret place.'

'Oh, right. OK.'

'I'll get this back to the office,' he said raising the evidence bag with the diary in it.'

Katherine walked him back round to the front of the house and up the drive to where he'd parked his car. She suddenly remembered something. 'When you arrived you said you were on your way here anyway. Why was that? Did you need something?'

'I didn't think there'd be anyone on site today. I wanted to walk round while it was quiet. There's something I can't quite put my finger on...' his voice trailed off.

'Sorry. The builders are working this weekend and I think next weekend, they want to catch up and get as much done before the heavy frosts start coming in and winter descends. Anyway, just so you know, there's someone staying here every night and I think during the day at weekends when the builders aren't working. Hmm, I'll have to check that. Anyway, he's got two big dogs, so you might want to give a little warning if you want to have a wander round, which you are welcome to. I wouldn't want you being attacked by the dogs!'

He laughed. 'Thanks for the warning. I'll remember that. Good idea having someone protecting your property, there are lots of tempting things here for opportunistic thieves, in addition to the inevitable ghouls who will want to poke round the site. Of course, if anything should happen whilst he's guarding the property, even if it seems like nothing, please can you let me know.'

'Of course. I'll get Dougie to pass that on. Bye.'

'Bye.' He slid into his car and reversed deftly out of the drive and headed off in the direction of the village.

# Chapter Eleven

All seemed to be slotting into place and running smoothly for Katherine. That was apart from her car which had started to play up and was getting progressively worse. It had taken her half an hour to get it started that morning and the last thing she needed was to repeatedly be late for work, when she wanted to start early to enable her to take Wednesday afternoon's off to keep abreast of the building works. After several attempts it started that Monday afternoon after work and she decided to see whether the village garage was as good as she had been told, it would also give her a chance to check out Tom Fullwood.

She pulled into the forecourt of the small, but tidy looking garage. She saw someone in navy overalls bent over the engine of another car and wondered whether it was Tom. She got out and walked over to him. Hearing footsteps, the man glanced up from what he was doing.

'Hello,' she said, taking in the stocky male with bulging biceps straining at the fabric of the overall, who stood in front of her. His eyes were close together and his nose had the slightly wonky appearance of one which had previously been broken. His hands were covered in grease and there were smudges on his face. Despite his hard exterior his deep brown eyes looked soft and kind, she thought.

'Hi, what can I do for you?' he smiled.

'My cars been playing up, being a pain starting up in the mornings.'

'Do you want to pop the bonnet up,' he asked wiping his hands on a greasy rag, which had been hanging out of one of his back pockets.

She did as he asked and watched as he poked and prodded a few things. She had no clue about cars and for all she knew, he could be planning to carry out a load of unnecessary work. But given what others had said about him and his honesty, she hoped that she would not be ripped off, as she had been at the last garage she'd used.

'Shouldn't be too tricky to sort out. When would you like it done?'

'As soon as really, but I work and need the car to get there and back. If it manages to keep going for the rest of the week, how about Saturday?'

'Sure, no problem. Drop it off first thing and I'll get it done during the morning for you. I think you only need a couple of small parts so it shouldn't cost too much, unless I discover something whilst I'm working on it. Do you live locally?'

She hesitated. 'I'm living in Wynenden Close temporarily.'

'Well, if you have any problems starting it this week, give me a bell and I'll nip round and try to get it going for you.'

'Oh, thanks!' she hadn't expected that.

'No problem,' he smiled, 'see you on Saturday.'

'Sure, great, OK. See you then.' Did he not need her name or a phone number? He must be very trusting, she mused, getting back into her car and driving off. Once home she reversed up the small drive, so that if the car did need help starting it was easier to access the engine.

The phone was ringing when she opened the front door. Dropping everything down and slamming the door behind her, she raced to get it before the answer phone kicked in. 'Hello?' she said breathlessly.

'Hello Katherine. Have I caught you at a bad time?' It was Ted.

'Oh no, not at all. I've just got in from work.' She was pleased to hear from him, having wondered how long it would be before he phoned after their drink a couple of weeks previously. She was determined not to chase after him, after all, it had only been a casual drink she reasoned.

'Sorry I haven't phoned earlier, it's very remiss of me. My only excuse is that work has been manic, but then it usually is, so perhaps that's no excuse and I should manage my time more effectively. Thanks for the other night, I had a really good time.'

'Despite Andrew Battle turning up!' she laughed.

He chortled. 'Yes, despite that. Anyway, I wondered if perhaps you'd like to do it again some time?'

'Yes, that'd be nice. Just let me know when you're free.'

He groaned. 'I'm afraid it probably won't be for a couple of weeks, hope that's OK?'

'That's fine, whenever, I know everyone's busy, particularly at this time of year with Christmas parties coming up and all that.'

'I wish! No such luck for me.'

'Oh dear, never mind, they can be rather boring some-times anyway.' She tried to console him, but actually she rather enjoyed socializing and all things festive, in the run up to Christmas.

'You're too kind. Anyway, the other reason I'm ringing is to forewarn you that Sir Geoffrey is going to be heading out to the farmhouse at some point soon. He's been talking about it for a while and is determined to do so.'

'That's fine. He mentioned it when I saw him, I just hope he likes what I'm doing. I know he saw the plans for the Garden Room and the proposed changes, but seeing them in the flesh can be rather different.'

'Don't worry, I think he's just curious. Anyway, I've got to go, pile of paperwork with my name on it waiting for me. I'll call you soon. Take care. Bye.'

'Bye.' She had a warm, fuzzy, feeling as she put the phone down.


When Katherine met with Dougie on the Wednesday to go through the inevitable queries which were cropping up, she mentioned that Sir Geoffrey would be paying a visit to forewarn him. The build was progressing well and she left them to it, promising to return on Saturday to iron out fur-ther queries.

Bright and early on the following Saturday, Katherine dropped her car down at Fullwood Garage. Tom was there beavering away, even though it was only 8 a.m. He was accompanied by a young, lanky, spotty, lad who turned out to be helping Tom every Saturday and was mad keen on cars.

'Morning,' she called, retrieving her rucksack out of the back seat.

'Morning,' he smiled, 'what time would you like to pick it up?'

'Um, I don't mind really. Sometime this afternoon?'

'That's fine, I'll have it ready by lunchtime. I normally close about 2 o'clock but I'll be here 'til about 4 o'clock today, so turn up when it suits you.'

'Thanks.'

'You off on a nice walk?' he enquired pleasantly, having observed the walking boots, jeans, thick jumper, waterproof jacket, hat, gloves and rucksack.

'I'm walking up to the house to see what the builders have been up to,' she blurted out before realizing what she'd said.

'Doing a house up are you? Where is it?' he asked good naturedly.

'Um, er, Wynenden Farmhouse,' she stuttered, but observed him keenly, watching for what kind of reaction her words would procure.

He paled slightly. 'Oh. That's a nice house,' he replied woodenly.

'It is,' she paused. 'Look, I'm sorry, I know,' she hesitated, 'about you and Cecilia and I'm sorry.'

'Thanks,' he said quietly. 'You were there when she ...' his voice crackled with emotion, 'when she was found?'

Katherine nodded. 'Sorry.'

He shrugged and gazed into the distance. Katherine thought he had a haunted look about him, ghosts from the past catching up with him.

'It must be difficult for you,' she ventured, 'after so much time. I gather you and she were very close.'

He sighed. 'We were soul mates. We were going to be together forever.'

'It must have been hard for you, trying to be together with her parents so disapproving of your relationship.'

His eyes snapped up and hardened. 'Huh, they didn't truly care about their daughter, she was just some kind of trophy, an accessory to the lifestyle they aspired to. They didn't really know her. I blame them for her death. If they hadn't tried to force her to be someone she wasn't, this would never have happened. If they hadn't sent her away...,' his voice trailed off.

Feeling she'd over stepped the mark, Katherine stood awkwardly and said nothing.

'Anyway,' he suddenly said in a business like manner, 'I'll have the car ready by lunchtime.' He turned and went back to the car he'd been working on.

'Thanks, I'll leave the keys here,' she said placing them on a shelf just inside the garage doors.

She walked briskly for the twenty-five minutes it took to get from the village to the house, mulling over the conversation, barely seeing the beautiful surrounding countryside with the last few richly coloured autumnal leaves fluttering down, the fields bare, preparing for another winter, the hedgerows empty of their summer offerings. By the time she reached the house she was warm and out of breath from the exertion, the walk had reminded her that she needed to get fit and do more exercise, more walks and back to the swimming which she loved, was what was required she concluded.

She was again amazed at how quickly the work was progressing. The roof timbers were up for the Garden Room and they had almost completed replacing the rotten timbers on the main roof. By next week they would be felt and battening both the roof's followed by the tiling. The full height glass windows, which would run from the base of the roof structure in the Garden Room down to the brick work, which was six courses high in reclaimed brick to match, as closely as possible, the original building, had been ordered and the house would then be completely water tight. Excitedly she could see it all coming together, as her builders performed miracles and her evenings spent poring over every detail was coming in to its own. The house was to be re-wired and re-plumbed and most of it would be re-plastered, due to poor repair. She knew exactly where she wanted everything to go, from light switches to radiators and underfloor heating, to taps, the whole lot. This, in turn, made life very easy for Dougie and his team and meant that it was purely problems which cropped up on a daily basis which needed to be resolved and there was no need to constantly chase for details or information. Dougie knew that when it came to ordering the tiles, floorboards, bathroom fittings - absolutely everything - all he needed to do was ask and Katherine had the information ready. There would be no delays on her part. The kitchen was already on order and would be ready in plenty of time for the kitchen to be fitted and finished.

Having gone through the latest batch of problems which needed addressing and which weren't able to be sorted out over the telephone in the last couple of days, Katherine walked from room to room with her paint charts. She stood in each room, trying to imagine what it would be like, what she wanted from the room and matching a colour to go with that vision. Taking into consideration the aspect of the room and the amount of natural light which came in, ensuring that she wasn't making mistakes such as choosing dark, cool, colours for a north facing room with a small window. She scribbled a note of each room and the colour options she had decided on in readiness to give to Dougie who would get sample pots and put the three choices she'd opted for each room up for her contemplation. The only rooms she couldn't address were the attic ones, these could be done once the roof was on and the new windows - for which she had been granted consent - were in. There was going to be one in each gable end and two heritage Velux windows at the back. This gave her an additional two large bedrooms with sloping ceilings and a decent sized shower room. These were in addition to the four double sized bedrooms on the first floor, main bathroom and ensuite bathroom to the master bedroom. She was just finishing up when she glanced out of the window to see Sir Geoffrey and Ted approaching up the drive. She flipped her file shut and went out to greet them.

'Hello!' Katherine called cheerfully.

Ted smiled in delight at seeing her. 'Hi. I thought you weren't here, your car's not here?'

'In the garage I'm afraid, it's being a bit temperamental.'

'Katherine, my dear, how very nice to see you.' The upper class clip of Sir Geoffrey's voice cut across the still air.

'Lovely to see you too,' replied Katherine pleasantly.

'Thought we'd come and see the house. See what you're up to.' She could see his moustache virtually bristle with excitement.

'Great! Come this way.' Nervously she led the way to the front door, offering a silent prayer that he would like what she was doing and not start making things difficult for her, even though he had no legal right to do so. She took them into the hallway and up the stairs, first to explain what was going to change - which wasn't a great deal - then it was downstairs to explain which walls were going to be removed as several, relatively modern, store rooms were to be knocked down to create a bigger kitchen, which would then create an "L" shape into the Garden Room. Finally she took them through to the room which would become the winter sitting room she had decided. She noticed Sir Geoffrey staring intently at the recently exposed fireplace. Ted raised his eyebrows at her questioningly.

'So...,' he cleared his throat, 'is that where the young girl was found then?'

'Yes, it was,' she replied, noticing that is eyes had misted up slightly.

'And she was there? Alone? All by herself was she?'

'Yes. Tragic, absolutely tragic. I'm trying not to think how awful it must have been for her.' She and Ted stood silently whilst Sir Geoffrey gazed, almost trance like, into the fireplace.

Eventually he muttered something imperceptible, then he snapped back to his usual self. 'Right well, jolly good job you're doing. Now where's this Garden Room you keep talking about?'

She led them out through the front door and round to the back of the house where they could see the builders beavering away, she raised her eyebrows at Dougie who was in a deep discussion with one of his men. She explained what they were doing and how it was all going to come together, pointing out where the heritage Velux and gable end windows would be once the main roof was finished and where the Garden Room would join the main house and which area of wall was to be knocked through to allow it to connect to the main house.

'Excellent, excellent. Good to see life being brought back into the old place. One of my favourites this. Used to come down here with my brother. Of course in those days one of the farmers lived in this house and his wife used to make the most magnificent cakes, we'd come down here and she'd feed us up with cake. Wonderful woman. The cook we had up at the house was absolutely dreadful at baking, she couldn't produce anything decent, her fruit cake was enough to break your teeth on.' He chuckled to himself at the memories. 'You found the Well then?' he asked.

'Well? I didn't know there was one.'

'Oh, yes, over there somewhere.' He waved his hand into the distance.'

Overhearing them, Dougie stepped forward. 'Sorry, to butt in. I forgot to tell you Kitty. The police uncovered it during their search. We've covered it over with boards at the moment and staked them into the ground, don't want any accidents with anyone falling down it.'

Oh, right.' She was a bit miffed that he'd forgotten to tell her this. A Well, how exciting! That would make watering her planned vegetable garden easy.

'Right, well, can't stand around here all day,' said Sir Geoffrey briskly. 'Come on Ted, we've got things to do.' He marched off in the direction of the drive trailed by Ted and Katherine.

'Nice to see you,' he whispered to her.

She felt a fuzzy glow inside her. 'Nice to see you too,' she grinned.

'Thank you for the tour Katherine. Jolly kind of you. You're doing a grand job, just grand, look forward to seeing it when it's finished. Good bye.'

Katherine smiled to herself, amused by Sir Geoffrey's lack of awareness, the pure assumption that he would be invited back to see the house when it was finished, but there was no arrogance there. She had a soft spot for both him and his wife, despite their old fashioned ways and mannerisms. Katherine was growing more fond of them the more she saw of them, but couldn't put her finger on why this was.

'See you,' called Ted giving her a big grin as he hopped into his Land Rover, having ensured that Sir Geoffrey was safely ensconced in the passenger seat.

She perched herself on a tree stump once they had left and happily munched her cheese and salad sandwich, re-lived that she had received Sir Geoffrey's seal of approval, but bemused that it bothered her what he thought of her project. She waited until the builders had finished their lunch break then went through her paint list with Dougie, he wouldn't need it for ages but she in no way wanted to be responsible for any delay on the work, and so in her usual organized manner, was prepared well in advance. With nothing more for her to do she walked back down into the village to collect her car, this time taking in the beauty and peace of her surroundings as she went. She arrived at the garage just after 3 p.m. to find that Tom was busy working on a vintage car, she wasn't quite sure which one as it seemed to be in rather a lot of bits. He pulled himself out from underneath it and brushed himself down.

'All fixed,' he said nodding towards her car, 'nothing major, the bill comes to £125.00.'

Pleasantly surprised by the relatively low cost, she fished her debit card out of her rucksack and slid the card into the machine. While it was going through they made polite small talk, Katherine unwilling to venture into anything more personal after her faux pas this morning. She was just slipping her card back into her rucksack when the deep growl of a car crept up behind and revved ferociously, making her jump.

'Oh, no,' she groaned, seeing the grinning face of Andrew Battle leaning out of the window of his Porsche 911.

'Changed your mind yet?'

'No.'

'Let me know when you do!' He put his foot on the accelerator and raced off in a roar of noise. Katherine winced at the sound.

'Friend of yours?' asked Tom looking at her suspiciously.

'No! Absolutely not!' she retorted indignantly.

'Making a pest of himself as usual then,' Tom rolled his eyes.

'Yes. What do you mean "as usual"?' She was intrigued to know Tom's feelings about Andrew.

He shrugged. 'Oh, he's always up to something or other, hassling someone or other.'

'You sound like you are speaking from personal experience?'

'Not me personally, but he always seemed to be hanging around when Cecilia and I were together in the village. Always making lewd remarks, that sort of thing. People like him get their pleasure, their kicks, out of demeaning other people, seeing them squirm, making them uncomfortable, suppose he's used to getting his own way and will do whatever it takes to get it.'

'And is that what he did with Cecilia or was it you he was getting at?'

'Huh! He wouldn't get to me, I've come across enough people like him. He's come from humble beginnings like me, I know where I've come from and I've worked hard, worked honestly and I'm proud if people know what I've done with my life. Him, he wants to forget, pretend like he always was a big shot, that he didn't grow up on a run-down estate, he's ashamed of his past. Do you know his mum still lives in the house he grew up in, still struggles to pay the bills but does he help? Does he heck! Never sees her, he's washed his hands of his family, he's a disgrace of a human being.'

Very eloquently put, thought Katherine agreeing with him. 'So was it Cecilia he was hassling then?'

'He hassled, and still does hassle, every female. Bit of a womanizer, convinced no female can say no to him and, bizarrely, a lot of woman say yes to him. It's like he has this strange animal magnetism, can't understand it myself, you see sane, intelligent women giving in to him, they must be mad! He's worked his way through many a wife in this parish too, he's got no morals.'

'Really! Gosh!' He was even worse than she had thought he was, ethically and morally bankrupt, by the sounds of it.

'So, watch out. Unless of course you like that sort of thing,' he looked slightly embarrassed by his vehement outburst.

She laughed. 'No, not interested and he's not interested in me, think I must be too old for him! He's interested in my house and he just won't give up. It's starting to become really irritating now.'

'The house? Why does he want that?'

'No idea, not got a clue. Perhaps it's the challenge? Sir Geoffrey refused to sell it to him and he sees that as a slight, don't know, but what I do know is that he won't get it. Anyway, thanks for doing the car.'

'No problem, you shouldn't have any more problems. See you.'

# Chapter Twelve

'So, please can you come?' pleaded the voice of her six year old goddaughter Alice. 'I'm an Angel and I even have a speaking part!' She was doing her best to persuade her godmother to come and see her in the Year 1 Nativity Play which they were putting on that week at school on Wednesday afternoon.

Katherine smiled as Alice continued to plead, it was nice to be so wanted. 'What time is it on Wednesday afternoon?'

'2.30 p.m. Mummy will save you a seat so you won't have to get there really early. Does that mean you can come?' she asked excitedly.

'Yes, I would be delighted to come.'

'Yippee! Mummy! Mummy! Katherine's coming! She's going to come!'

Libby came on the phone laughing. 'You've certainly made her day, I don't think I need to go, I'm not as popular as you!'

Katherine laughed back. 'That's only because I get to do the nice things and don't have to be the nagging mother!'

'Oy! Don't be so cheeky! It's in the job description! Nagging is a very important part!' she joked.

'It's lovely to be asked and it's great that happens to be on the one afternoon when I can be available.'

'It won't muck up your meeting with Dougie will it?'

'No, I had a long meeting with him yesterday and if I eat my sandwich in the car on the way back from work I can go straight to the farmhouse, have a quick meeting and then whizz up to the school for the nativity. It will be lovely. You'd think that working in a prep school I'd have seen enough of them, but I never do, never get out of the office to see the plays or performances and besides, it always means so much more when there's a child you're closely associated with in it.'

'Well, thanks, you've really made her day. Fortunately Henry's only got a Carol Service this year otherwise you'd have to clear your diary to come and see him too! So, I'll see you up there. To get a good seat you have to get there so ridiculously early, I'll save you one.'

'Great, look forward to it. Bye.'

And so, after a quick meeting with Dougie and a brief admire of the tiles being put on the roof, she headed off to the Prep School at Wynenden School to watch the much anticipated Nativity. She parked her old Golf in amongst the substantial collection of new four wheel drive cars, the usual motley crew of Range Rovers, Land Rovers, Volvo's and the like along with a couple of Bentley's and a Ferrari, but a healthy sprinkling of what Katherine perceived as 'normal' cars scattered throughout the car park, reflecting the apparent financial and broad range of parents and backgrounds at the school. She was used to it and not in anyway intimidated, the car park at the school where she

121

worked was filled with an almost identical collection. Katherine followed the stream of parents and grandparents down to the hall, took the programme which was offered to her by one of the older Prep School children and searched the throng for her friend, eventually spying her deep in conversation with another mum.

'Hi,' she said softly, not wanting to interrupt the conversation.

'Katherine! Hi!' Libby kissed her on both cheeks and introduced her to the other mum. They chatted pleasantly until the Prep School Headmaster came out and made a little speech about how much hard work had gone into this performance and thanking the parents and grandparents for attending. The lights went down and for the next half an hour they all sat in rapt attention at the small children doing their utmost to perform the Nativity. So small and so sweet, they earnestly performed and were rewarded by deafening clapping from proud parents and grandparents. This was followed by another short speech, from the Prep School Headmaster, congratulating the children and informing the adults that cups of tea and coffee along with cake and mince pies would now be served at the back of the hall.

'They were so sweet!' exclaimed Katherine, 'and Alice was wonderful!'

Libby burst with pride, as did the other parents. 'I know! It is absolutely amazing what they do. The Head of Music and Head of Drama work miracles. It's certainly nothing we experienced at school is it?'

'You're telling me! We were lucky to get even a hint of music or drama, but that's one of the things you shell out so much money for each term.'

'And worth every penny as far as I am concerned.' They edged their way to the back of the hall, caught up in the tidal wave of adults heading in the same direction. Libby handed Katherine a cup of tea and offered her a piece of cake. Finding it difficult to decide between lemon drizzle and chocolate she eventually settled on chocolate and wasn't disappointed. The sponge was soft and moist and the butter cream was rich but not too sweet. Libby had settled on the same and they momentarily lost themselves in the enjoyment of the cake.

'Gosh that was good,' commented Katherine licking her fingers then wiping them with a paper serviette.

'Another advantage of sending the children here,' grinned Libby, 'they really do make the best cakes.'

'Worth every penny of your umpteen thousand pounds a year you spend here then!'

'Oh, look, there's someone you might be interested in,' whispered Libby.

Katherine frowned, surely she wasn't matchmaking?

'Over there, the tall slim man, perfectly cut suit,' she continued in hushed tones.

Katherine glanced over and saw a very convivial looking male in a beautifully cut suit, pristine shirt and silk tie, dark brown hair sprinkled with grey round the edges, cut in a very traditional short style but with a slightly floppy fringe. He was chatting animatedly to some other parents. Got to be a banker or something, she thought.

'He's the Headmaster,' whispered Libby.

'Oh.' Katherine felt slightly crestfallen. 'Must be getting paid too much if he can afford suits like that,' she retorted. 'Hang on, I thought it was the Headmaster who gave the little speeches prior to and after the Nativity?'

'Oh, he's the Headmaster of the Prep School. Over there is Robert Codell the Headmaster of the Senior School who also oversees the Prep School. He's been here for years, I think he must have been here when Cecilia was a pupil, though not as Head. He was appointed Headmaster two years ago, prior to that I think he had been the Deputy Head for about eight years.'

'Hmm, I wonder if he knew her. He must have known of her, but I wonder if he actually taught her?'

'Ooh, he's coming this way. Tell you what I'll introduce you if I get a chance. I've met him a few times, his wife teaches Year 1, she teaches Alice sometimes, she must have been behind the scenes helping today,' she stopped whispering and smiled as he came directly towards them. 'Mr Codell, nice to see you again.'

There was a beat before he replied as he went through his rolodex memory for the correct name. 'Mrs Lumsden. How are you?' he replied pleasantly, a dazzling white smile on his face.

'Very well thank you and you?'

'Very well indeed.'

'This is Katherine, a friend of mine, Katherine Muier. Katherine this is Mr Codell the Senior School Headmaster.'

They shook hands politely and made pleasantries to one another.

'Katherine has just moved into the village,' she continued.

'Oh really, how nice. It is a lovely village, whereabouts are you in the village?'

'I'm just renting somewhere at the moment.'

'She's doing up a farmhouse,' interrupted Libby. 'Perhaps you know it? Wynenden Farmhouse?'

Whilst the smile stayed, the blood seemed to drain out of his face and he coughed in distraction. 'Oh yes. Lovely house I believe, been past it a few times when we've been out for a walk,' he replied tightly.

'Thanks. Yes it is lovely, well hopefully it will be when it's finished, though obviously we've been delayed a bit what with...'

'Ah, yes,' he seemed to have recovered himself, 'unfortunate business that.'

'Did you know her?' asked Katherine.

'She was a pupil here and I did teach her for a while. Shame, great shame, she ended up the way she did. Well, if you will please excuse me, I had better circulate. Nice to meet you,' he nodded at Katherine, gave them another dazzling smile and eased his way towards another group of parents.

Katherine looked at Libby and raised her eyebrows, she did the same back. When he was safely out of earshot, Libby whispered to her friend. 'What did you think of that? Looked like he'd seen a ghost!'

'I know,' whispered Katherine back. 'Wonder what it is?' At that point they were interrupted by an overly excited Alice flinging herself at her mother.

'What did you think?' her bright little eyes looked up in to her mother's, seeking approval.

'I thought you were wonderful! The best Angel ever!' she hugged her daughter tightly to her and kissed the top of her head.

'I thought you were fantastic Alice! It was an absolute delight to watch you, the whole thing was really special, thank you for inviting me.' She stroked her goddaughter's hair and squatted down to hug her, relishing the tender moment.

'Did you really? Wasn't it fun! It was so exciting, but scary too!'

'I don't think you're going to get her to bed on time tonight!' laughed Katherine. It's going to take an age for her to come down from this.

Libby smiled indulgently at her daughter. 'I know, but it's worth it!'

# Chapter Thirteen

There was something niggling away at Katherine but she couldn't work out what, just couldn't put her finger on. No matter how hard she tried her brain refused to retrieve what was bothering her. She flicked restlessly between TV channels, her concentration virtually nonexistent, the phone interrupted her musings.

'Hello?' she said absent mindedly.

'Hi Katherine, it's Ted, how are you?'

'Hi!' her focus immediately switching to the caller. 'I'm ok thanks, how about you?'

'I'm fine thanks, my head is finally coming above the parapet and I wondered if you fancied going out for that drink we talked about?'

'I'd like that. When were you thinking of?'

'How about tomorrow night? I know it's short notice again,' his voice sounded hopeful.

'Tomorrow would be great. Where do you suggest? The Grouse & Peacock again?'

'We could do, or there's the Cow & Mistletoe, it's a bit further away, nice though, old like The Grouse & Peacock, log fires and all that.'

'Great, not been there either. What sort of time were you thinking of?'

'If I pick you up about a quarter to eight, would that be OK?'

'I'll be ready. See you tomorrow,' she put the phone down, a little tingling of excitement buzzed through her. Why was it that, even though she was forty-seven, she felt like a teenager, she wondered?

After another frantic day at work Katherine was glad to get home and glad that it was Friday. The end of any term was always manic; there were reports and invoices to get out, paperwork to prepare for the next term and a million and one other things that all needed to be done before school closed the following Thursday for Christmas. Katherine wouldn't be back in the office for three weeks as she was lucky enough to mainly only work term time, unlike some of her colleagues, and the children were off for almost four weeks. But despite her tiredness she was buzzing with excitement at the thought of going out for a drink with Ted again. She flopped down onto the sofa with a cup of tea for half an hour to recuperate and recharge her batteries and flicked on the television for half an hour of "rubbish" as she called it. There were never any programs of substance on at that time of day and sadly those types of programs were in the minority these days anyway, an unsavoury tidal wave of "reality" type programs having washed many interesting dramas and cultural programs out of the way.

With tea and "rubbish" finished, she hopped up and trotted into the kitchen, popping a defrosted shepherds pie she'd made and frozen a couple of weeks previously into the oven. Whilst it was heating up she ran herself a nice hot bath filled with some reviving bubble bath and soaked luxuriously. Eventually she heaved herself out, ritually cleansing her face and moisturizing it while she drip dried under the towel. She slipped into pre-chosen clothes of slim fitting, knee length, chocolate brown coloured fine needlecord skirt, soft cream silk blouse and a sage coloured round neck cashmere cardigan, she settled on a pair of slim, long, rich conker-coloured suede boots with a slight heel. A pair of pearl earrings and a simple gold chain with a gold coffee bean on it and a spray of her favourite Chanel perfume finished the ensemble. She perched in the kitchen and ate her supper carefully so as to ensure it didn't splash her pristine cream blouse.

Prompt as ever, Ted knocked on the door at 7.45 p.m. precisely. As the evenings were cooling down, Katherine wrapped her pale pink cashmere scarf around her and slipped into her trusty navy pea coat. Again the drive to the pub was made up of small talk giving Katherine a sense of déjà vu. The pub turned out to be just as picturesque as the last; lots of beams, wooden floors, couple of open fires roaring away, but was quieter, less a noisy hubbub and more a serene murmur, but that could have been down to the fact that it was not a Saturday night. They had no problem finding a table as the pub was barely a quarter full. Because of the ancient design of the pub there were lots of nooks and crannies and plenty of tables with comfortable chairs or sofas where one could sit and chat without fear of being over heard. Again they chose a table by one of the fires, there was a small cluster consisting of a two seater sofa and a wing chair. Katherine seated herself on the sofa whilst Ted went to the bar to buy their drinks. She thought it was ridiculous that she felt so nervous about Ted potentially sitting next to her on the sofa, but she spread her coat next her anyway to avoid this, inwardly berating herself for being so pathetic.

'So, how was your day?' he asked placing a large glass of white wine in front of her and flopping himself down into the wing chair opposite her.

She relaxed now that the hurdle was over with and chatted about her day, what was going on at the school and asked him about his work and what had been keeping him so busy. The conversation inevitably came round to the farmhouse and she told him excitedly about what the builders had been doing and how well it was all progressing.

'Any news?' he asked sipping his apple juice and sparkling water mix.

'About Cecilia?' He nodded. 'No, nothing, there's no reason why I should be told anything I suppose, best to just let the police get on with their jobs.' She frowned, there was something and she couldn't put her finger on it.

'You look troubled? What is it?' he asked.

'Oh, nothing, I don't know ...' she trailed off. 'There's something I can't put my finger on and I don't know what.'

'Relevant to the case?'

'I think so, but I'm not sure.'

'About someone or something?' he probed.

'Again, I don't know. It's just a feeling.'

'It's not Andy Battle hassling you again is it?'

'No..., though he had apparently been making a nuisance of himself with Cecilia.'

'Really? How do you know that?'

'You remember I took my car into a garage for repairs?' He nodded. 'I took it to Fullwood Garage.'

'Ah,' the penny dropped.

'We got chatting, it kind of slipped out which house I was renovating and he mentioned Cecilia. Apparently Andrew was always hanging around, making lewd comments and that sort of thing. I can't help feeling there's more to it than that. What if he had done something to Cecilia?'

'Like what?'

'I don't know. Threatened her? Attacked her? Sexually assaulted her even.'

'They're pretty serious allegations, I'd be careful who you say this too,' his brow wrinkled. 'I mean I'm not saying I don't think he's capable of any of those things but what I think, and what he is actually like, could be two entirely different things,' he said generously. 'I'm a bit prejudiced against him as he has been quite ruthless in his pursuit of Wynenden Farmhouse.'

'I get that, I'm really just surmising out loud. I don't know how old he is? He must be, what? In his thirties or forties? And she was sixteen when she died, only by a few months, so he must have been maybe ten or twenty years older than her, that's a pretty big difference at such a tender age. Another thing Tom said, was that he seems to think that Andrew has this animal magnetism about him, that women can't resist him, can't see it myself but...,' she shrugged, 'what if he appeared older and sophisticated to Cecilia? What if it ...,' she stopped herself suddenly, she was going to say "if it was his baby she'd been pregnant with" but realized just in time that few people knew about this fact, rumours yes, but fact no.

'What if?' he looked quizzically at her.

131

'Oh, nothing, just wondering if there'd been something going on between them.'

'I would have thought with all the gossips around, someone would have heard something and besides he's the sort of person who would brag about it.'

'Yes, but not if she were under aged when this was going on. She didn't turn sixteen until she was away. He may be arrogant and full of himself, but he's not stupid, he'd not want to be classed as a sex offender, a paedophile would he?'

'No, I suppose not.' They sat thoughtfully for a minute mulling over their discussion.

The door to the pub burst open followed by a blast of cold air, interrupting their contemplations; a man weaved his way unsteadily to the bar and leaned heavily on it. 'Double whisky please,' he slurred loudly. The barman looked at him for a moment before silently filling the glass. The man slapped a twenty pound note down onto the bar top and without waiting for his change threw the spirit down his throat, slammed the glass down and demanded another. This one he grabbed and staggered over to a chair, dropping himself messily into it.

'You? 'Whas this? You found summing ...' he slurred loudly in the direction of Katherine and Ted from across the room. It was Rupert Stillingfleet.

Katherine shifted uncomfortably in her seat. 'Oh, hello Rupert. Um, how are you?' What a stupid thing to say! I'm a complete moron, she berated herself.

'How d'ya think? My daughter's dead and what you gonna do about it?' he swayed unsteadily in his chair, sloshing his whisky over himself as he did, about ready for a tumble.

'I think, the police are doing all they can,' she replied quietly, aware that they were now the focus of the whole pub, thank goodness it's not full, she thought.

'Thas not, goodenough,' he slurred 'whose gonna bring her back eh? Justanswermethat.'

'Sorry,' she replied meekly unsure of whether Rupert thought she was a policewoman or not.

'Come on, let's find you a nice table to sit at,' Ted got up and firmly took Rupert, who had staggered to his feet by this time, by the elbow and guided him to a quiet table on the far side of the room, as far away from them as was possible.

'He's in a bad way, isn't he?' she whispered to him when he returned.

'Yeah, poor chap. I don't really know him, lots of people gossip about them being stuck up, but they've always been fine with me, hardly ever see them mind you. How do you deal with something like that? Your daughter disappears and ten years later she's found just a few minutes from your house?' He shook his head. 'Awful, a living nightmare I would imagine.'

'Yes. I guess he's using alcohol to numb the pain.' They sat in a glum silence for a while, the evening kind of spoilt for them and being caring people themselves they could empathize with Rupert and the pain he must be feeling. Eventually, they decided to leave and went back to Katherine's house for coffee. Katherine sincerely hoping that he wouldn't take this as an invitation for anything more. They chatted amiably for a while and sometime after midnight Ted left, giving her a gentle kiss on the cheek in farewell.

Knowing that the builders weren't working that week-end Katherine decided to go the village Farmer's Market and then head up to the farmhouse later on. The weather had turned cold and there had been a heavy frost overnight, the whiteness sparkled in the low morning sun. She shivered and pulled the collar of her coat up higher to keep out the north wind which was gently blowing and bringing the temperature to well below freezing. She was glad she'd put on her pale pink cashmere beanie which matched her scarf and had been a present from Libby last Christmas. Huddled figures hurried up towards the village hall and with relief Katherine burst through the doors into the warmth of the building. It was packed. With Christmas rapidly approaching people were out looking for presents which were slightly different, something which couldn't be found in the high street run-of-the-mill shops. Determined to see every stall this time, Katherine queued patiently for her bread as, yet again, it was rapidly selling out and the queue seemed longer than on her previous visit. She then strolled from stall to stall admiring the many different hand made products and chatting to the stall holders. There was one stall selling unusual designs in silver and she bought a pair of earrings for Libby which were made up of intricate fine twists of silver interwoven with small, circular, amethysts. Pleased with her purchase she decided to have a cup of coffee before inspecting the remaining stalls. She joined the queue and studiously avoided looking in the direction of the long table, she purchased her coffee and hurried past, smiling and saying "hello" at speed before she could be stopped. Fortunately for her the long table was full with the usual mélange of people and the smaller tables near them were all full up too. There were a couple of seats free at a table about as far as it was possible to be away from them and she politely asked the two middle aged women sitting there whether it would be alright for her to sit there.

Katherine sat and sipped her coffee and observed the hive of activity which was going on. The hall was full of people; young, old, middle aged and they all seemed to be buying - good news for the stallholders. Of course with Christmas approaching there were a lot of festive products, fabric stockings hand-stitched and ready to be hung up on Christmas Eve, cupcakes with festive toppings such as Father Christmas, snowflakes and reindeers, jars of home-made mincemeat for mince pies, mince pies, Christmas Puddings, holly wreaths. Katherine tried hard not to listen in to the two women's conversation but being in such close proximity, it was tricky not to. Piecing together what was being said in the snatches she'd caught, she came to the conclusion that the woman called Jane was actually the Headmasters' wife at Wynenden School. Jane was saying how busy he was, always the same at the end of term, how tired he was getting, how he needed a break, how he'd been on edge for the last few weeks.

'I can't understand it,' she said, 'he doesn't normally get quite so stressed but for some reason he is.'

'Maybe he just needs a break. He works so hard, he always has done.'

'Yes, I suppose so,' replied Jane doubtfully.

'And there has been the added pressure of having to make time for the police.'

Katherine's ears pricked up. The police?

'Yes, they do seem to have made rather a lot of visits.'

'Natural I suppose, they must want background on the girl. I know they went into all that when she went missing but that was a long time ago and now that it has become a murder enquiry I suppose they are going to want to go through everything again with a fine toothcomb, they must have to build up some kind of fresh profile again and go over what she was doing in the months prior to her death.'

They absolutely had to be talking about Cecilia. Katherine felt compelled to stay and listen but at the same time felt guilty at eaves dropping into their conversation. Still, she reasoned, if it were that private they shouldn't be discussing it in public.

'Add to that,' continued Jane's friend, 'the fact that Robert was her Form Teacher and taught her English, he's the one who is best placed to give them some background on her.'

He taught her! No wonder he went so pale when I mentioned her, thought Katherine. I wonder what his opinion was of her?

'It is a tragedy, poor girl didn't deserve to die like that. Robert always said she was a handful. It was a shame, she was such a bright girl, could have gone far but would get behind in her work, he said.' Jane glanced at Katherine and smiled.

'Do you live in the village?' Jane's friend enquired pleasantly.

Katherine blushed a bright red. 'Well, yes I do um ...' It was time to own up, she'd just seen Betty come through the main hall door and if she didn't say anything then she was sure that Betty would. 'I, er, bought Wynenden Farm.'

The two women looked agog at her for a moment, too nonplussed to say anything.

'You must be Katherine,' said Jane, 'Robert mentioned that he'd met you. You were there weren't you, when she was found?' Katherine nodded. 'How dreadful.'

'Golly!' was all Jane's friend could muster.

'Mmm, it wasn't very pleasant.'

'I hope they catch whoever did it soon. Her poor parents are going out of their minds. I popped in to see them a couple of days ago. Distraught, totally and utterly distraught. Her mother is beside herself.'

'Not nice at all,' added Katherine. 'I didn't know the girl, but it must have been a shock for the whole village.'

'When she went missing no one really paid any attention to her mother who insisted that something was wrong. Cecilia had run off a couple of times before and always returned. Maybe if we had believed Audrey, Cecilia would still be alive?'

'Maybe Jane, but you can't think like that, it won't change anything now and let's face it, if she had not been so wild maybe we would have taken her mother's claim more seriously. You weren't the only one who didn't believe her.'

'I suppose,' Jane looked none too convinced.

Hesitantly Katherine spoke, choosing her words carefully. 'In what way was she "wild"? I keep hearing this about her, but "wild" could mean anything, I'm just curious to know what kind of person she was.'

'Well,' Jane looked thoughtful, 'she was very willful, she did what she wanted to do, she was always plastered in makeup, every morning the teachers would get her to clean it off and yet later on in the day she was covered in it again. She seemed to have no respect for rules. She seemed very forward with members of the opposite sex and on several occasions was brought home by the police for underage drinking and being found in clubs and bars. But there were times when she could be really sweet. A complicated child is how I would describe her.'

'Hmm, seems like she was quite a handful.' And yet to Katherine it was diametrically opposed to what Tom had told her. She glanced at her watch and, feeling that there was nothing further to be gained by continuing to chat and already feeling guilty about gossiping, she decided to have a quick look at the remaining stalls before the market closed. 'Lovely to meet you,' she said picking her cup and saucer up and rising to go.

'You too, Katherine. I'm sure we will see you around the village now that you're here. Robert mentioned you were renting somewhere?'

'Just a little terraced house on the estate. Bye then.'

Replenished with some homemade pumpkin soup she'd purchased from the market, Katherine again wrapped herself up well against the weather and set out for the walk up to the farmhouse. The leaves in the lanes were crisp and crunchy underfoot from the frost which had remained, squirrels scampered around collecting the last few remaining nuts to store away for the long winter ahead. All was peaceful and quiet when she arrived at the house, no builder and now the roof was nearly finished and the remaining tiles locked securely in the house and ghoulish day-trippers had diminished, no Mick with his dogs, they'd be back later on for their overnight shift. His car was still there next to his caravan, but this was a rouse for any passing rogue to believe that people were present at the proper-

138

ty - Mick's wife having picked him, and the dogs, up once it was light.

Katherine stood at the head of the drive and enjoyed the silence, the stillness of the moment, the wind gently whispered in the trees, teasing the last few leaves off their branches. It had been a while since she had had the place to herself and slowly she walked around the five acres, admiring how large it all seemed now that they'd been cleared of 30 years' worth of overgrowth. She relished taking in the house from every angle. The roof was nearly finished; the frames were in for the windows at each gable end, plywood temporarily fixed against them until the glazing went in, and the heritage Velux windows too. The roof on the Garden Room had been completed, the four oak posts at each corner of the extension stood resplendent and the frames for the tall, wide windows and French doors were all ready for the glazing which would arrive on Monday, additional support from steels in place which would be hidden from sight by the  time the building was completed. Once this was done pointing work to the brickwork on the main house would begin and the Garden Room would be knocked through to the main house, as part of this the store rooms would be knocked down too.

Taking her keys out she let herself into the house. It was silent and eerie; she shivered slightly and forced herself to not think creepy thoughts. Internally little had changed but she still revelled in the opportunity to walk around without the constant banging and crashing of the builders. Finally, she walked into the winter sitting room and stared at the fireplace. Would she always look at it and think of the girl? She hoped that with time she wouldn't, because otherwise how could she live there? She sighed and left, locking the door securely behind her. She took one last look at the Garden Room, admiring the work that had gone into it and strolled back around to the front of the house.

'Argh!' she jumped as she bumped into the 6'2" frame of Andrew Battle. 'Do you have to do that? Sneak up on me,' she snapped, furious that he was on her land again.

He smiled at her lazily, enjoying her discomfort.

'What are you doing here anyway? You're trespassing. Please leave,' she glared at him.

'I just thought I'd have a look round,' he looked amused.

'You can't just "look round", not now, not ever! Now please leave!' She walked briskly up the drive expecting him to follow her, but he didn't move. 'What do you want? Just leave me alone!' she shouted.

He strolled casually towards her. 'You know what I want,' he leaned close to her, entering her personal space, making her squirm and stagger backwards. 'I want this house and I won't stop until I get it,' he'd moved in closer again, she could feel his warm minty breath on her face.

'Are you threatening me?' she stammered.

He smiled at her, each time she shuffled backwards, he leaned in closer to her, his sapphire blue eyes were hard and cold. 'Merely pointing out a fact.'

Something snapped inside her. 'Is this what you do? Go round bullying people until they give in?' He shrugged and grinned at her. 'Is that what you did to Cecilia Still-ingfleet?'

His eyes flashed dangerously. 'Why are you talking about her?' he snapped.

Touched a sore point, thought Katherine, herself so wound up she could barely control her anger. 'What did you do? Force yourself on to her? Not give her any choice?'

He glared at her, then instantly changed, he laughed at her. 'You don't know what you're talking about.'

'Admit it, go on!'

'I didn't have to force myself on to her. She was gagging for it. Couldn't keep away from me. She was a right little goer,' he licked his lips surreptitiously at the memory. 'For someone so young, she sure knew what she was doing.' He glanced at Katherine's shocked face and laughed. 'Jealous are you? Want a piece of me too?' he looked her up and down.

'What?' she exploded. 'You arrogant, self-centered, hateful man. You know what you are? You're a paedophile! You need locking up! She was fifteen! How could you? How could you take advantage of such a young girl? You're sick,' she spat.

'Like I said, she was ripe for the plucking. She pestered me for weeks, on and on she went, raising her skirt length higher, lowering her top, silly tart. Very versatile, as I remember, particularly liked it in the back of my cars. Of course I didn't quite have the collection I've got now, but we certainly made the most of what I did have,' he grinned at her.

She couldn't believe how proud of himself he was, she felt sick to her stomach, bile lurking sourly in the back of her throat, ready to leap out, it took all the power inside her to restrain it. 'Get off my land! Get off it!' she shrieked. 'I'll report you. You won't get away with this.'

He gazed at her for a moment, his eyes piercing into her, then laughed again and walked past her. 'Go ahead,' he replied casually, 'you can't prove it. She's dead!' With that he sauntered arrogantly to his Range Rover and roared off.

Katherine stood there stunned, shaking from the shock. She slowly walked up the drive trying to absorb what he'd told her, in a daze she walked back to her little terrace and let herself in. She leaned against the kitchen sink still wrapped up against the outside chill and gazed unseeingly into the postage stamp sized garden. Eventually she put the kettle on to make some sweet tea to help with the shock, picked the phone up and dialled the police, asking for DI Allix.

# Chapter Fourteen

DI Allix turned up accompanied by DS Windsor a couple of hours after receiving Katherine's phone call. DS Windsor, as usual, looked neat, smart, un-crumpled and unruffled by life. Her boss, in comparison, looked slightly creased around the edges and took up Katherine's offer of a cup of coffee, leaving DS Windsor poised and ready with her notebook and pen.

They listened in silence as Katherine recounted what had occurred up at the farmhouse earlier that afternoon, DS Windsor neatly taking notes throughout. When she had finished DI Allix sat there looking thoughtful, she could see his mind whirring. Did he believe her? Did he think she was making it up? She began to doubt herself. Would anyone believe her?

'Well,' he said, finally breaking the silence. 'We'll bring him in for questioning, he's a slippery character who knows his rights. We need some hard evidence to prove it and he knows it. Threatening you is something else we can bring him in on, but again it's your word against his. I know I believe you, but it could be a hard one to prove with no witnesses. Like I said, he knows his rights. If he should behave in this manner again, please let us know immediately.'

Katherine shuddered at the prospect. 'I just hope he doesn't come up to the farmhouse again or maybe I'll just have to make sure I don't go up there alone. But what am I going to do once the work is complete and I've moved in? I can't hide from him for the rest of my life,' she looked pleadingly at the two of them.

'I can but hope that after a warning from us he'll leave you alone, but as I've said, if he doesn't, let us know,' he looked kindly at her.

'Mmm, I hope so. I just can't understand why he's so keen to buy the house. It seems as though he's obsessed. Perhaps you could find out?'

'Whatever his reason, he's not likely to tell us, but I will do a little digging to try to find out.' He rose to go and DS Windsor snapped her notebook shut purposefully. 'I'll keep you posted but I would ask you to keep this information to yourself. Whilst I feel what you are saying is true, it could be hard to prove and I'm sure Cecilia's parents are distressed enough.'

'Yes, of course. I won't tell anyone. I saw Rupert Stillingfleet last night. He was in a bad way, had had far too much to drink.'

'Hmm, where was that?'

'The Cow & Mistletoe.'

'I hope he wasn't driving? It's remote that pub, certainly not within walking distance of his house.'

'I don't know I'm afraid. I left before he did but it looked as though the barman was keeping an eye on him, I suppose he didn't want any trouble in the pub.'

'Right, well I'll be in touch. Thank you for informing us. Good bye.'

'Bye.' She closed the door behind them and heaved a sigh of relief. Checking that the door was locked, she put the chain on as added security, as far as she knew Andrew did not know where she was temporarily living but she wasn't going to take any chances. Feeling drained she reached for the cooking brandy again and poured herself a generous quantity. For a moment she hesitated, remembering Rupert Stillingfleet, she didn't want to become like him and be reliant on alcohol when times were tough. Don't be silly, she told herself, one drink isn't going to hurt, but then perhaps that's what alcoholics told themselves as they started out on their unwitting road to addiction?

Feeling brighter the next day she pottered round, went for a brisk walk around the village - keeping within view of houses in case Andrew should make a sudden appearance - and settled down to spend the afternoon writing Christmas cards. With three weeks to go, other than purchasing the Christmas cards, she had not given it much thought. She synced her phone to her Bose speaker, went on to Spotify, searched for a suitably Christmassy album, selected play and allowed the Christmas music to get her into the mood and busily wrote. Stopping to make a cup of tea, she impulsively picked up the phone and rang Libby.

'Hiya, it's me. How's it going?'

'Hi Kitty, you beat me to it, I was about to call you. You free next Friday morning?'

Katherine did a mental diary check, school would have broken up at lunchtime the day before and she was officially off duty after the staff Christmas lunch began which was once all the children had been safely packed off for the holidays with their parents. 'Yup, thinks so. Why?'

'I'm having coffee with a friend; she's got another friend coming who I think you would be interested to meet.'

'Really? Why?'

'She's got two children; a six year old and a twenty-six year old.'

'Wow, that's a bit of an age gap, but what's that got to do with me?'

'Ah, well, her eldest daughter went to Wynenden School. Not only was she in the same class as Cecilia Stillingfleet, she was her best friend!' Libby sounded triumphant with this piece of news.

'Really? Gosh. Does she know that Cecilia was found at my house?'

'Yes, she's quite keen to meet you apparently. Anyway, if I pick you up about 10 o'clock I'll drive you there,' she paused, 'I feel I ought to warn you that there are going to be half a dozen young children running around.'

'I'll bring my earplugs then!'

'Great! Anyway, how's your weekend been?'

Katherine went on to recount what she had already told the police and managed to persuade Libby that she was fine and that there was no need for her, Katherine, to pack the house up and move in with them until the farmhouse was ready.

'Really, I am absolutely fine, it's OK,' she said sounding braver than she actually felt.

'You sure?' asked Libby suspiciously. 'Are you sure you're not just trying to keep me happy but underneath you're a quivering wreck? What about if I come over and stay for a couple of nights?'

'No, absolutely not! I'm fine and your family needs you. I'll see you on Friday as planned OK?'

'You quite sure? I mean totally 100% sure?'

'Yes! Now buzz off and go and play with your gorgeous children or something and leave me in peace to write my Christmas cards. Bye!' she put the phone down laughing, feeling perked up from her chat.

With the mad final push to the end of the term over with, it was with relief that Katherine awoke on Friday morning safe in the knowledge that the next three weeks were hers; no work, no racing into the office. The Christmas lunch had been fun, all staff having let out a collective sigh of relief that the term had ended and ended well. She was sure it was something to do with the shortened daylight hours of winter which made everyone seem more tired, certainly the children were exhausted and in need of their much needed break.

After a leisurely breakfast, Katherine showered and dressed in readiness for her morning out with Libby and the children. She was intrigued to meet the friend of a friend whose daughter had been best friends with Cecilia, hoping to gain some insight into the girl. Though they had arranged for Katherine to go with Libby in her car, she decided to take her own car and follow Libby, giving her the freedom to go straight up to the farmhouse afterwards and to not hold Libby up if her plans changed. They set off in convoy and fifteen minutes later arrived at a neat, modern, mellow-brick house set in the middle of an acre. Henry and Alice leapt out of the car as soon as the engine had been turned off and banged on Katherine's window, eager to see her. She got out and hugged them both before they raced off up the drive to knock on the door.

The door was opened by a pleasant looking woman with long auburn hair which curled luxuriously around her shoulders, her freckled face was welcoming and she greeted Katherine warmly, ushering both her and Libby in out of the cold. Libby introduced the woman as Marcia.

'Welcome to the mad house! I'm afraid my two were already hyped up with Christmas coming but when I told them this morning that Henry and Alice were coming over and Sammy too, they seemed to disappear into another stratosphere!' They walked past a play room which was filled with the noise of the children all talking at once. 'I think we'll go and hide in the kitchen, it'll be quieter than the sitting room.' The sitting room being the room adjacent to the playroom.

They walked into a light airy kitchen which opened up into a conservatory creating a large rectangle, kitchen area at one end, dining area in the middle and opening out into the conservatory beyond that. In the conservatory sitting on one of the wicker based sofas was a small plump woman with a very short, severe, blonde hair cut. She rose when she saw the trio and walked over to them smiling shyly.

Marcia introduced Libby and Katherine to Suzie and they politely chatted whilst Marcia busied herself with her Gaggia coffee machine making cappuccino's for them all. She then produced six beakers, some orange juice and some homemade star shaped biscuits with the decorations having most obviously been created by her children. For the adults she popped some mini mince pies onto a plate and they carried their refreshments over to the conservatory and chatted politely as they settled into getting to know one another. After several interruptions from the children, Marcia finally brought up the subject of Cecilia.

'I have to confess that I had forgotten all about Cecilia until news of the discovery of her remains came out,' she said.

'There's no reason why you would have remembered her,' replied Suzie, 'I too had not thought about her for a long time, though Claire had - that's my eldest daughter,' she added for Libby and Katherine's benefit, 'it's distressing to think what that poor girl must have gone through.'

'I know, it's hard to believe that anybody could do such a thing. I mean you read and hear about murders all the time in the media but it doesn't seem as real as when it actually happens so close to home.'

'I think we've become too de-sensitized, it's become so frequent in the news that we don't pay as much attention as perhaps we would have years ago. There doesn't seem the reality that the person who was killed was a real person, someone's wife or daughter, husband, son, mother, father,' added Marcia.

'I hate it. I tend to want to bury my head in the sand, pretend it's not happening, because if I think about it too much I think about my children and what if something like that happened to them? It makes me feel sick and I want to hide them away, which would not be healthy for them.' Libby shivered as she said this; just talking about it gave her the creeps.

'It must have been so shocking for you Katherine, to find her? Libby told me that you had.'

'Horrible. In some ways it didn't seem real, like that sort of thing couldn't happen in a house I owned. I think about her so much, every time I enter the farmhouse I see her and yet I know virtually nothing about her. The local gossips classed her as "wild" but this was the opposite to what her boyfriend told me.'

'You've met Tom?' asked Suzie.

'Yes, as you know he owns the garage in the village and my car was playing up. We started chatting and he eventually told me about her, he said they were made for each other, that they were soul mates.'

'He was a lovely lad, I only met him a couple of times and haven't seen him since. My daughter Claire was Cecilia's best friend, they'd known each other since they started at the Prep School in Reception. They were glued to each other, spent hours talking and doing what teenage girls do. She came to our house a lot, Claire only went to Cecilia's house a half dozen times in the whole of the time that she knew her. Cecilia didn't really get on terribly well with her parents, though from what Claire said she got on better with her mother than her father. I don't think she was terribly happy at home and I know her parents were totally opposed to her relationship with Tom, they saw it as her ruining her life.'

Katherine sipped her second cappuccino her mind popping with questions. 'So, what was she like when she was older, a teenager?'

Suzie blew thoughtfully through her lips. 'Well ..., I suppose I would sum her up as complex. She was, from what Claire told me and my observations, very strong willed, I worried that she might lead Claire astray but she didn't. Some people found her abrupt and obnoxious but she was always very kind, very sweet when she was with us. There was a sort of need about her, almost a desire for her to be a part of our family and she was a really good friend to Claire, you knew that no matter what, she would always be there for her and stand up for her. That's why it was so strange when she disappeared. I know no one believed Cecilia's mother when she said she had gone missing, even her husband, I think, thought that she was over reacting and told the police so too. But she didn't tell Claire where she was going and she *always* did, she'd run off a couple of times but I found out later that she had always told Claire. Mind you, I did give her a telling off for not letting me or her parents know that Cecilia was alright. That's why when she did go missing Claire was so insistent that something was wrong, when I grilled her she swore that she didn't know where Cecilia was and I believed her, of course now we know why,' she looked sadly into her coffee.

'Did, or does, your daughter have any idea as to why Cecilia was killed?' asked Katherine.

'I've asked her and it's something she has asked herself a million times, but there's no reason she could think of. She did say that if it had turned out to be suicide she would have been less surprised.'

'Really? Why's that?'

'Cecilia always had the air of a troubled child but I could never find any reason for it. Claire told me after Cecilia went missing that there had been something going on at the school.'

Libby's ears pricked up at mention of the school where her children were educated. 'What sort of trouble?'

Suzie glanced nervously at Marcia who nodded encouragingly. 'Well, it's rather delicate, I mean I can't prove anything and because I couldn't I didn't take it further at the time. I asked around subtly but back then these things weren't really talked openly about and if it was, it was put down to the child being hysterical. Certainly no one would have believed Cecilia, I struggled when Claire told me but I know with both the girls they may have omitted to tell me the truth sometimes but neither of them out rightly lied to me or my husband, and there is a difference.'

Katherine and Libby held their breath; gripped by what Suzie was saying but both for different reasons, Katherine because she thought it might have some relevance to Cecilia's death and Libby because there was a pit of dread in her stomach, what had happened at the school where she was sending her beloved children too?

Suzie cleared her throat apprehensively. 'Please bear in mind that what I'm about to tell you is in the past, I don't really want it being dragged up and causing trouble,' she glanced at Katherine and Libby who nodded in understanding. 'Cecilia was a bright girl, could have gone far, her parents had high expectations of her, but she didn't always settle down to her studies and got behind, particularly in English.'

Katherine made a sharp intake of breath, stopping Suzie in her tracks. With a jolt Katherine remembered all the entries in Cecilia's diary for "extra English!" They looked questioningly at her. 'Sorry,' she murmured, 'please, go on,' she urged Suzie.

'Because she was behind in her English, it was suggested she have extra English lessons. These she had with the Head of English, who at that time was Mr Codell.'

'What? You mean Robert Codell, the current Headmaster?' squeaked Libby.

'Yes. Um, that's why this is um, er, delicate,' she paused, 'according to Claire, which is what she had been told by Cecilia, he was giving her more than extra English lessons...' her voice trailed off and she blushed.

It took a moment for the penny to drop and when it did they sat stunned and opened mouthed. Libby had gone pale and felt faint and it was Katherine who spoke first.

'Do you mean,' she gulped, 'do you mean that he was abusing her? That he was having sexual intercourse with her?'

Suzie nodded.

'That's awful,' whispered Libby.

'So what did you do when you found out?' asked Katherine.

'I didn't rush in to anything. I was stunned, so shocked, I mean, he taught my daughter English. She assured me that he hadn't done anything to her and that she hadn't heard rumours of a similar thing happening to anyone else. Anyway, my husband and I discussed it and discussed it and eventually we both went to see the then Headmaster. He all but laughed in our faces,' she said bitterly, the memory still vivid.

'What! How could he do that? Surely he had to take your concerns seriously? Weren't there procedures he had to follow?'

'If there were, he wasn't going to follow them. If I'd known before Cecilia disappeared, then maybe we could have spoken to her parents, taken it further, but we didn't, no one knew where she was and without her to back up what Claire had said there was no proof, no evidence. But

I know Claire and, yes, I know that all parents tend to think that their child could never make something of such magnitude like this up, but I knew she wouldn't have. I spoke to her recently about it again, she's twenty-six now - her own person - and she still maintains that that is what was going on. In fact she's now wondering if it had anything to do with Cecilia's disappearance, her death. That's why she said if it had turned out to be suicide she would have been less surprised, but murder? Neither of us can believe it.'

'I think I'd better make some more coffee,' commented Marcia, 'you look like you need it.' She herself was not surprised, Suzie had told her a few days previously and knowing that Libby's friend was there when Cecilia was found, had thought that there may be some use in Katherine and Suzie meeting. It still disgusted her to the bottom of her stomach what Cecilia had allegedly been subjected to, such despicable behaviour.

Libby's mind was racing, there was no way she could let her children stay on at a school where a man like that was in such a position of authority. How could they be sure that Cecilia was the only one? He could have been getting away with it for years and he always seemed so nice, so pleasant and his wife was lovely. But what if she were in on it too? What if they were grooming the younger children? She felt she would explode in distress. Katherine squeezed her friends hand, well aware of what would be going through her mind, she too felt fiercely protective of Henry and Alice.

'So if the Headmaster didn't believe you, what did you do?' asked Katherine.

'We took Claire out of the school immediately and sent her to another one. We couldn't take the risk. It was awful. We thought about going to the police, but who would take the claims of a school girl, particularly one whose friend had gone missing, over that of a well respected teacher with an unblemished record? There was no hard evidence. Believe me, I've worried over the years, I've kept my ears open to gossip and if there had been a hint of it, just a whisper that he may still be doing this, I would have been straight down to the police station.'

'Now we know that Cecilia is dead, it could be relevant, very relevant.'

'I know. I knew I had to go to the police, when Marcia said that it was a friend of a friend of hers who owned the house where Cecilia was found, I thought it would be helpful to meet, I didn't want to go straight to the police. As it was your house, I thought you might know more? Have an inside on the case or at least know who I should speak to?'

'Sure. I really don't know much. The DI in charge seems nice, not scary or anything and seems to take any information given to him seriously, you could speak to him?'

'If you know him, could you speak to him first?' she looked beseechingly at her.

'Well, er, I suppose I could, though I don't know him well, but it's you he'd need to speak to and your daughter, I guess he would want some kind of statement from her. Is she prepared to give one do you know?'

Suzie nodded. 'Absolutely, she wants justice for her friend. She may have gone missing ten years ago but she still feels the loss and feels it afresh now that her body has been found and she most definitely wants Cecilia's killer found. Maybe Mr Codell had nothing to do with it, maybe Cecilia did make it all up – though I would be surprised –

155

either way it seems that now is the time to take it further, though the thought of it fills me with dread.'

'OK well I'll give him a call this afternoon. If you let me have your phone number, your mobile number and your address he can get in touch with you.'

'Sure. Marcia have you got a piece of paper and a pen?' Marcia brought a pad and a pen along with more coffee.

'But my children go to that school. What am I going to do?' Libby looked close to tears.

'Not rush into anything, that's what you're going to do. The children are off for four weeks, there's a different Headmaster at the Prep school, I don't think you should do anything rash. Talk to James, but don't rush into anything,' said Katherine with more confidence than she felt. 'And don't, whatever you do, go telling any of the other parents, for the time being anyway, ok?' Libby nodded meekly back at her.

Feeling a need to lift the distressed mood, Marcia changed the subject and started to chat about Christmas and asked what everyone's plans were, doing her best to lighten the atmosphere. After a little while, Katherine excused herself as she had a meeting with Dougie at the farmhouse, she thanked Marcia for her hospitality, hugged Libby and reaffirmed to Suzie that she would speak to DI Allix that afternoon, she needed time for it all to sink in, to put her thoughts into a cohesive order and for the shock to start to wear off.

She was just getting into her car when her mobile rang. She could tell from the number on display that it was Dougie. 'Hi Dougie, I'm on my way,' she assumed he was chasing her for their meeting even though she wasn't late.

'Kitty, you need to get here as quickly as possible,' he replied urgently.

'Why?' she frowned.

'The police are on their way, just get here quickly,' the phone went dead.

The police? Alarmed, Katherine jumped into her car and drove off at speed.

## Chapter Fifteen

By the time she got to the farmhouse there were both marked and unmarked police cars in the drive. Katherine could see DI Allix talking to Dougie near the front door. She leapt out of the car, her mind frantic, she was on the cusp of saturation point and couldn't take any more. She hurried up the drive only to be stopped by a police constable, irritated Katherine explained who she was but was still blocked, told to wait where she was until confirmation had been received to say that she could proceed.

'For goodness sake!' she exploded 'it's my house, just let me past.'

DI Allix and Dougie heard the commotion and hurried over. Reassuring the police constable that Katherine had a legitimate reason to be there, DI Allix took her towards the house. Dougie looked distressed and the rest of his workmen were sitting in their vans.

'What is it? What's going on?' demanded Katherine, fearful of what she might be told. She looked from one to the other. 'Well?'

DI Allix spoke softly. 'I'm afraid they've found another body.'

Katherine's mouth gaped, this couldn't be happening, it really couldn't! She swayed unsteadily and closed her eyes. Assuming that she was about to faint both Dougie and DI Allix grasped her.

'It's OK,' she said faintly, 'I'm not going to pass out. It's just...'

'I know. It's a shock,' said DI Allix gently.

It's more than that, thought Katherine, so much more, you have no idea. Today had to be one of the worst days of her life. Snapping her eyes wide open she asked, 'Who? Who is it? Do you know?'

DI Allix looked sadly at her. 'It's a baby, it's not a recent death.'

She looked into his eyes and saw reflected her own fears. A baby? Could it be that Cecilia had not had an abortion? Had actually had the baby? But what sort of monster could murder a young girl and then murder her baby? 'Where is it?' she whispered.

'In the house. Forensics are there.'

'But I don't understand, why wasn't it found when they searched before?'

'It was bricked up, there must have been an alcove at some point in one of the store rooms. To look at it you could see no difference, all the walls matched with the same whitewash, when we started knocking the walls down we ...' Dougie trailed off, tears pricking his eyes.

A small moan emitted from Katherine's lips.

'I'm sorry,' said DI Allix simply.

'Where? Where is it?' she asked. Silently he turned and led her through to the back of the house careful to keep a distance and not to interfere with forensics. In amongst the rubble lay a small blue bundle, she froze when she saw it. 'I can't, I can't look at it,' she turned to rush out of the room but not before she had noticed that there was a small gold necklace with a butterfly laying close to the bundle. 'It's hers isn't it?'

DI Allix sighed deeply. 'I can't know for sure until DNA test have been carried out to match the baby to Cecilia but if I were to make an educated guess, I would say yes. The fact that it would appear her necklace was with the baby would give a possible indication that it could be her baby.'

'But who would do such a thing? Who? To murder a young girl, that's, that's ...' she searched for the right words, 'horrific. Wicked. But to murder a baby? How could anyone do that? A poor, innocent baby, not able to defend itself, that person has got to be evil, pure evil.'

DI Allix rubbed his brow, there were moments when he really hated his job and this was one such moment. 'Let me arrange for someone to take you home. I'll come and see you later on.'

Katherine didn't refuse, she felt weak and sick with the pain which was ripping through her. Then, in another wave, she remembered what she had been told that morning. If this was Cecilia's baby, could it be Robert Codell's? What about Andrew Battle? And Tom Fullwood assumed that it was his baby, did he know that the baby had not been aborted? She allowed herself to be propelled out to her car, a police constable was going to drive Katherine's car and stay with her until DI Allix could see her.

'I'll see you later on,' reassured DI Allix.

Katherine nodded. 'I need to speak to you.' He looked questioningly at her. 'I found something out this morning, something I think you ought to know about.'

'Really?  What was that?'

'Not here.  Not now,' she replied numbly.

'OK, later then.'

In a daze, Katherine was driven home.  The police constable persuaded her to lie down and brought her a cup of hot, sweet, tea which Katherine meekly drank.  She lay fully clothed on top of her duvet staring at the ceiling unseeingly.  Her brain was going into meltdown with the barrage of information which had been thrust her way today.  She refused offers of food but acceptingly took another mug of sweet tea.  She shivered all over and dragged the half of the duvet from the other side of the bed over her, cocooning herself up, she drifted in and out of consciousness.  A bang brought her back to reality, it was dark outside and light was shining up the stairs from downstairs.  She sat up disorientated until, like a slap in the face, she remembered.  There were soft footsteps on the stairs and the female police constable who had accompanied her home was silhouetted in the door way.

'DI Allix is here to see you,' she said gently.

'OK, I'll be down in a minute.'  She watched the woman disappear down the stairs and went into the bathroom.  Her hair was all over the place and a grey, haunted, face looked back at her.  She splashed her face, brushed her hair and teeth in an attempt to freshen up.

There were quiet voices coming from the sitting room and she could see DI Allix sitting on one of the sofas rubbing his face again in his hands.  A second later he saw her and rose.

'Katherine, how are you?'  He looked intently at her.  To him she had always seemed strong, the sort of person who picked herself up and moved on, but looking at her now he wasn't so sure.

She shrugged in response. After all, what could she say? She didn't even know herself. She sank down into the sofa opposite DI Allix and took the mug of tea pressed into her hands by the police constable, who in turn then went and sat in the chair to the right of Katherine and got out her notebook and pen.

'The baby has been taken away and I'm afraid the builders won't be able to work until we have finished.'

She sighed, what did it matter what the builders did? Two lives lost, how many more would they find? 'Have you been to see Cecilia's parents?' she asked.

He nodded sadly. 'Yes. They're, well ...' he grappled to find a word which could describe the agony and the pain that Cecilia's parents were going through.

'They must have known about the baby. Cecilia was around for a few days after she got back from France before she disappeared.'

'They did. Why they didn't tell me I don't know. They had no idea that she had had the baby. They assumed that she had had the abortion and it was all done and forgotten about. When she turned up on the doorstep with a tiny baby they were stunned. They kept the baby in the house, too ashamed to let Cecilia take it out. It was a boy, by the way. That was why Mrs Stillingfleet was so insistent that something was wrong when she went missing. Cecilia had taken the baby with her, she had no money, not taken her passport, no clothes, no baby clothes or supplies. Mr Stillingfleet maintains that he thought she'd just run off or run away with Mr Fullwood and would be back within a couple of days when they discovered it wasn't as easy as they thought.'

'I don't get how they could fail to mention that she had a baby with her? It's pure stupidity.'

DI Allix didn't say anything though he agreed. 'It would perhaps explain why they have not organized Cecilia's funeral yet, unsure as to whether the baby would be found or whether the baby was elsewhere being brought up, unaware of his start in life.'

'I'd wondered about that. I'd assumed they'd want to lay her to rest as soon as she was released and was surprised when they didn't.'

'You said earlier that there was something you needed to tell me?'

'Yes, it seems even more relevant now, particularly if it is true. Did you get anything out of Andrew Battle by the way?'

'No, he denied everything. Whether he knew about the baby or not I don't know but I will be pulling him in for a chat to ask him, he'll be aware of DNA testing, it might make him talk.'

'And what about Tom? Have you seen him yet? He's going to be devastated, he assumed the baby was his. I got the feeling there was something he wasn't telling me. Maybe he knew that the baby had not been aborted? Maybe they were going to run away together?' she mused.

'I'm going to see him next. Please, tell me what it is you know.'

Katherine sat for a moment, ordering everything into place so as not to miss anything out and then proceeded to tell DI Allix everything she had been told by Suzie. She handed him the piece of paper with her telephone numbers and address on it.

'I wish she'd come to us at the time,' he sighed.

'Hindsight's a great thing, but surely you can see why she didn't come to the police?'

'Hmm,' was all he responded, his brow creased even deeper. 'Well, thank you Katherine, I will most certainly be following this up. In the meantime, as before, if you could keep what you know to yourself it would be appreciated. A statement is being made later to the press about the discovery of the baby but no details will be released. And, rest assured, I will let you know what the outcome is with Mr Codell. I can understand your friends fears but there may be nothing in this, in which case she could be panicking unnecessarily.'

'Thanks. Well, I suppose I will speak to you soon then.' She showed them out, slid down the closed door, slumped on the floor and burst into tears. Too much trauma piling up had opened the floodgates and was intermixed with the mourning of her own loss, for the much wanted baby she'd miscarried.

# Chapter Sixteen

After a restless night's sleep Katherine awoke on Saturday morning tired, lethargic and cringingly ashamed of her breakdown the night before, relieved that there had been no one around to witness it. She couldn't believe that she had allowed herself to become so distraught. Yes, the situation was unpleasant but it wasn't her daughter or her grandchild who had been found at the farmhouse. She'd become too emotionally involved and whilst she knew that the draw of the situation prevented her from detaching herself completely, she also knew she had to take a more practical and less emotional view of it. If she remained too emotional about the situation she was afraid that there would shortly come a point where she would find owning the farmhouse untenable and she had to make the conscious decision, despite the discoveries, to keep the dream of her house at the forefront of her mind.

Her immediate instinct was to hide and stay in the house but instead she got up, got dressed straight away, had breakfast and set off to see Tom Fullwood. It wouldn't do any harm to have chat. She was aware of the odd twitching of curtains as she walked down Wynenden Close and she couldn't blame them. With so many comings and goings at her house and the fact that she owned the farmhouse where the biggest drama of the village was taking place, she wouldn't have been surprised if people had come out of their houses and out-rightly stared at her. She pushed her chin into the air with determination and marched briskly to the main road, past the post office and stores, the restaurant, the butchers –where she gave the butcher a cheery wave – past the doctors' surgery and vets and finally crossed the road to Fullwood Garage.

The tall lanky lad, of whose name she had not discovered, smiled at her and muttered something to Tom who was bent over the engine of a car. He glanced up at her, the dark circles and bags under his eyes prominent.

'Hello,' he said wiping his hands on a rag, 'car still alright?'

'Yes thanks. No problems with it,' she paused hoping that the lad would make himself busy elsewhere.

Tom looked at her intently, his eyes flicked to the young lad. He reached in his pocket and took some cash out. 'Steve, why don't you walk up to the shop and get some biscuits? Take your time.' Steve opened his mouth to protest then closed it thinking better of it, took the money and headed across the road in the direction from which Katherine had just come.

'You've heard?'

He nodded and let out a deep sigh, his stocky frame seeming to deflate.

'I'm sorry.'

'Thanks.'

'Did you know before Cecilia came back that she had kept the baby?' she asked gently.

He shook his head. 'No. I had no idea. She wrote a couple of times but she never mentioned it. When she came back I asked her why, she said she hadn't wanted to risk her parents finding out. Not that I would have told them. She said it had taken a while to persuade her aunt and uncle, who she was staying with, that she should keep the baby, not have an abortion. They hadn't wanted to go against her parents' wishes but they're staunch Catholics and abortion is against everything they believe in, which is how she managed to persuade them. They sound nice her aunt and uncle, totally different to Cecilia's parents.'

'So when she brought the baby back, what happened?'

His sad eyes looked at her. 'Her parents went ballistic apparently, particularly her father, they wanted to give it up for adoption but Cecilia was having none of it. They refused to allow her to go out with the baby in case anyone saw her. They wanted to get rid of the baby and pretend that nothing had happened, Cecilia would go back to school and everything would carry on as normal.'

'And what did Cecilia think?'

'She hated the idea, she wanted to leave school, stay with the baby. When I first saw him I was so shocked. I couldn't believe it. She had to smuggle him out, though I suspect her mother knew, we met up at Wynenden Farm. She didn't tell me, she just said she needed to see me, so we met where we had often met, there was no one to bother us, to disturb us there. I walked in and there he was,' his face softened at the memory, 'so small, so peaceful, I'd never seen such a tiny baby and the enormity that he was mine, that I was the father, well, it blew me away,' he shook his head as though still amazed.

He's got no idea that he may not have been the father, Katherine thought bitterly to herself, poor man, hoping he never finds out, but fearing he may well do. 'So what was she going to do? If her parents wanted the baby adopted and Cecilia to go back to school, presumably they weren't going to let her stay at home with the baby and support them?'

'No, we were going to go away together. She knew that she could go back to her aunt and uncle, they had been so supportive of her through the late stages of her pregnancy and after he was born, she felt sure that they would help us.'

'When were you going to go?'

'Cecilia said she knew she could get some money, I don't know where from, she assured me that it was OK, and when she had it the three of us would go to France. She said she hoped to have it the next day and she would call the day after and we could go that day or the day after that. But she never called. I waited and waited. When she didn't call I phoned her parents, her mother started haranguing me, accusing me of taking Cecilia and the baby. I was bewildered, I told her I had no idea where Cecilia was which was why I was calling. She'd already been on to the police but when she was finally convinced that I was telling the truth, she called them again and again, she phoned round the village, phoned her friends, no one had seen her. I didn't know what to think, I felt sure she wouldn't have left me, but part of me wondered whether she had gone back to France and would call me when it was safe for me to join her. Over time it ...' his voice trailed off.

'I'm sorry, really I am.'

He shrugged again. 'At least I know now. I know that she didn't leave me, but I hope they find the bastard who did this to her and to our baby,' he spat vehemently.

'I'm sure they will. Have you told the police this?'

'Yes, last night,' he thought wistfully of his wife Tracy and lovingly of their six month old son, grateful for the support she had shown him as ancient history was raked over, distressing for him and uncomfortable for her.

'If there's anything I can do just let me know,' she had no idea what she could do for him that would ease his pain but it seemed like the right thing to say.

He looked up at her with a haunted look in his eyes. 'I'd like to go to the house. On my own if that's ok?'

She understood, the need to be with your loved one, the place where your memories lay. 'Sure, when the police have gone. I'll let Mick, who's keeping an eye on the place when the builders aren't there, know.'

'Thanks.'

She left him deep in thought and wandered off back into the village. Where was Cecilia going to get the money from? Did she tell anyone else about the baby? There seemed to be a lot of contradiction to her. To Tom she was the loyal girlfriend and mother of what, he believed and may well turn out to be, his baby. There was the kind and polite girl Suzie knew. There was the girl who was wilful and wild. Then there was the image of her as a girl who slept around and liked wild sex and, in addition to this, there was the possibility that she was a girl being abused by her teacher. Katherine couldn't get her head round it. How could one person behave in such a different manner to so many different people? Who was the real Cecilia?

169

And if she had been such a sweet child, what had made her change? It can't surely have been purely down to teenage hormones? Puzzled and confused, Katherine strolled up the green and into the village hall. Surreptitiously she bought her bread, some soup and a cake and was praying that she would be able to slip out of the hall unnoticed, when Betty appeared right in front of her. Her heart sank.

'Kitty! How are you?' Betty looked concerned, in a motherly way, at her.

'Fine thank you. How about you Betty?' replied Katherine with a false brightness.

Before she knew it, Betty was propelling her over to the table where her friends sat. Their eyes lit up at the sight of Katherine and she felt a frisson of irritation. 'Now, you really must come and have a cup of coffee with us,' said Betty patting Katherine's arm. Katherine opened her mouth to protest.

'I'm sorry Betty, but I'm going to have to take Katherine away from you. Important things to talk about.' Katherine felt weak with relief. It was Ted. She turned and grinned at him. 'Now Katherine, we really must finish that discussion, come along,' he said in a businesslike manner directing her away from Betty and her friends who were looking crestfallen, like birds who had been savouring the juicy worm in front of them before devouring it, only to have another bird come swooping in and take it from under their beaks.

'Sorry Betty, thanks for your kind offer,' smiled Katherine as Ted led her away to a table as far away from them as possible. He quickly purchased two coffees and returned before Katherine could be pounced on again.

'Phew! Thanks for that Ted.'

He laughed. 'I know a damsel in distress when I see one.'

She laughed back and saw the warmth in his sparkly blue eyes and the crinkle of his smile lines around his eyes and mouth. 'Well I was certainly that damsel today. I was feeling as though I was about to be thrown to the lions! They mean well, but I really couldn't cope with them today. I know what they're after.'

He nodded. 'I heard on the news this morning. It's unbelievable, so tragic. I'm assuming that the baby was Cecilia's?'

She hesitated. 'They won't know for definite until tests have been done.'

'I feel for her parents, no wonder Rupert's in such a bad state,' he said referring to Rupert's heavy drinking.

'Mmm. Horrific. I suppose I'm going to get another summons from the House then?' she said referring to Wynenden Park.

Ted's brow wrinkled. 'Quite possibly. They're away this weekend so I shouldn't think they even know.'

'Nice quiet weekend for you then?' she looked hopeful.

'Been working this morning and have got a family party tonight in Oxfordshire. Haven't had a chance to catch up with my brother and his family, or my parents, for sometime. It'll be really nice to see them all. My nephew must have grown a lot.'

'I didn't know you had a nephew? How old is he?'

'About 10 months now. I've not seen him for four months so I guess he's changed a lot.'

'Certainly will have, they seem to change every minute at that age. Have you just the one brother?'

'Yup, younger by five years. My parents converted one of the barns on the farm and moved into it. They're only a few minutes away from my brother and his family who are in the farmhouse, they're loving it, playing the doting grandparents.'

'You never been tempted then? Marriage? Children? The whole works?' she was intrigued.

'Tempted, but never found the right woman to make an honest man of me,' he grinned at her. 'What about you?'

'Well, divorced - you know that, children,' she looked wistfully away, it wasn't the right time or place to talk about what happened, she shrugged. 'I've not been blessed.'

He saw the sadness in her and wanted to know more. He found her intriguing, she wasn't needy like some women could be, she was independent, her own woman and he liked that. 'So,' he felt it wise to change the subject 'are you all ready for Christmas? I can't believe it'll be Christmas Eve a week tomorrow.'

'Me either! And no, I'm not in the least bit ready. I'm normally so organized and would have had the cards sent weeks ago, presents all wrapped and cake made too but all I've done is write a few cards! I can't believe how unorganized I am!'

'You have had rather a lot on your plate, so I suppose you can be forgiven,' he joked.

'You're too kind!' she poked him on the arm. 'Anyway, enough about my disorganization. How about you?'

He grinned and held his hands up. 'OK. Guilty. I haven't done any shopping either but I have written my cards, was posting them this morning in fact.'

She rolled her eyes at him. 'Hypocrite!' she laughed.

'Reluctantly, I've got to go. I've got to be in Oxford-shire by mid afternoon at the latest. If I'm not, my brother is going to be on the war path, surprise birthday party for my mother.' He rose to go. 'Shall I escort you safely off the premises?'

She grinned up at him. 'Thanks, I think I need protect-ing.'

'What have you got planned for the rest of the weekend then?'

'Not sure, I ought to go shopping but I don't think I can face the crowds, so I'll leave it until Monday or Tuesday. Other than that, not a lot, I might go to the Carol service in the Church tomorrow afternoon, get in the festive spirit and all that, after all it is about the birth of Jesus.'

'Very virtuous, enjoy it and catch up with you next week I hope?' he looked questioningly at her.

'I hope so. I'm sure I could squeeze you in amongst all the Christmas shopping I have to do!'

'You're too kind,' he joked back. 'Well, take care,' he hesitated, tempted to kiss her.

She saw his hesitation, paused and then murmured. 'You take care too, enjoy the party. Bye.'

He stood staring after her, then slid into the seat of his Land Rover, waved as he drove off and focused on the many tasks he needed to complete before leaving for Ox-fordshire.

Katherine hummed Christmas carol's to herself as she strolled home, glad of the welcome diversion. She was still humming, whilst she heated up the soup she'd pur-chased for lunch at the market, when the phone rang.

'Hello?'

'Hello?' stuttered a female voice, 'is that Katherine? Katherine Muier?'

Instantly on her guard, Katherine cautiously said, 'speaking.'

'It's Audrey, Audrey Stillingfleet.'

Flummoxed that Audrey should be phoning her and mystified as to how she had got hold of her telephone number, she hesitated before focusing. 'Oh, hello Audrey. I'm so sorry. Really sorry.'

A sob emitted from down the line. 'Thank you.'

'I can't imagine what you and your husband are going through,' she continued simply.

Audrey sniffed. 'Thanks. I wonder. I know you must be busy. But I wondered if you could possibly come here, to the house? I'd really like to speak to you and I can't face going out, can't face anyone.'

Taken aback, Katherine was perplexed, after all what on earth could she say that would help Audrey?

'Please,' Audrey's voice was plaintive down the phone.

'Um, OK. I suppose so, but I don't know what I can do to help?. I don't know anything.'

'Thank you. Could you come this afternoon? Any time.'

'Er, yes, I suppose so,' she glanced at the clock, it was 1 p.m. 'what about 3 o'clock?'

'That would be perfect, thank you. Do you know where we are?' She gave Katherine directions and called off.

Katherine looked dubiously at the phone then went back to stirring her soup.

# Chapter Seventeen

3 p.m. found Katherine pressing the buzzer to the intercom at the gates of Audrey and Rupert's house. They were grand and slightly over the top wrought iron gates, some would call them pretentious, given that what lay beyond them was not a stately home but a mediocre modern 5 bedroom red bricked house set in an acre and a half of garden. The intercom stuttered into life and the gates slowly swung open. Katherine got back into her car, for she had driven as the house was on the periphery of the village boundary and she wasn't entirely sure just how far out of the centre of the village it was. In fact, she could have walked it in about thirty minutes and part of her wished that she had, it had turned into a glorious afternoon with the sun shining brightly and the blue sky clear and crisp.

Audrey was waiting on the doorstep for her, dressed in a short denim skirt, with sky high red heels and a low fronted cream wool jumper fitting snugly over her amble bosom and plastered in make-up. Despite the effort Audrey appeared to have made, Katherine could still see behind the mask of makeup, her eyes were red and puffy and her nose looked raw.

'Thank you for coming,' she said, ushering Katherine in.

Katherine smiled and followed Audrey as she click clacked her way across the marble entrance hall to the kitchen. Everything was white and pristine, nothing was out of place and there was no clutter anywhere to be seen. The kitchen too was all white, bar the stainless steel work surfaces on top of the glossy white contemporary units.

'Can I get you something to drink? Tea, something stronger?'

'A cup of tea would be nice please,' she replied politely. From what little she had seen of the house so far there seemed to be no indication that Cecilia had ever lived there, no cutely painted pictures from her younger years stuck up on the wall, no height marks made on a door frame, no photos that Katherine could see. She waited awkwardly whilst Audrey made the tea who got out a tray and laid it with fine bone china cups and saucers, a teapot, a jug of milk, sugar cubes in a matching bowl with tongs, a couple of side plates and a few slices of stollen. When she'd finished the ritual she led Katherine into the sitting room, this too was all white, white walls, white carpet, white upholstery. Nervously Katherine took her cup of tea, terrified that she would spill it and make a mark on something. How on earth had they coped with a teenager in the house? What sort of a life would a teenager have had if she had not been able to make a mess? There were a few precious ornaments dotted around and one photograph of a girl who, Katherine assumed, was Cecilia.

Audrey saw her looking at it. 'That's her, my gorgeous Cecilia,' her voice cracked. 'That was taken about a year before she... she...' sobbing she continued, 'before she died, before it all started going wrong,' she finished.

The girl looked bright and happy, long, straight, blond hair, green eyes and freckles, a big smile, she looked carefree. How could things have changed so much? What had happened to set the wheels in motion for this tragedy to unfold? Katherine looked at Audrey who was doing her best to recover her composure and sipped her tea quietly.

'She was always such a lovely, happy child and then she started to change. I put it down to hormones at first but it just got worse, she constantly fought with her father, she was rude, abusive even, ran off. I couldn't understand where my precious little girl had gone to?' Audrey looked bewildered.

'I'm so sorry,' again Katherine wondered why she was here.

Audrey blew her nose on her handkerchief. 'Maybe we neglected her? The cleaning business was getting busier and busier and we spent more and more time there, we wanted to make it grow, make money so that we could provide Cecilia with a comfortable start in life, one where she didn't have to get into debt to go to University, buy a car for her, help her to buy a little cottage somewhere. Maybe if I'd spent more time with her, she wouldn't have changed so much. But we were doing it for her, to pay for the school fees, give her the best start in life.'

'I'm sure she knew you were doing your best for her,' Katherine hoped a few kind words would bring a little comfort, after all nothing she could say or do would bring Audrey's daughter back.

'Tell me a little bit about her, before she went to France,' she said diplomatically, 'and what happened when she came back?'

Audrey's eyes drifted off to another place as she remembered. 'She had this boyfriend, Tom, they'd been together for a few months, he seemed nice enough but Rupert didn't want her seeing him. He was convinced that Tom would lead her astray, keep her from her studies, she had to focus, he told her, get good qualifications, work hard, she shouldn't have a boyfriend at her age, he told her. They fought and fought. I didn't see the problem, I thought if they were left alone, let the relationship run its course, it would all blow over. I tried to tell Rupert that the more he made of it, the more she would dig her heels in and that's precisely what happened. Then she became pregnant, just a short time before she was due to turn sixteen. Rupert wanted to report Tom to the police, for having sex with a minor, but somehow Cecilia persuaded him otherwise. She stubbornly said she was going to keep the baby, that she and Tom were going to bring it up together, he was only just sixteen, what hope had they got? Of course Rupert went ballistic, he arranged for her to go to a clinic and to stay with his sister and her husband in France, let things die down a bit, get a bit of space between Cecilia and Tom. He was sure that when she came back she would have forgotten all about him. I had my doubts but went along with it. I just wanted her to be happy and did feel that if there was some distance between her and her father things would calm down a bit, let Rupert calm down and give Cecilia a change of scenery, with a bit of TLC from her aunt and uncle I thought there might be a chance she would revert back to being her old self.'

'So what happened when she returned with the baby?'

'I was shocked, but a part of me was delighted, there was my grandson, how could any mother not feel something for their grandchild? He was gorgeous, absolutely gorgeous. So small, so sweet, hardly cried, I fell instantly in love with him and Cecilia was so good with him, took total care, fed him, bathed him, there was a maturity about her which was astounding for her years. Rupert ,on the other hand, wanted nothing to do with him, he wanted the baby put up for adoption. Cecilia begged and pleaded, I begged and pleaded but he wasn't going to shift his view. I didn't know what rights Cecilia had, or Tom for that matter, I just hoped that the baby could not be adopted without Cecilia and Tom's permission, that there would be nothing Rupert could do.'

'It must have been very tricky for you, being pulled between the two people you love.'

'It wasn't pleasant but Cecilia was my daughter and as a mother I would do anything to protect her, if I had to choose between my husband and my daughter, there would be no contest.'

It just goes to show, thought Katherine, that you should never make assumptions or judgements about people. From what everyone else had said, Audrey and Rupert put themselves first before their daughter and treated her like a trophy. Audrey was painting a totally different picture. Even if Cecilia had had the love and support from her mother and some kind of love from her father, albeit in a very Neanderthal way, what had changed? What had made her rebel? A thought popped into her head, had the change coincided with Cecilia starting her extra English lessons?

179

Had abuse changed her? At that moment Katherine could think of no sensitive way to bring it up.

'What happened on the last day that you saw her?' asked Katherine gently.

Audrey sniffed and wiped her eyes. 'Rupert had banned Cecilia from taking the baby out in public, he didn't want anyone to know. Cecilia was desperate to see Tom, to show him the baby but it wasn't wise for Tom to come to the house. The day before she went missing I'd let her sneak off with the baby to see Tom, they met up at your farmhouse. She wasn't out for too long, didn't want to run the risk of Rupert finding out. Anyway, that was fine, Rupert was none the wiser. The next day, Rupert said he had meetings all day and would be back late, Cecilia asked if she could take the baby out again, I agreed as long as she steered clear of the village and public places, she gave the impression that she was going back to the farmhouse and I assumed that she was therefore meeting Tom. She went out in the morning and said she would be back by early afternoon. She took the baby in one of those papoose things and plenty of nappies, clothes, a blanket and water and a snack for herself, so she was well prepared and she was feeding the baby herself so there was no problem about bottles or feeding him. When she hadn't come home by mid afternoon I started to feel cross. Cross that she had let me down, she'd promised she'd be back by mid afternoon. By late afternoon I was starting to get worried and by early evening I was frantic. I tried to phone Tom but couldn't get hold of him. Rupert came back late, must have been about 10 o'clock, but by then I had phoned the police. They arrived shortly after he got back. He told me not to tell them about the baby, I didn't know why. He then persuaded them that it was not unusual for Cecilia to run off, they were very kind but you could see them thinking that I was some kind of over protective, hysterical, mother. But I knew Cecilia wouldn't keep the baby out, the evenings were chilling down and she adored him, she took such care of him, I just *knew* that she wouldn't do anything to put his health or safety in jeopardy. As soon as the police had gone Rupert and I had a massive row, it was horrible, he stormed out and I didn't see him until late the next day. I couldn't sleep, I just couldn't. I phoned round her friends, I asked around the village but no one had seen her. I phoned Tom and vented my frustrations at him, accusing him of keeping her away from home, he denied it, it was when he started to sound worried that I believe him, he said he had not seen her all that day. It was days before the police took me seriously, then the village realized and everyone was out searching fields and woodland and still Rupert wouldn't let me tell anyone about the baby and he threatened Tom, I don't know what he said to him but Tom didn't tell the police either.'

'Surely though with his daughter missing he wouldn't care whether people knew about the baby or not? Just to get his daughter back would have been enough?'

'I know, but he insisted. Kept saying she'd turn up and then the baby could be adopted out. And as time went by it became harder. I mean how could I tell the police months down the line that my daughter had had her tiny baby with her and that they had both gone missing?'

'Hmm,' pondered Katherine.

'I never gave up hope that they would come home, that they were still alive. Every year on her birthday, and on the baby's birthday, I'd make a cake and light candles. I always hoped, always,' tears were streaming down her face.

'And now? What happens now?'

'I don't know. I don't know how I can go on? My baby's gone. If we bury her it's like acknowledging that she's dead, if we don't I can continue to pretend, pretend for the rest of my life that she may still come home.'

I don't think she even knows about the allegations made about Robert Codell. How on earth is she going to cope if they turn out to be true? That the school they worked so hard to pay for was quite possibly responsible for the downfall of her daughter. That her daughter had been abused. Katherine gulped; it would be enough to push anyone over the edge.

'You have Rupert. Can you not support each other through this?'

'Huh! Rupert! All he does is drink. Have you not wondered where he is? He's out, no doubt getting plastered. He started drinking when Cecilia disappeared, not a lot but over time it has got progressively worse and these last few weeks there's barely a moment when he's sober. I've had to go and sort the mess out that he's making at work, fortunately we have a team who are very supportive, but it's getting ridiculous, he turns up at the office half cut, he's making a fool of himself. He drinks from the moment he wakes up until the moment he passes out. I've tried to talk to him about it but he flies off the handle, he won't acknowledge that he has a problem. I don't know what to do? So, as for support. I've got no one. I'm alone and no one to share my pain with.'

No wonder she phoned me, thought Katherine, she's desperate. Katherine could only assume that it was because her daughter and grandchild had been discovered in Katherine's farmhouse that she'd felt there was some kind of connection, a link between the two of them.

'There must be someone you could talk to? A friend perhaps?'

She shook her head. 'No, Rupert's managed to chase them all away and I have buried myself in work and neglected the few friends I did have.'

'What about the vicar? Couldn't he help?' Wasn't that what members of the clergy were supposed to do? Be there in a crisis?'

'Maybe. He did phone and leave a message but I've not got back to him. Maybe I should phone him?' she brightened momentarily.

'What was your grandchild's name?' Katherine realized that the baby had always been referred to as "he" or "baby" rather than by name.

'He didn't have a name. Not that I know of, Cecilia said she wanted to choose one with Tom. I don't know if they did. I suppose I could ask Tom, I never really thought of it which is peculiar.'

'You could,' though Katherine remembered Tom referring to the baby by gender rather than Christian name, 'and if the baby did not have a name maybe you could choose one for him?'

'What a good idea! Yes. You're right. I must speak to Tom and if they'd not chosen a name, then we could choose one.' This small idea gave her a mission, something to think about, something to keep her going.

Katherine rose to go. 'Thank you for the tea and for the cake.'

'Thank you for coming,' she took both Katherine's hands in hers, they felt warm and soft in her own thin, boney and ice cold ones, and looked directly at Katherine. 'Thank you.'

Katherine left still feeling slightly bewildered, trying to discover who Cecilia really was as a person, was proving to be decidedly tricky, there continued to be so many contradictions. It would appear that the driving force behind the desire for the Stillingfleet's to put Cecilia's baby up for adoption was from Rupert and opposed to what Audrey wished. The picture painted by the village was one of them being as bad as each other, whether the passing of time had given a rosy hue to Audrey's as to her view of her relationship with her daughter, was something Katherine was unlikely to find out. Feeling none the wiser Katherine drove home with her mind feeling in a fog, arriving home she decided that it was no good focusing all her efforts on Cecilia and decided to devote the rest of the afternoon, and as much of the evening as was necessary, in completing the writing of her Christmas cards.

# Chapter Eighteen

At 3.30 p.m. the next day Katherine slipped into one of her smarter coats, in this case a pale, moss green, velvet one.  She wrapped her pale pink cashmere scarf snugly around her neck, did the buttons of the coat up and slipped on a pair of pale pink cashmere gloves which matched her scarf.  Satisfied that she looked smart enough, but well defended against the cold, she set off at a brisk pace to the Church for the afternoon Carol Service.  Katherine had not been into the Norman towered Church which nestled neatly at the top of the Green adjacent to the village hall.  She assumed that, like a lot of Churches, there would be little or no heating and the building would have held onto the frosty weather which the country was being gripped by.

She wasn't sure whether there would be many people in the congregation as when the media talked about the Church of England it always seemed to refer to it's dwindling in number of those attending.  She was pleasantly surprised therefore to see, maybe not a steady stream but certainly a steady trickle of, cars driving up and parking in the Church car park which was shared with the village hall, and a few who, like her, were going on foot.

She was greeted, firstly, by a blast of hot air as she walked into the Church and then a couple of cheerful faces welcoming her to the Church. She was amazed to see that the Church was at least three quarters full with more following her in and with still ten minutes to go before the start of the service. Katherine tried to sneak to a seat at the back of the Church in order not to be prominent in her presence. However she was guided to a seat at the end of a pew about half way up the aisle. She murmured pleasantries to those immediately next to her then looked around to take in her surroundings. The Church had a large Christmas Tree to the left of the pulpit, it was covered in baubles, tinsel and white lights which twinkled and sparkled in the built-in lights and candle light of the Church. To the right of the pulpit Katherine could see a Nativity scene laid out, she squinted closer at it and realized that Jesus was not in the crib, perhaps they waited for the day itself to put him in there, she pondered. She looked around her and though, in general, the congregation was of the older generation, there was a respectable gathering of all ages, quite a few families with younger children and babies who were making their presence known by their over excited chatter and the frequent "Sshh" emitting from their parents.

Across the aisle and in the front row she saw Sir Geoffrey and Lady Percevall-Sharparrow, she hoped that they wouldn't see her for she knew that if they did she would be grilled on the spot in front of so many strangers and cringed at the thought of what would be excruciatingly embarrassing, that was assuming they had been informed about the discovery of the baby. Katherine had hoped that as they were away for the weekend they would not be back in time for the service. Her eyes continued to stray around the congregation for any familiar faces, she was startled to see Andrew Battle sitting with his arm around an exceedingly young looking woman - different to the one she had seen him with in the Grouse & Peacock - he glanced in her direction, saw her and gave her a lazy smile. Feeling churlish not to, she smiled politely back then studiously studied the service sheet she had been given on the way in.

The organ which had been playing some pleasant music stopped and the vicar appeared in front of them all to welcome them to the Carol Service. Most of the lights were turned off and the magical glow of the candles lit the Church. Lots of carols, several readings, a brief sermon, some prayers and the service was over before she knew it.

Katherine now felt truly in the Christmas spirit, the service had uplifted her and she followed the sea of people flowing towards the door, managing to avoid Andrew and doing her best to keep out of Sir Geoffrey's sight. Tea, mulled wine and mince pies were to be served in the village hall so after a quick shake of the vicar's hand and words of thanks for the service, she wrapped herself up again against the frosty air and strolled down the path towards the village hall. She noticed a small group of people over by a familiar looking car, silhouetted in the dark. As she came parallel to them she was startled to see that it was DI Allix. DS Wilson was beside him and even more startling was the fact that it was Robert Codell he was talking to. His wife Jane was beside him seeming distressed. Though Katherine could not hear what was being said, the back door of DI Allix's car was opened and Robert Codell ushered in. DI Wilson got in on the other side and sat next to him, as DI Allix slide behind the driver's wheel his eyes alighted on Katherine. He held them momentarily in a greeting and then swiftly drove away, leaving Jane Codell standing, bewildered.

Unsure as to whether to go and see how she was, Katherine was saved by Jane's sudden movement, she ran to her car, jumped in and raced off, narrowly missing knocking down a group of elderly ladies who had been cautiously making their way from Church to village hall. Fortunately, it appeared that no one else had noticed Robert being driven off; at least that's one less piece of gossip to go round, for the time being, thought Katherine.

Ensuring that the group of elderly ladies was alright, other than a little flustered, Katherine went ahead of them into the village hall. The bright lights after the darkness outside made her blink momentarily. The hall was filling up and there were people ferrying trays of tea, mulled wine and mince pies around. Gratefully she took a cup of tea and a mince pie and moved towards the edge of the room feeling slightly like a fish out of water. Everyone seemed to know each other and were chatting happily to one another. She normally didn't feel quite so socially inept, but she felt awkward, she could hardly start a conversation with "oh, yes, I own the house where the bodies were found" could she?

She didn't notice a figure slide next to her until there was a slight clearing of a throat. Katherine turned and saw the pale face of Audrey Stillingfleet looking back at her. Surprised to see her as, by her own admission, Audrey had said she was too nervous to venture into the village, she smiled warmly at her.

'Hello Audrey. Did you enjoy the service?' was the inane question Katherine thought of.

'Hello Katherine. It was OK, nice to see the Church so full. Lovely to see children,' she gulped and tears welled up in her eyes.

How hard it must be to see so many happy families, children, parents, grandparents and to know that you will never be part of that exclusive group, thought Katherine about Audrey. Then, like being hit by a bolt of lightning, Katherine realized that it applied to her too, she too would never be a part of that exclusive group, at forty-seven she knew the boat had past her by and not through lack of trying.

'You alright?' Audrey looked anxiously at her. 'You look like you've just had a fright.'

Katherine blinked. 'I'm fine, she stuttered, 'really, I'm fine,' she took control of herself. 'Is Rupert with you?'

Audrey shook her head. 'No. He ...' her voice trailed off.

Probably drunk again, mused Katherine. She became aware that people were looking at them, not in an obvious, out-right sort of way, but surreptitiously Katherine knew they were talking about them, well about Audrey anyway. As if sensing it too, Audrey shifted round so that her back was facing out to the centre of the hall and she was facing Katherine and the wall.

'Don't worry,' whispered Katherine.

'It's the first time I've ventured out to a village event, since, well, you know...' Audrey glanced at Katherine. 'I took your advice yesterday and telephoned the vicar, he was so nice, he came round yesterday evening and we had a long chat, it really helped. It was he who mentioned the Carol Service, so I thought I'd take the plunge, you know, get it over and done with, do it when something joyful is being celebrated.'

'You're very brave. People mean well, I'm sure they all feel for you.'

'I know, it's just hard, I don't want people's sympathy or pity and one moment I want to talk and talk about Cecilia and the baby and the next moment I don't and wonder what they are thinking of me? Hiding the fact that Cecilia had had a baby? That we didn't tell the police? Rupert isn't helping either by being drunk all the time and he's driving whilst drunk, I've begged and pleaded with him not too but he won't listen.'

Katherine squeezed Audrey's hand and felt silly that she had felt so nervous about talking to people when she arrived. She had nothing to hide from and nothing to feel awkward about, it was pathetic, she thought, and poor Audrey was in a living hell. Perspective had been firmly put in its place.

'Everyone is going to have their own opinion and there will be a small number who will criticize and be cruel about you behind your back, but they will be the minority and unfortunately that's life, but they aren't the people who count. For each one of them there will be dozens who are not like that. Maybe they won't be able to understand why you did what you did, but they will empathize with your situation and feel your pain. Putting it off will make it seem bigger, seem worse, when you do start integrating back in to village life, getting it over and done with will help, making that first step. But you've done that already, you've come here, it can't be any harder.'

'You think so?'

'I know so,' said Katherine with confidence. 'I'm sure you will receive many offers of support too, you're not alone.' Even though you may feel it with your husband being so unsupportive she added silently. 'Come on,' she said decisively, 'let's get you a cup of tea and a mince pie.' She took Audrey by the arm, turned her around and marched purposefully towards a young girl who was carrying a tray with cups of tea and a plate of mince pies. 'Here you are,' said Katherine, passing Audrey a cup of tea, swapping her empty cup for a full one and placing a mince pie on the side of each saucer.

It was mere seconds before someone had approached them and was offering Audrey their condolences, a steady flow of people continued and Katherine slipped back into the crowd. She turned and bumped straight into Tom.

'Hello,' he smiled at her, his face even more drawn and tired than the day before. 'This is my wife Tracy,' an exhausted looking young woman shook her hand and smiled. 'And this, is our son Joe,' he took the cute six month old from his wife and kissed and cuddled him, looking immensely proud.

'Pleased to meet you,' replied Katherine to Tracy. 'He is such a sweetheart.' She cooed at the baby who was grinning his little head off, dribbling and burbling.

'Thanks, we think so.'

At that precise moment Katherine caught sight of Sir Geoffrey and Lady Susan out of the corner of her eye, she could see them approaching through the throng. 'I've got to get going,' she excused herself, 'lovely to meet you.' She slipped through the crowd, out into the fresh night air and walked as quickly as her legs would carry her back to her house.

It was a while later that evening when her phone rang and she put the TV on mute before answering. It was Ted. They chatted amiably about their respective weekends, Ted having had a great time with his family, the surprise party being a roaring success.

He cleared his throat. 'Anyway, I'm afraid Sir Geoffrey was just on the phone to me.'

Katherine felt a fizzle of disappointment, she'd thought he'd phoned her because he wanted to, not because he had been instructed to.

'Sir Geoffrey would like to see you. Apparently he tried to catch you this evening but he didn't manage to.'

She felt irritated. Why should she jump whenever he said she had to? She was grateful for being able to purchase the farmhouse but she wasn't going to spend the rest of her life leaping to command every time he demanded it.

Ted felt uncomfortable asking; he liked Katherine and didn't want to have to be the go between. 'Anyway he's asked if you could come up to the house tomorrow morning, as early as possible. I did say I thought you might be rather busy what with Christmas coming,' he added hurriedly.

'Really, I can't do tomorrow morning or even the afternoon, well that's not true, I could if I really wanted to or it was urgent or it was life threatening, but it's not and I don't see what I'm supposed to know that they would be interested in. Why don't they speak to the police?'

'I know, but…' he was stuck between a rock and a hard place.

'Tell him I will be up on Tuesday morning at 10 a.m. but that if I can possibly manage it I will come up later tomorrow afternoon, though it's very unlikely.'

'Thanks.' He knew he'd upset Katherine and he also knew he would get a blasting from Sir Geoffrey for not making sure that Katherine was there first thing tomorrow.

Katherine felt slightly remorseful at having snapped at Ted. 'I don't mean to be grumpy,' she said.

He brightened slightly. 'Don't worry, I thought you were rather restrained, all things considered,' he joked tentatively; he could feel a thaw down the phone. 'I was going to phone you anyway, it's just unfortunate that Sir Geoffrey got to me first. I've only been back half an hour. Do you think you could fit me into your busy schedule for a drink? Coffee even if that's easier?' he was hopeful.

'Ooh, I don't know,' she replied teasingly, 'I'll have to check my diary,' she paused momentarily for effect, 'I could squeeze you in on Tuesday evening, if that works for you?'

'It will!' he replied determinedly.

'Great. Well if you're not at the house when I come up on Tuesday I will pop into the stables to arrange a time.' The stables were where the Estate Office was, once housing twenty horses there were now none and part of the stables had been converted to provide office space outside of the main house.

'Look forward to it. Bye.'

She put the phone down and still felt a bit guilty. She could have gone to see Sir Geoffrey first thing before she went shopping but she didn't want to. Besides, she reasoned, if I get delayed, the later I go shopping the bigger the queues will be.

And she was right, she'd set off early to do a blitz at the Bluewater Shopping Centre and even though she was there for nine o'clock, cars were streaming in and rapidly filling up the parking spaces, by 10 a.m. she knew it would be full.

There weren't a huge number of presents she needed to buy, her parents were dead, she had no husband and no children which just left her with a small number of presents to get for a few friends and, of course, for her godchildren with whom she would be spending Christmas. With the prolific amount of toys which children had these days Katherine did what she always did when it came to buying them presents, she checked with Libby. On the list this year was another doll with accessories for Alice and a specific set of Lego for Henry. To accompany these Katherine spent some time choosing a book for each of them, fortunately both children loved to read which Katherine put down to the fact that their parents loved to read and also read stories to them each night before bed.

The crowds were thronging and were starting to make the Christmas shopping experience unpleasant. Katherine normally shopped at the end of November, when it was close enough to Christmas to feel Christmassy but far enough away to avoid hideous queues. Even purchasing a take away coffee was a mammoth event. Gritting her teeth Katherine continued in a determined manner, gradually ticking off each present one by one. Hungry and grumpy she purchased a sandwich and drink from the Waitrose within John Lewis, along with a pre-prepared luxury fish pie and pre-prepared vegetables for that night and collapsed into her car, her feet throbbing. There were cars lurking up and down each row, like vultures waiting to pounce on their prey. Determined not to be put off by this Katherine sat and munched on her sandwich and sipped her drink, she started to feel slightly human again. With relief she drove out of the centre thankful that she wasn't in the massive queue which now tailed all the way around the perimeter road of Bluewater and up and down the A2.

Her feet were still throbbing by the time she got home. She dropped the bags on the floor, popped the fish pie into the fridge, made a camomile tea to calm her and lay on a sofa with her feet propped up on one arm of the sofa. An hour later she felt revived and knew that she should go up to Wynenden Park to see Sir Geoffrey but she could not face it. The morning had been tortuous enough and whilst her mood had improved, she felt that a visit to him would be enough to put her in a foul mood again.

She felt restless, a need for fresh air and open spaces after the claustrophobia of the morning. Feeling guilty she changed into jeans and a warm jumper and put her walking boots on, on went the hat, the scarf, the gloves and the thick black waterproof coat. The cocooning of the walking boots soothed her feet and she wished she'd worn them shopping, going for comfort rather than style. Pocketing her keys and a torch as the evenings drew in so early, she hurried off up the road. Walking past the shops in the village she headed out in the direction of Wynenden School hoping that she would not be spotted by Sir Geoffrey or Lady Susan. Before reaching the entrance to Wynenden School she crossed the road and took a footpath across the fields.

She wondered what had happened during the interview DI Allix must have had with Robert Codell the previous evening. Had he found out whether Robert had been abusing Cecilia? Had he denied it? If he had abused Cecilia and he denied it would they ever be able to prove what he had done?' She was deep in thought when she reached the lane she needed to cross in order to join the next section of the footpath. The sun was starting to lower itself in preparation to set and she knew she needed to hurry if she were to be back in the village before dark. She climbed over the style and walked down the lane towards where she would find another style and be able to join up with the next footpath. She stood aside to let a car go past, not looking to see who was approaching. The car pulled up beside her and her heart sank.

# Chapter Nineteen

'You need to be careful out here on your own, these lanes are awfully narrow, wouldn't want anything to happen to you if a driver didn't see you.'

Katherine shivered, was he threatening her again? It was Andrew Battle in his Range Rover. She slipped her hand into her pocket and subtly felt around for her mobile. With horror she realized she had not picked it up from the kitchen work surface.

'Afternoon Andrew,' she said politely, trying to hide her nerves. He grinned at her.

'Decided to sell yet? Another body. Tut, tut, people are going to think you are storing them up there,' he laughed at his own sick joke.

How could anyone be so unpleasant? Had he had no feelings for Cecilia, the girl he had had sex with on numerous occasions? Had he no respect for the dead? She looked at his self-satisfied face, his perfectly groomed physique dripping in wealth and something snapped inside her.

'Have you no respect for the dead? For that poor girl and her baby?' she snapped furiously. 'Your baby,' she snarled.

A startled look swept fleetingly across his face, his eyes flashed dangerously. 'What are you talking about? You're determined to get me into trouble with the police, you and your *false* accusations,' he emphasized.

'False! You confessed to me that you had slept with her on many occasions. Just because she's not here to defend herself you think you can get away with it! She was under aged, or did that not mean anything to you?'

He sneered at her. 'You can't prove anything. And just to make it perfectly clear to you, I did not kill her or her baby.'

'But you were seen,' Katherine blurted out the lie before she could stop herself, he'd infuriated her so much she couldn't help it.

His eyes narrowed and pierced into her. 'You're making it up. Besides, so what if I was seen with her?'

'You met her at the farmhouse on the day she went missing, didn't you?' she noticed that he had shifted uneasily in his plush cream leather seat. She had no idea where these ideas were coming from, but having started she had to pursue them. She was sure he was lying.

His face changed back to a smirk. 'You think you've got it all sussed don't you? You think I murdered her? Hah!' he laughed. 'Why would I murder her? She was nothing to me! Sure she was a good screw and a bit of fun but that was it, end of.'

'So why did you go to the farmhouse?' Katherine was convinced that her gut feeling was right, she knew he was hiding something, but murder? That she was not so sure.

He stared intently at her for a few moments, weighing up his options. 'Well, no one is going to believe you and you can't prove anything, I know you're lying about me being seen. She phoned me, said she needed to see me urgently. Of course, I thought she wanted to re-kindle our acquaintance, there seemed to be a certain irony to me that she wanted to meet at the farmhouse. I wanted that house, why not baptize it with my pleasure early?'

Katherine shuddered in disgust and tried to push the unsavoury images away which were popping into her head.

'When I got there I found that she had this squawking baby with her. I was furious. I'd cancelled a meeting to see her, she wasn't up for it, far from it. Said the baby was my son. I told her to get stuffed, I wanted nothing to do with her or the baby She said if I paid her twenty grand in cash by that afternoon she need never see me or the baby again, she'd disappear and I'd never hear from her again.'

She must have known what his reaction would be, thought Katherine, sure that he would want nothing to do with her or the baby.

'I laughed at her, told her she had to prove it was mine and then come after me for money. There was no way I was going to pay a penny to her, I was livid, left her to it and never saw her again.' His gaze had drifted off whilst he spoke.

Katherine was stunned that she had been right. That her wild guess of him seeing her at the farmhouse on the day she disappeared was correct. Her mind was racing with unanswered questions, then spoke. 'When was this? When did you see her? Morning? Afternoon? Evening?'

'Mid morning, why?'

'Because if you saw her and you didn't kill her, then whoever came after you must have. Did you tell the police this when she went missing?'

'You must be joking! Why would I do that? Besides, she told me she was going to disappear. I assumed she had done that, done what she said she was going to do.'

'Did you see anyone else? Anyone when you left?' she asked hopefully.

He frowned then shook his head. 'No. There was no one about. I passed Geoffrey in the lane, had a chuckle to myself, he would have been furious if he'd seen my car at the farmhouse.'

'And that was it, no one else?'

'No. Now I've wasted enough of my time. Tell the police what you like, they can't prove anything and I will deny it all anyway. Soon enough they'll believe that they have a deluded female on their hands.' With that he closed his window and roared off.

They wouldn't would they? Katherine was worried. If she told DI Allix what Andrew had just told her he might start thinking that she was wasting his time, that it was self-interest and she had some kind of personal vendetta against Andrew.

As she walked back across the fields in the growing dusk, Katherine's mind was crammed with questions. If Andrew had been summoned to meet her at the farmhouse, who else had? Who was the father of the baby? Was it Tom? Andrew? Robert? Had Robert Codell met her there? Had he been abusing her or was it untrue and a pack of lies? Who had the most to lose by the revelation that they had had sex with an under aged girl? Her answer to this one had to be Robert. He was her teacher, ten years ago he was about to be appointed Deputy Head and was no doubt ambitious and had his eyes on a Headship some-where. If it came out that he had had a relationship with one of his pupil's, let alone an under aged one, he would be ruined, he would surely be jailed and his career as a teacher would be well and truly over. But what if it's not true? What if Cecilia made it up? Who would have the most to lose? Katherine's gut feeling was that Andrew was not guilty, he was too arrogant and Cecilia's threat to expose him would be seen as an irritation rather than anything else. Or would it?

So deep in thought was she, that she arrived back home without having been aware of getting there. The more she puzzled, the more questions popped up, she was sure she was missing something. Should she tell DI Allix of her conversation with Andrew? She decided to sleep on it and call him in the morning after her visit to see Sir Geoffrey.

# Chapter Twenty

Katherine braced herself for her meeting with Sir Geoffrey, why she felt nervous she did not know. A thought had sprung into her head overnight. If Andrew had seen Sir Geoffrey driving up the lane in the opposite direction, maybe Sir Geoffrey had seen someone arriving at the farmhouse or driving down the lane towards it? She knew it was ten years ago but was hopeful that he might remember something, anything.

She pressed the bell and waited. Again it was some time before she heard the approaching barks of the dogs. They arrived in a clatter at the door before anyone else and she saw the dogs' heads popping up and down as they barked and jumped to see who it was. She was delighted when Ted appeared and opened the door.

'Hello. I thought you might be busy on the Estate?'

'I was, but Sir Geoffrey asked me to come in.'

'Oh, right. How are they?' she asked tentatively, trying to ascertain the mood that Sir Geoffrey and Lady Susan were in, for she felt sure that his wife would be there too.

Ted frowned and searched for the right word. 'Tense, I think, is how I would describe them.'

'Tense? But why?' This did not bode well for their meeting she felt.

'I...' he thought better of it, 'I'm not entirely sure.'

Katherine still wasn't really sure why she was here. She had no information that would be of use to them and felt that their time would be better spent in talking to the police. Ted led her through the myriad of corridors again until they arrived at the same drawing room they had been in on Katherine's last visit. He held the door open for her and she walked into the room which, fortunately, was warmer than the rest of the house, as it had a blazing log fire roaring in the fireplace. Sir Geoffrey was pacing up and down and Lady Susan was sitting down, gazing into space. Sir Geoffrey turned and greeted Katherine as she entered and ushered her to a seat.

'Be a good chap Ted and make us some coffee will you.' It was an order rather than a request.

With Ted dispatched to do as he was told, Sir Geoffrey stood astride in front of the fire warming his back and looked intently at Katherine. She shifted uncomfortably under his gaze. Lady Susan, Katherine observed, looked deflated, not her usual robust, jolly hockey sticks, type of self. After a moment Sir Geoffrey spoke.

'So, Katherine,' he said, 'more rum goings on at the farmhouse eh?'

'Yes. I'm afraid so.'

'Tell me, what happened?'

She looked from one to the other, both were focused entirely on her. 'Well, I, um, don't know really. I wasn't there. I received a phone call from my builder asking me to come to the farmhouse as quickly as possible and that the police were on their way. When I got there the police had already arrived,' she paused unsure as to what they wanted.

Sir Geoffrey cleared his throat. 'And did you,' his voice trembled slightly, 'did you see the baby?'

Katherine noticed that at the mention of the baby Lady Susan gripped her hands tightly and her face took on a frozen appearance. Katherine closed her eyes and shuddered at the memory. 'I didn't see the baby itself. I didn't want to. I just saw a blue bundle and then I left the room.'

'Just tell me about the bundle. What was it like?'

Katherine shivered at the question. Why was he so intent on getting information about the baby? It didn't seem right to her, but she dutifully answered the question as best she could. 'It was small and wrapped tightly, though I think an edge of the blanket had come lose when it was, um. You know. Er. Discovered.'

Fortunately, she was temporarily saved from further questions as Ted arrived with a tray laden with coffee and some digestive biscuits. Katherine gratefully took her cup and saucer, filled with instant coffee, and clung to it as though it were a security blanket.

'Is there any more you can tell us about the baby?' persisted Sir Geoffrey who had now sat down next to his wife.

Ted caught Katherine's eyes and raised his eyebrows questioningly and she gave an imperceptible shrug in response.

'Not really. I think the police are the ones you should talk to, they will have more information. Oh,' she suddenly remembered, 'other than the fact that it was a boy.'

'How can the police be so sure that the young girl was the baby's mother?'

'Well, they obviously have to wait for DNA tests to be carried out to confirm it, but lying close by to the baby was a necklace which had been given to Cecilia for her sixteenth birthday by her parents. Her mother has also confirmed that the blanket is identical to the one Cecilia had with her when she took the baby out.'

A silence fell and Sir Geoffrey and Lady Susan looked at each other, sharing something, but Katherine knew not what.

'It's very sad,' said Ted quietly. 'Poor girl. Poor baby.'

Katherine sighed. 'Terrible.'

'Actually,' Katherine decided to plunge straight in, 'I know that Cecilia and the baby were at the farmhouse on the day she went missing and I understand, Sir Geoffrey, that you drove up the lane that day? I don't suppose you saw anyone? Anything? Anything at all which might help the police? Cecilia had met someone at the farmhouse, he or she may not have anything to do with her murder but they might unknowingly hold a vital clue.'

'Did you call the police, Ted?' asked Sir Geoffrey suddenly sounding weary.

Katherine was startled. Police? If he'd called the police? Why had she had to come up here?

'Yes I did Sir Geoffrey. DI Allix will be here sometime later this morning.'

It was Katherine's turn to look questioningly at Ted. He, in turn, shrugged and mouthed that he didn't know why.

'Are you sure there's nothing else you can remember Katherine,? Nothing else about the baby?'

'No. Really I don't. I'm not sure what you want to know? Why are you so interested in the baby?' she asked, being slightly impertinent.

Sir Geoffrey gazed at his wife. She took his hands, squeezed them and nodded. 'Go on,' she whispered hoarsely, 'everyone will know sooner or later.'

What on earth is going on? Again she raised her eyebrows at Ted who gave her a "I really don't have a clue" look back

Sir Geoffrey got up and went to a beautiful antique, mahogany, bureau and took out a piece of paper. He handed it to Katherine, who studied the piece of paper and felt confused, as though she were being particularly dense. She handed it to Ted who studied it too. He then looked up at Sir Geoffrey, a look of comprehension in Ted's eyes.

'I'm sorry. I don't understand? What has this got to do with the ...' her voice trailed off. Oh my goodness! It couldn't? He couldn't? But how? She gaped at Sir Geoffrey astounded.

He sat down next to his wife and hung his head in shame. His wife gripped his hands in comfort.

'You're the, you're the ...' she stuttered. He nodded. Katherine looked at Ted who was shell shocked.

'Are you sure? I mean, I don't understand?' there was anger starting to build in her now. How could he? How could he do it?

'Yes.'

Katherine and Ted sat in stunned silence for a few minutes trying to get their heads round what had been revealed to them.

'Why don't you explain. Start from the beginning,' prompted his wife gently.

He cleared his throat and ran his finger round the inside of his shirt collar nervously. 'I thought she was older. She looked it, looked nearer to twenty from what I could tell,' he glanced apprehensively at his wife who nodded, encouraging him to go on.

'I. We. We'd had a huge argument. Like one we'd never had before, nor since. I was furious, absolutely livid, I stormed out and marched across the estate. I ended up at the farmhouse, I had a bottle of Scotch with me, I'd swiped it in fury. Thought I'd go into the farmhouse and quietly get sozzled. Anyway, I go in only to find this girl in there, crying her eyes out she was, her face was red, nose raw, eyes swollen. I was in such a bad mood I shouted at her for trespassing, which made her cry even more. I can't cope with tears, too emotional for me, got to keep those things in. I offered her my bottle of Scotch and she took a swig then produced a bottle of vodka she had with her. She wouldn't tell me what precisely was wrong, just said her life was a mess, how she hated everything around her, hated her family, she seemed to hate life in general. I assumed she'd had a row with her boyfriend or whatever, usually the cause of being over emotional in a female. We got through the Scotch and started on her bottle of vodka. We got pretty drunk.' He cleared a frog from his throat and glanced nervously at his wife again, she gripped his hands and looked intently at him. 'The next thing I knew... I woke up a few hours later and I was,' he blushed heavily and ran his finger round the collar of his shirt again, 'I was not er, terribly well, er, attired, should I say.'

Katherine and Ted gaped in astonishment, their mouths hanging open.

'Anyway, made a complete fool of myself. Thoroughly ashamed of my behaviour. Told Susie straight away. Never had secrets from her and wasn't about to start. Susie was a jolly good girl about it, forgave me. I didn't deserve it, but she forgave me,' he said gruffly, showing publicly the most affection for his wife that he had ever done. 'Thought that was the end of it. Moved on. Until I had a phone call from the girl months later, said she had to see me, it was important and I had to meet her that day. 12 o'clock she said. As you can imagine, I had no desire to see her, let alone go to the farmhouse where my, shall we say, indiscretion, occurred. Spoke to Susie and we decided I should go, see what she wanted. Susie knew she could trust me. Never had been unfaithful before and wasn't going to be again. A silly drunken mistake. Haven't touched a drop of the hard stuff since.'

'So you were on your way to see her,' thought Katherine out loud.

'Yes. I met her. She seemed a lot younger than previously. With her was a tiny baby. In warm clothes, he was dressed all in blue. She'd put the changing mat on the dusty oak floor and the blue blanket on top of that and he was lying on that, looking around, little legs kicking,' he drifted off at the memory. 'She told me he was mine, that I was the father. She needed money. She was going to stay with friends but she needed money for the baby and needed it that afternoon. I don't think she expected me to be interested in the baby, but I was. It was something I, something *we*,' he corrected himself, 'had always wanted, a son and heir. There he was. I couldn't believe it! Out of such a mistake came something so precious. I told her I wanted to be involved in his life, that he would be the heir to the Estate. But despite being bowled over and stunned by the events I still held on to reality. I knew that if she could have a drunken, er, whatever, with me, then it wasn't beyond the realms of possibility that she could do it with someone else. I had to have proof that he was mine. She told me that she needed some money and that when she got back we could sort it all out, maintenance and the like. I explained that it would take a day or two to get some cash for her, it's common knowledge that we're asset rich but cash poor. I couldn't rustle up a few thousand just like that. Besides, I needed to speak to Susie, she needed to be involved, to be alright about the situation. She said she needed the money again, was quite agitated about it, there was nothing I could do, I simply could not get my hands on such money so quickly. I told her she should give me a ring the next day and I would let her know when the cash would be ready. Eventually she accepted what I was saying and said she would call me. The baby was crying by now so I asked if I could pick him up. She hadn't named him. I asked if he could have one of my family names, it was a tradition. She didn't object but was vague. She let me pick the baby up. He was so tiny, so fragile, it was incredible to think that the small infant I held in my hands was mine. My flesh and blood,' his eyes sparkled at the memory. He had a sharp little nail so she carefully bit it off. I asked if I could have it, she thought it was weird but agreed. He wobbled as I held him, his neck so floppy, I stroked his hair, it was only afterwards that I realized one of them had clung to my jacket. I calmed him down a bit but she insisted she had to feed him and could I leave. So I did. Told her she could stay there as long as she liked. My mind was whirring with plans, if he was my baby I wanted to be involved, wanted Susie to be involved. I knew in my heart when he looked into my eyes that he was mine. I told her to phone me the next day. I knew she lived in the village, I'd asked her for her address, her phone number but she said she didn't want to give them to me, her parents weren't happy about her having had the baby. She said it would take them time to get used to the idea of her being a mother, but that when the time was right she would tell them who the father was. I accepted this, I was in shock. You don't expect to wake up one morning and have your world turned upside down do you?' He looked questioningly at them.

Feeling as though she was on the set of a movie and that this was all make believe, Katherine felt that her mind was about to explode from information overload. Ted sat there still looking stunned. He'd worked for his employees for ten years and never in a million years would he have expected this.

'What time did you leave her?' asked Katherine, as her brain processed what she had been told and segments started to fall into place.

'It was probably about 2 o'clock. She was alive and well and so was the baby. I came straight back here and told Susie. I showed her the sliver of finger nail and the hair and it was she who suggested they be sent off for DNA testing, it would cost, but it would be worth it to be one hundred percent sure that he was my son. Susie could see things more clearly, was more practical. She's been an absolute rock. Arranged for a couple of thousand pounds in cash to be ready for collection the next day, thought that was enough for nappies, clothes and the like, keep the baby going. She went and collected the cash the next morning whilst I waited for the girl to telephone me. We had discussed the situation. We wanted to be involved in the baby's life, wanted the baby to know his heritage. I waited and waited for her to call, the cash was ready, but she never called. Susie went down to the village to see if she could find her, thought it would be more subtle than me going. She heard a whisper in the post office that the girl had gone missing. There was no talk of the baby. We didn't know what to think, maybe the girl had gone early, thought she'd be in touch. The girl's mother called the police in, it was then that we discovered how old she was, that she was sixteen. I was stunned and horrified, I had no idea, she looked so much older. We were both still convinced that she had gone to her friends early, assumed that if her parents were having to adjust to their daughter being a mother and weren't happy about the situation, that she might have found life at home too hard. After a week the village got together and started searching the surrounding area, I got Ted to organize staff from the estate to search every inch of it. I checked the farmhouse. There was no sign of them and nothing seemed disturbed but it must have been. To think that they were bricked up there, how could I not have noticed? We waited and waited in the hope that she would contact us, that she would get in touch, time passed and we worried that something really had happened to her, but we never gave up hope. The hope that, one day, my son would walk through the door. Susie sent the nail clipping and hair off for analysis and eventually it came back confirming what we had suspected, that the baby was mine, I was the father.'

'Did you not tell the police about the baby?'

He shook his head. 'No. Like I said, we assumed that she had gone to stay with her friends, we didn't want to make things worse for her, and then, as time went by, it was harder to do so. Foolish, totally foolish, we should have told the police everything right from the start, maybe,' he choked, 'maybe my son would still be alive and the girl would be too.'

'I don't think so, I don't think you could have done anything. It's believed both she and the baby were murdered that day. Which is why, if there is anything, absolutely anything, no matter how insignificant a fact, you need to tell the police and you need to tell them what you have just told us.'

The once stiff backed, brusque, sometimes pompous, sometimes arrogant, but on the whole kind man, looked small and deflated. Katherine admired Lady Susan for standing by her man, for putting her faith in him, but was not overtly surprised as she was of the dying breed who stood by their man no matter what, who took their marriage vows and stuck to them – for better, for worse, for richer, for poorer – Katherine felt humbled. Perhaps there was more she could have done to save her marriage? But when the husband runs off with another woman and doesn't want to return and stick to the commitment he made to his marriage, there was not a lot that could have been done.

'I know. That's why I asked Ted to contact the police. I will do *anything* humanly possible to find out who killed my son and did the same to that poor girl. I will not rest until justice is done,' he sat up slightly and held his head high, determination surrounding him like an aura.

Katherine understood now why she had been summoned. The first time, when Cecilia had been found and Sir Geoffrey kept asking if there was anything else, he was obviously asking about his son. Perhaps the fact that the baby had not been found with his mother had maintained their hope that his son was still alive? Living the life of a happy ten year old? For the body of the baby to be found must have been devastating, though perhaps not entirely unexpected, the hope whipped away from them in a flash. If Sir Geoffrey was the father, had Tom known about it? Had he somehow found out? Having dismissed him in her own mind as a suspect, he now came to the forefront. What would he have done if he had found out that his girlfriend had slept around? That he was not the father of her child? Was she really going to go to France with him? Or was she going to go on her own? Katherine only had his word that the plan was they would both go. Had he told the police yet what he had told her?

'Katherine?' she became aware of Ted trying to get her attention.

'What? Oh, sorry, I was thinking, there's a lot to take in.' It was clear to her that Sir Geoffrey had had no idea Cecilia was fifteen when she became pregnant. Presumably the DNA test would be done again? She was sure he was telling the truth and that it wasn't the DNA test for another baby, but the police would need confirmation. Would Sir Geoffrey be arrested? Be charged with illegal activities? The situation was too dreadful, a complete mess and what would Cecilia's parents do when they found out? What would the whole village do? Would it ostracize them both? Would Susie suffer because of her husband's one indiscretion? If Tom didn't know, how would he take it?

213

Katherine had a nagging ache beginning in her head and she was sure it was going to turn into one of the worst headache's she'd ever had. Her blood was pumping athletically around her body, as though she had just run a marathon and she felt slightly light headed. She focused and found both Sir Geoffrey and Lady Susan peering at her with concern.

'Are you alright Katherine?' asked Lady Susan speaking for the first time. 'You look awfully pale. I've sent Ted off to make some more coffee, I'll put extra sugar in yours, you look like you need it, for the shock.'

Katherine smiled weakly and wondered in amazement at how Lady Susan could put the needs of Katherine before the agony that she must be going through. She must surely be aware of what was going to happen? The consequences? The pin had been pulled out of the grenade and all she could do was wait for it to explode.

It wasn't long before Ted returned, this time with large mugs of coffee, something for them to all grip on to. Lady Susan added several spoons of sugar to them all and whilst it tasted disgustingly sweet, Katherine found a strange comfort in it.

Sir Geoffrey had spent the last few minutes pacing up and down, his brow furrowed in deep thought. His wife patted the seat next to her and he obediently sat down and took the mug of coffee offered to him. 'It's no good,' he said, 'I can't think of anything that could be of use to the police. I really wish I could.'

'Is there nothing? Did you drive straight home? Saw nothing? Saw no one?'

He frowned again, working through his journey back from the farmhouse, it was ten years ago which didn't help.

'I got into the car, was in a bit of a daze, turned left and drove up the lane, saw that chappy, who is now Headmaster at the school, out for a walk, got home, spoke to Susie. That was it.'

Katherine had frozen when he'd mentioned "that chappy" could it be a coincidence that he was there? That he was near the farmhouse? 'Do you mean Robert Codell when you say "that chappy"?' she asked trying to keep the tremble from out of her voice.

'Yes. That's the one. Jolly good fellow. Ah,' Sir Geoffrey's eyes lit up, 'maybe he saw something?'

'Possible,' Katherine managed to croak. There was no doubt in her mind now that she had to tell DI Allix about Andrew Battle. If he were telling the truth that he had seen Cecilia first. Then Sir Geoffrey had seen her next. Could it have been Robert Codell? She felt a chill go down her spine and she gripped her mug tighter.

In the distance the dogs started to bark and a faint ring was heard. Ted went to answer the door and returned a few minutes later with DI Allix and DS Wilson. If DI Allix was surprised to see Katherine there he did not show it. She could see Sir Geoffrey and Lady Susan bracing themselves for what lay ahead. Katherine excused herself, smiling wanly at Sir Geoffrey and Lady Susan and murmured to DI Allix that she needed to speak to him. He promised to call and she left them to it. Ted guided her through the ancient building to the front door. They stood looking at one another, still in a state of shock over Sir Geoffrey's revelation.

'Will I see you tonight?' Ted asked hopefully.

Katherine frowned for a moment before remembering that they were supposed to be going for a drink that evening. 'Er. Yes. I've got this dreadful headache, so assuming I can get rid of it, yes.'

'How about I cook you supper instead? Save you having to do it yourself and my house will be quieter than a noisy pub?'

'That would be nice, thank you.' It would also give them the opportunity to talk about the days dramatic turn of events without fear of someone overhearing them and spreading it around. Discretion was of the utmost, Katherine felt.

'Would you like me to pick you up? You could have a drink then?' He looked quizzically at her.

'No, thanks, I'll be fine. What time would you like me to come over?'

'Sevenish? Whenever suits you, I'll be there.'

'OK, see you later then.'

On autopilot she drove home, took a couple of paracetamol and lay down on her bed, her head banging so loudly it felt like it was being used as a drum. She drifted in and out of sleep, vaguely aware of her head calming but waking when it started pounding ferociously again. She took two more paracetamol and drank a couple of glasses of water then went back to bed. By 5 p.m. she awoke again, her head pounding less, but unsettled by the dreams and semi-consciousness she had drifted in and out of, everything to do with Cecilia was being spun round like a washing machine on full spin. Robert Codell was the unknown quantity, until she knew for definite whether he had been abusing Cecilia or not she would not know whether he had the motive to kill her. She reminded herself that he could be innocent. That it could be made up. Information like that, if incorrect was dangerous and damaging, the potential to ruin one man's life and his family was easily done in one quiet, whispering rumour. The damage done, trust lost and suspicion prevalent. There would be no case of "innocent until proven guilty" in the position he held, people would automatically assume him guilty.

Groggily she got up and had a shower, letting the warm water run down her and wash away the griminess which she felt. She washed her hair vigorously, endeavouring to remove the nagging headache which still lurked at the back of her head. She slipped on a casual dress, nothing too dressed up, with long sleeves, a scoop neck and soft fabric which wrapped itself around from the front underneath the bust and tied in a bow at the back. The fabric was a mix of blues and greens in a small swirly pattern and flowed loosely around her. Her stomach rumbled as she had not had anything to eat since breakfast, by now it was 6 p.m, not wishing to spoil her appetite, but unsure of what time Ted would serve supper, she munched on a piece of toast and restrained herself from having several more pieces as it had whetted her appetite. She took another couple of paracetamol and hoped that they would be enough to finally dispose of her headache.

Ted's house was a small farmhouse on the edge of the Wynenden Park Estate, it came with the job. Katherine pulled up in front of the picturesque house, a slightly smaller version of the one she had bought, but in good condition. The door opened and a black Labrador came bounding out. 'Ella!' commanded a voice, ensuring that the dog came to an obedient halt rather than jump up at Katherine. The dog wagged her tail enthusiastically and Katherine stroked her head and murmured to her.

'Sorry. Meant to keep her in but she beat me to it!' laughed Ted.

'Oh, she's lovely, very friendly.'

'You ok with dogs then?'

'Grew up with them, just never owned one myself because I was always working, didn't think it was fair to keep a dog cooped up all day.'

He grinned, relieved. Ella was a major part of his life and it was important that anyone who came into his life liked dogs too. 'Come in, it's freezing out here.' He ushered into the kitchen and took her coat.

Katherine was surprised at how neat and tidy the house, from what she could see, was. She'd expected a bachelor pad to be filled with junk; no surface clear, chaos reigning. So it was most pleasant to see the kitchen tidy, work surfaces with food or cooking implements on them rather than piles of unwashed dishes and neglected paperwork. The old oak units had a refined air about them despite having seen better days, they suited the age of the house. There was an ancient dark blue Aga emitting warmth on the far side of the room with pots simmering on the top.

'Drink?' he asked.

'Something soft please.'

'Apple juice, orange juice or elderflower cordial?'

'Elderflower please.' She sat at the rectangular oak kitchen table and watched him as he deftly poured the drinks, got the ice out then checked the food on the Aga.

'Smells delicious,' she commented.

'Thanks. Hope it's ok. Didn't know what you liked and forgot to ask you this morning. You're not vegetarian are you?' he looked panic stricken.

'No, don't worry, love veggie food but I love meat too.'

218

Relief spread over his face. 'Phew! I did try and phone you this afternoon but you must have been out.'

'Sorry, I collapsed on the bed, my head was so bad, had a bit of a snooze, didn't hear the phone ring and I completely forgot to check the answer phone.' She wondered if she'd missed a call from DI Allix.

'How's your head now?'

'Much better thanks. So what did you decide on in the end?' she nodded towards the Aga.

'Roast lamb, roast potatoes, veg, gravy, hope that's OK?'

'Mmm, delicious! And I am very impressed that you can cook.'

'Don't speak too soon, you haven't tried it yet!'

There was a momentary lapse in conversation which Katherine eventually broke. 'How did it go after I left this morning?' she asked tentatively.

His face saddened as he thought of his employers. 'Difficult. DI Allix was as surprised as we were, though he did a good job of keeping a neutral face. Sir Geoffrey told them exactly what he had told us. He accompanied them down to the station to make a statement, which took a while, I drove him and waited. Of course what was worse, and something I don't know if he will recover from, was when he was told that Cecilia was just fifteen when she conceived their baby. I genuinely don't think he had a clue that she was so young. He's a real gentleman, he would *never* knowingly have had sex with her if he had known she was under aged, alcohol or no alcohol, intoxicated or not. I still can't believe he did what he did in the first place, it's so out of character. So unlike him. Unfortunately no one's going to believe him, once this gets out I dread to think what's going to happen.'

Katherine shook her head sadly at the whole situation. The hard fact was that he would be classed as a paedophile, the point that he had no idea she was under aged, that it wasn't pre-mediated, not calculating, was consenting by both parties – albeit drunkenly - and a one off indiscretion in an unblemished record of fidelity, would be irrelevant. 'What are you going to do?'

He shrugged and looked lost. 'I don't know. I don't know how the rest of the staff will take it, what their reaction will be? On the plus side most of them have worked for him for twenty or thirty years, they should know him, know that it was completely out of character. However, security could be an issue. There's not enough money to pay for increased security, so if people come onto the Estate to cause trouble, to get to Sir Geoffrey,' he shuddered. 'I'm going to have to do the best I can and more.'

She didn't envy him one bit, it was going to be ugly there was no doubt about that. 'This all happened shortly after you started. Did you not think there was something strange in his behaviour?'

'I've asked myself that a million times, but I was new to the job, I didn't really know Sir Geoffrey and Lady Susan and they're not the type of people who wear their hearts on their sleeves. It takes a while to build up a relationship and trust of people like that. If I'd been with them for ten years at that time then yes, I think I would have picked up on something and I think they might have confided in me. They know they can trust me, that I won't betray them.'

'They're very lucky to have you, to have someone so loyal.'

'Thanks.' His face looked drawn and tired with worry. Katherine wanted to hug him, to make him feel better but she was apprehensive and nervous of the response she may receive, that he might reject her. 'Well, this supper is not going to cook itself. I'd better make the gravy.' He leapt up and into action.

'Anything I can do to help?' offered Katherine.

'Nope. You sit there and relax, there's not much left to do, I had it all ready. That's the beauty of having an Aga. I'll just make the gravy then serve.'

The food was delicious, the meat tender and succulent, potatoes crispy, Katherine felt herself being restored and the remnants of her headache drifted away as the stress from her body released itself. They spent the rest of the evening sitting at the kitchen table, long after the apple pie and custard had been finished. Well past midnight and with a wave of exhaustion hitting her she left, thanking Ted profusely and hesitated on the doorstep, unsure as to whether to kiss him or not. He kissed her softly on the cheek and she glowed all the way home.

# Chapter Twenty-One

Tuesday morning was a glorious winter's day. A heavy frost covered the ground, the sky was pure blue and the sun strong. Katherine had discovered a message on her answer phone from DI Allix when she returned home the previous night. He said he would try to get hold of her on Tuesday and that it was all clear for the builders to go back to the farmhouse. She phoned Dougie as soon as she got up to let him know, rather apologetically, he informed her that his men were on another job for a few days which would be finished immediately before Christmas. He'd assumed that they would not be allowed back to the farmhouse until after Christmas and he needed to keep the money flowing in and the cash flow healthy. Disgruntled that Dougie had done this, she did reluctantly understand his reasoning but it meant further delays, every day mattered, at this rate her house wouldn't be finished before summer and she'd wanted to move in during the Easter holidays. He agreed to meet her for a quick chat at the farmhouse about mid morning, so she walked up there after breakfast, breathing in the clean, fresh, crisp air, clearing the cobwebs from her head.

He was there, ready and waiting for her, they briefly ran through a few points and discussed the kitchen. Katherine did her utmost to not think about the little bundle she had seen on her last visit, doing her best to force it from her mind, hopeful that when the works were complete it would eventually become a distant memory.

'I'll get the paint samples and drop them off here later along with brushes,' Dougie was saying. Whilst the house was in no way ready for samples to be painted onto the walls, Katherine felt the need to do something practical so that she didn't feel time was being wasted. Most of the house was going to be re-plastered and the samples would be covered up, but it would give her an idea of whether the colours she had selected would suit certain rooms or whether she needed a complete re-think. In some ways she felt that by painting the samples on the walls it would start to brush away the horrors of the previous months and bring a fresh start to the work.

'That'd be great, thanks. I'll come up tomorrow and make a start. If I don't speak to you before Christmas have a lovely one and I'll see you all back here next Wednesday.'

'Will do. You have a good one too Kitty. See you.' He hurried out leaving Katherine to absorb the silence which descended on the house. She leant on the ancient metal sink which, along with a wobbling strip of work surface, was all that was left of the old kitchen, and drank in the view of the overgrown garden and distant fields through the dusty window. The kitchen was south facing and the sun was just starting to edge its way round into the kitchen. Once the old kitchen was knocked through to the garden room light would flood in all day as it had windows on three sides facing east, south and west. The frost twinkled like diamonds in the soft winter sunlight, the acres of her land covered in a sparkling, crisp, white, blanket. She started to feel cold and zipped her coat up higher, then went out through the back door and locked up. The frost crunched under her feet as she walked around. Something made her glance up as she turned the corner of the building and was startled to see Robert Codell leaning on the gate at the entrance to the drive. He was gazing at the house and took a few moments before he noticed Katherine walking towards him, he turned to go, pretending he hadn't seen her.

'Hi!' called out Katherine loudly, determined not to miss her opportunity and contemplated what she might say.

He paused then turned back. He looked pale and tired, dark swathes were under his eyes and he seemed to have aged about ten years since she had last seen him. 'Hello,' he replied politely.

'Nice day isn't it?' continued Katherine.

'Mmm, yes,' was his vague reply.

'Would you like to have a look round?' asked Katherine suddenly feeling that if he found himself where the crime took place, it might jolt a memory, his subconscious making him blurt something out or at least prick his conscience if there was anything there which needed doing so. The amateur, and rather foolish, detective side of her coming out.

He looked confused. 'No. No thank you,' he turned to go.

'Are you sure? I thought you might like to see what's being done, particularly as you saw it before hand?'

His face froze and the muscles round his jaw tightened. 'No. Never been in it before,' he muttered.

Katherine pretended to look surprised. 'Really? I'm sure someone mentioned that you'd been in the house? Not for years though...' she looked vaguely off into the distance, pretending to recall some piece of information. 'I'm sure they said it was around the time that Cecilia went missing, but perhaps that was during the search for her?' She knew she was playing a dangerous game, but her god-children were her world and if the man standing in front of her had a fondness for young girls she was going to do everything to ensure that he did not remain in a position of responsibility with unlimited access to children. If she were wrong then she'd have to plead temporary insanity, stress, whatever he wanted to call it, and apologize – a lot - and hope that she, in turn, didn't get into trouble.

'Cecilia? I think you must be mistaken,' his voice had taken on a hard edge.

'Maybe I am, sorry, but I was sure someone said that you were up here on the day she disappeared? Must be my mind playing tricks on me, so much has been happening,' she tried to look innocent, weary and care worn and at the same time play the sympathy card.

He snapped. 'Look, I don't know what game you are playing but drop it. Understand?' He took a step closer to her and Katherine nervously felt for her mobile phone in her pocket and grasped her hand round it.

She took a deep breath and carried on, feeling a bit like someone poking a snake with a stick, waiting for the snake to strike. 'But you were,' she paused, 'close to Cecilia, weren't you?' her voice had dropped. She saw the fury in his eyes and tried not to flinch.

'I have no idea what you are talking about,' he replied through gritted teeth.

'You gave her extra English lessons didn't you?' it was a rhetorical question, 'except that you gave her a little more than extra English ...' her voice trailed off, the implication clear.

He leapt forward and grabbed her by the throat. 'You're playing with fire,' he hissed at her, his face so close that she could feel his garlicky breath on her face. 'She did nothing she didn't want to...' his voice trailed off and he shoved her back, glared at her and marched off down the lane, leaving Katherine shell shocked.

She stood stock still, her mind grinding slowly as she laboured to processes his words. Had that really just happened? He'd confessed, surely he had confessed? But it wasn't enough to convict him. He could deny it, say that he was referring purely to the English work. But she knew. She knew he was referring to far more than that. Her legs turned to jelly and she started shaking. She grabbed hold of the gate and lent heavily against it. Her head swam, breaths come fast and furious, her heart pounding, she tried to take long deep breaths to calm herself but it made it worse. She lent her head against the gate waiting for it to pass, it took some minutes of focused, calm, breathing before her heart slowed a little and she stopped hyperventilating. She straightened up, closed her eyes and breathed deeply in through her nose and out through her mouth, she did this a few times until her heart started to slow further. With some clarity she used her mobile to put another call though to the police station, asking for DI Allix to phone as soon as possible.

She shut the gate behind her and hurried down the lane in the direction of the village, praying the Robert wasn't lurking down there waiting to do something to her. She glanced nervously about her as she went, walking as fast as she could so that she was almost running. She reached the Wynenden Road with relief and slowed to catch her breath. Katherine crossed over the road to the pavement and walked at a slightly slower pace through the village, feeling some modicum of security from having buildings around her. She had a sudden craving and need for a sugar fix and diverted into the post office. Fortunately Betty was not there and the other woman with whom she job shared was the total opposite to her work colleague, quiet, unassuming and uninterested in gossip. Katherine picked up a copy of The Times, a copy of the Christmas issue of the Radio Times and several bars of chocolate. She smiled and murmured pleasantries, paid quickly and as soon as she was out of the shop ripped the cover off a chocolate, caramel and biscuit bar and sank her teeth into the sweet chocolatey, biscuity, gooey confection. The sugar rush hit her and she felt her spirits rising.

She was about to turn into Wynenden Close when a car pulled up beside her. The passenger window went down and she saw Audrey Stillingfleet's pale face looking out at her. Despite the trauma she was going through she had still applied her full make up, though Katherine thought it wasn't quite as perfectly applied as it had been when she had seen her previously. 'Hello,' she said.

'Hello Audrey. How are you?' Katherine bent down to talk to her.

'Oh, you know. OK.'

'How's Rupert?'

Audrey's face darkened. 'Drinking even more. He's not been going in to work at all, which is perhaps a blessing given the state he is in, it's getting out of control and I don't know what to do about it,' her voice trembled.

Poor woman, thought Katherine, she had enough trauma to deal with over her daughter and grandson and was quite sure she could do without having to deal with a drunken husband, having to be strong for them both, run the business, the house, all the weight was on her shoulders and if she didn't get support soon, Katherine felt sure that Audrey would, unsurprisingly, have a breakdown. 'If you need to talk, you know where I am, call any time. Have you spoken to Rupert's doctor or your own doctor?'

'I tried. I even managed to persuade one of them to come out, didn't tell Rupert, but as soon as the doctor arrived Rupert stormed out. The doctor could see what state Rupert was in but there's not a lot they can do without his cooperation. I'm worried about his drink driving, what if he crashes into another car or someone else and kills them?'

'Have you mentioned this to DI Allix?'

'Yes, but unless they catch him drink driving there's nothing they can do. They don't have the resources to sit outside the house all day waiting from him to leave or return. They've far more important work to do.'

'I'm sorry I can't do more to help. You take care of yourself and please do call if you need anything.'

'Thanks Katherine. Bye,' with that she put her BMW into gear and drove off to clear up yet another mess of Rupert's making at work.

Poor, poor woman, thought Katherine gazing after her. What a miserable life she has got, no chance of any kind of a Happy Christmas for her, what has she got to celebrate? Nothing. Katherine continued up Wynenden Close to home.

In desperate need of a caffeine fix when she got back, Katherine selected an extra strong coffee pod and popped it into her machine and watched it whir into life and fill her cup with the dark liquid. She gained comfort, as she usually found, from clutching the warm cup and sipping the hot liquid. She checked her answer phone and her mobile to make sure she had not missed a call from DI Allix and impatiently waited for him to call, couldn't he tell it was urgent? Having continued to pace up and down for an hour waiting for his call and restraining herself from phoning again, she decided to change her focus reasoning that "a watched pot never boils" and made herself cheese on toast. Flicking through the Radio Times she saw that the classic old film 'White Christmas' was on in half an hour, nothing like a bit of festive schmaltz to get into the Christmas spirit she thought. It was five days until Christmas Eve and definitely time to get on with wrapping presents, she brought them all down from the spare room, which was crammed with unpacked boxes like the rest of the house, and sat on the floor in the sitting room with White Christmas playing on the television. She focused herself totally on the task in hand to ensure that she didn't think about Robert or why DI Allix hadn't called. When a pile of enticingly wrapped presents sat neatly in the middle of the floor she made a cup of tea, took a shop bought mince pie from the cupboard and curled up on the sofa to watch the remainder of the film.

As the credits rolled there was a sharp rap on the door. Cautiously Katherine peered out of the sitting room window to see who it was, fearful that it might be Robert Codell even though he didn't know where she was currently living, it was DI Allix.

He smiled when she opened the door. 'Sorry it's taken a while for me to catch up with you,' he said pleasantly, 'but I've been a little bit busy as you could imagine.' He took up her offer of a cup of tea then settled himself on a sofa, laying his coat next to him. As dusk was falling, Katherine switched the lights on and drew curtains.

DI Allix sipped his tea and waited for her to sit down. 'So, what was it you needed to speak to me about?'

Where did she start? So much had happened in the past forty-eight hours. She felt rather embarrassed about her behaviour now she was recounting her conversation with Andrew Battle and then moved on to Sir Geoffrey. DI Allix listened intently, nodding now and then and occasionally intercepting with a question.

She then paused, took a sip of her tea and broached the subject of Robert Codell. 'I don't know how far you've got with your enquiries? I saw you taking him away on Sunday evening.' She looked questioningly at him.

'I can't really discuss him with you, but suffice to say, as the main witness is dead it could be rather tricky to prove anything. We are however continuing to make enquiries.'

Katherine fiddled with her fingers, feeling rather foolish. 'I, um, I saw him this morning,' she said nervously, fearful that she would get into trouble for stirring things up. 'I was up at the house, had had a meeting with Dougie , I stayed at the house on my own for a little while then left. As I was leaving, I saw Robert leaning on the gate at the head of the drive, I know he saw me but he turned to go, so I called out to him. I… Well … I didn't out rightly accuse him of, you know, with Cecilia, but I heavily hinted, talked about her extra English lessons, implied that he had given her more than the lessons…' her voice trailed off again. She looked anxiously at DI Allix who said nothing, feeling she was a complete idiot for doing what she'd done and trying to keep the embarrassed blush, which was creeping over her face, in check. 'Anyway, he denied ever having been up at the farmhouse and then he grabbed me around the throat and told me, and I use his precise words "She did nothing she didn't want to…" then he pushed me back and strode off. I know it was a really stupid thing to do, but I couldn't help myself, I don't know what came over me? I suppose the over protective side of me came out and my godchildren go to the Prep School and will probably go on the Senior School. I don't want them being at risk. I had to find out and by his reaction, his anger and what he said, I'm sure he abused Cecilia and maybe others.'

DI Allix sat silently for a minute, Katherine felt like a naughty child about to be reprimanded. 'I know you meant well,' he said with unnerving calmness, 'but it is best if you keep out of it. There's a difference between coming across information, which might be useful in an investigation, and deliberately goading someone into saying something they don't mean to. Whilst it would appear that the implication from the way he reacted, and what he said, would suggest an inappropriate relationship with Cecilia, there is no concrete evidence.'

'I know. I'm sorry. And I'm not a gossip. I won't go round saying things about people which aren't true and I'm only telling you this because you are the police and my priority is for the safety of my godchildren. Apart from anything, Robert Codell was seen not far from the farm-house on the day that Cecilia disappeared. She could have contacted him, just as she did Andrew Battle and Sir Geoffrey, and demanded that he meet her at the farmhouse. Maybe she even asked him for money just as she had asked the others? After all, if he had abused her she wouldn't have to say much to remind him what a vulnerable position he was in, how one word from her could potentially mean the end of his career, mud sticks. I would say that that was a pretty strong motive for murder.'

'I understand. I really do and several lines of enquiry are being followed up. I must again ask you not to say anything about your thoughts on Robert Codell, or anything else to do with the case, to anyone, no matter how tempted, especially not to the parents of your godchildren. I don't have to tell you what the consequences would be if rumours abounded, true or not, his life would be ruined, an innocent man treated as guilty for something he may never have done. I don't want a witch hunt going on.'

'Don't worry, I won't, I will be keeping my eyes and ears open, but my mouth firmly shut,' she swiftly changed the subject. 'Do Audrey and Rupert know that Sir Geoffrey is the father of their daughter's baby?'

'Not yet. I want absolute proof before I break it to them. DNA tests are being carried out and as soon as I have the results I will tell them, I see no reason to not believe Sir Geoffrey but I have to be sure.'

'How are they? Sir Geoffrey and Lady Susan? You know that he thought Cecilia was older, twenty or so, he had no idea that she was under the legal age of consent. It *definitely doesn't* make it right, but I do feel for him and

Lady Susan. One moment of total out of character madness and stupidity could absolutely shatter their lives, more than it has already done, but then similar could be said for Cecilia. If she hadn't got pregnant she may still be alive.'

He restrained himself from giving her another lecture on interfering, hoping that she had listened and learnt her lesson. Annoyingly her interference had produced some interesting pieces of information, ones which the police had so far failed to tease out.

'It's a delicate situation and will be handled sensitively. I can't say any more than that I'm afraid.' He rose to go. 'Thank you for your help.'

Katherine saw him out and felt disquieted, she knew she was right and she was sure Robert was capable of murder.

# Chapter Twenty-Two

Settling on a change of scene for the next morning, Katherine took herself off to the small town of Cranbrook some ten miles from Wynenden. It was a pretty little town with a strong community spirit centred around two roads which formed an "L" shape through the centre of the town. Along these were a wide ranging assortment of shops and banks, you could purchase pretty much anything you wanted to from haberdashery to food to clothes to jewellery and everything in between. Katherine wandered in and out of the shops picking up a couple of interesting kitchen implements in the well stocked cook shop, treating herself to a soft cream silk floaty top in one of the boutiques and then went for a cappuccino in the small Italian coffee shop and deli, the welcome was warm and the coffee excellent. It was packed and Katherine had to share a table with an elderly gentleman who was reading a newspaper. By the jovial banter which was batting backward and forward between him and one of the staff she assumed he was a regular.

She sat in the bay window which afforded her a view both up and down the bustling street and watched the world go by. There seemed to be a large number of over excited children, which was hardly surprising given that Christmas was only a few days away, their mothers looking slightly haggard and worn down by the whole event before it had even happened. It was nice to see a small town thriving, though there had been times of struggle and would no doubt be again, and keeping its individuality rather than giving in to the multitude of big brand shops which seemed to dominate so many high streets. On top of that was the bonus of free parking, a virtually nonexistent occurrence in this day and age. Katherine vaguely remembered reading something about the local council trying to introduce parking charges and there being a huge outcry against it, petitions were signed, letters written and with much celebration the proposal was over turned.

She suddenly spotted Robert and his wife Jane strolling down the street in deep conversation. Katherine turned inwards and prayed that they wouldn't see her let alone come into the coffee shop for a drink or something to eat. She waited a few moments before peeping round and breathed a sigh of relief as she saw their backs disappearing down the street. The last thing she wanted was a public confrontation and she had promised that she would steer clear of any antagonistic behaviour. Katherine gulped down the last of her cappuccino, paid and hurried up the street in the opposite direction to the one which Robert and Jane had just gone. She nipped into the paper shop and treated herself to a couple of glossy magazines and dose of Hello! magazine, plenty of fluffy reading to keep her going throughout Christmas. She had been so engrossed in the building works and brochures for the umpteen items which were required for the farmhouse, that she had had little time to flick mindlessly through such magazines. She always liked to have what she thought was a proper read before she went to sleep, a book to stretch her mind rather than something trashy to whizz through. The classics were her favourites, she loved a spot of Dickens or Hardy and even a splash of Dostoevsky from time to time. At the moment she was deep in her annual festive read of Dickens' much loved "A Christmas Carol" she could never resist reading it at this time of year and was now a firmly entrenched tradition for her.

With a pleasant and relaxing morning under her belt, she wolfed down the take away homemade soup and sandwich she had purchased in one of the delicatessens in Cranbrook, changed into a pair of old jeans, shirt, jumper and coat and set off to the farmhouse in her car, trusting that Dougie had delivered the paint samples and brushes to the farmhouse earlier as promised. She would have preferred a walk in what was yet another crisp, dry, day but if she were to get the samples up before dusk fell she wouldn't have time.

She frowned as she pulled up to the entrance to the drive. The gate was open and there was a black Porsche 911 sitting, parked haphazardly, abandoned in the drive. She was sure it wasn't Andrew's but couldn't place it. Katherine scanned the area and could see no one. She hesitated, perhaps she should go home or maybe she could phone Ted? What would she say to him though? That there was a strange car in the drive and could he come and help her? What a wimp, he would think she was, particularly when no doubt there would turn out to be a logical explanation. Even so, something unsettled her.

She locked her car door and kept the keys in her hand in her pocket, ready to use as a weapon. Her heart started to pound as she stepped silently, closer and closer to the house. She could hear nothing. She paused. Silence. She continued to creep, round the side of the house, silently approaching the back door, it was open and the kitchen window had been smashed. She froze on the spot. Dougie wouldn't have done that. Her breath was coming fast and furious. Very quietly she edged her way to the kitchen door and listened. Faintly she could hear a noise, it sounded like sobbing. Katherine strained to hear, there were moans mixed in amidst the sobs. She slid quietly through the gap in the kitchen door, breathing in so as not to nudge it and make it squeak. She edged slowly, stealthily, through the kitchen, walking round the rubble, the sound seemed to be coming from the winter sitting room. Quietly she crept, moving closer and closer until she was in a position to glimpse a figure through the open door.

There was a great lumpy mass sitting on the floor with his back to her, the collar of his black raincoat was pulled up high around his fleshy neck, his grey hair straggling over it. Surrounding him on the floor were empty bottles. She saw him tilt his head back and glug more from a still full bottle of whisky. She knew it was Rupert Stillingfleet and relaxed slightly. He was rocking backwards and forwards, sobbing and muttering words under his sob filled voice. Katherine hesitated, should she leave him to his grief? Or should she call Audrey to come and pick him up?

It felt intensely personal, too intrusive standing there listening to the poor man mourning the loss of his daughter and grandson. She decided to leave him for a while, but as she turned to creep out she accidentally tripped over a raised floorboard and fell against the wall. Rupert's hulk spun round. 'Sorry,' murmured Katherine.

'It's you,' he slurred, 'fancy a drink?' He waved the now half empty bottle at her. 'I've got plenty,' he flapped his hands towards a couple more full bottles of whisky. 'Come here, come and join me.'

Politely Katherine went over to him. He was sitting opposite the opened up fireplace. He pushed a bottle over towards her which she took and held on to, he was too drunk to notice whether she was consuming any or not. She sat in silence as he continued to mutter to himself, wondering what she should do? Maybe he needed someone to off load to?

'I'm sorry about Cecilia and about your grandson. I can't imagine how awful it is for you,' she said gently opening up the lines of communication, if talk was what he in fact wanted.

He swayed slightly as he sat there, his bloodshot eyes exacerbated by his tears and not focusing properly from the alcohol.

'So am I,' he slurred, 'she was my baby.'

Katherine nodded.

'Problem was, she was growing up, growing up you know. She wasn't my baby anymore.'

'I'm sure a lot of fathers feel like that about their daughters,' she encouraged.

'But she was mine! Mine, I tell you!' he shouted.

Katherine shifted nervously, hoping that the alcohol wasn't going to make him violent.

'She was my baby! How could I let anyone else have her? She was mine! How could she let anyone else touch

238

her? It wasn't right! She was for me, me alone!' he sobbed.

Katherine shivered. He couldn't? He surely couldn't be saying what she thought he was saying? Her heart slammed rapidly against her ribs and she felt bile rise up into her throat.

'Don't you see?' He swigged from his bottle and raw eyes looked pleadingly at her. 'She was mine to keep.'

Katherine tried to keep calm, but inside her head she was screaming "how could you do that to your own daughter?" it disgusted her to her core. She wanted to vomit. The thought of him touching her in that way. It was sick.

'Did I fail her? Could I not satisfy her? Is that why she turned to others?' he spat vehemently. 'I knew! I knew she slept with other men. That stupid boyfriend of hers to start with. There were others, I followed her. Secret liaisons all over the place. Why couldn't she be satisfied with me? I was the one who loved her, it should have *only* been me who touched her.' He took another long glug of whisky and threw the empty bottle skittling across the oak and picked up another, fumbling to twist off the lid.

A stream of swear words ran through Katherine's mind, along with panic, not knowing what to do.

'How could she get pregnant? It wasn't right! She needed to stay pure for me. Why did she have to dirty herself with other men? I could have provided her with everything! That baby,' he spat, 'she should have got rid of it, I arranged it all, make her pure again, for me, give her another chance, a chance to redeem herself but she had to come back with it, that devil child! She shouldn't have kept it. She had her chance and she blew it, she couldn't carry on, she ruined everything!' He took another swig.

239

Oh shit! Thought Katherine. He can't mean? She shoved her hand in her mouth and bit hard on it to prevent her from screaming.

'I followed her,' his eyes gazed at the fireplace, misty with the memories, 'saw her meeting that scum she called her boyfriend. Knew she'd be up here again, came up in the afternoon, all I could hear was the screech, screech, screech of that devil child, wouldn't shut up, I had to shut it up, I couldn't think, it was getting in the way, without it we had a chance, she could be my little girl again, she tried to fight me off, but it didn't take much to shut the baby up. Then she started screaming at me, shouting at me, I tried to make her feel better, held her to me, she struggled, but she knew better, she knew I could make her pure again, she felt me, we were one, but all she did was scream, she hit me!' he looked indignant.

Blood was dripping from Katherine's hand as she drew blood from biting so hard, tears streaming down her face, not from the pain, but from the evilness of what had been done.

He drank, long and hard from the bottle, it dribbled down his chin, but even when he finished he didn't seem to notice. 'I tried to get her to shut up, I did, I managed too but then she went limp in my arms, my baby, she shouldn't have struggled...'his voice trailed off.

Katherine sat rooted to the spot. If she ran, would he do the same to her?

'It's too late now. It's all ruined. She was supposed to remain here, resting in peace but you, you and your stupid builders ruined it! Everyone knows now that she's gone, they know about the baby, her purity gone. It's over.' He took another long swig and staggered to his feet. Katherine inwardly flinched not daring to move. He staggered out of the room and she heard him stumbling through the kitchen. She grabbed her phone and dialled the police station.

'Please, get DI Allix, anyone, up to Wynenden Farmhouse. NOW! Rupert Stillingfleet murdered his daughter Cecilia and her baby, he's here, hurry!' She broke off as Rupert staggered back into the room, Katherine cowered against the wall, but he swayed on the spot, leant over, swiped several times at a full bottle of whisky on the floor, finally grasped it and staggered out. She heard him again stumbling through the kitchen, then it went quiet. The blood was roaring in her ears and she was sweating profusely but shivering from cold. She caught a movement out of the corner of her eye through the window. He was stumbling towards his car. She couldn't let him drive in that state! Instinctively she ran out through the back door, round the house and up the drive as fast as she could.

'RUPERT!' she shouted. He turned and saluted her as he fell into his car. 'STOP!' He revved the engine of his Porsche, cranked it with a grinding into gear and put his foot down, then clumsily negotiated his way out of the drive, narrowly missing her car and the gates, swerving all over the road, she could hear the roar as he raced at terrifying speed up the lane. Katherine slumped on the ground and wept, not caring that the damp and cold from the grass was seeping through her jeans. Minutes later there was a squealing of brakes as several police cars flew into the drive.

DI Allix was amongst them. 'Where is he? Where's Rupert?' he asked urgently.

'You know?'

'He left a suicide note for his wife. Confessing to everything. She got it about half an hour ago, we were there when your call came through. Where did he go?'

'He went that way,' she pointed to the left, 'I tried to stop him, he's drunk so much, but I couldn't.'

'Stay here,' he commanded, indicating for a couple of police officers to look after Katherine. The rest of them jumped into their cars and drove off.

It was half an hour later before DI Allix returned, his face, worn, sad and defeated.

In the meantime a blanket had been wrapped round Katherine and she was sitting in the warmth of a police car. 'Did you find him?' she asked, fearing the worst.

He looked grim. 'Yes. He'd crashed his car into a tree, he's dead.'

Somehow Katherine had known, the way he had spoken, the way he had raced off, she could kick herself for not having tried harder, for not taking his keys off him earlier.

'There's nothing you could have done,' said DI Allix softly as though reading her mind. 'He'd planned this. If you had stopped him he would have found some other way to kill himself, maybe not now, but later.'

'Did his letter tell you everything?' her pained eyes looked deep into his.

'It did.'

She started at a sudden thought. 'What about Audrey? Did she know that he was abusing their daughter?'

'I would say from her reaction, no. She's not in a good way as you can imagine.'

'She's lost everything. Her daughter, her grandson and now her husband and all she has is the knowledge of what he did to her. Is anyone with her?'

'Her doctor is at the moment, she's had to be sedated.'

'So she doesn't know Rupert is dead yet? Poor, poor woman, how will she ever recover from this? Her life shattered, blown apart beyond recognition. This is the sort of thing you would expect to see in the vilest of movie's, the sort of film some sicko would go and watch,' she shook her head, her body and mind so numb with shock she could barely move.

'Let's get you home, into the warm,' he instructed the two police officers to take Katherine home and to stay with her. He in the meantime had to return to the crash site. The only ounce of relief in the situation was that Rupert had not killed someone else by his drunken driving, he had driven straight into a tree, deliberately DI Allix was privately convinced, the alcohol drunk in preparation to numb the last few breaths of life.

# Chapter Twenty-Three

It was several hours later when DI Allix arrived at Katherine's house. She had persuaded the policeman and woman that she really was alright to be left on her own after she had changed out of her damp clothes and been plied with sweet tea. She sat shell shocked on the sofa, the darkness drew in and the sitting room was only lit by the occasional flash of car headlights coming up the road. With no lights on in the house, but her car on the drive -having been driven back by one of his colleagues - it was with trepidation that DI Allix knocked on her door. In a daze she dragged herself off the sofa and opened the door. She looked drawn and haunted. Guiding her back into the sitting room, DI Allix switched on a couple of lamps, drew the curtain and went into the kitchen to make some tea. Whilst the kettle was boiling he came back into the sitting room, picked up a rug which was over the arm of the chair and offered it to her, she was shivering even though the heating was on and she was well wrapped up in a thick jumper.

He handed her a mug of sweet tea and sat down opposite her. 'Do you feel up to talking?' he asked gently, 'it can wait until tomorrow.'

She shook her head. 'No. It's ok. I'd rather go through it now. Perhaps it will be cathartic?' She recounted from start to finish what had happened that afternoon, from the moment she drove up to the farmhouse to the arrival of the police.

'Thank you. Perhaps tomorrow, if you are feeling up to it, you could come down to the station and make a formal statement.'

She nodded. 'What did the letter say? The one Rupert wrote.'

It correlates with what you have told me. He mentioned the abuse, the murders, it was a rambling letter but it confirms - without doubt - that he was responsible.'

'It's so tragic, it's dreadful how one man's sick, twisted actions have such devastating consequences. He's ruined so many lives. How can anybody abuse their own child? It's pure evilness. Did Audrey really have no idea at all?'

'I don't think so. When she's fit enough to be interviewed we will have to question her, but I really don't think she was aware at all otherwise she would have tried to stop him. It's clear her priority has always been her daughter and I suspect she would have chosen her daughter over her husband.'

'But Cecilia's behaviour changed, surely she must have suspected something?'

'She put it all down to puberty, to hormones kicking in, the abuse didn't start until she was eleven.'

'Audrey's going to have to live with that for the rest of her life, always wondering "if only". How do you get over something like this?' Katherine shook her head in bewilderment.

'I don't know, it won't be easy for her, but hopefully with help and support, in time, things will become a little easier for her.' Sadly DI Allix knew that Rupert wasn't the only parent to abuse his child.

'So what happens now? What happens to Rupert?'

'As there is a signed confession and he confessed to you, albeit in a drunken state, the case will eventually be closed. Funeral arrangements for Rupert can go ahead as normal.'

'Who on earth is going to arrange it? Even if Audrey felt up to it, would she want to? He's taken away everything from her. I don't think many, if any, will attend his funeral, not after what he did.' She winced at the thought of what sort of gossip would be spreading around the village once it became public knowledge. She hoped that Audrey would not be ostracised for what her husband did, but Katherine knew that there would always be a few who would consider her guilty by association and responsible and not accept that she was as much a victim now as her daughter was then.

'Is there anyone I can call? Ask them to come and sit with you?' enquired DI Allix.

'No, I'll be fine. I'll give a friend a call once you have gone. Does Sir Geoffrey know yet? He ought to be told, you know, as he was the baby's father, though I assume you are still waiting for the DNA tests results you have requested?'

'Not yet, he's my next stop.'

'It might be an idea if Ted were present, as moral support, Sir Geoffrey has asked him to be present on other occasions. Would you like me to phone him for you?'

'That would probably be helpful, thanks.'

'And what about Tom?   Does he know yet that it was Rupert who murdered his girlfriend?   That Rupert was abusing her?'

'Not yet.   After I've seen Sir Geoffrey I will go and see him.'

'Poor man.   He said she was his true love, it's going to shatter him when he finds out that he wasn't the only man having sex with her, no doubt he'll feel betrayed and it will probably disgust him,' she shivered in revulsion at the thought of Rupert doing what he'd done to Cecilia.

'It won't be pleasant and even worse for him when, assuming we receive confirmation, he is told that the baby wasn't actually his.   I'm not planning on breaking this to him until the DNA report has confirmed what Sir Geoffrey's report states.'

A thought struck her.   'So why was Andrew Battle so interested in the house?   I had thought initially that it was because he had something to do with Cecilia's death, but in my last conversation with him he mentioned that he was already interested in purchasing the farmhouse at the time of her disappearance?'

DI Allix gave a small smile.   'I think I may have discovered the reason.   He owns fifty acres of land which surrounds your property, the land is not held directly in his name but in one of many of his companies, though it is not easy to find this out.   It appears he bought the land, which was not a recent part of the Wynenden Estate, with a view to developing it and creating a massive housing estate, houses all packed together, as many as he could fit in.   The only problem was that, despite there being separate access to the site, the council deemed it as unsuitable for such a large development and in secret initial talks it was suggested that his best bet for getting the housing estate passed by the planners - allegedly along with a little palm greasing -was to purchase Wynenden Farmhouse and create an access through the land belonging to it. I imagine that the reason why Sir Geoffrey refused to sell to him was because he suspected Andrew might try and do something like that.'

'Ahh, no wonder he's so keen to get his hands on the farmhouse!' She smiled, then it faltered. 'Does that mean he is going to harass me until I sell the house and the land to him? Or even worse, what if he gets planning permission to build on the land he owns anyway?' She could see her country idyll, which was already teetering on the edge, being swallowed up by some monster estate.

'If he does continue to harass you, just let me know, he won't be allowed to get away with it. As for him getting planning permission to build on the land with the current access, it would be unlikely, even if he tried to slip it through the planning department it would become public knowledge and I doubt that anyone in the village is going to want a massive housing estate swallowing it up. Also, I think it is in a conservation area which should make it virtually impossible. He has gone to great lengths to hide the fact that he owns the land. I wonder how the village would feel if they discovered who the land owner really was and the true intention of its usage is?' His eyes twinkled at her.

She was slightly startled by his suggestion, but grinned at the thought. It truly would scupper Andrew's plans if the village found out, she didn't like to gossip, but if it were fact, nothing made up, a small comment casually dropped into a conversation for the greater good, would be round the village within minutes. It was certainly something for her to ponder upon.

'I'll see you at the station tomorrow then,' he got up.

'OK. Sometime in the morning. Whatever time suits you just let me know, I'd rather get it over and done with then try and forget about it as much as I can. I'll give Ted a call now,' she said as she showed him out.

'Thanks. Bye.'

She picked the phone up and dialled Ted's number. He perked up when he heard her voice and she too felt some comfort from speaking to him. After the pleasantries were over, she continued. 'Ted, I think it would be a good idea if you went up to the house. DI Allix has just left here and is on his way to see Sir Geoffrey.'

'Why? What's wrong?' his voice filled with concern.

'I can't say, it's best if you hear it from DI Allix. Just go and be with Sir Geoffrey and Lady Susan. They're going to need your moral support. Don't worry, he's not going to be arrested or anything.'

'You sure? I'd best get up there then. Speak to you later. Bye.'

Next, Katherine phoned Libby and asked her simply to come over. Without questioning the reason why, Libby arrived an hour later, having left the children with James as soon as he got back from work.

Katherine spent the evening pouring her heart out to Libby, trying to cleanse herself of the horrors of the day. Libby was astounded and horrified, but comforted her friend as best she could, leaving her in a better state than when she arrived. Ted phoned later in the evening, in a state of shock himself about what had happened, to see how Katherine was. Having reassured him that she was fine she took a long hot bath, tucked herself up in bed and immersed herself in her book – A Christmas Carol – removing herself from the present reality.

After a fitful night's sleep, Katherine reluctantly drove herself down to the police station and spent a lengthy while giving her statement. When she appeared into daylight again, the grey cloud had dispersed and the sun was trying to peep through. She took a deep, long, breath and exhaled slowly, clearing her mind. In some way, though the horrors of the previous day and weeks and months were still with her, and would be for some time to come, she felt that she could start to move on. The only thing which still worried her was the thought of Robert Codell and whether he had had a sexual relationship with Cecilia. There was nothing more she could do, it was in the hands of the police and she trusted DI Allix to persevere until he was satisfied that Robert was innocent or not.

Feeling the urge to be around normal people, people carrying on with their everyday lives with nothing as dramatic as what she had experienced going on in their lives, she drove to the town of Tenterden and wandered round the shops, dipping in and out, absorbing the normality of life going on around her. She stopped and had a cappuccino in a small delicatessen and flicked through one of the newspapers provided for customers, drifting into and out of other people's conversations, snippets here and there, all mundane stuff. Revived from her drink she decided to brave Waitrose and do her Christmas food shop so that she need not go near a supermarket for the next week or so. With only two whole days left until Christmas Eve there was a frenzy of buying going on, it was trolley to trolley in the aisles, Katherine hadn't expected it to be quite so busy, having assumed that the manic buying would start at the weekend. It always left her feeling slightly sick at the sight of other people's trolleys at that time of year, people seemed to go to extremes of excess, gorging themselves as though they had never been fed and didn't know where their next meal was going to come from, she winced at the thought of the waste which would be left, perfectly good food which would simply be thrown out, it was disgraceful really.

She told herself to stop moralizing and get off her high horse and battled her way round, doing her best to keep a smile on her face and remain polite, despite other harried and hassled shoppers. She had already ordered a turkey and some sausages and bacon from the village butcher and was going to collect them on Saturday and drop them off at Libby's. It was her contribution to the meal and despite Libby's protests that she need not do it, she had insisted and would drop them off to give Libby plenty of time to do whatever preparations she had in mind.

Feeling as though she had just done ten rounds in a boxing ring, Katherine wearily drove home, her mood lowering as her blood sugar level dropped, knowing that she needed food to boost her. She left all but the frozen and chilled food in their bags on the kitchen floor to be packed away later and flopped on the sofa with a glass of water and her seasonal sandwich of turkey and cranberry sauce which she had purchased from the supermarket. She dozed off and started when there was a rap on the door, feeling slightly confused and dazed, it took her a few moments to come too, noticing with relief that it was still light outside and she hadn't been asleep for hours. A quick glance at her watch told her only an hour had passed, to be precise.

She opened the door rubbing her eyes and was greeted by a huge bunch of red roses. Ted's face peeped round the edge of them. She smiled broadly.

'Hello! Come in,' she was delighted to see him.

'I thought these might cheer you up, you know, what with all you've been through,' he looked worriedly at her.

'That's so kind of you. Thank you, they're beautiful!' She took them from him and he followed her into the kitchen, stepping round the remainder of the as yet unpacked shopping. She searched around for a vase and then realized they were all still packed, improvising she took out a large, and quite elegant, glass jug and arranged the roses in them, they looked perfect. 'I can't remember the last time someone bought me flowers, they're gorgeous, thank you,' she kissed him shyly on the cheek and he grinned at her. He made her feel like a teenager again.

'Good, I'm glad. From what DI Allix said, you had quite an eventful day yesterday.'

'That's an understatement! It's not one I *ever* want to repeat. How are Sir Geoffrey and Lady Susan?' she asked with genuine concern.

His face clouded momentarily. 'Shocked, but at least they know. They were coming to terms with the fact that his baby was dead, but to be told that his baby was murdered by the father of the mother of his child, and that the very same person had been abusing his daughter and was someone who had lived in the village for a long time, and was deemed a respectable member of the community, was beyond belief. They look so dazed and bewildered, so vulnerable, I've never seen them like that before, it's really taken it out of them and of course they still don't know what will happen to Sir Geoffrey, whether he will be charged or not and they're fearful of the reaction from the village. Fortunately they are going away for Christmas and New Year, they're going to her brother and his family for Christmas and then to some friends in the south of France for New Year. It should give them time to start to get their heads around what has happened and hopefully get a boost in support from their friends and family before it becomes public knowledge.'

'I do feel sorry for them. I've become kind of fond of them, I suppose because I've caught a glimpse of the tenderness they have for one another and the fact that, despite appearances and brusqueness, they are very kind and caring people. What he did was so wrong, sex with an under aged girl and on top of that, cheating in a marriage is a big no no as far as I am concerned ...'

'I can understand why,' he murmured remembering what she had told him about her ex-husband.

'To do it with an under aged girl – even a consenting one - is disgusting even though he genuinely had no idea she was under aged. I know it's no excuse, but so many teenage girls do look years older than they really are which is a danger in itself. It's not too difficult to see how he misjudged her age, perhaps out of naivety, I doubt he's had much to do with teenage girls or the younger generation in general. He's not like her father who deliberately had sex with her by forcing himself onto her, it's not like he had a sick incestuous relationship with her.'

'I agree, nothing is every black and white. It's in no way right what he did, but compassion needs to come into this. I'm just not sure how much of that compassion is going to be shown to them,' he looked grim.

They sat thoughtfully for a while, having moved from the kitchen to the sitting room with their mugs of tea. Katherine was beginning to feel that she was going to be awash with tea the amount she'd recently been drinking.

'Anyway,' he started brightly, 'you're off to Libby's for Christmas then.'

She smiled at the thought of Henry and Alice and the huge excitement and anticipation they would be filled with on Christmas Eve and then Christmas Day. 'I'm looking forward to it, the children are so sweet, I'm staying over that night and coming back on Boxing Day. Means I can have a glass of bubbly without worrying about driving. Tell you what, if I had ever been a drink driver I would never want do it again having seen Rupert. But let's not talk about him anymore. You're off to your brother's house aren't you?'

He grinned. 'Yup, can't wait, going on Saturday and coming back the following Wednesday. Quick days work on Thursday to check the Estate and then I'm off until after New Year. What are you doing at New Year?'

She shrugged. 'Don't know, haven't thought that far ahead. How about you?'

'I've been invited to dinner at a friend's house, think there are going to be about thirty of us. Would you like to come? They are always hopeful that I will bring someone with me, think they might be shocked if I do!'

She blushed, it seemed as though the kernel of a relationship might be growing. 'I'd love to. It'll save them playing matchmaker for you,' she grinned.

# Chapter Twenty-Four

Six months later and it was moving in day. Previous days of torrential rain had given way to a soft, warming late spring sunshine. Katherine was up early, she'd spent the previous week cleaning the farmhouse from top to bottom and with Ted's help ferried the boxes with kitchen utensils, crockery and an assortment of other bits to the farmhouse. The boxes were unpacked and the kitchen was ready, it was everything else which remained to be transported from one house to the other and then unpacked.

Katherine had hired a local firm who had promised to arrive at 8 a.m., by 7 a.m. she was itching for them to arrive, eager to get the move going and finally settle into her new house. Dougie and the builders were still at the farmhouse, laying a terrace, rebuilding the tumbledown brick outhouse which she would use as a garden store, then they would move on to building a new two bay, oak-framed cart shed which would serve as a garage and finally, once that was complete, they would lay the drive and redo the fencing, it would be autumn before she finally had the place all to herself, but she didn't mind, it would be comforting to have other people around whilst she settled in.

Fortunately for Katherine the removal men turned up on time and before too long the boxes and her furniture were loaded up to accompany what she had had in storage, which had already been loaded into the van before they arrived at Katherine's rental house. She still had a week left on the rental of the terrace and was leaving the cleaning of it until nearer the hand over date. She slammed the door behind her and jumped into her car, having made quite sure that the removal men knew where to go, she didn't want a last minute hitch.

She led off, constantly checking that they were behind her and a few minutes later they arrived at the farmhouse. It took several manoeuvres for the driver to reverse the van into the drive but within minutes the four men were swarming like worker bees, whizzing boxes and furniture into the house. Each box had been labelled with the room name it was to go to and Katherine went round ticking them off her list. Her furniture was next but it looked sparse in what was a vast space compared to what she was used to. She was impatient to start ordering new furniture but had restrained herself, for it would only be once she was settled into the house and really living in it, that she would truly know what she needed and that could differ to what she thought she needed, besides which with a keen eye on the budget and for a bargain, the sales were coming up shortly and she was hopeful that she might pick up some good deals.

She tried not to moan about the muddy footprints the men were depositing on freshly cleaned floors, just another task to add to the long list of things she needed to do. By late lunchtime the men had finished, she waved them off, closed the front door behind her and did a little jig of excitement, punching the air in triumph. She was finally in, despite everything, she'd done it. There was a knock on the door behind her and she assumed that the removal men had forgotten something. It wasn't them, it was Ted holding up a brown paper carrier.

'Lunch,' he announced, smiling broadly at her.

She grinned back, delighted to see him. 'In that case you can come in!' She kissed him softly on the lips. He scooped his free arm around her and squeezed her. Their relationship was developing slowly and growing stronger as each day went past.

'You can be the first to try out my new seats at the centre island, you are honoured!' she joked. The kitchen was stunning; pale limestone tiles of different sizes fitted neatly together on the floor, the cream painted units brought more light to the kitchen and the multicoloured black granite top sparkled as the sun caught different fragments of colour in its rays. There was a pristine white double butler's sink by the window, which afforded a beautiful view of the garden whilst doing the mundane washing up. It all smelled new, clean and fresh and resembled in no way the rubble strewn place of horror where Cecilia and her baby were found. Katherine had kept the lines clear, clean and simple throughout the house. There were no dramatic or violent colours, just pale creams, soft yellows and gentle pale greens. She had used Farrow & Ball paints throughout and was amazed how the paints changed colour in different light, one moment a soft yellow would look just like that and a while later when the sun had moved round or gone in, it looked like a very pale green. It brought an individuality and uniqueness to the simplicity. Apart from the kitchen, larder and laundry room whose floors were cov-

257

ered in the pale limestone tiles, the rest of the floors were covered in wide, pale, oak floorboards. The fireplace in the winter sitting room had been sandblasted, the oak Bressemer beam brought back to life to show off the stunning piece of oak it was and a small wood burning stove placed within the fireplace.

'I'm surprised you managed to get away,' she commented.

'It was Geoffrey who encouraged me to take the time out,' he still marvelled at the change in Sir Geoffrey and Lady Susan. They had been humbled by their experience and even more so when the village found out that he was the father of Cecilia's baby and the implications which came with it. Far from vilifying him and ostracizing the pair of them, they were forgiving and supportive. He had been fortunate to avoid a full blown Crown Court case and both he and Susan had made radical changes to their lives. With there being no doubt that they would never be parents - the hope finally being dashed with the discovery of the dead baby - they moved forward, galvanized into action to make the Estate work and be successful and not be reliant on an offspring to do so. A combination of Ted's ideas and their's were being put into action. For ten years Ted had been coming up with innovative ways to enhance the coffers of the Estate, but they had all been rejected, now they were not only welcomed but encouraged. Events were being organized, the farms were going to be fully utilized and Sir Geoffrey and Lady Susan had announced that fifty percent of any profit would go to charities to support abused children and women. And finally they had insisted that they be referred to as plain Geoffrey and Susan, no use of their titles to be used. A transformation indeed and one which had rejuvenated them, they were more active, more sprightly and used their commanding skills in a positive way.

At Sir Geoffrey's insistence, Tom was contracted to service all the Estate vehicles, his way of attempting to make amends. After initial resistance Tom had accepted, wanting to keep the past in the past and felt he would be a fool to turn down what could, potentially, be a very lucrative contract, he had a wife and child to support, with another baby on the way.

'I trust Andrew's leaving you alone now? He's not exactly number one favourite around the village since the revelation of his plans for the land around here. Don't think he's got a hope of developing it. Can't imagine how it came out?' he grinned at Katherine.

'Quite a surprise eh?' she joked back. Ted had been one of the few she had told in confidence ,before finally letting it slip one day at the Farmers Market, within an hour it was all round the village and the forces were being rallied, the 'Battle against The Battle' as it was now being referred to, swept into action.

'I saw Audrey in the deli,' he added.

'How was she? I haven't seen her for a couple of weeks.' An unlikely bond had formed between the two, they were polar opposites in personality, but previous events had given them a link, a weak one, but a bond between them which was growing stronger and a solid friendship was developing. Audrey had thrown herself into work, was taking part in village life and was doing her very best to build a new life for herself.

'She seemed ok, asked after you, said she'd pop up in a few days to see you.'

'Gosh, that's a big step forward, she's not been here since, well, you know...'

'Mmm. When I popped into the shop, Betty was still full of the latest on Robert. That piece is going to play and play.'

Katherine shivered in disgust. An investigation had revealed that he had, indeed, been abusing children. Several girls had come forward dating back over the past twenty years and a case was being made against him. She sincerely hoped that he would be convicted for what he had done but felt dreadfully sorry for his wife Jane, who, like Audrey, had had no idea what her husband had been up to. She had taken indefinite leave from her job at the school and her husband had been suspended, until he was convicted by the courts they could not sack him, but Katherine was aware that even if, by some total miscarriage of justice, he was not found guilty, then he would not work there again, or at any school, she suspected and fervently hoped. She reflected on how many lives had been ruined by his actions. Not just the girls themselves, but their parents and possibly the relationships and future relationships the girls would have throughout their lives.

Whilst they chatted, Ted unpacked the simple lunch of sandwiches, crisps and smoothies which he'd picked up from a nearby deli, whilst Katherine produced plates and glasses.

'My first official meal here since moving in!' She raised her glass and chinked it against Ted's.

'To your new home! May it be filled with many happy years,' he responded.

Katherine smiled and sighed contentedly. Finally she was in her new home, the home of her dreams and whilst she would never forget Cecilia and her baby, it was time to move on, to create a new episode in the history of the house, for she knew that every house had its secrets – good and bad – it was just she had discovered those of the farm-house, when most people never found out. She gazed at Ted and sincerely hoped that he would be a part of the making of the history of her house, that they would have a long term future together. She felt sure that he would never let her down as her ex-husband had, but then, when she had married Rex she had not expected it to end the way that it had. One never knew what the future would bring, life was an adventure and it was time that her life had a positive adventure.

# OPPORTUNITY FOR DEATH

## Praise for *Opportunity for Death*

*'A must for mystery addicts! Read it!' - Dorothy Simpson*

*'Superb read. A classic whodunit brought up to date.'*

*'Start to finish in an evening, not able to put down.'*

*'Intriguing and totally absorbing. A wonderful and fascinating tale of the intrigues of English village life... beautifully written and well told, a brilliant book to disappear into.'*

## Praise for *In The Past*

*'An excellent summer read. I'm a fan of Agatha Christie and Dick Francis. Once I started I found it really difficult to put down. The story kept me guessing right up to the very end. I would definitely recommend it as an excellent summer garden read. I enjoyed it so much I've ordered the next one.'*

*Engaging and gripping. Would love to read more from E M Elliot.'*

*'A really enjoyable and page turning read from start to finish. Looking forward to the next one please!'*

# OPPORTUNITY FOR DEATH

## BY

## E M ELLIOT

For Mum

Following in your footsteps…

# 2006

# Chapter One

Bella Sparkle nosed her metallic blue VW Golf into the gravelled parking area beside the house, turned off the engine and sat gazing at what was to be her home for the next six months. The mellowness of the aged brick basked in the late spring sunshine and the pale pink climbing rose weaved its way up the front wall and draped itself over the top of the doorway. The quintessential English country cottage, she thought smiling to herself as she hopped out of the car and walked up the path to the front door. She breathed in the sweet scent of the roses, whilst taking in the twee, white, picket fence, neat parcel of lawn on either side of the path and abundance of lavender which enveloped Bella in a cloud of heady scent as she brushed past it.

From appearances, there was nothing remarkable about Bella. If you were to pass her in the street she probably wouldn't even register in your mind, her average height of 5'5", her average size of 12 to 14, her long browny/blonde hair scraped back into a ponytail. But, if you looked closer, looked deep into her eyes, you would be struck by their azure blue colour, the depth of which shone brightly, and realise that, here, was a person who was exceptional. You could not help but be drawn to her, open up to her, tell her things which you could not bring yourself to tell anyone else, even though you may never have met her before. She exuded a quiet calmness, confidence and serenity, even when she did not necessarily feel it herself.

So, here I am, she thought fitting the key into the lock. This will be such fun she told herself, six months in the country, close to my best friend. She tried to ignore the ambivalence which niggled within her, opened the door and stepped into the light, spacious hall of the semi-detached cottage. The stairs rose in front of her and she glanced through the door on the left to a spotless dining room with mahogany table and chairs for six, which gave the impression of never having been used. To the right of the staircase was the sitting room. Bella pushed open the white painted door and smiled approvingly, the room ran the depth of the house, a large window over-looked the front garden, an open fireplace held a small wood burning stove which waited patiently for winter to come and its chance to burst into life again. It had a warm, cosy, lived-in feel, a bookcase full of books, television, DVD player, coffee table, lamps, paintings on the walls and half a dozen china ornaments. The sunshine outside reflected off the creamy walls and into the room, the cream and green striped curtains added a touch of colour without dominating. Best of all were the two French doors which led out into the garden. Bella fumbled with the bunch of keys in her hand until she found the correct one, unlocked them and pushed the doors open onto the south facing garden and stepped out onto the flagstone patio.

Nice. Very nice, she thought, wandering across the lawn admiring the well stocked borders which were bursting in a riot of colours and perfume.

Keen to get unpacked, Bella had a quick whizz round the rest of the house; the immaculate, wood based, granite topped kitchen, three bright and airy bedrooms and one clean, functional white bathroom.

She'd been lucky to get the place. Having sold her house in Norfolk, and desperate to get away for a change of scenery, her best friend Mia Thurgood had persuaded her to rent somewhere near to her and, having persuaded Bella to do so, set about finding somewhere a bit more special than the usual practical rental property. As luck would have it a couple she knew were off to Hong Kong for at least the next year. Keen to rent it out just to friends, or friends of friends, they happily agreed to rent it to Bella, once the usual checks had been carried out, then the contract and deposit had subsequently been dealt with. So Number 2 Church Cottages, The Green, Monhurst, Kent became Bella's home for the coming months.

It was a beautiful location looking out over an expansive green, the lane off the main road through the village looped round the green to enable access. The ancient Norman church was off to the right at the top of the green and the barn-like Village Hall was on the far side, far enough away for noise not to cause a disturbance from the many events held there. Further down, and directly opposite the cottage, was The Old Rectory, a magnificent Georgian property of generous proportions.

It all seems so peaceful and quiet, thought Bella as she unpacked load after load of luggage and boxes that had been shoe-horned into every available space in her tardis like car. Hope I won't be bored though, she mulled ambivalently, doesn't look like anything goes on here.

As dusk drew in, Bella finally flopped down onto a comfortable wooden garden chair with a glass of perfectly chilled Sauvignon Blanc and relaxed. All she had to do now was to come up with a plan to keep herself occupied for the next six months or so. A sense of unease rippled through her. Making herself snap out of it, she picked up the village magazine and local paper, which Mia had given her earlier at lunch, and flicked through them – Farmers' Markets, Village Fêtes, Open Gardens – there seemed so much to do, but she wasn't sure if she'd be able to adjust to the change of pace having just left life in an urban environment.

Giving herself a telling off and to be positive, and not be negative, she ran a relaxing bath, soaked for an hour, sank into bed, snuggled under her duvet and fell straight to sleep.

The morning sun slanted through the gap in the spriggy Laura Ashley curtains. Bella yawned, stretched, and rolled over to look at the clock. 9 o'clock! She couldn't remember the last time she'd slept right through the night, let alone to such a late hour.

With a burst of energy she leapt out of bed and trotted into the pristine white bathroom for her morning ablutions. Those completed, she dressed herself in a pair of mid-grey, loose-fitting linen trousers and a plain, pale blue, semi-fitted, cotton top with three-quarter length sleeves. She glanced at herself in the full length mirror and sighed at the reflection. Who would believe that two years ago I was a size 8 with incredibly toned muscles and a stomach that most women would die for? It seemed a long time since she'd been that person; the one who took pride in her appearance, exercised religiously, ate a healthy, well-balanced diet, and was happy, she thought sadly. She didn't feel that the person in the reflection was really her. Hair, which needed a good cut and highlights, skin that should be having more than a touch of moisturiser slapped onto it and, worst of all, the muffin top. That bane of most women's lives, particularly in middle age, the roll of fat that hung over the top of the waist of trousers or skirt.

She mused that maybe now was the time to start doing something about it? The daily runs and weight sessions were a long way off. 'I'd probably keel over with a heart attack if I tried to do that now,' she muttered to herself.

But perhaps brisk walks and a bit of cycling might be a good start – she'd noticed a bicycle in the garage when she put the car away the previous night - and there were always the weights, which had found their way mysteriously into the car and not into storage with the remainder of her possessions that she'd not sold or given away. My subconscious trying to tell me something, she wondered.

Well, today will be the first day of my new exercise regime, she decided, running downstairs to the kitchen. A brisk walk around the village will help me orientate myself and perhaps discover whether this place is really as quiet and inactive as the first impression has given. Muffin top no more! There was nothing wrong with being a size 12 to 14 or larger, in fact a lot of men seemed to prefer women with a bit of shape to them, but having been the same size and weight her whole life up until two years ago, psychologically Bella just didn't feel herself with the extra weight and also worried about long term health problems if she kept piling on the pounds.

Bella opened the cupboard, took the half eaten box of sugary cereal out and banished it purposefully to the bin, then reached for the more healthy, unopened muesli box that she'd bought. As she poured the boiled water into the cafetière, deemed old fashioned by some, she caught the delicious aroma of fresh coffee wafting through the air, the telephone rang. Bella frowned. No one knew the number, as she had not got round to sending out change of address cards. Must be for the owners, she concluded. Deciding that whoever it was would only ring back, and she'd have to get used to answering it for the owners of the house, she picked it up and pressed the answer button.

'Hello?'

'Bella. It's me. How are you?'

'Hi Mia. I wondered who'd be phoning. I'd forgotten that you had the number. How are you?'

'Good thanks. You settled in?'

'Yup. Just working out my plan of action. How about you?'

'Wading my way through Fred's accounts at the moment - always a joyous event: not! Anyway, I was ringing because Fred and I are going to some friends for lunch on Saturday, and you've been invited too. Sophie and Harry have invited about a dozen friends. Should be fun, they're great, really nice people. I think you'll get on well and it'll give you a chance to meet some local people. I suspect you'll find it rather interesting... it certainly won't be boring!'

Bella could feel her friend grinning down the phone. 'That sounds lovely, I'll look forward to it. But what do you mean, "I think you'll find it rather interesting"?   I know you don't say things like that without meaning something!'

'Ah, well you'll just have to wait and see!  They live up at Beacon Hill Farm.  Turn right from the green, follow the road along and take the next right.  After a short distance the house is off to the right.  You can't miss it - there are no other houses near it.  Sophie said about 12 o'clock.  I'll see you up there.  Don't forget to call if you need anything and don't forget our trip out next week!'

Bella laughed.  'As if I'd forget!  Well, I'll see you on Saturday.  Have fun with the accounts!'

'Thanks.  You're too kind!  Bye.'

Bella smiled to herself as she munched her cereal in the morning sunshine.  It was good to have her best friend so close, knowing she could drop in and see Mia anytime, but also knowing that she didn't have to live in Mia's pocket during her stay in the village.

True to her word, after breakfast Bella slipped on her canvas shoes and set off for a brisk walk round the village.  She turned left at the bottom of the green and walked along the lane, leaping unnecessarily into the hedge every time a car went past; she may have been brought up in the country but living in a small town for the past 18 years had de-sensitised her from village and rural country living.  Fifteen minutes into her walk she was puffing and panting as though she had run a marathon.  Sense overcame her keenness to get fit, after all Rome wasn't built in a day, she persuaded herself as she crossed the lane and turned to walk back towards the village.

Bella revelled in listening to the gentle peacefulness of the countryside; birds tweeting joyously, full of lots to say for themselves, bees humming, bugs buzzing. As her mind drifted off she was startled by the distant roar of a vehicle, which suddenly hurtled round the corner swerving in all directions. Bella leapt into the hedge, this time justified in doing so, and gaped as the cumbersome beast of a Range Rover roared past her. All she could remember when it had gone was a flash of green and the number plate W1NE. Idiot! she fumed. Some people just shouldn't be on the roads! Bella tried hard to quell the anger that rose in her and by the time she'd reached the centre of the village she was slightly calmer, but still muttering to herself.

Bella pushed open the door to the village Post Office, making the bell tinkle announcing her arrival. 'Morning,' said the middle aged woman in her late fifties who was behind the counter.

'Oh, er, morning,' replied Bella, looking around to locate the newspapers. She picked one up and went to pay.

'Lovely day out there isn't. Shame I'm stuck in here on a day like this. By the time I have a day off it'll be raining! Usually does,' the shop assistant chattered on. 'Passing through are you?'

'No.' replied Bella, fearful that if she were too chatty the woman would want her life story.

'Local then?' The woman seemed oblivious of Bella's reluctance.

'Renting a house in the village.'

'Oh, lovely. You must be renting 2 Church Cottages?'

How on earth does she know that?

'Yes, that's right.'

'Friend of Mia and Fred's aren't you?'

She nodded mutely. Was there nothing that this woman didn't know? Bella fervently hoped that village life wasn't going to be a claustrophobic prison of nosiness.

'I'm Sharon and that's my husband Ron,' she said waving in the direction of the Post Office section of the shop. Unaware that there was anyone else in the shop Bella turned and smiled in the direction to which Sharon was waving her hand. A small, thin, grey-haired man smiled back at her; he had kind eyes and looked hen-pecked.

Probably enjoys being shut in the Post Office section, provides some sort of barrier to his wife, mused Bella. No! I mustn't be nasty, they're only being friendly, thought Bella.

'I'm Bella. Bella Sparkle.'

'Bella. What's that short for? Isabella?'

Really?! The inquisitiveness of the woman was astounding. Bella did her best to quell her grumpiness, after all it wasn't Sharon's fault that she was in a bad mood because of some lunatic driver. 'It's short for Christabel,' she replied evenly.

'Ooh, I say! Very posh name,' giggled Sharon. 'Don't you like it? I think it's lovely. Do you mind if I call you Christabel instead of Bella?'

What was the point? thought Bella admitting defeat; she'd probably call me that no matter what I said.

'Most people call me Bella,' she attempted weakly.

'Christabel it is then,' said Sharon cheerily. 'Now, would you like me to have that paper delivered to you every day? The Times Monday to Saturday, and would that be the Sunday Times on Sunday?'

'Er. No, thanks. I'd quite like to walk down myself. Thanks anyway.' She didn't want to make any kind of commitment to this woman, imagining the drama that would unfold if she fancied a different paper one day. A thought suddenly sprang to mind. If Sharon was so nosy, it was likely that she would know everyone in the village. 'I don't suppose you happen to know who owns a green Range Rover with the number plate W1NE, do you?'

Sharon laughed. 'That'll be Rupert. Why d'you want to know? Almost get run down by him did you?'

'Well. Yes as a matter of fact.'

'No surprise there then.' At that moment the door opened and someone, who was as chatty as Sharon, walked in allowing Bella the chance to slip away before introductions were given and her life story expected.

Carefully she crossed the road and strolled back up to the cottage, intrigued to know more about this Rupert person who would appear to be a well known character. Must ask Mia on Saturday, she's bound to know, Bella thought, making a mental note to herself.

Bella slowed as she arrived at the gate to the cottage. It all looked so perfect. Just how one would imagine an English country cottage to look like. Who'd have thought, six months ago, I'd now be living in such a pretty little cottage, she mused? Inwardly she made a note to cut some roses and lavender to bring into the house, they were so fragrant and bright and chirpy. Just looking at them, and breathing in their heady scent, made her spirits lift. Unlocking the front door, Bella tried studiously to ignore the pile of boxes she'd abandoned in the sitting room, and which still needed unpacking, their heavy presence trying to guilt her into doing what she knew she had to. After her first flurry of enthusiastic unpacking the day before, she'd convinced herself that it was too late to carry on last night, when really she just wanted to sit back and enjoy being at the cottage. Reluctantly she set the newspaper down on the kitchen table, opened the windows up throughout the house to allow the warm breeze to flow through, and braced herself.

The first box was full of just a small selection of her favourite books  A few classics in the form of Thomas Hardy, Charles Dickens and Jane Austen, along with a few chic-lit books and a lot by her absolute favourite author – Agatha Christie. She sat on the sofa and picked each one out individually, turning it over and reading the back as though she'd never read the book before. There was something about a book which she found seductive. It had the power to fill you with so many emotions, take you away from your own life, make you reflect on how little people ultimately change over the centuries. Consistently there was greed, hate, love, fear, passion, adultery, murder, jealousy. Without exception there was always a book to suit her mood.

She often felt empathy with the authors. Their observations about human behaviour and life in general reflected her quiet observations of those she met and what happened around her. The likes of Miss Marple and Poirot fascinated her and secretly she felt that, although they were fictitious characters, she was a little bit like them, observing what most would miss.

The books she had before her now were her stalwarts. Her loyal companions who were there through thick and thin, unwavering in their ability to whisk her away from her own life, to distract her from the past two years, the worst two years of her life. She knew that, no matter what, she could dip into any one of the books and they would comfort her, cushion her temporarily, and distract her from her own emotions.

Bella got up and removed three shelves worth of books from the bookcase, which belonged to the owners of the cottage, and ferried them backwards and forwards to the dining room, placing them carefully on the dining room table which she knew she would not use. She was intrigued by their collection of books, which indicated total opposites in terms of taste: Jackie Collins to thick, nonfiction, tomes on history. Neither was her normal literary fodder, but she thought she might dip in and venture outside her usual taste should the mood take her. With the shelves clear, she set about lovingly placing her own books on them. Bella stepped back, she admired, with satisfaction, her selection, the room felt much more like home already.

Next up was a box filled with what she classed as "useful bits": a sewing kit, knitting needles and wool (though it had been several years since she had last attempted to knit), note pads, pens, sticky notepads to put by the phone, small spanner set, a set of screwdrivers, candles and matches, a torch and other such assorted paraphernalia. She buzzed round trying to find homes for them all, resorting to either one of the spare bedrooms, or in a cupboard in the kitchen. The next box had some paintings in it which she decided not to put up, and staggered upstairs with it to the spare room she had designated for the overflow of her things, and which was now no longer looking like a spare room but more like a storage unit.

Finally, and hesitantly, she opened the last box. Gingerly she removed the first photograph and unwrapped it from its protective paper, aware of the apprehension rising within her as she did so. She turned the photo over and gazed lovingly at it, feeling the tears well up in her. Her fingers traced the outline of the couple staring back at her. A familiar tear splashed down onto the glass and she wiped it away with the clean, white handkerchief she'd retrieved from her pocket. Though she could not live without having the wedding photograph of her and Hugh somewhere in the house, it still brought such raw pain when she saw it, that sometimes she wondered whether she would be better off hiding it away and keeping it in a drawer. Every time she glimpsed it, she wondered why? Why on earth had it had to happen to her? To them? She wasn't sure if she would ever understand. The happy smiling couple in the photograph, taken twenty-two years ago, seemed a lifetime away.

Bella stood up and tried to decide where to put it. If she left it in the sitting room visitors would no doubt ask questions, and she wanted any information about her private life given on her terms, not as and when anyone enquired. Ruling out all the rooms downstairs, she wandered up to the spare bedrooms, putting it down on bedside tables and chests of drawers in turn and standing back to observe each time. None of them seemed right. She'd had it out in the sitting room at her previous house. It had seemed right there, always there, but here it was different, she'd come to Kent for a change, for an escape. Eventually she walked into her bedroom and put it on the bedside table. Though it evoked pain in her when she saw it, for some strange reason it felt right to have it there. Satisfied, she went downstairs. Maybe it would help her if it was more visible? Deciding she'd had enough unpacking for one day, she folded the top of the box over, pushed it behind a chair and spent the rest of the day pottering around, familiarising herself with the kitchen and its many utensils and reading the paper quietly in the garden, enjoying the peacefulness of it all. She looked forward to the lunch on Saturday and felt a gentle, light contentment begin to settle on her.

# Chapter Two

Saturday dawned as another gloriously sunny pleasant day. Clear blue skies, without the hint of a cloud, and brilliant warm sun glowing high, would provide the perfect backdrop to the lunch party. Bella was eager for it to come round, keen to meet all the, she anticipated, interesting people who would be there, but also slightly nervous, after all, if they're so fascinating she was sure that she would seem boring to them.

Bella was ready by 11.45 and itching to go, but etiquette dictated that she wait a while to ensure arrival at about 12.15 to 12.30. She smoothed her flowing, pale green and white, spriggy, floral dress down. Whilst not exactly shapeless it hung loosely off her frame and, in her opinion, hid her well padded shape. The upside of having put on weight was that her breasts had ballooned simultaneously to the rest of her body, giving her a generously proportioned bust which rippled lusciously above the scoop neck of the dress. Low heeled, soft green, suede mules completed the outfit, and Bella felt confident that if the lunch was either casual or more formal she would fit in at one end of the scale.

She waited until 12.05pm, locked the door and got into her Golf and drove cautiously up the road, turning right as instructed and then, eventually, right again into the drive of a fabulous period farmhouse. A perfectly manicured circle of lawn centred the drive, four cars were neatly lined up off to one side. Bella pulled in next to a blue VW Beetle that looked distinctly like the one which was often parked outside the detached cottage just up from Bella's cottage, next to the church. With relief Bella saw Mia and Fred's silver Volvo estate sitting in the row of cars and, with a flutter of nerves, picked up the hand-tied bouquet of flowers from the front seat, and headed to the front door. Before she could get there a smiley-faced woman in her mid thirties, with long curly blonde hair came round the side of the house clutching an equally smiley six month old baby.

'Hi! You must be Bella. I'm Sophie and this is Jemima.' On cue the baby beamed even more brightly and giggled.

'Hi Sophie. Here these are for you,' she said proffering the flowers.

'They're beautiful! Thank you, but you didn't need to bring anything!'

'It's a pleasure. Thanks for inviting me. Would you like me to carry them for you?'

'Please. If Jemima gets close to those she'll be pulling them out and tweaking the petals off before I can arrange them. Come round the back and meet the others.'

Bella dutifully followed her through a wrought iron gate and round to the back of the house, gasping at the stunning view. From the terrace you could see for miles, across the village and to the distant hills.

'It's beautiful! You have such a lovely house and what amazing views.'

'Thanks. We're very lucky. Bella, this is my husband Harry. Darling, this is Bella.'

A short, slim man with short, blond, grey-splattered hair, turned to greet her. His eyes, like his wife's, were green and sparkly and he had laughter lines which crinkled as he spoke. 'Nice to meet you Bella. What can I get you to drink? Wine? Pimms? A soft drink?'

'Something soft would be lovely thanks. Whatever you've got.' Harry disappeared off into the house leaving Bella to greet Mia and Fred.

'Good to see you,' kissed Mia. Fred engulfed her in a hug.

'You too. Thanks for this.' Her best friend looked as elegant as ever in a simple cream linen shift dress. Though they were the same age, at 42, Bella always felt that Mia looked younger than her years, and certainly more youthful than herself. They were the same height but Mia was slimmer and her cropped, glistening, brown hair was always perfectly kept, never a hair out of place. It framed her petite face, with small button nose and full lips, which looked as though she'd had collagen injected into them, but were actually as nature had created them.

'Come on. Let me introduce you to the others.' Offered Harry, who had returned with a tall glass filled with elderflower pressé and ice bobbing on the top.

'Thanks,' she said as he and Mia led her over to the other invitees who'd arrived.

'This is Jennifer. Jennifer this is Bella. Bella's renting 2 Church Cottages. Bella, Jennifer lives in Willow Tree Cottage up by the Church.'

'Hi Bella, I thought I'd seen you in the village. Certainly Sharon in the shop has been announcing your arrival! Though she keeps talking about "Christabel" do you prefer that or 'Bella'?' She grinned at her.

Bella rolled her eyes and laughed. 'Bella is just fine. No one has called me Christabel since I was a little girl. It seemed futile arguing about it with her.'

'Very wise, there's no point, just admit defeat where Sharon is concerned.'

Bella instantly felt like she'd found a new friend in the tall young woman who stood in front of her, despite the fact that she was the sort of woman most females would be jealous of. Jennifer exuded a sensuousness that many men found irresistible, her lengthy rich glossy chestnut hair curled seductively down, mirroring the curviness of her body. Long, slim, shapely, tanned legs were revealed below a knee length, pale yellow, fitted skirt and a fitted white cotton blouse which clung snugly to her breasts and was unbuttoned to reveal a hint of what nestled beneath.

'Have you settled in then?'

'Pretty much. It's a lovely village. Quite quiet though.'

'Never judge a book by its cover! I think you'll come to realise that all is not as it seems...', she smiled mysteriously.

'Really? I don't suppose you'd like to expand on that?' Bella's curiosity was roused.

'Oh, I think that would spoil the fun,' she laughed, 'wouldn't you agree Mia?'

Mia nodded and grinned.

'Hi,' said a skinny, ferrety-faced man joining their group. Though gaunt and with a razor sharp slender nose and smudges of dark under his eyes, Bella could see that his soft brown eyes exuded a warmth and gentleness. His blue and white checked cotton shirt was fraying around the collar and cuffs and his pale beige chinos looked well lived in.

'Bella, this is Seb. Seb, this is Bella,' introduced Jennifer.

'Ah! You're Mia and Fred's friend who's renting the cottage,' he smiled warmly at her. Bella liked him immediately. She didn't know him, but she wanted to. There was something vulnerable about him which appealed to her. 'Settling in well? Suppose I shouldn't ask as I imagine this lot have already grilled you? Must be getting tedious having to keep offering the same response.'

Bella laughed. 'I don't mind. Everyone's been so friendly. How do you all know each other?'

'Mia, Sophie, myself, Cressa - who's over there talking to Sophie - Kimberley (who we all call Kim) and Florence all play tennis together. Jack plays at the club too with Harry and Fred, and when we all get together the husbands or wives come too, that's how it started,' replied Jennifer. 'Though some of us go back a lot further than that.'

'So is Cressa your wife then Seb?' asked Bella politely. Jennifer sniggered. Seb shot her a filthy look.

'No. I'm not married, never have been and shouldn't think I ever will.' Bella felt a twinge of disappointment. What was his story? There was an air of them all seeming to know something, but also that they weren't going to divulge the secret. 'Cressa is married to Jack. You see that short, rotund chap talking to Harry, that's Jack.' Everyone chortled except Bella. Wasn't it a bit rude to describe him like that? Still, they obviously knew each other well, besides he wasn't that fat. At that moment Jack turned slightly and Bella caught sight of his rather expansive stomach which eclipsed Harry. She could see what they meant.

'Hey! Cressa! Come over here and meet Bella,' called Jennifer. Another very tall, slim, elegant woman glided serenely across to them despite the cocktail-stick-thin, towering spikes of her heels sinking into the grass with a little 'pop' at each step. She was the polar opposite in appearance to her husband.

'Pleased to meet you Bella.' She proffered her hand with long elegant fingers, which Bella shook accordingly, noting how soft it felt.

'Likewise. Jennifer was just telling me that you play tennis together.'

'We certainly do.' There was a reserved air about Cressa, slightly aloof, as though she wasn't quiet comfortable in the presence of her friends. Bella's brow wrinkled slightly in puzzlement.

'And this is Florence,' announced Sophie, joining the swelling group.

Bella's head was starting to swim with so many rapid introductions. She'd never remember all their names at this rate! Out of all the women, Florence was the one who looked misplaced and the dowdiest. Bizarre, considering the fact that she must be the youngest observed Bella. Florence wore a plain, pale blue, cotton skirt, which didn't fit properly and a slightly over-sized white shirt, which was left untucked. Bella felt that she looked like an ugly duckling waiting to blossom into a swan. She was very petite, and had a beautiful heart-shaped face with rose bud lips, and the most perfect and clearest complexion that Bella had ever seen. Her eyes were a deep emerald green, flecked with gold, which were enhanced by the rich goldenness of her lengthy, rather unkempt, straight, blonde hair. A change of clothes, and a good hair cut, and she would be stunning, by far the most beautiful woman here. Peculiar then, that she should dress like that. There was something about her which puzzled Bella. Something she couldn't put her finger on, but given that she had only just met her - and the others - it was hardly surprising.

Bella was distracted from greeting Florence by a commotion coming from the side of the house. Raised voices could be heard but though she strained to catch a few words she couldn't hear precisely what was being said, however she could feel a subtle shift in the previously jolly atmosphere. She noticed Seb clenching his jaw and his hands were screwed up into a fist. Hmm, intriguing, mused Bella.

Jennifer rolled her eyes. 'Here they are, no doubting that.' She saw Bella's enquiring look. 'Rupert and Kim,' she added.

Rupert, trailed by Kim, made a beeline for the group, shaking Harry's hand on the way. Suddenly he stopped short. Observing, Bella could see his face pale almost imperceptibly but not the cause. Curiouser and curiouser. He recovered quickly and pounced on Jennifer, giving her a squeeze and a long wet kiss on each cheek. Bella shuddered. In his mid forties and well over six feet tall he towered over the rest of the group, which was fortunate for him because with his height he could carry off the substantial weight around his middle and get away without looking too portly. His face was puffy with large dark circles under his dull, brown, bloodshot eyes, his nose was bulbous and red with broken capillaries fanning out over his face. Bella was convinced, by the look of him, that he was

291

an alcoholic. There was something decidedly slimy about him, which made her dislike him instantly even though, as yet, she had not been introduced. His slicked back, black greasy hair added to his unappetising appearance.

Having extracted herself from his clutches, Jennifer introduced Florence to him, as this was the first time Florence had met him because she had only joined the tennis club a few months beforehand.

'Have we met?' barked Rupert peering intently at her. 'You look familiar.'

'No,' replied Florence meekly. 'We definitely have not met, I would have remembered.'

He stared intently at her before his lecherous eyes alighted on Bella. 'And who do we have here?' he said leering at her.

Bella shivered in repulsion. 'Bella Sparkle,' she replied making a huge effort not to grimace when his chubby fingered, clammy hand grasped hers.

'Now I know we haven't met, or I would have remembered,' he licked his lips surreptitiously. Bella felt like a helpless rabbit caught in the talons of an eagle.

Mia stepped in to save the moment. 'And this is Kimberley, Kim to us, Rupert's wife,' she said pointedly looking at him.

A much younger woman, at least ten years, thought Bella. What on earth is she doing with a lech like him? Kim was quite tall, skinny - bony even - with short, blonde, stylishly cut hair and very pretty. Her skin was clear, but there were bags and dark circles under her dulled blue eyes. The stress of being married to Rupert reflected in her face.

'Hi Bella, nice to meet you. Mia told us you were going to live in the village for a bit. D'you play tennis?'

'I haven't for several years. I'm not very good I'm afraid.'

'Not very good!' snorted Mia. 'You used to thrash me!'

'That was a long time ago. I am definitely not as fit as I used to be.'

'I don't know about that, you look pretty fit to me,' oozed Rupert.

Bella mentally vomited, but smiled politely. How on earth did Kim put up with him? Or perhaps more importantly, why? Perhaps he has hidden qualities, ones which no one else sees? Or possibly it's the size of his bank balance? Maybe he's really rich? Don't be so judgemental and cynical, Bella chided herself. You don't know them and apart from that nobody's perfect.

'You must come and play with us! We have a lot of fun!' continued Kim.

'Thanks. I'd like that, as long as you keep your expectations of my ability on the court low,' she grinned.

Harry discreetly topped up glasses, whilst Sophie disappeared into the kitchen to complete the final preparations for lunch, leaving Jennifer holding Jemima. 'She's so cute isn't she?' Jennifer said jiggling the little tot in her arms, making her smile and giggle the cute infectious giggle that only babies do.

A few minutes later Sophie called everyone to the exquisitely laid table, under a wooden arbour covered in a honey scented honeysuckle, providing much needed shade out of the now scorching sun. It was laden with poached salmon, a riot of multi-coloured salads, and an interesting selection of breads.

'This looks delicious Sophie. How on earth have you managed to produce such a banquet whilst looking after Jemima?'

Sophie smiled, pleased that all her hard work had not gone unnoticed. 'I just prepared things while Jemima had a sleep, and did a lot last night, and Harry's looked after Jemima this morning.' Harry in the meantime had taken Jemima off for her nap, with her having already been fed with pureed carrot and parsnips and some milk before everyone arrived. Two additional seats remained empty.

'Who's missing?' asked Kim.

'Ariadne and her friend,' replied Sophie.

'She's always late, never turns up on time. We could be waiting until supper time and she still might not turn up,' whispered Seb to Bella who was seated on her right. 'Just wait until Ariadne arrives, then the entertainment will really start...' He grinned broadly at her and raised his eyebrows.

# Chapter Three

Mid-way through the meal, the noisy chatter and laughter was suddenly silenced by the dramatic arrival of the much awaited Ariadne, who swept in blowing kisses to everyone, as though she were accepting an Oscar.

'Darlings! It's so wonderful to see you,' she breathed.

Sophie jumped up and hugged her friend. Bella was struck by how different they appeared. Ariadne was like a beanpole in both height and physique, and so thin that Bella thought that if she stood sideways you wouldn't see her. Her hipster cut-offs were excruciatingly tight, there was no way she could have got into them other than by being literally poured in. Matching was an equally tight white top, which stretched so tightly over her surgically enhanced breasts that it was surely only a matter of time before the fabric ripped under the strain. In every way she seemed perfect. The perfection, it has to be said, that the fashion and film industry tried to brainwash ordinary mortals into believing is the only way to look. Ariadne's skin was flawless and wrinkle free, despite being 35 by which time most women have a few fine lines beginning to appear. Her nose was perfect. Her chin was perfect and her lips were an apparent luscious perfection. Her golden blonde hair was iron-straight down to her mid back, with not a single hair out of place. Her sapphire blue eyes sparkled like an oasis in the perfectness which was Ariadne. She looked totally perfect, but completely unreal thought Bella. Bella was roused out of her Ariadne-esq trance by the flourishing introduction of the guest whom she had brought with her.

As her eyes swept round to look at the guest, Bella did a double take at Rupert, who had momentarily stopped pouring wine down his throat in order to dribble and lech at Ariadne, managing a quick grope of her bottom whilst he greeted her. But Rupert's face was turning as white as a sheet, even whiter than earlier. Bella shivered. As the guest approached him he hesitantly held out his hand to receive the one which was offered and shook it. Bella pushed her attention back to Ariadne who was announcing that the guest was Kit, her agent, who was an "absolute darling", and she couldn't live without him.

'Nice to meet you,' said Kit giving Rupert a firm shake and, to Bella's observation, what appeared to be a rather intense stare. Am I imagining it, thought Bella, or do they already know each other? Rupert seemed to relax, relieved even, at these words and muttered a greeting in return.

Bella focused on the exceptionally handsome man that was Kit. Again, he seemed to exude a similar perfection to Ariadne. He was exceedingly tall, well over 6'4", she guessed, slim with perfectly toned muscles she imagined, but not too muscular. Short, trim, chocolaty brown, perfectly groomed hair framed his face. He looked incredibly attractive in his faded jeans and white shirt which exuded casual expense. Bella felt her stomach flutter as he took her hand in his, and smiled at her as though she were the most beautiful, and only, woman in the world for him. Her legs turned to jelly and she was glad she was sitting down. She blushed at her silliness, berating herself for responding like a teenager at her age, over him simply because of his looks. She glanced furtively around, relieved that no one seemed to have noticed. He slid lithely into the chair at the end of the table and, feeling her eyes upon him, glanced up and held hers for just a moment. Bella melted.

'Trust Ariadne to bring an Adonis with her. She always does this,' muttered Seb to her, oblivious to the fact that Bella was smitten by the said Adonis.

Bella munched cautiously on her food, now even more highly aware of her size in comparison to Ariadne, who must be at least a Size 0 if not a Size 00. And how on earth can anyone wear white and keep it looking so blindingly pristine? She herself had given up on white a long time ago. It didn't seem to matter what she did, she only had to breathe and there would be dirt on it and, though she never normally spilt her drink, you could guarantee that as soon as she was wearing white, her first sip of coffee would end up all over it. Yet there was Ariadne sitting, chatting, laughing gaily as the centre of attention, sipping wine, picking at a lettuce leaf and not a hint of anything ever having been dropped or spilt onto the blinding whiteness. Had she had lessons in how to wear white? Is this what they learnt in Hollywood? Bella gloomily felt more and more dowdy as the minutes passed.

Sensing a little cloud of dejection over her, Harry – who was sitting on her left – whispered to her.

'You okay?'

Bella nodded.

'You sure? Don't let Ariadne spoil things for you. The others have all got used to her, but you should have heard them after Sophie had first introduced her to them. The girls spent weeks mauling Ariadne to bits. But don't be taken in, because although she may look "perfect", as others would tell us, she's not a very happy person.'

'Really?' Bella tried to suppress the glee which popped up.

'Not a happy bunny at all.' Bella felt too embarrassed to ask why, as she hardly knew Harry, but was grateful for his attempt at cheering her up.

Kit in the meantime was gazing intently into Jennifer's eyes, his honey voice whispering things to her that, no matter how much Bella strained, she could not hear. Jealousy nudged at her and she wished she were Jennifer. Bella looked round the table as the lunch continued like a play unravelling itself before her. Rupert was drinking copious amounts of wine and glaring at Kit as though he could kill him. Kim was chatting quietly to Fred, with the occasional nervous glance in Rupert's direction. Cressa was listening intently to Ariadne, who was in turn trying to command everyone's attention. Sophie was dividing her time between Jack and Rupert. It was an interesting set up with Ariadne sitting next to Harry, Harry next to Bella, then Seb, Jennifer, Kit, Mia, Rupert, Sophie, Jack, Florence, Fred, Kim and Cressa who had Ariadne on her other side. Bella could only assume that Sophie and Harry had spent a long time devising the seating plan in order to keep certain people away from one another, as it was obvious there was a lot of history simmering away beneath the eclectic mix of people.

Seb was an affable chap who chatted away to Bella and, whilst she enjoyed their conversation, she got the feeling that his mind was elsewhere. Every so often he surreptitiously glanced at Kim and regularly, without hiding it, glowered at Rupert who was becoming more and more drunk as the minutes ticked by. Perhaps Sophie and Harry hadn't organised a seating plan after all, if the filthy looks Seb was giving Rupert were anything to go by? Wonder what the history is there? And it wasn't just Seb who had a problem with Rupert, Jack too was wincing and scowling every time Rupert's monotonous, drunken monologue became too loud. Maybe it was just because Rupert was so drunk? The more he drank, the more of a bore he became and the more self-righteous and self-opinionated he became. And the more lecherous.

He was making Bella feel queasy at his lewd behaviour, and not so subtle suggestive language towards, mainly, Jennifer but also Ariadne. Both were doing their utmost to ignore him. In fact, everyone seemed to ignore Rupert as though this were a regular occurrence and something which just had to be endured and they wouldn't allow to spoil their lunch. His face became redder and Bella was convinced that his bulbous nose was growing before her very eyes. Drops of spittle flew in all directions as he spoke, and his eyes now had a glazed look about them. Mia caught her eyes and smiled, raising her eyebrows as if to say "I told you it'd be interesting". Bella grinned back. Mia was going to have a lot of explaining to do. She wanted a full run down on everyone in the group.

By mid afternoon as the heat of the sun was starting to wane they all moved to sit on the terrace in the sunshine. Bella estimated that by this time Rupert must have imbibed at least three or four bottles of wine. Anyone else would have been paralytic but he still managed to stagger up from the table, admittedly bumping into it as he negotiated his way around it, but nevertheless he made it across to the other side of the terrace, where he dropped his heavy load onto the wicker double seat next to Jennifer, who immediately looked panic stricken. Rupert leaned towards her, put an arm around her shoulders, and pulled her to him. Jennifer did her best to struggle out from his clutches, but was thwarted as his other hand slid its way surprisingly swiftly up her legs and under her skirt, his head lolling over her breasts. Enough was enough and Harry and Fred extricated Jennifer from his clutches.

'Come on Jen,' slurred Rupert, 'you know you want it. Stop playing hard to get and let me give you a good seeing to.'

She ignored him and moved to a seat as far away from him as possible, smiling apologetically at Kim, who looked resigned to this kind of behaviour. Poor thing, thought Bella, why on earth does she stay with such an odious specimen of a male, it's so humiliating for her.

Seb, who had been standing silently beside Bella, could restrain himself no longer. 'Can't you at least show some respect for your wife?' he snapped.

Rupert looked at him and swayed gently; a malicious sneer coming over his face. 'Don't be such a bad loser Seb. She's my wife, not yours.' This was followed by a phlegmy cackle.

Seb leapt forward, but Harry and Fred, anticipating this move, grabbed him, both muttering to him. 'He's not worth it. Let it go.'

Curiouser and curiouser, mused Bella.

Kim subtly slid beside Seb, squeezed his arm and just as subtly went back to where she'd been standing. 'Here's the coffee,' chirped Sophie, setting the heavy tray down on to the large wicker table. She poured and passed out fine bone china cups and saucers until she got to Rupert, who was given a large sturdy mug.

'Don't give me that rubbish!' he snapped. 'I want a proper drink.

'Think you've had enough Rupert. Have the coffee and this glass of water,' said Harry setting them down in front of him.

Ariadne, sensing trouble brewing, glided onto the sofa beside Rupert and purred, 'Come on now Rupert, you know I don't like it when you drink too much.' She gently stroked his face with the back of her hand as though she were trying to soothe a troubled child. Rupert's demeanour changed instantly, turning on what he believed to be charm but any sane woman would see as lechery. Ariadne picked up the mug and passed it to him. 'Come on, drink this for me and then I'll pass you the water.' She made the simple act of drinking coffee and water a seduction scene. But whatever it was it worked. Rupert meekly took the mug and drank it, his eyes wandering over her breasts as he did so. It made Bella cringe just to watch, but there was an imperceptible sigh of relief from the rest of the group, at Ariadne's rescue of the situation.

'He is such a jerk,' muttered Jack. Cressa kicked him to shut him up, not wanting the situation to be inflamed again.

'Here she is, all bright and awake from her lovely sleep,' announced Sophie returning with the beaming Jemima.

'She's such a cutie, here let me have a cuddle,' requested Mia putting her hands out to take the bundle from Sophie.

Momentary peace settled over the group until Rupert, realising that he was being placated rather than onto a promise with Ariadne, got up to go. 'Sophie, Harry, fun as ever, see you around.' He rummaged in his pocket until he found his keys. 'Kim, I'm sure you'll find your own way home. See you,' he called to everyone, waving his arm in the air as he walked in a zigzag towards the drive.

'He's not going to drive is he?' asked Bella aghast.

Harry and Fred looked at each other. 'Suppose we should try.'

'Of course you should!' shrieked Bella.

Everyone looked startled.

'The thing is, every time someone tries to stop him they get hurt,' said Cressa. 'Oh! Like that,' she continued as Fred staggered back having been punched in the face by Rupert. Mia leapt up to see to her husband and Sophie raced off to get some ice to put onto the undoubted bruise which would shortly be appearing.

Bella meanwhile was open-mouthed, not sure whether she was more shocked at what she had just seen, or the fact that this was a regular occurrence when anyone tried to stop Rupert drink driving. 'But he could kill someone! He can't be allowed to drive in that condition!' she shouted, tears pricking at her eyes. 'We should call the police.'

'We've tried that and everything else,' murmured Kim sadly. 'By the time the police arrive Rupert's at home and denying ever having been out. They're too busy dealing with other crimes to come out every five minutes to see Rupert. Sooner or later they will catch him drink driving, it's just astounding that he's not been caught yet.'

'But it's a disgrace! It shouldn't be allowed to happen,' snapped Bella.

By now the others were raising their eyebrows and wondering how a stranger could have the audacity to pass judgement on them? All except Mia and Fred. Fred whispered something to Mia, who left nursing her husband and came over and put her arm around the distraught Bella.

'Hey. It's okay. We're doing our best to stop him,' she whispered.

'But it's not okay.'

'And who are you to judge us?' snapped Cressa in response, 'you don't know us.'

An uneasy silence followed. 'You should tell them,' whispered Mia, 'they'll understand.'

Feeling cornered, but of her own doing, Bella reluctantly spoke. 'I don't mean to offend you, and you're right I don't know you and I shouldn't judge you, but my husband was killed by a drink driver, so I know all too well what the consequence can be.' She gazed miserably at her lap and fiddled with her fingers.

'I'm so sorry,' murmured Sophie squeezing Bella's shoulders and kissing her on the top of her head. 'It must have been so awful for you.' The others sat looking stunned, a reality brought to the scenario they had been allowing to play out for years, that Rupert could be the cause of someone else's death.

'I didn't want to spoil the day. I'm sorry.'

'You haven't spoilt it. I think we've become too complacent about Rupert, something really needs to be done and it's me that needs to do it,' replied Kim. 'I have tried, it's not easy and it won't be, but he has to be stopped.'

So taken up were they with Bella's revelation, that they had not heard the crunching and scraping coming from the drive as Rupert attempted to depart, damaging most of the cars in the drive as he did so.

Shortly afterwards Bella decided it was time to go and let them enjoy the rest of the day without her dragging them down. She thanked Harry and Sophie profusely and promised the girls that she would attempt to play tennis with them in the next few weeks. 'See you next week,' she said softly to Mia, 'sorry for upsetting your friends.'

'You've got nothing to be sorry about. I'll call you later.'

Bella didn't notice the slight dent in her bumper as she got into her car, she was too busy struggling with her conscience. Should she leave it to Kim to deal with her husband or should she take matters into her own hands? It was a decision she had made by the time she'd got home. She would never forgive herself if Rupert killed someone and through her disinclination had let it happen. She picked up the phone and set the wheels in motion.

# Chapter Four

Sunday morning dawned as bright and beautiful as Saturday had the previous day. Bella lay in bed listening to the church bells chiming away, calling the village to its doors. She toyed with the idea of going to the morning service, but decided she wouldn't be ready in time. Maybe next week, she thought, lazily stretching in bed before getting up.

The day passed peacefully. Other than purchasing a paper in the shop before breakfast, Bella did not stray from the house, spending most of her time reading in the gloriously warm sunshine, the birds tweeting enthusiastically in the trees as though communicating some major gossip to one another. She did a good job of not thinking about Rupert but eventually she couldn't help it, it was niggling away at her. Had he been dealt with yet? Had the route to him permanently being stopped from drink-driving been set in motion? She hoped so.

With only a shopping trip with Mia planned for the week ahead, Bella contemplated some other activities, perhaps a trip to the village farmers' market? A trip or two to the famous and well reputed Sissinghurst Castle and Gardens, created by VitaSackville-West and Harold Nicholson, she felt was most definitely an absolute must as they were reputed to be spectacular.


After another good night's sleep, Bella strolled down to the shop the next morning - the warmth of the day just starting to take the edge off the chill over night - as was becoming her routine to collect a newspaper to read over her leisurely breakfast. The bell pinged as she opened the door. Sharon was chattering at full steam to another woman, pausing briefly to call out, 'Morning Christabel,' before returning to her gossiping. Bella picked up her newspaper and briefly glanced at the magazines, deciding not to purchase one after all. Though she wasn't paying attention to the gossiping, her ears were alerted when she heard Rupert's name.

'Are you sure?' squawked Sharon.

'Absolutely.' replied the short, stout woman dressed in a screamingly loud floral print ensemble in a myriad of mismatched, violently bright colours, which did absolutely nothing for her.

'Dead! I can't believe it!'

Bella paled and felt a wave of dizziness wash over her, steadying herself on the side of the counter.

'You alright Christabel? You've gone as white as a sheet.'

'Fine thanks,' croaked Bella. 'What were you just saying about Rupert? Do you mean Rupert Ireton?'

'Yes. Haven't you heard?' replied Sharon, as though she herself had known for hours and not just been told herself.

Bella shook her head numbly, hoping that she'd heard incorrectly.

'He's dead. Killed himself by driving into a tree apparently.'

'A tree?'

'Yes. Apparently he was way over the legal limit, must have been totally plastered to think that a tree was the road. I always knew the likes of him would meet a sticky end. Serves him right,' she continued spitefully, 'drinking and driving, it's a wonder he didn't kill anyone and he treated that lovely wife of his like dirt. I can't imagine what she saw in him.'

'His bank balance I should think,' muttered the other woman meanly.

'That's awful! What a terrible thing to happen. How's his wife?' snapped Bella.

'Kim? You mean you know them? Tell us then. What're they really like?' Sharon was keen for more information, any snippet of gossip to add to her tale.

'I ...' stuttered Bella. 'Can I pay for this? I've got to go.' With that she shoved the correct money haphazardly onto the counter and hurried out of the shop, before she could be plied with further questions. Racing back to the house, her heart pounding furiously, she fumbled with her keys. 'Come on! Open!' she snapped at the door. Eventually the key turned in the lock, Bella flung the paper on the hall table and grabbed the phone, dialling Mia's number quickly. The phone rang and rang at the other end, eventually Mia answered.

'Hello?'

'Mia, it's me.'

'Oh, hi Bella. How are you?'

'I'm fine. Mia I've just heard the most awful thing. I don't know if you know, but I thought I ought to let you know.'

'I know Bella. Rupert,' she sighed heavily.

'It's terrible. When did it happen?'

'Saturday night about 10pm. Seems he was so drunk he just veered off the road and hit a tree. Died instantly.'

'How's Kim? She must be shattered?'

'She's devastated. Anyone would be.'

'Let me know if there's anything I can do to help.'

'Thanks Bella. Everyone seems to be rallying around. We're making sure Kim isn't on her own. She's completely numb with shock, as you can imagine. Something like this always gives people a reality check about what matters in life. But then you know that more than most.'

Bella sighed deeply. 'Yes, I do. You take care. I'll pop up and see you soon okay?'

'Thanks. I'm going over to Kim's in a bit. I'll probably be there for the rest of the day, so maybe tomorrow? Bye.'

'Okay. Bye.' Sadly Bella put the phone down, wandered into the kitchen and gazed trancelike into the garden, painful memories rising to the surface, ones that she had tried so hard to forget. Feeling slightly sick and with her appetite for breakfast having deserted her, she drank a large glass of water and made some fresh coffee in the hope that a shot of caffeine would perk her up, and took it into the garden. She gripped the mug to her and sipped it thoughtfully. Vaguely she became aware of a persistent ringing noise and eventually realised it was her doorbell. She hopped up and went to answer it. Standing on the doorstep were a man and a woman. The man looked familiar but, momentarily, she couldn't place him.

The man looked startled as he realised who she was. 'Bella!' he cried.

'Dave! Nice to see you again!'

The woman next to him looked puzzled. Bella, this is Sergeant Swart. Sergeant Swart this is Bella – Mrs Sparkle. The women smiled politely at each other.

'I'm afraid we're here on official business Bella. May we come in?'

'Of course. Come through.' She led the way as Inspector Dave Ormandy stooped his towering, wiry figure under the top of the door frame. His colleague however was diminutive in height, well-rounded and red-haired, followed her boss in, closing the door quietly behind her.

Bella led them into the sitting room, indicated for them to take a seat and offered them a drink which they duly refused. Puzzled she sat down. It had been a long time since she'd seen Dave. He and her late husband Hugh had trained together, but they had lost touch when she and Hugh moved to Norfolk and Dave moved with his wife to Kent fifteen years ago. Discreetly Sergeant Swart pulled out a notebook and pen, poised, ready for action.

'I'm sorry about Hugh,' said Dave. 'It's just not right that he should have died at such a young age, particularly in those circumstances. He was such a good man and an excellent policeman.'

'Thanks.' Bella tried to keep the tears which were welling up at bay. Rupert's death had brought a renewed wave of the pain she had felt when her husband had died, feelings which had been, overall, starting to soften in their ferocity, but which, from time to time, reared their ugly heads.

His manner changed as he moved into official mode. 'We're here about Rupert Ireton.'

Bella nodded. 'I heard in the shop this morning that he had died. Apparently he crashed his car into a tree because he was drunk?'

'Mr Ireton's car was involved in a road traffic accident on Saturday night, he died instantly from injuries caused by his car hitting a tree. You telephoned the police station late on Saturday afternoon to report Mr Ireton for drink driving. What led you believe he had been drink driving?'

Bella recounted the events of Saturday afternoon, including how Harry and Fred had tried to stop him, but that Rupert had punched Fred and apparently habitually lashed out and hurt anyone who tried to stop him.

Dave paused, conscious of how sensitive he needed to be. He cleared his throat. 'How did it make you feel that he was going to drive whilst heavily under the influence of alcohol?'

Bella blinked. Why the change? 'I felt angry of course. Furious that he was putting other people at risk by his actions, that what happened to Hugh could happen to someone else because of Rupert's blatant disregard for others.'

'Furious enough to do something about it?'

'Of course! I telephoned the station and reported him. Why all the questions? It's not my fault Rupert was so drunk he drove into a tree.'

'At the moment we're keeping an open mind as to the cause of the accident.'

Bella had been married to a police officer for long enough to know what this meant. 'Keeping an open mind? Do you mean to say you think Rupert's death wasn't caused by him being drunk and driving off the road?' She looked expectantly from one to the other.

'Until we can be certain that the cause of death was an accident, or deliberate on his part, as a result of him being too drunk and driving off the road and into a tree, we have to keep an open mind.'

'So you think it may have been deliberate? That he was murdered?' Bella's jaw dropped in shock. 'You can't mean that? I mean, why? Why would anyone want to kill him?'

'Like I say, we're keeping an open mind at the moment. What were your observations of the group you were with on Saturday? Were there any tensions? Any grudges? Arguments? Anyone who could have been pushed too far by Mr Ireton?' He looked expectantly at Bella's kind face, and waited patiently.

After a few moments Bella replied quietly, '*If* it transpires that Rupert's death was not an accident, or deliberate on his part, but was caused by the actions of another person, I will then give you my thoughts and observations of that day. Until such time, I feel it inappropriate to say anything.' She looked determinedly into his pale blue eyes.

Point taken, he thought. 'If you change your mind,' he scribbled down a number, 'you can contact myself or Sergeant Swart on this number.' He rose, terminating the visit. Awkwardly they went to the front door. He hadn't wanted to upset an old friend, but he still had a job to do, he just hoped that she'd realise it. 'Thank you for your time Bella.' It would be an insult too far to be formal and call her Mrs Sparkle. 'Just one thing,' he paused turning on the step, 'did you go out on Saturday night?'

She shook her head. 'No, not at all. Apart from going to the village shop, I've not been out at all since I got back from the lunch party.'

'Sir,' called Sergeant Swart from the direction of Bella's car. They walked over. He immediately saw what she had discovered.

'How on earth did that happen?' yelped Bella. 'My poor car!' She touched the dented bumper and scraped boot.

'How long has it been like that?'

'I don't know. It's the first time I've seen it. I've not been out at all. Looks like a green car's hit it.' As she spoke she had a sinking feeling. Surely it couldn't be?

'We might need to take a sample from this. Don't go getting it fixed just yet,' he said.

Numbly, Bella shook her head. She stood there watching as they drove off, wondering what to do. Should she tell Mia? Did anyone else know that the police were considering that Rupert may not have died as a result of an accident, or that it may have been deliberate on his part? She really didn't want to be involved, but somehow she'd managed to get tangled up in what was probably the biggest incident to hit the village in years. As she turned to go back inside she saw Jennifer hurrying into her cottage up the lane. Decisively she grabbed her house keys from the hall, slammed the door behind her and scurried up the lane. She lifted the wrought iron knocker and knocked loudly on the green front door.

Jennifer opened it, her face pale, eyes red rimmed, and gazed at Bella. She attempted a half smile, 'Hi Bella,' but made no indication to welcome her visitor in.

'Hi Jennifer. How are you? I guess you've heard about Rupert?' Jennifer nodded in acknowledgement. 'Can I come in?' Jennifer politely stood back, closed the door behind Bella and led Bella through to a large kitchen, which ran the whole width of the back of the house. The limestone floor sparkled in the sunlight and reflected off the maple wood units. At one end, to the left, was a large four oven pale blue Aga. The kitchen opened out into a large sitting area, which was constructed in brick with an oak frame, infilled with glass. It was stunning, having a contemporary edge to it, but perfectly blending with the Georgian era house.

'Coffee?' she offered, breaking the silence.

'Please.' Bella watched as Jennifer silently filled the kettle, put it on the hot plate of the Aga to boil and whizzed up some coffee beans in a chrome coffee grinder. She then took up the classic Aga pose – standing with her back to the Aga, leaning into the warmth – and smiled wanly at Bella.

'Gorgeous house and this kitchen is stunning. How long have you lived here?' enquired Bella.

'Thanks. About three years. Did the kitchen and extension last year.'

'Whoever carried out the work has done a great job and you've got fab taste.' Silently Bella wondered how someone so young – for Jennifer could barely be thirty, she estimated – could afford such an expensive house. She hadn't got the impression that Jennifer was a city high flyer who earned vast sums of money and received a massive bonus each year. In fact, she didn't know what Jennifer did to earn a living, not that it was any of her business she reminded herself.

'Let's go and sit through here.' Jennifer nodded in the direction of the sitting area as she loaded the cafetière of coffee, jug of milk, cups and saucers onto a wooden tray. Bella wandered through and sat in a deep, comfortable, chocolate brown, designer leather contemporary sofa. The glass doors were folded back on themselves allowing the gentle breeze to float in from the garden and tickle her feet. Jennifer placed the tray down on the large bespoke oak and glass coffee table, which mirrored the construction of the room, and poured a cup out for them both, assuming correctly that Bella did not take sugar. She sank back into another sofa, not identical, but similar to, and complimenting, the one which Bella was sitting in, and sighed heavily. 'I can't believe it, I really can't believe that he's dead. It seems impossible. Rupert was Rupert and he was indestructible.'

'I feel it always seems more shocking when someone you actually know dies,' replied Bella diplomatically, remembering how Rupert had behaved towards Jennifer.

'I know he could be a pain, but he didn't deserve to die. Not like this. Not so young. I know he wasn't really young, but he wasn't old, not like he was in his eighties or nineties and lived a long life and heading towards the natural end of his life.'

'Mmm, no. What was he - fifty? Fifty-five?'

'No. Forty-five. Looked older than he was, but I suspect that was due to the vast quantities of alcohol he consumed.'

Bella waited, hoping that Jennifer would volunteer more information. She sipped her coffee and listened to the peaceful buzz of bees and other insects outside in the garden, the gentle chattering of birds providing a background ambience.

'You know,' said Jennifer, 'I was one of the very few women who had not had an affair with Rupert. There was something about him that made him very alluring. Can't quite put my finger on it, but he never had a problem attracting women. I think that's why he found me so much of a challenge. I resisted him. Part of me was curious, but I would never have an affair with a married man, and certainly not with the husband of a friend.'

'He was obviously very interested in you. How did Kim feel about him playing around? It must have been hard on her and so humiliating.'

'Yup. I don't know why she put up with it. They married after a whirlwind romance. He swept her off her feet and six months later they got married. I think he stayed faithful for the first year, but after that he slowly got up to his old tricks again. I know in her own way she loves... loved... him,' she corrected herself, 'but I got the feeling recently that she wasn't going to put up with it for much longer.'

Bella's ears pricked up. 'Oh? Why do you think that?'

Jennifer screwed up her face as she contemplated Bella's question, her long slim nose wrinkling as she did so. 'I'm not sure. She just seemed brighter, as though she knew the end was coming and her future looked freer.' Her hand flew to her mouth in shock. 'Oh! What have I said? That sounds horrible! As though she were wishing him dead and she wasn't, I meant she was just going to move on with her life.' Jennifer looked horrified.

'It's okay, don't worry I know what you meant.' Bella hastily changed the subject. 'Is the Farmers' Market any good? You know, the one held in the Village Hall?'

'Um. Yes. Pretty good,' she replied distractedly.

Bella drained the remainder of her coffee and decided it was time to go. 'Thanks Jennifer, do pop down anytime you like. You know, if you want to talk or anything. No, don't get up,' she said as Jennifer rose to let her out, 'I can see myself out. You sit, you still look a bit shaken by what's happened.' She patted her in a motherly way on the shoulder and quietly let herself out. Was it possible that Kim had had something to do with Rupert's death? She seemed such a nice person, surely she couldn't have done it? What would be her motive? Bella pondered this as she strolled back down to her cottage. Freedom from him? But if she had killed him it was a big risk to take - if she were found guilty she would be locked up for many years. Did she think it was worth the gamble? Or money? By the looks of things Rupert was pretty wealthy, but I suppose you can't judge someone's wealth just by the way they choose to portray themselves, appearances can be deceptive.

Back at the house, Bella busied herself in the kitchen making herself a sandwich stuffed with cheese and tomato, simple, but her favourite, her appetite now having returned. Her mind was whirring as she chewed. Who else would have had a motive to kill him? After Saturday's performance there were probably quite a few and that was just those who were there, it didn't take into account the many people Rupert must have come into contact with in the course of running his business, or was it businesses? She chided herself for assuming that it was murder rather than the more likely reasons of an accident or suicide, the police were just doing their job and being thorough. Still, it gave her something to focus on and forget the worries of her own life.

# Chapter Five

The next morning Bella drove along the Monhurst to Brookhurst Road on the way to Mia's house for coffee. Mia and Fred lived with their sixteen year old daughter Tess in a small, three bedroom barn conversion. It had been a labour of love, ten years in the making, combining Fred working on it at weekends, interspersed with the expertise of a local builder, and hard saving to pay for it. It was prettily situated down a long drive, between the villages of Monhurst and Brookhurst, and set in two acres of garden and a paddock. The bedrooms were complemented by a main family bathroom, and an en-suite to the master bedroom. Downstairs was a large sitting room with wood burner and a study corner tucked off to one side, a cloakroom, a dining room which was used as a music cum family room and a large kitchen/breakfast room with utility off it. Not massive, but beautifully finished, and in a glorious location with views over the fields towards Brookhurst.

'Hi!' called Mia from the oak front door, looking slightly subdued compared to her usual bright, sparkly self.

'Hiya,' replied Bella kissing her on the cheek, 'how are you?'

Mia Shrugged. 'Okay I suppose.'

Mia efficiently made coffee. The house was spotless as usual, the cream kitchen units looking as though they were brand new and the black Aga shined away as though just fitted. She carried the cafetière and milk out onto the terrace, Bella following with the pink spotted mugs. It didn't matter how many times Bella visited, her breath was always taken away by the beauty of the view that the property afforded which stretched as far as the eye could see over fields, gently undulating hills and - on a clear day - even to the coast and adjacent sea; every time was always like the first.

'So, how is Kim coping?' asked Bella.

'She's distraught. But I think it's guilt which is making it worse for her more than the fact that Rupert is dead.'

'Guilt? For what?'

Mia pursed her lips. 'Well,' she said cautiously, 'I know you'll keep this to yourself,' her eyes flicked briefly to Bella's face for confirmation, though she knew her friend well enough. 'Kim was planning on leaving Rupert.'

'Aha! So Jennifer was right.'

'Jennifer? What do you mean?'

'Oh. Um. It was just a passing comment that Jennifer made yesterday when I saw her. She said she had a feeling that Kim had decided to do something about her marriage. Didn't say what, don't even know if she actually knew or was speculating.'

Mia shrugged. 'Kim was being careful, but I suppose it's natural that the others would pick up on something.'

Bella waited expectantly. Eventually she prodded Mia. 'Well? What was she going to do?'

'She didn't go into details. She just said that she'd decided their marriage was no longer a marriage and that it had run its course. She felt that no matter how hard she tried Rupert never reciprocated. He was constantly criticising her and putting her down, nothing she did was right. She tried to change to please him but even that didn't work. I was worried about her. She seemed to be turning into a shadow of her former self, no self confidence, becoming reluctant to go out, even missing tennis sometimes which was unheard of. And I'm not totally convinced that he wasn't hitting her.'

Bella gasped, shocked, but somehow deep down she wasn't surprised. 'How awful! It sounds like a nightmare of a marriage. Abuse doesn't just have to be physical. I don't know which would be worse, mental or physical abuse, each in their own right horrific, but to be, quite possibly, on the receiving end of both – well, I don't know how she coped. Don't know how anyone would cope.'

'I'm not sure what specifically nudged her to evolve back to how she used to be, but it was as though she'd suddenly had her "off" switch flipped. Like she'd hit rock bottom and couldn't take any more. She started turning up to everything again, dressing more like she used to and generally looking happier. When we quizzed her on it she would just smile and say nothing. Finally, we were on our own one day and she blurted out that she was going to leave Rupert. I had the feeling there was more to it but it was as though she suddenly realised she'd said too much. Don't think Rupert knew. I don't think he'd take very kindly to being left, his ego wouldn't be able to cope with the humiliation. He's always been the one who's done the loving and then the leaving.'

'Hmm, interesting. Well she's certainly free of him now.'

'Bella!'

'I didn't mean it in a nasty way, you should know that. I just meant that whilst it is a horrible situation for her to be in, ultimately it will be less complicated and messy. She won't have to put up with his temper, which no doubt would have rocketed when she told him she was leaving him, or put up with him turning up drunk and pleading for her to come back or other such scenarios.'

'I suppose. It just doesn't sound very nice when it's put like that, but you're right.'

For a moment Bella paused, wondering whether she should tell her closest friend about the visit from the police. If she did it would open a can of worms. If she didn't, and Mia found out later that Bella had known more than she'd let on, she'd be cross and hurt. Deciding that the last thing she wanted to do was to cause friction in her friendship with Mia, she told her.

Mia's stunned face said it all. Total and utter shock. The news had hit her as though being slapped in the face. 'You have got to be joking? Please tell me that you are joking?'

Bella shook her head. 'Sorry. It probably was just an accident. You know what the police can be like, don't want to commit themselves to anything until they're sure. They're just being cautious.'

'Do you think Kim knows?'

'I've no idea Mia. I'm sure she would have told you. I think it would be best not to say anything to her. What would be the point of upsetting her further when it's highly unlikely that it was deliberate? It's not going to achieve anything. Best to keep quiet.'

'Yeah. I suppose so,' Mia replied slowly, wondering if she were in Kim's position would she want to know? 'But why would anyone want to kill Rupert?'

'I think we're jumping the gun a bit,' answered Bella, beginning to regret telling Mia. 'There's nothing we can do. It's down to the police - if there's anything to tell they will tell her. All you can do is be there to support her Mia.'

'I guess so. I'll have to tell Fred though.'

'Yes, but no one else. Please promise me. It's speculation as far as I am concerned. There are enough rumours flying around at the moment, there's no need to add fuel to the fire.'

'Okay. Anyway,' continued Mia changing the subject, 'how are you settling in?'

Bella grinned. 'Fine. I thought when I moved here that life was going to be too quiet in the village but it's proving not to be the case! It's an interesting group of friends you've got.'

Mia laughed. 'Eclectic, I think is the word you're looking for. Life is never dull with them. Obviously, I'm more friendly with some than with others but on the whole they're a nice bunch.'

'I look forward to meeting the rest of them. In the meantime, you can fill me in on those I have met. I definitely got the feeling on Saturday that the relationships between everyone are complex and intriguing...'

'You could say that! But right now I've got to get off and see Kim. Said I'd pop in about lunchtime and, as it is about that time, I'd better be going.' She gathered up the coffee paraphernalia and hurried back inside.

'You can't leave me hanging on like that Mia!' chided Bella. 'Tantalising me and then leaving it. That's so cruel,' she laughed.

'You never were good at waiting were you Bella,' smiled Mia with a twinkle in her eye. 'Come on, out you go,' she playfully pushed her friend out of the front door, set the alarm and locked it behind her. 'Catch up with you later in the week,' she said kissing Bella on the cheek.

'Only if you promise to spill the beans,' grinned Bella. 'Thanks for the coffee. Let Kim know I'm thinking of her. If there's anything I can do, give me a call. Take care.' She followed Mia's ancient silver Volvo Estate down the drive, they both turned right towards Monhurst with Mia then turning left into Coppice Lane.

Kim's house was a large Tudor Farmhouse constructed with an oak frame, Flemish bond brickwork and a Kent peg tile roof. Rupert and Kim had completely refurbished the house when they bought it, just before they married five years ago. Within the strict guidelines of being a Grade II Listed house, they obtained consent and were allowed to open up a couple of rooms without affecting the character or disturbing the original structure of the property. The house now had five substantial bedrooms and a family bathroom. The master bedroom had been opened up to access the sixth bedroom, which was now a dressing room and an en-suite bathroom; a large sitting room, a smaller sitting room, both with inglenook fireplaces with wood burning stoves, a study, a cloakroom, a boot room, a dining room, a massive kitchen/breakfast room and a laundry room all surrounded by 10 acres.

Cressa opened the door to Mia, her tall frame - heightened by her spiky high heeled shoes - towering over her. Cressa was looking pale and drawn despite her make-up and hair being perfect as usual.

'How is she?' asked Mia in a muted tone.

'Not good. I've just put a call in for the doctor to visit.'

'That bad? I thought she was getting by, all things considered.'

'She was, until the police came this morning.' Cressa looked grim, her thin lips pursed together tighter than usual.

Mia's heart flip-flopped. Police? Surely it couldn't mean? 'Police?' she stuttered, 'What did they want?'

Cressa ushered her through the relative gloom of the hall, compared with the bright sunshine outside, to the kitchen which was flooded in sunlight due to the extra window and French doors Rupert and Kim had been allowed to put in. 'Drink?' Cressa poured herself a substantial glass of white wine. The bottle was half empty, it looked as though she'd started early.

Mia shook her head. 'Water will do thanks.' Cressa removed a bottle of still water from the fridge and poured the liquid into a simple crystal glass. Mia took it, grateful to have something to do with her hands. 'So, the police?' she prompted quietly, above her she could hear the floorboards creaking as someone moved around. Kim she presumed.

'You'd better sit down.' Cressa pulled a chair out and sat at the large oak table which dominated the centre of the ornate oak kitchen. She fiddled with the stem of her glass, took a long gulp and spoke. 'The police believe that Rupert's death was not an accident.'

'Not an accident?' whispered Mia.

'No. They think the crash was deliberate. That Rupert was killed deliberately. That he was murdered.'

'Murdered?' echoed Mia hoarsely. 'That can't be so? I mean, how can he have been murdered? It was an accident, Rupert was drunk and lost control of the car. It was a dreadful accident.'

'Apparently not. The police believe that he was forced off the road, and that it wasn't an accident, it was deliberate.'

'But how can they possibly know? I mean, what if both cars were going too fast and they had to swerve to avoid one another? How do they know that that didn't happen?'

'They did explain but I was too shocked to take it all in. There's some complicated way they can work things out and all indications are that it was deliberate. You'd have to ask them to explain it to you, if you want to know precisely how they have come to this conclusion.' Cressa was getting paler by the minute.

'You okay? You look unwell.' enquired Mia, concerned by Cressa's appearance.

'I'm fine,' she snapped. 'Do you want me to stay or are you okay to wait with Kim? The doctor should be here soon. Kim's taken herself off to her room and doesn't want me up there. Don't think she wants anyone up there.' Still stunned, Mia nodded without thinking. 'Jen's going to be along later. If you need anything give me a call.' Cressa picked up her keys, patted Mia on the shoulder and hastily exited.

Mia heard the front door close, and then silence. She became aware of the clock ticking in the kitchen, then, despite everything, her stomach rumbled. How could she possibly think of food at a time like this? She stood up and cautiously went upstairs, tapping gently on Kim's door. 'Kim? It's me, Mia. Can I come in?' There was silence. She tapped again. 'Are you okay? Can I get you anything?'

Again silence, then a very quiet 'You can come in,' permeated from behind the door. Mia lifted the latch and braced herself.

Kim was standing staring out of one of the windows. Mia walked quietly across the pristine white, deep pile carpet, which had been laid over the oak floorboards and slipped her arm around her friend's shoulder. Kim looked at her, her eyes red rimmed from crying, her nose and lips swollen and raw from the sobs.

'Cressa told me. I'm so sorry.'

Kim tried to speak, but her throat was so sore it came out as a croak. Mia went to the oak bedside table and poured a glass of water from the glass flaçon. Kim sipped it, allowing the water to soothe her throat. She tried again. 'Thanks. It just seems to be one shock after another. It's bad enough that Rupert is dead, but to think that it was deliberate, that someone killed him,' she shook her head as though trying to get rid of the suggestion. Mia led her over to the capacious oak framed bed and sat her down. She looked so frail, as though she might collapse at any moment. 'Why would anyone want to kill him? I mean, I know that he rubbed a lot of people up the wrong way, but not enough to make someone want to do that. I just don't understand.' She looked beseechingly at Mia who shrugged, at a loss as to know what to say.

'I've no idea either. I think that the police must have got it wrong, that it really was just a dreadful accident.'

'I wish that were so but they seemed pretty convinced. They explained in detail how they'd come to that conclusion, but I can't really remember what they said. I was so stunned.' She sobbed and pulled out a sodden white handkerchief from her jeans.

'So what are the police going to do? If they think he was killed deliberately, how are they going to find out who did it?'

Kim sniffed. 'I don't know. But they'd better find out who did it. I want justice to be done. I know he was impossible to live with and that I was going to leave him, but no one deserves to die like that, no one!' she shouted vehemently.

'Sssh,' soothed Mia, stroking Kim's hair as tears began to stream down Kim's face again. 'I'm sure they'll find out. We'll make sure that they do.' There was a knock at the front door. 'That'll be the doctor. I'll just go and let her in.'

'I don't need a doctor! I need Rupert's murderer to be found! Why did you ask her to come?'

'I didn't. Cressa did. She obviously felt that you might need the doctor.'

'Well, I don't,' she shouted, 'I just need Rupert back.' Mia slipped out of the room and downstairs to let the doctor in.

# Chapter Six

The next morning the sky had clouded over, and there was a grey heaviness which replicated the feeling of many in the village. News of the murder had sunk all but the most gossipy into a suspicious malaise. Bella had felt like she was a tasty morsel being fed to a group of particularly ravenous piranhas when she went to collect her paper that morning. Mia had phoned her, to update her late yesterday afternoon once she'd returned from Kim's house. As if sensing this by some telepathic force, Sharon at the shop had gone at Bella like a dog with a bone, desperate to tease every last titbit out of her. Unfortunately for Sharon, Bella was having none of it. Through gritted teeth she smiled politely, and refused to answer any questions from the posse which had secured itself in the corner of the shop.

Having recovered from the ordeal over breakfast Bella decided to risk it, and go to the Farmers' Market in the village hall, hoping sincerely that she wouldn't be pounced upon again for information. She strolled up to the entrance door and was intrigued to see that the plaque on the wall stated that the hall had only been opened in 1998. This surprised her because the hall looked like a very old barn, which had been converted for use by the village. Whoever had designed it and built it had done an excellent job, it blended in perfectly with the surrounding area.

There was a general hubbub of noise coming from within and she was greeted by a large, light, high ceilinged area, crammed full of stalls, laid out around the inner perimeter of the hall with another rectangle of tables in the centre. The goods on offer were produced or sourced locally; there were eggs, cheese, flowers, yoghurts, milk, cakes, jams, chutneys, vegetables, fruit, meat, fish, everything one would ever need to survive on very nicely. Bella chatted to the stall holders as she wandered around, purchasing a variety of produce with which to stock up her cupboards and fridge. All of the stall holders seemed to be local and enthusiastic about selling their produce, in particular they were keen for local residents and visitors to the area to support local businesses, and not rely so heavily on the large supermarket chains. There was an elderly couple who grew their vegetables in their garden and produced just enough to sell at the market. There was the city high-flyer who had made so much money that he'd given it up when he was burnt out at forty-five, and decided to live the good life keeping bees and making his own honey. There were young mums who were trying to juggle the impossible task of fitting in some kind of work to earn money, around looking after their children, and many other fascinating individuals with their own stories to tell and motivation for being there. It was fascinating.

Laden down with bags so full that she had enough food to feed several people for a week, not just herself, she popped her hoard down onto a chair in the area outside the kitchen, which had been set up with tables and chairs for people to sit and enjoy a catch-up and have a drink. Bella queued and ordered a cup of coffee. She eyed the selection of cakes that were on offer, decided that as she'd been useless with her healthy eating and fitness campaign so far she may as well not start the regimen with purpose until tomorrow, and chose a large piece of moist chocolate cake. She took a mouthful, pushing the guilty feeling far away and savoured the sweet, sticky cake – perfect, she concluded.

'Hi,' called a voice, dragging Bella away from her chocolaty reverie.

'Jennifer! Hi, how are you? Please join me,' Bella grabbed the bags from the spare chair and piled them on top of one another on the floor. They promptly all fell over and apples rolled in all directions. 'Typical!' she laughed. Jennifer scurried around helping her to pick them up.

'I'll just get a coffee then I'll join you.'

'That was delicious,' sighed Bella as Jennifer sat down. 'Probably the best chocolate cake I've ever tasted.'

'I know, they're scrummy.' Jennifer looked paler than two days ago. Her hair was lank and unwashed, and the dark circles under her eyes were taking on a purplish hue.

'Tell me,' said Bella, 'I'm slightly mystified. Why are all those people queuing up at an empty table?' She'd been observing them whilst eating her cake, more and more people had joined it, until now there were about 20 standing patiently, one behind another.

Jennifer laughed. 'That, Bella, is known as "The Bread Man Phenomenon".'

'The what? What on earth is that?'

'There's a local baker who bakes the most incredible bread. A huge variety of different breads and suchlike which you can't seem to find anywhere else locally. His prices are reasonable and everything is freshly made every morning. Everyone knows this. If you go to other local Farmers' Markets, you will find that there is always an empty table with a queue of people waiting patiently.'

'But if the table's empty, why are they queuing?'

'Because he's always late. He always turns up. But he's always late. His bread sells out so quickly that quite often, if you don't queue, then you won't be able to get what you want.'

'In that case I'd better buy some, if there's any left by the time I get there! Oh, is that him?' There was a flurry of activity and people parted as though royalty had arrived. Several trips were made to bring in the crates of bread and other baked offerings, all the time the queue waiting patiently. They watched in silence for a minute. Jennifer, used to this weekly scene, allowed Bella to observe it without distraction as she was obviously fascinated by other people's behaviour. 'I wonder if there'll be any left?' Bella murmured.

'Why don't you go and queue. I'll get us another coffee and look after your bags.'

'Oh that's kind, thanks very much. I've got to see what all this fuss is about!' Ten minutes later she returned bearing two loaves of bread, the type of which she'd never heard of before, and a couple of white crusty rolls.

'Get what you wanted?'

'I guess so. There was a bit of a kerfuffle going on. The person in front of me had just bought the last somethingorother and someone else behind me wanted it! Thanks for the coffee.' She picked the cup up and studied Jennifer - she was convinced Jennifer wanted to tell her something. 'I guess you've heard the update about Rupert?'

Jennifer nodded and fiddled with her cup, tears welled up in her eyes. 'I can't believe it. I just can't.' Bella waited quietly. 'It's just ...' Jennifer looked furtively around her to ensure no one was listening. She lowered her voice so that Bella had to lean forward to hear her, 'It's just that I think I was the last one to see him alive.'

Bella's eyebrows shot up in surprise. 'Really? How did you work that one out?'

Again Jennifer checked that no one was listening. 'He came to the house. He came to see me. He was pestering me. He'd taken my rejection earlier on badly. He was determined to get me into bed. He was very persistent.'

'And did he?'

She shook her head. 'No, he tried, stuck his tongue down my throat, hand up my skirt that sort of thing, but I managed to fend him off. I gave him a slap round the face and told him that if he didn't leave me alone I'd call the police.'

'And what did he do then?'

'He laughed. Said he'd be back, that sooner or later I'd realise that I wanted him, that I was just playing hard to get and would surrender to him. All sounded a bit like he'd swallowed a ghastly romantic novel the amount of clichés he was reeling off.'

'So then he left?'

'Yes.'

'What time was that?'

'About 9pm.'

'And the crash was at about 10.05pm?'

'I think so.'

'There's quite a time difference between him leaving you and his death. After all, Coppice Lane is only a couple of minutes away, maybe five, from where the car crashed and it's not the most direct route to his house.'

'Have you been there?'

'Where?'

'To their house?'

Bella shook her head.

'So how do you know what the quickest route would be?'

'Mia told me.' Mia had told her, but Bella didn't want to admit that she'd had the maps out to study the local lanes, far more satisfying than looking on the internet she felt, or that she'd driven down the various routes which would take you to Kim and Rupert's house. As soon as she'd found out that it was murder, her mind had whirred into overdrive, sure that somehow she would be able to tease out some useful piece of information and give her some focus and purpose for being in the village.

'Oh, okay,' Jennifer looked suspiciously at her.

'Anyway. What I was saying was that there's quite a time difference between his leaving you and the accident. It's possible that he went on somewhere else. Maybe the pub?'

'No, I don't think so. I got the impression he was on a mission. The funny thing is that though he'd drunk a lot during the afternoon, by the time he came round he didn't seem at all drunk. In fact, for Rupert, I would say he was stone cold sober.'

'Hmm. Have you told the police this?'

'No. Don't think it's relevant really.'

'I think you should. The more information they have, no matter how irrelevant you feel it is, could help them. It's a bit like doing a jigsaw, you need all the pieces in order to fit them together to solve the case; better to have too many pieces than not enough and have great big gaps missing.'

'I suppose…' replied Jennifer reluctantly.

'Give them a call when you get back. After all, you want to find out who did kill him don't you?' She looked questioningly at her.

Jennifer shifted uncomfortably in her seat. 'Of course.'

Wisely, Bella changed the subject and chatted aimlessly about the Farmers' Market until they'd both finished their coffee, then wandered back with her on the way home.

'Take care. Thanks for the coffee. Come down and see me sometime,' suggested Bella as they arrived at the pristine white picket gate to Jennifer's front garden.

'Thanks, I will.'

'And please do phone the police and tell them what you've told me.'

Jennifer sighed heavily. 'Okay,' she replied reluctantly.

'Bye.' Bella carried on towards her cottage, the weight of her over-stuffed bags starting to strain on her hands, she gathered speed the closer she got. She dumped them on the doorstep and stood shaking and rubbing her hands together, there were bright red lines dug into the palms of both her hands and fingers. She was just reaching into her bag for her keys when a voice behind her said.

'Hello Bella. Need a hand?'

She turned to see Dave, Detective Inspector Ormandy, smiling at her, his eyes crinkling as he did so.

'Please. I've definitely bought too much. But there were so many lovely things. It was just too tempting!'

'At the Farmers' Market?'

Bella nodded.

'I've heard it's very good. Never had a chance to go, always working.' He grinned ruefully and bent down to pick up the pile of bags as Bella opened the door.

'Come through to the kitchen. Thanks, just put them on the table and I'll sort them out. Coffee?' She was not entirely sure whether this visit was for official business or not.

'Please. That'd be nice.' He leant against the sink, and watched Bella as she put the kettle on and packed her purchases away into their respective homes. 'Looks like you've bought everything being sold. Did you leave anything for anyone else?' he teased, feeling as though it hadn't been fifteen years since he'd last socialised with her.

'Very funny. I did leave the odd crumb for other people. Shall we sit outside?' she suggested as she unlocked the back door. 'I think we might be in for a storm later, it seems to be getting so muggy.'

'Here, let me.' He lifted the tray and followed her out onto the patio, set it down on the wooden slatted table and settled into one of the matching chairs.

'So, is this an official visit or unofficial visit?'

He smiled. 'I wish it were unofficial but I'm afraid it's not. When I saw you on Monday you said that if it turned out to be murder, you would give me your thoughts on the people you were with at the lunch that Saturday.' He fished out a list from his pocket and put it in front of her; everyone at the party was on it.

Bella shifted uncomfortably. Just because she knew Dave from long ago, didn't mean that what she said wouldn't be off the record and not used as some kind of evidence. She felt unfaithful to those who had befriended her on Saturday and she didn't like it. 'I did, so I suppose

I'll have to, though I want you to know that I really don't like doing this. I hate gossip and that's what it feels like.'

'I know, but any information which may be relevant, or may not even seem to be relevant, will help.' He wished he didn't have to do this as much as she did. He liked her and didn't want her mixed up in police business. 'If you could go through each person on the list and give me your thoughts about them, their relationship with Rupert or anything else which struck you I'd appreciate it.' He waited patiently.

She looked miserably at the list and sighed. 'Okay. Well to start with I think they all know each other through tennis. All the women are members of the local tennis club and play regularly. Some of the men do too I think, Fred, Harry and Seb do but I can't quite remember - one of them will be able to tell you anyway - and I think the other men are members but don't necessarily play - just come along to the social side of things - of which I think there are many. I can't imagine Rupert ever played but I really have no idea.' She sat pondering, Dave nodded encouragingly. 'Fred and Mia are my friends. They're great, really nice people and I know they won't have anything to do with it. Fred tried with Harry to stop Rupert from driving off after the party as he was so drunk, that's when Fred got hit by Rupert. Rupert must have had several bottles of wine to drink. Then there's Sophie and Harry who are delightful and their daughter Jemima, didn't see any tension there between them or anyone else, though obviously they invited everyone and must have known who would or wouldn't get on with one another. Umm ...' she pursed her lips as she recalled the afternoon. 'Obviously there was Kim and Rupert. Rupert seemed to treat her like dirt, and didn't take her feelings into consideration when he was busy dribbling all over Jennifer and Ariadne. Kim was quite quiet. Ariadne seemed to know everyone and was so glamorous, a real Hollywood Star, and her agent Kit who was also very attractive,' she blushed as she thought of him, something that did not go unnoticed. 'He was busy flirting with Jennifer and I don't think Rupert liked that. Seb is nice, got the feeling he wasn't impressed by Kit or Ariadne, and there was definitely something going on between him and Rupert.'

'Something? What do you mean?'

'I don't know, but I got the feeling there was some history there. Could be he just didn't like Rupert's arrogance, he seemed quite an unassuming person Seb. He also seemed a bit protective of Kim. But then, I felt protective of her too after the way Rupert treated her. Florence seemed quite pleasant, she was very quiet though and I didn't get much of a chance to talk to her Think she moved to the village a year ago and has been going to the tennis club,' she paused to sip some coffee, glad that it was decaffeinated so she wasn't buzzing from an overdose of caffeine. Her eyes ran down the list. 'Ah, Jack and Cressa, again I didn't get to talk to them that much. Jack was giving Rupert filthy looks but I don't know why and there seemed to be tension between him and Cressa, but that could just be their normal relationship. Oh, and Jennifer, she's lovely, she lives just up the lane, the cottage by the church. She's nice. Rupert was all over her, seems she was a bit of a challenge to him. She refused to have an affair with him...' she hesitated, 'in fact I think she's going to give the police station a call.'

Dave looked questioningly at her. 'Is she? Do you know what about?'

Again Bella hesitated. 'Yes, but I think it's best coming from her, she only told me this morning. It may or may not be relevant but I said that, relevant or not, you would need to know.'

'Is she still at home do you know?'

'I walked with her back from the market, so she was there a little while ago unless she's gone out again.'

'Okay. Thanks. I'll pop in and see her before I head back, and don't worry I'll make it clear that you haven't told me what it is.'

'Thanks. I'd hate for any of them to think I can't be trusted, or that I'm an enemy or spy in the camp. Well I don't think there's anything else to add to what I have told you. I'll let you know if I think of anything.'

'Thanks.'

'So how did he die then?' she was intrigued to know.

'Well, it appears that another car was coming in the opposite direction and forced Rupert off the road. It wasn't helped by the fact that he was over the legal limit. It's a straight piece of road and easily wide enough for two cars to pass, there's no bend or anything. We're also trying to trace all the cars that Rupert appears to have driven into. Seems he bumped quite a few at the party, but there are unmistakable marks, dents and paint from another car on the front wing of the car he was driving, which would be consistent with his car being hit by another.'

'Hmmm,' Bella's mind was digesting the information.

'I'd appreciate it if you kept that to yourself.'

'Don't worry. You can trust me, I won't tell anyone.' And he knew he could trust her. Bella decided to change the subject. 'So, how's Alison?' Bella had known Dave's wife Alison years ago when they all socialised together.

A dark shadow flitted across his face. 'I don't know. She left me two years ago for another man. A younger man. Huh.'

'I'm sorry, I didn't know,' she felt like a fool now, and very embarrassed.

'How would you? It's okay. It's in the past, got to move on and all that. Didn't get the work/life balance right. Can't really blame her, I devoted too much of my time to work and not enough time to her and our relationship, so she found comfort elsewhere. Wasn't helped by the fact that we'd tried for years to have children and couldn't.'

'Oh, I'm sorry.' What else could she say? She knew how painful it was to desperately want children and not have any. She and Hugh had tried for years and eventually she'd finally become pregnant, they were overjoyed. Tragically, three months into the pregnancy Hugh was killed and the stress and strain had caused, or contributed to, a miscarriage. The part of Hugh that had been her sole comfort after his death died too; it had taken a long time for her to recover, to start seeing a point to life again, and even now there were times when life seemed too dark for her.

Dave had heard on the grapevine that Hugh and Bella had not had children. And he could see no evidence in the house of the paraphernalia which normally accompanied children. He knew too well what a sensitive subject it could be and refrained from enquiring.

'I threw myself into work even more when she left. Divorce came through last year. I'm trying to get a better balance, take time off, have holidays etc. I've even started cycling, gets me out of the house. Seems kind of quiet there on my own.'

The big important detective looks like a little lost boy, thought Bella. 'I'm hoping to start cycling. I have got to lose some weight and there's a bike in the shed.'

'You don't need to lose weight! You look great as you are.'

Bella blushed, flattered by the compliment. 'Thanks. I've put on a lot since Hugh died, comfort eating, you know...'

'I did the opposite. Stopped eating. Kind of got used to having my meals all prepared for me, didn't appreciate it at the time. You only realise what you've lost once it's gone.' He sighed wistfully. 'Still,' he tried to brighten up, 'got to go with the flow and all that. I'm quite a dab hand at cooking now. Went on a course, bought Delia Smith's Complete Cookery Course book to start with and progressed from there and there's so much one can access on the internet, it's a revelation! Perhaps,' he hesitated, 'I could show you some of my culinary skills? Maybe dinner or lunch one Sunday?' He looked hopefully at her.

'I'd like that.' She felt all weird, a cross between excitement, being flattered, nervousness and guilt. Was she being asked out on a date? She'd not been on one since Hugh had died and wasn't sure if she ever wanted another relationship. Or was it just old friends catching up?

As if sensing her unease he hastily added, 'It would be good to catch up,' unsure himself whether he wanted simply friendship or more, surprised that he'd asked her. He stood up to go. 'I'll be in touch to arrange a date. And thanks again for all your help.'

'That's okay,' she'd momentarily forgotten that he'd been here on business, it had so easily slipped into pleasure. 'If I remember anything else, I'll give you a call.'

'Thanks I'd appreciate it. I'll go and see if Jennifer Galbraith is in. Bye Bella.' He smiled at her again, the warmth of it radiating from his face.

'Bye.' She closed the door behind her and wondered what had just happened.

# Chapter Seven

The next week passed by quickly as Bella started a crash diet, began cycling furiously and caught up with Mia. By the end of the week her muscles ached so much she didn't think she could get out of bed, her stomach rumbled most of the day and she felt permanently grumpy from the lack of food. The upside was that she had lost 4lbs in weight. As she stood on the scales she got a little buzz from seeing 4lbs less on it. The feeling was momentary as she wondered whether it was really worth it. Eating virtually nothing, and exercising hard was not the best way, nor the most effective way, of losing weight. Eating sensibly and building the amount of exercise up slowly would have a longer term benefit she felt sure and questioned why she had not started on that path instead.

The morning of the funeral arrived and, resisting the temptation to go mad and stuff herself with food, Bella opted for a small bowl of muesli, decaffeinated coffee and a glass of orange juice. A pure banquet in comparison to the previous seven breakfasts. As each morsel of food hit her stomach she could feel her blood sugar level rising, along with her normal good nature. Replenished, she got ready for the funeral. Mia had asked if she could attend, and though she'd felt rather awkward as Rupert had been a virtual stranger to her, it did feel like the right thing to do. She'd disposed of her 'funeral outfit' after Hugh's, she couldn't bear to see it in the wardrobe every day as it reminded her so much of one of the worst days of her life. It had therefore been a bit of a challenge to find something suitably sombre, which fitted her and was cool enough to wear in the searing June heat. Eventually she'd found a navy blue linen dress that came down to her calves, had a relatively high neck – up to her collar bones – and sleeves that came to the top of her elbows; with this she was going to wear a navy blue blazer-style jacket. Not a particularly stylishly put together outfit, but one which would suffice.

Mia knocked on the door at 10am. Fred, having parked in Bella's drive, was waiting by the car. The funeral was to be held at the village church along with a burial, followed by a wake in the village hall.

'Ready?'

'As I'll ever be,' replied Bella.

'Looks like the church is going to be crowded,' commented Fred, nodding in the direction of the queue of traffic inching its way up the far side of the green to the church and village hall car parks.

'More likely to be filled out with the local gossips and people gawping. So macabre,' added Mia.

'Hmm, suppose so. I managed to escape the clutches of Sharon at the shop this morning. Think she and her cronies are coming along for a nose. I guess there's bound to be a natural amount of curiosity. After all Rupert was a bit of a character by all accounts and a prominent businessman, and both he and Kim took part in lots of village activities. Until they find out who killed him, it'll rumble on for a while.' Unfortunately Bella knew all too well about the consequences of living in a close knit community, albeit an urban one, and being the focus of local people and local media attention, as Hugh had been a well respected policeman in the town where they had lived. The pressure had really been on his colleagues to find out who was responsible for his death. Fortunately, there had been several witnesses and it didn't take long for them to track the culprit down. Justice had been done when the case was successful, and the drink driver was sent to prison for his deadly misdemeanour.

'You okay?' asked Mia softly, squeezing Bella's arm.

She nodded. 'I'm fine.' She cleared her throat. 'It'll be quite interesting to see who's there. I imagine the police will be lurking in the background - doesn't the person who committed the crime usually have a compulsion to be there at the funeral, or have I been watching too many detective programmes on television?'

Mia and Fred laughed. 'Haven't got a clue.'

They walked in silence the rest of the way. When they arrived inside the church they found it was packed, with people even standing at the back of the church and down the sides. Fred craned his neck and saw Cressa waving at him. They weaved their way down the aisle towards her and slipped into the pew next to her. Bella smiled and politely said hello. She noticed that two pews were taken up with those who had been at the lunch party, all except Sophie and Harry.

'Where are Sophie and Harry?' she whispered to Mia.

'Coming with Kim and her parents.'

'Oh. Has she not got any other family?'

'No. She is an only child, as are her parents, and her grandparents are dead.'

'What about Rupert's family?' she scanned around looking at who was there.

'Not invited.'

'What?!' squeaked Bella, hastily lowering her voice as people turned to stare at her. 'Why not?'

'Apparently they had a big falling out - about thirty years ago. He's not been in touch with them since, and they haven't with him.'

'But he would have been only fifteen years old, thirty years ago. Surely it can't have been just teenage angst which caused the falling out?' Bella's curiosity was piqued.

'Don't know,' whispered Mia, 'don't think he has ever really talked about it. Kim doesn't really know much. She tried to persuade him to ask them to their wedding, but he went ballistic. I don't think she dared mention it again.'

'How very peculiar. I know families fall out and all that, but he was still a child.' Her brain ticked away as she ran through numerous scenarios as to why the fall-out could have occurred, but couldn't come up with anything which sounded vaguely realistic. The organ started playing and everyone fell silent, turning round to see the coffin being carried slowly up the aisle, Kim and her parents clutching on to one another for support with Harry and Sophie bringing up the rear.

Throughout the service Kim sat up ram rod straight. It seemed to Bella that she was doing the comforting to her parents, not the other way round. Fred read the lesson and Harry gave a carefully worded eulogy. Bella found that the service wasn't as excruciatingly painful as she had feared it would be; she'd been worried that it would rip open old wounds and she would become a weeping wreck again.

The sky had clouded over and there were heavy dark clouds and an oppressive air by the time the service moved outside. It was as she was standing beside the open grave that she noticed Ariadne and Kit. It would have been impossible not to have. Ariadne was dressed completely in black in a tight-fitting, knee length skirt, tight-fitted jacket, which was buttoned low and no blouse, her breasts appearing desperate to burst out – Rupert would have loved it - and on her head she had a clutch of black feathers with a net veil which just covered her eyes and stopped at the top of her nose. She looked like a 1930s movie star. Kit next to her was sharply dressed in a hand-tailored black suit, black shirt and black tie. There was a lot of whispering and pointing from the outer echelons of the mourners as they recognised the globally known movie star. Trust her to steel the limelight and detract from the true reason for the gathering, thought Bella.

Bella vaguely heard the Vicar going through the motions of the final stages of Rupert's burial as he was committed to his grave. Kim gripped her weeping parents to her and stood as though a stone statue, her face blank and as pale as alabaster. Bella saw Seb hovering slightly behind her with a pained expression on his face, and couldn't work out whether it was over Rupert's death or Kim's pain. Cressa and Jack stood just along from Kim on the other side of Mia and Fred. The apparent emotional distance that was between them may as well have been as wide as the Grand Canyon. Strange couple - she couldn't work them out.

As the mourners started to disperse and those invited headed off to the wake, Bella noticed the waif-like figure of Florence standing under a tree slightly apart from where the rest of them had been.

'You okay?' asked Bella gently as she looked into her ghost-like face.

'Fine. Thanks,' she replied tightly.

'Would you like to walk over to the village hall with me?'

Florence shook her head. 'No. Thanks. I've got to go.' And with that she fled like a startled rabbit in the direction of the church car park.

Weird, thought Bella shrugging. Suppose grief shows itself in different ways. I wonder if Rupert had had an affair with her?

'Hi Bella.'

Bella spun round, startled.

'Sorry to make you jump.' It was Dave.

'That's okay, I was deep in thought. Seen anything interesting?'

He smiled. 'Have you?' he bounced back to her.

'I find watching people fascinating,' she replied, deliberately avoiding his question.

He looked intently at her and decided not to push the subject. 'Sorry I haven't phoned. Been a bit busy at work,' he smiled guiltily.

'I guessed as much. What's happened to your new resolution to achieve a good work/life balance?' she joked.

He laughed. 'I know, I know. Bit difficult when you're investigating a murder though.'

'I suppose. Forgiven then.' She became aware that Sharon and a few of her fellow gossips were edging closer, having ascertained who Dave was. Bella gave Dave a beady look and raised her eyebrows trying to indicate that they were being listened too.

He understood and without turning round swiftly turned on his official voice and said, 'Well if you do think of anything, please contact myself or one of the officers working on the case.' He gave her a wink and walked off without even bothering to see who was behind him.

Seizing their moment, Sharon and her posse surrounded Bella. 'What did he have to say then? Any breakthrough? Go on, you can tell us. We're as discreet as anything. Won't tell a soul.'

Bella tried hard not to laugh. As if they could ever be discreet! 'Nothing to tell I'm afraid ladies.'

Fred, having observed the scene, called out to Bella and wandered over. 'Sorry to interrupt. Bella, I think Mia needs you.' He took her by the elbow and led her purposefully across the churchyard.

'Thanks,' giggled Bella, 'it was like being surrounded by vultures.'

'My pleasure,' he grinned back, releasing her elbow.

'Quick, let's get out of here before they follow us. Hope they're not coming to the wake.'

He shook his head. 'Nope. Don't think so. I believe that so many people were expected to turn up that it's by invite only, otherwise they wouldn't all fit in.'

'Good idea having it here at the village hall, right by the church and no mess to tidy up at the house afterwards, and more importantly no intrusion by a lot of people you don't know or barely know but felt obliged to invite.'

'Yeah. It's been organised by the tennis club committee. They got the caterers in they use for their events.

Kim's still paying but everything has been organised for her. One less thing to worry about. There's always so much to think about when a loved-one dies, even worse when it's not been from natural causes or an accident.' He gave her arm a comforting squeeze, appreciating that the whole affair would be reminding Bella of Hugh's death.

'Mmm, I know.'

A queue of people was edging slowly into the village hall when they arrived. They stood chatting easily together as they inched their way forward. Eventually they made it inside and squeezed their way over to Kim to offer their support, then jostled their way back across the room to make way for the many other people who wished to speak to her. Jammed up against a wall, Fred was sent off on a mission to acquire drinks and food for the three of them. Bella scanned the room - if you didn't know it was a wake you would think it were some kind of fun social gathering. It was as though as soon as the service was over everyone felt that was that, all done and dusted, and they could get on with having a jolly good time. Were they there celebrating Rupert's life or had he been forgotten the moment they walked out of the churchyard? The person who caught her attention was Seb who was still hovering behind Kim in an attentive, almost husbandly, way.

'Mia.' she poked her friend in the side to get her attention, for the noise in the room was rising at an incredible rate. She flapped her hand indicating that she wanted to speak into Mia's ear. 'What's the story with Seb?' she asked.

'What do you mean?' replied Mia warily.

'I don't know, it's just that he's so attentive, like a husband or lover might be.'

349

Mia looked round furtively and, not recognising anyone close to her, she bent her head to whisper to Bella. 'It's common knowledge, but old news now, best not to be resurrected.' Bella looked expectantly. 'Before Rupert came on the scene Seb and Kim had been together for several years; they were engaged and were due to get married. Rupert came along, swept her off her feet and before we knew it they were getting married. Seb was devastated - Kim was, and I suspect still is, the love of his life - he's not had a relationship since. He was also furious - he was convinced that Rupert was doing it to spite him or seeing it as some sort of challenge. Most of us agreed with Seb, because as soon as Kim and Rupert were married it seemed as though Rupert was bored and ready for a new challenge. Obviously none of us knew what went on behind closed doors. Kim kept painting a rosy view of their marriage for a long time and maybe it had been good in the beginning - it's not for me, or anyone else, to say otherwise. Personally, I think Kim and Seb were a perfect match.'

Bella's eyes were virtually out on stalks at this nugget of information. What if Seb had finally decided to get his revenge? What if he were so obsessed with Kim that he'd do anything to get her back? Surely this was a motive for murder?

'Now don't go bringing this all up,' warned Mia knowing full well the look on Bella's face, 'It's ancient history.'

'But it could be relevant?'

'Bella, I don't want to fall out with you over this. Seb would never in a million years hurt anyone. So just leave it, okay?'

Before Bella could reply, Fred turned up balancing three drinks and three plates of food on a tray, it was a miracle that he'd been able to get through the sea of people. Following closely behind him was Jennifer.

'Hi. Bit of a squeeze isn't it?' she said.

Bella noticed her white pinched face was covered in red blotches, and her nose was red and swollen from crying. She was clutching a glass of champagne for support.

'You seen the others?' bellowed Mia over the noise.

'Yeah, Jack and Cressa are busy having an argument in the lobby. Ariadne and Kit are holding court on the other side of the room. Seb's over with Kim. Harry and Sophie were following me but it looks like they've got caught up with someone, and I've not seen Florence since the service.'

'I think she's gone home. I asked her if she wanted to walk over with me but she ran off like a frightened rabbit.'

'Strange. Oh well, perhaps she felt intimidated, she's quite shy and I guess she doesn't really know anyone here apart from us. I'll give her a call later.'

They chatted for a while, eventually the hall began to thin out. Walking as though she were doing the red carpet, Ariadne, followed by Kit, ambled towards them and arrived with a flourish and the heavy scent of exotic, oriental perfume. She kissed everyone, including Bella, called them all "darling" and acted as though this were a reunion after many years apart. Taking centre stage as usual, Bella observed, wondering how much of it was an act and how much of it was who she really was. Watching Bella watching Ariadne, was Kit, who slid over to be beside her and whispered a lazy "hi" in a slightly dubious American accent. Bella smiled politely.

'It's good to see you again,' he murmured. Bella's heart fluttered, and she told herself not to be so ridiculous.

'You too,' she replied in a slightly strangled voice. 'So sad about Rupert.' She was sure she saw a flicker of something in his eyes.

'It's always sad when someone dies,' he replied in a hard voice.

'Yes, but to be murdered. Not nice at all.'

Kit shifted from one foot to another, seeming uncomfortable with the direction of the conversation.

'Did you know him well?' asked Bella feigning forgetfulness, as Kit had supposedly been introduced to them all as an unknown quantity.

He stared hard at her, his dark brown, almost coal black eyes piercing into her, making her shiver, but not from lust. 'No,' he replied curtly. He turned and went back to Ariadne, slipping his arm around her microscopic waist and switching his lazy smile back on. Bella was left standing slightly bewildered. Why so hostile? If he hadn't known Rupert, what was the problem? Her gut instinct was telling her that he wasn't telling the truth - somehow, somewhere, he and Rupert had met before and it was blatantly obvious that he didn't want anyone to know.

Unbeknown to Bella, Harry had caught the conversation. He smiled at her and raised his eyebrows, she felt slightly better and moved over to chat to him. A little while later she became aware that Kim, her parents and Seb were hovering near the door, everyone else had gone. Bella murmured a few more words of condolence and decided to slip away, leaving the cohort of friends together with Kim

# Chapter Eight

Bella changed out of her funereal outfit and into a pair of beige linen trousers with an elasticated waist along with a loose-fitting linen top in a slightly darker shade of beige. She poured herself a glass of chilled sparkling mineral water, straight from the fridge, and wandered out into the garden, strolling round, contemplating the flowers in full bloom, a gorgeous splash of colour, her mind still whirring in the background, mulling over and over earlier conversations. Should she tell the police? Was it all speculation and gossip? Did her suspicions about Kit have any foundation?

Like a light bulb going on, she realised she could find out more about him on the internet. Surely a well known agent, with exceedingly famous clients, would come up in a search? It would be hard to believe that in this day and age of 2006 with the internet booming, that he would not have a media presence of some kind. She hurried inside, grabbed her laptop - yet another technological growth area, Bella had read, and being one of the lucky 67% to own a laptop - from the kitchen table and took it outside. She drummed her fingers impatiently, as the computer started itself up, irritated that it seemed to take so long. Finally she typed in her password, logged on and started the search.

First hit was his agency website, which had the usual self-appreciating guff meant to fool everyone into thinking what an amazing agency he owned and ran. She then spent the next two hours typing in his name in different configurations, then trawling through whatever came up, which ranged from glowing reports from appreciative starlets, to backstabbing and bitching from those who had either been dumped, or never been taken on in the first place by his agency, or rivals. She was beginning to get frustrated that nothing distinctly personal about him was coming up. There seemed to be nothing about his past prior to becoming an agent, other than the rosy picture which was painted in interviews or press releases. There was no real information about his family, childhood, adolescence, what he did before becoming an agent, nothing that could indicate a link between him and Rupert. She'd managed to ascertain that he was two years younger than Rupert, but that was it.

Sighing heavily, she decided to make a sandwich as it was now mid afternoon and she'd barely eaten anything since breakfast, a few nibbles at the wake and that was all. She took the butter out of the fridge, and just as she was about to sink the knife into it- thought better of it - a few calories she could do without. Instead she chopped up some cucumber and tomato, ground some pepper over it and looked at the calorie-light sandwich unenthusiastically. But at least it was food. She took it outside and munched on it thoughtfully. The sun was trying hard to break through the dark gloomy sky, rather like someone constantly switching a light on and off.

One last go, she decided as the food gave her a bit more energy with which to concentrate. Her hands hovered over the keyboard as she waited for inspiration to come, as to what to type into the search engine. Eventually she typed in "Kit Kerr gap year work". Bingo, she thought, as new information popped up. Quickly she clicked on the link and waited to see what would appear. A flashy website for a well respected vineyard in Australia popped up. Hmm, wonder what the connection is, she mused, clicking on link after link, in the hope that it would bring some morsel of information up. Maybe he'd just bought some wine from there and because he was well known it came up? She felt a twinge of disappointment, but clicked on the "Our Beginnings" section. Up popped a blurb about how the vineyard had been started thirty years ago. The owners had scraped together enough money to buy the vineyard and replanted and nurtured it for ten years, before it had started to flourish and make money. These days the grapes were picked by machine or by hand, depending upon the grape variety and which wine it was to be made into, but twenty years ago all the grapes were picked by hand. People backpacking around Australia contacted them for work and would spend the harvest season crammed into basic accommodation, with meals and a small amount of money paid, in exchange for long days spent toiling in the vineyards. Along with the information were ancient photographs of the backpackers and the owners, from the first year they'd introduced the scheme. Bella peered intently at the photographs, one by one, excitement rising in her, convinced that she would find what she was looking for. She stopped at one. Could that be him? She peered closer - she was sure it was him. Twenty years younger, but those eyes looked distinctly familiar. She saved it to a file and hurried inside to print it off, enlarging it before she did so.

The sun was now fully out, making the light perfect for looking at the rather grainy picture. Yes, she was convinced it was him. She buzzed with excitement, then very carefully studied each and every person in the picture again, peering at them closely, trying to take into account the fact that it was taken twenty years ago. There at the opposite end of the row to Kit, was a young man she was convinced was Rupert. It had to be. That had to be the connection. But if they knew each other twenty years ago, why would they deny knowing one another?

A memory flashed into her mind as she suddenly remembered the look on Rupert's face when Kit had arrived. He'd gone deathly pale, not the face of someone seeing a long lost friend from the past. What had gone on? And who would know now? She could tackle Kit, but had a feeling he would stonewall her. Kim? Not the right time to be asking questions about Rupert's past. Mia? Maybe she would know but Bella was doubtful. If something had gone on, which neither Rupert nor Kit wanted anyone to know about, then it was doubtful they had told anyone.

Jennifer? Maybe in his scheme to bed her, he had told her things he'd told no one else in order to get her to trust him? A possibility, but a dubious one. Bella resisted every urge within her to go straight round to Jennifer's house, now was not the time. Jennifer was upset from the funeral, and asking probing questions about Rupert's past would not result in any answers. Tomorrow would have to do.

Restraining herself until 10am the next day, Bella hurried up the lane to Jennifer's house, printed out copy of the photograph tucked safely in her pocket. She rapped loudly on the door and waited. Silence. She rapped again. Just when she was about to give up, the door opened and a miserable looking Jennifer stared back at her.

'Oh, hi,' she said unenthusiastically.

'Hi Jennifer, how are you?'

She shrugged. 'Okay I suppose. Do you want to come in?'

Bella could tell from the way she asked that it was politeness, rather than desire, which had prompted the question. Still she was keen for answers, and responded with an affirmative. Jennifer led the way through to the kitchen which was looking unkempt; unwashed crockery and detritus piled up in the sink waiting to be cleaned, dirty work surfaces covered in crumbs and debris.

'S'pose I ought to tidy up,' she commented lethargically. 'Can't seem to muster up the enthusiasm.'

'Well, it's understandable, you're still upset about Rupert's death, and with his funeral only being yesterday, it's hardly surprising,' soothed Bella.

'Guess so. Silly really, but somehow I feel guilty.'

'Guilty?'

'Yeah. As though I denied Rupert his dying wish. Ridiculous I know, and completely illogical, but that's how I feel, and maybe if I had slept with him he wouldn't have been driving down that road and he'd still be alive.' She poked a few dishes in the sink and turned away from them, there were still a couple of clean mugs, they'd do.

'Unlikely. Would it have made any difference if you'd known he was going to die?'

'Probably not,' she sighed, 'just one of those irrational things. I'll get over it.'

Eager to keep the subject on Rupert, Bella tried to subtly turn the conversation to his past. 'How well did you know Rupert?'

'About as well as anyone I suppose. Why?'

'Oh, er, just curious really. I noticed his family wasn't there yesterday? Mia said they'd had a falling out about thirty years ago, didn't know why. Do you?' she asked hopefully.

'No idea. Not something he talked about. Don't even know if Kim knows. She tried to persuade him to ask them to their wedding but he went ballistic apparently. Why the interest?'

She hesitated. Be honest or not, she dithered. 'Curiosity, I suppose. I got the impression that Kit knew Rupert.'

'Don't think so. I believe that Saturday was the first time any of us had met Kit.'

'Hmm. It's strange that's all. When I chatted to Kit about Rupert at the funeral, he went all peculiar on me, clammed up and walked off to speak to someone else. Like there was something to hide. Also, I noticed, though it may have been a coincidence, that Rupert paled dramatically when Kit arrived on that Saturday.'

'I think you're probably reading too much into it. I'm sure if Rupert knew Kit, then Kim would know about it, and would have said so.' She looked at Bella, her interest roused. 'Was there anything else that made you think that?'

Bella didn't want Jennifer to think that she was a snoop, and shifted uncomfortably, but she felt that Jennifer might at least be able to give an opinion as to whether, or not, it was Kit and Rupert in the picture. She took the picture out of her pocket. 'I don't want you to think that I always go nosing around in other people's business, but there was something about Kit yesterday, something almost sinister it sent a chill through me, so I did a bit of research on the internet. I found this picture, I'm sure that it's Kit. Here, have a look. What do you think?'

Jennifer peered at the photo. 'Well,' she paused, 'I suppose it could be him, but it could be anyone. I've only met him twice, and if this was taken twenty years ago when you suspect Kit and Rupert first met, he will have changed a lot.'

'Hmm. Have a look at the others. Is there anyone else there that looks familiar?'

Jennifer studied it closely. One by one, she looked at each person. Suddenly she frowned and pursed her lips. 'I…' she hesitated. 'It …' she looked up at Bella, who was holding her breath in anticipation. Could she really have found the connection?

'What is it?' Bella didn't want to put words in to Jennifer's mouth.

'This person,' she pointed, 'looks a bit like Rupert. I mean, again I didn't know him twenty years ago but this person seems to have his features; thinner, yes, but I'm sure it's him.'

'I thought so too, but I only met him once,' Bella replied excitedly.

'So if they did know each other why the big secret?' Jennifer echoed Bella's very thoughts.

'What happened so long ago that made them both be economical with the truth? And if they could be deceitful about that, could Kit lie about where he was when Rupert died?'

Jennifer gasped and clutched her throat. 'You don't think…'

Bella shrugged. 'I don't know, but why be so shifty? Do you know where he says he was, when Rupert died?'

'Um. I think Sophie said something about him having gone out for cigarettes.'

'So it's possible. Did he get any?'

'Cigarettes? I don't know. Sophie might. I'll give her a call.' She picked up the phone and asked Sophie, who must have been wondering why she was being asked such a peculiar question. Jennifer put the phone down, her eyes sparkling. 'Sophie says that she remembers he didn't get any because Ariadne had a bit of a strop about it as she'd run out and was desperate. She remembers that he was a bit distracted when he returned, snapped at Ariadne, telling her she could go and get them herself if she were that desperate, and stomped off to his room, from where he did not reappear until the next morning. Ariadne had to go out and buy some. She was in a foul mood and livid with Kit. Ariadne went out at about 10.20pm, about ten minutes after Kit got back, and she returned at 10.35pm. Sophie's sure about the time, because she was shattered after the party and just wanted to go to bed but felt obligated to stay up until Ariadne got back.'

'So, he could have done it. The timings fit,' said Bella excitedly.

'Yes. But I think we might be rather getting ahead of ourselves and jumping to conclusions, don't you?' She asked rhetorically.

'True, but you have to agree that it's a bit suss.'

Jennifer nodded, and they lapsed into a thoughtful silence. Bella's mind was whirring as she tried to decide what to do next. It was Jennifer who broke the silence. 'I can't really see any way of finding out more. I mean, I suppose we could ask Kim, but I'm sure she would have said she knew him if they'd met before, or if Rupert had told her about him.'

'Yeah. I couldn't find anything else particularly relevant about Kit on the internet, so I guess there's no point searching again. Do you think I should tell the police?'

'Tell them what though? It's pretty circumstantial, don't think they'd take you seriously.'

'Maybe not.' she paused. 'Only thing is that the Inspector who is heading up the case, trained with my late husband. I hadn't seen him since he moved to Kent fifteen years ago, but we knew each other quite well before then. I think he'd listen to me, and maybe look into it, even if he thinks it's not relevant.'

'I suppose you could tell him, though I'm reluctant to have the police digging around in something which may be irrelevant, and might just resurrect things from the past which should be left well alone.'

'Suppose…'

Jennifer sighed deeply. 'But if it were my husband who'd been killed, I'd do anything to try and find out who did it but I really don't want Kim upset any more than she already has been.'

'I can see that, but it's a bit late for that. Rupert's dead.'

'Mmm. I think perhaps I, or we, should speak to Kim first, tell her what we think we've discovered. She might look at the photo and say it's absolutely not Rupert, and produce a picture of him when he was that age to disprove our theory.'

'Okay. Sounds like a plan. At least then she will be aware of what's going on, and not think that we're sneaking around behind her back. Even though I barely know her I would hate to upset her, or anyone for that matter. I'm not doing this because I enjoy digging around in other people's lives and being nosey. I guess with what I experienced with my husband it has struck a chord and I know how desperately I wanted the culprit found and brought to justice and would like the same for Kim.'

'I didn't think you were. If you're a really good friend of Mia's, then I couldn't imagine her having a friend who was a meddling busybody. And I am really sorry about your husband.'

'Thanks. Kit acting so strangely seems to have triggered something in me,' she paused, still reticent about divulging too much about her past. 'So you know that my husband died two years ago. He was killed by a drink driver. It helped me a great deal to know who was driving that car, and that justice was done. It would have been so much worse for me if that person had never been caught. I would have looked at everyone as though they were the one responsible, and would have wondered if he or she had done it before - done it again - made other people suffer the way I had suffered. I feel I can empathise in some way with Kim given the way Rupert died.'

'It must have been so painful for you,' replied Jennifer softly. Bella nodded and tried to hold back the tears which were pricking at her eyes. 'I think I can understand why you want to find out what Kit is hiding. It may be perfectly innocent but, combined with the fact that he came back without cigarettes, it does seem a little suspicious.'

'Shall we go to Kim's now?'

'Not sure. Bit soon after the funeral.'

'Hmm, true.'

'Still, if we're barking up the wrong tree, I'm sure she'll understand, and if we're not then the police can look into it and tell us that we've got over-active imaginations when they find nothing. I'll give her a call first, see how she is.'

Kim was apparently holding up well and, intrigued by Jennifer's mysterious phone call, invited her and Bella to pop round.

Fifteen minutes later, having driven together in Jennifer's VW Beetle, they pulled up in front of the magnificent house. Bella was bowled over by its beauty, she was always rather in awe of anyone who lived in such a huge house. She tried not to gawp as Kim ushered them through to the sitting room, where she had already prepared a pot of coffee for the three of them. Considering she had buried her husband the previous day, she looked remarkably well. Her skin seemed to glow more than it had done at the lunch party, and there was a slight air of confidence about her which Bella had not noticed before.

Jennifer explained, to an intrigued Kim, what Bella had discovered, and handed her the photograph. She and Bella held their breath as the minutes ticked by, Kim studying it intently. Silently she rose and walked to a bureau at the back of the sitting room. She rustled around for a moment or two and fished something out. She sat back down and studied the photograph again.

'I'm sure it's Rupert. Not so sure about Kit, as the first time I'd met him was at the party, but it does kind of look like him. Here, have a look at this.' She offered them an old photograph of Rupert. 'That was taken about fifteen years ago I think, you can see the similarities.'

Sure enough there was Rupert looking remarkably similar to the man in the photograph Bella had printed off. She felt a frisson of excitement.

'He must have recognised Kit,' said Kim. 'If they were working on a vineyard together for several weeks, I find it hard to believe that he wouldn't have. But I have no idea who Kit really is. I mean I know who he is now, Ariadne's agent/friend/lover, whatever he is, but nothing about his past. Tell you what, I'll give Ariadne a call and ask a few subtle questions, maybe she knows if there is a connection.' Kim disappeared off in the direction of the study, Bella and Jennifer could hear the muted tones of her voice drifting through the open door.

'Does Kim know that Rupert came round to your house shortly before he died?' asked Bella.

Jennifer shook her head and chewed on her bottom lip.

'Do you think you should tell her? You've told the police and it may well come up at some point when they're talking to Kim.'

'I was kind of hoping that if I buried my head in the sand it might go away and I wouldn't have to tell her. After all, it's not going to achieve anything, it'll probably just upset her further.'

'Tricky. But would it be better coming from you or the police?'

'Since you put it like that, I suppose I have no choice,' she replied reluctantly.

At that moment Kim hurried back into the room. 'No luck I'm afraid, she doesn't know anything. She was starting to get suspicious so I changed the subject.'

'What would you like us to do then Kim?' asked Bella.

'It's a bit of a mystery, but I can't believe that it has any bearing on Rupert's death,' she paused as her mind ticked through the options. 'I suppose, as long as the police are discreet in their enquiries, then it would do no harm. I don't want to go upsetting Ariadne, but if Kit has nothing to hide then even if he found out it shouldn't be a problem.

'You sure?'

Kim nodded.

'Okay, I'll give Inspector Ormandy a call when I get home. He's a good man, he'll be tactful.'

They spent a while chatting, Kim seeming quite animated, though rather overwhelmed by the amount of paperwork there was to sort out. There were Rupert's businesses to decide what to do with and his personal finances. She was seeing Rupert's solicitor that afternoon about the will, and was hopeful that he would give her some guidance as to how to proceed. Surprisingly, Kim was keen to arrange a game of tennis as she was eager to get some "fresh air and exercise" as she put it. A date for Friday of that week was arranged, Jennifer offering to contact Cressa, Mia, Sophie and Florence, the venue being Kim's own tennis court, rather than up at the club where she would have to deal with other people's sympathy towards her. Jennifer couldn't bring herself to tell Kim about seeing Rupert before he died, justifying not doing so by reassuring herself that it was too soon after the funeral to break such news to her.

The next day Bella picked Mia up and they went off for the morning to the small town of Cranbrook. Mia berated Bella all the way about digging around in other people's business, but eventually conceded that actually Bella had done the right thing. She was concerned that this crusade to find Rupert's killer had too much to do with Hugh's death, that Bella was having trouble re-building her life. Despite Bella's reassurances that this was not the case, she decided to reserve judgement and keep a closer eye on her friend.

They parked the car in the free-of-charge car park and walked down the hill into the pretty little town which, though small, had everything you could possibly need. Several banks/building societies, post office, supermarket, book shop, hardware store, hairdressers, grocer and health food shop, optician, dentists, charity shops, clothes shops, restaurants, travel agents, the list was endless but the beauty of them all was that they seemed to complement one another and that there was a real sense of community, something that was disappearing in the country as each year went by.

Bella had to go to the bank so left Mia basking in the sunshine whilst she popped inside. Bella busied herself at the cash point, obtaining a balance and withdrawing some cash. As she moved to the side in order to place everything into her purse and allow the next person to use the cash-point, she heard a vaguely familiar voice at the counter behind her. She glanced round, it was Cressa, who hadn't seen Bella.

'Look,' she was saying in a fierce, patronising voice to the remarkably patient cashier, 'all I want to do is get a statement from my husband's account. We've banked here for the past twenty years, you know who I am, you know who my husband is, we have our joint account and all I am asking for is a statement from his own account. It's quite simple.'

The cashier patiently reiterated that she would not be able to do that as the account was in Cressa's husbands name, and only his name. Cressa became more and more agitated. Bella tried to slip out through the door unnoticed, feeling awkward, unfortunately Cressa saw her. Bella smiled, blushed deeply and scurried out before Cressa drew her in to her campaign.

'What's up? Machine eat your card?' laughed Mia as she saw a flustered Bella come hurrying out.

'No, thank goodness. It's a bit embarrassing,' she went on to explain what had happened.

'I despair with those two. They have always seemed like such a solid couple, but all they do is bicker now. I don't know what's going on but Cressa hasn't been a happy bunny for a while.'

'Should we wait for her?'

'No. She could be a while. If Cressa wants something she will do virtually anything to get it, so that poor cashier might be there for a while, in fact, Cressa has probably asked to see the manager by now. Come on let's go and get a cup of coffee.'

They wandered down the High Street and round into Stone Street, reaching a small Italian delicatessen situated in a very old, beamed building. They walked in past the delectable range of fresh pasta, meats and cheeses and up the steps to the few small tables, which were partially occupied, the ones outside being fully occupied, and sat down at the remaining available table by the window, affording Bella a good view up and down the street.

It was while they were sipping their drinks, Bella a cappuccino and Mia a latte – and very good it was too – that Mia saw Cressa stride by. Catching sight of them out of the corner of her eye, Cressa diverted briskly into the deli and marched up to them.

'Cressa! How are you?' ventured Mia as Cressa pulled up a chair to join them. She barked her order for a cappuccino and sat down heavily on the chair.

'Furious! That's how I am! Absolutely furious!'

'Oh dear. Why's that?' Mia had a sinking feeling, once Cressa was in a foul mood and ranting there was no stopping her.

'That bloody bank! I've banked there for twenty years and they won't even do me a simple favour!' She ranted and raved for five minutes with both Bella and Mia doing their utmost to make soothing noises.

'Surely Jack can get his own statement can't he? Or he can look at it online?' asked Mia bravely.

'Pah! It's not for him. It's for me.'

Mia frowned. 'But why do you need to see his bank account?'

Suddenly to their dismay Cressa's face crumpled and big fat tears rolled down her face.

'Cressa! What's wrong?' asked Mia. Cressa continued to sob. Bella ordered more coffee for the three of them, not sure what else to do as she was not well acquainted with Cressa.

'It's Jack,' she sniffed, 'he's gone all secretive on me. I used to do all our banking, I could access everything online, Jack left everything to me. Then one day he changed his password and I've not been able to access his account since.'

'Have you talked to him about this?'

Cressa nodded. 'Yes, but all he does is get tetchy. Ever since then we've been arguing. I think,' she blew her nose loudly, 'I think he's having an affair.' She looked beseechingly at them.

'An affair? Jack?' Mia looked incredulous. Of all the people she knew he was one of the least likely candidates to have an affair she felt. 'No, I don't believe it. He wouldn't do that. Just because he wants a bit of privacy over his account doesn't mean he's having an affair.'

She sniffed some more. 'I think he's paying me back.'

'Paying you back? What on earth for?' Mia was completely confused by now.

Cressa looked miserably at them. 'For what I did,' she replied in a hoarse whisper. Bella and Mia waited silently. 'I …' she gulped, 'I had a brief affair, in fact not even an affair, a stupid, stupid fling.'

Mia's jaw dropped in astonishment. Cressa? An affair? Surely not?

'You're disgusted by me aren't you? I can't say I blame you, I hate myself.'

Bella was wishing she were anywhere else but there. This was way too personal for her to be hearing. It was absolutely none of her business.

'When? Who? Why?' stuttered Mia.

'Eight years ago.'

'Eight years ago? That was such a long time ago. I can't believe Jack would wait until now to get his revenge, he's just not like that.'

'I thought we'd got over it, we were having a rough patch, as any marriage does, and Jack was away on business a lot and not talking to me, not really, not about what mattered - our marriage. I made a stupid mistake, had a fling for two weeks when he was away. Realised as soon as I saw him what an idiot I had been, regretted it ever since. I had to tell him, we'd never had any secrets, nor have we since until now. He went mad, he was so angry and hurt it was awful.' she shook her head in shame at the memories. 'I've always loved him, never stopped, I was so, so stupid.'

'But you've moved on since then. He forgave you didn't he?'

'Yes. It took a long time but he did, and I thought our marriage was stronger than ever, that's why I'm so confused and normally we talk about everything. I don't know what to do.'

'Who was it?'

'Who was what?'

'Who did you have a fling with?'

'It doesn't matter now.'

'I suppose not. Did you tell Jack who it was?'

She nodded, then blurted out. 'It was Rupert.'

'Rupert!' exclaimed Mia and Bella in unison.

'Oh Cressa! How could you? Of all the people!'

Of all the people, what, thought Bella. I'm definitely missing something here.

'I know, I know, you don't have to reprimand me.'

'I'm surprised he didn't go and thump Rupert.'

'I think he went round and had a good old shout at him. Thank goodness Rupert, for once, had some sense and didn't laugh at him, otherwise I think Jack would've killed him.  Oh, no, I didn't mean that!' she flustered realising what she'd just said.  'He wouldn't, he didn't.'

He wouldn't wait eight years, thought Bella, he would have done it there and then, unless he was the type of man who brooded on something and preferred his revenge "served cold".  But what was Cressa scared of?

'Of course not,' soothed Mia.

'It's just...' she broke down sobbing again.  Bella and Mia looked at one another, mystified.

'Just what?' whispered Mia.

'It's just ... Just ... I'm so scared,' she whispered.

'Scared?'

'The night Rupert died Jack went out just before 10pm and came back about five minutes later.  The accident happened just down the road from us.  What if...' she looked at them, terrified.

'He wouldn't have, trust him Cressa, you know him.'

'I know, but he's been acting so weird.'

'Have you told the police?' asked Bella.

She shook her head.  'No, I said he was at home all night,' she replied fiercely.

'Um,' Bella was trying to think of a sensitive way of phrasing it, 'he might have seen something which could be relevant.  Could be important?  You can't not tell them.  It could be the difference between finding Rupert's killer and not.'

Mia shot Bella a fierce look to shut her up.  Now was definitely not the time.

'Maybe.  But I'd do anything to protect Jack.'

Mia suddenly had an idea.  'Did Jack's car have a dent, a scrape, or anything on it?  I'm sure that whoever ran Ru-

371

pert off the road must have some sort of damage to their car.'

'No!' relief flooded over Cressa's face. 'Not a scratch, neither of us has on either of our cars. The police came and checked them over when they came to talk to us. Mia, you're brilliant. I've been worrying all this time  Thank you. Thank you!'

'My pleasure.' Phew, thank goodness that disaster has been averted, thought Mia.

Meanwhile Bella was mentally crossing Jack and Cressa off her suspect list.

A little later, after Cressa had fully cheered up, they waved her off and ambled back up the High Street to Bella's car, popping into a variety of shops on the way.

'So,' started Bella, 'what did you mean by "of all people"?'

'Hmm? Don't know what you're talking about?' replied Mia distractedly, as she glanced in the window of the well equipped cook shop.

'You know. About Rupert? About Cressa having a fling with him?'

'Oh, don't start Bella, it's not relevant.' She was becoming exasperated by all Bella's questions and her current obsession with behaving like a sleuth in an Agatha Christie novel.

'Don't be so tetchy! It's obvious that, whatever "it" is, it's public knowledge, it's just that I don't know!'

'Oh all right, but don't go blabbing about it, it'll just drag up unpleasant memories for some people. I don't know the full details, I never asked, but basically about ten years ago Jack and Rupert went into some kind of business deal together. Now, I don't know what happened, but Jack later pulled out, and a few months after that Rupert made a killing from the deal. Only problem was that none of the profits went to Jack. Jack claimed he was ripped off by Rupert, but there was no hard evidence so he couldn't take him to court. Rupert had stuck to the law – only just – but there was no doubt he knew that the deal, which was turning sour, had the potential to more than reverse itself. Trouble is he didn't tell Jack, and Jack needed to make sure he got his money back as he was committed to paying school fees.'

'Somehow that doesn't surprise me, Rupert doing something like that. I wonder how many other people he treated like that?'

'Yeah well, best keep those thoughts to yourself eh Bella?'

'Don't worry, I shan't say a word.'

# Chapter Nine

The thunderstorms during the night had cleared the mugginess from the air and the day felt fresh and bright with a warm sun and beautiful blue sky. Bella picked through her resolutely dull and dowdy selection of clothes, which definitely needed a transformation, attempting to find something suitable to wear for tennis. It had been several years since she'd last played – she and Hugh had played tennis a lot together – and though she'd tried to squeeze into her old size 8 tennis dress she hadn't even managed to get it down over her arms. Feeling gloomy, she reluctantly settled on a pair of navy Bermuda shorts and a pale pink polo shirt. Not, she felt, particularly appropriate for a game of tennis, she was sure the rest of them would be kitted out in their perfect white tennis apparel. On the upside, at least her feet hadn't swelled like the rest of her, and she could get them into her trainers.

In the kitchen she carefully wiped down her rather dusty tennis racket and munched on a banana to give her an energy boost. Whilst she was looking forward to an afternoon of exercise and fun with a group of nice people, she was worried that her rusty tennis skills and lack of fitness would spoil it for the others.

Bella shut the house up, and saw Jennifer drive past in her blue VW Beetle as she was locking the front door. She waved, but Jennifer didn't see her. Climbing into her own VW Golf, she followed in Jennifer's wake. Unlike the lunch party when everyone arrived in dribs and drabs, all the girls turned up virtually simultaneously. A bright cheery, chattery group was assembled in Kim's drive.

Kim greeted them from the front door and they wandered over having retrieved rackets and balls out of their respective cars. She ushered them through to the kitchen, where a copious quantity of cold drinks awaited them.

'We'll go out onto the terrace,' said Kim. She touched Bella on the arm and indicated for her to wait back. When they were alone Kim spoke. 'Have you heard anything?'

'No, sorry. I haven't spoken to Dave, I mean Inspector Ormandy, since I told him what we'd found out. I'm sure as soon as there is anything to tell he'll let you know, and don't worry, I did emphasise how sensitive this was.'

'Thanks.'

To Bella, Kim didn't seem as bright as she had the other day. The dark circles had returned under her eyes and these were accompanied by hefty bags. Still, it was only to be expected she reasoned. 'You okay?' she offered.

Kim smiled tightly. 'Fine. Thanks. Let's join the others shall we?'

'Florence not coming?' asked Cressa as they rejoined the group.

'No. She had to go into work or something, which is a shame. She doesn't normally work on a Friday, which is why I arranged it for today.'

'What does she do?' asked Bella.

'She's a nurse at a local doctor's surgery. Only works four days a week though, which is why she's been able to play so much tennis with us,' replied Jennifer.

Cressa was busy planning the rota of play, so that all six of them would have a good game on the single court. She organised everyone into pairs, and the tennis started. Those not playing were quite happy to sit back and bask in the sunshine, chat and watch the others running around exerting themselves on the court. Bella was paired with Mia, which was a relief as she'd played with her before. After three hours all of them were hot, sweaty and tired, but the endorphins seemed to have kicked into all of them, so it was an even happier group who sat in the shade of two large cream canvas umbrellas and sipped on Kim's home-made lemonade.

'That was great, thanks for asking me, hope I didn't slow you down too much?' said Bella. She was surprised at how quickly she'd got back into the swing of things, helped by the fact that there was only one court and time was therefore limited for each game.

'Not at all! In fact, I think it's just as well we stopped or you might have wiped the floor with us!' replied Sophie who was thoroughly enjoying an afternoon without having to worry about Jemima, much as she loved her, as Harry was at home looking after her.

'D'you manage to get everything sorted out that you wanted to at Rupert's solicitors the other day?' enquired Jennifer.

Kim looked miserable. 'I don't know.'

'Don't know? Did you not get to see him?'

'I did, but ...' her voice trailed off. The others stopped chatting.

'What's wrong Kim?' pressed Sophie.

'It's just weird. I still can't believe it.' The others glanced nervously at one other, wondering what on earth Rupert had done this time?

'He hasn't gone and done something stupid has he Kim?' continued Sophie, 'I mean, he has left you everything hasn't he? He hasn't left it all to a cats home or something?'

'No. Nothing like that. There's more than enough money. More than I thought actually, and the house is 100% mine, but I don't know what's going to happen to the business.'

'The business? What do you mean?' Rupert had spent the last ten years building up a reputable wine business. He had converted an oast house into offices and a shop, which was situated midway between the house and the village, in addition he'd had many fingers in many pies, with different subsidiary companies dealing with different aspects of his mini empire.

'The will states that 50% of his business assets i.e. excluding his personal effects, share of our house and savings etc, be bequeathed to a Charlotte Willingham.'

'Who?' they chorused.

'I don't know. That's the weird thing, I have no idea who she is, or what she meant to Rupert. His solicitor doesn't know, or is not allowed to tell me. The only thing he would say, was that she was a beneficiary of his will before he married me, and obviously remained in it after our marriage even though we both re-did our wills.'

'And you have absolutely no idea who this Charlotte person is?' asked Cressa.

Kim shook her head. 'No idea at all. It's confusing. I mean, why didn't he tell me about her? I wouldn't have objected if there was a good reason. I'm more than well provided for. I don't truly know about all the ins and outs of his business dealings, and am not that interested in any of them, other than the wine business. I really don't want to lose that, so until Rupert's accountant and solicitor can work out the value of the companies, I won't know if, after any taxation implications, the value of my share of the other companies will provide me with enough to buy out her share of the wine business - assuming she is willing to agree to that. I've got no idea if she would be happy to settle for cash, or want to sell any of the businesses or want to be involved or anything. If Rupert had left me 51% then I would have had the majority share and therefore have more control and say over how, and in what form, the business assets are distributed.'

'She isn't a member of his family is she? A long-lost sister, or cousin or anything?' suggested Mia.

'Nope. I know the names of all his family. I might never have met them, but at least he told me their names, as far as I know, though now I am beginning to have doubts.'

'Perhaps it would be worth contacting them? Maybe they might be able to shed some light?' offered Sophie.

'It's possible, but they don't even know who I am. Rupert and his family had not had contact for thirty years.'

'So they don't know he's dead?'

Kim shook her head. 'I have asked his solicitor to track them down and inform them. I thought about doing it myself, but I have no idea why they've not had any contact, and I could be getting involved in some sort of horrific situation, and I've got enough to deal with at the moment anyway. It'll be a shock for them, but maybe they think he's been dead for years, I don't know? I can't get my head round the fact that they've had absolutely no contact with their son since he was fifteen. I did manage to prise out of Rupert that he hadn't run away from home and therefore they've not spent the past thirty years wondering where their little boy is. I don't suppose I'll ever know why this situation arose, and perhaps it's best this way.'

'Have you thought of hiring a private detective?' suggested Cressa.

'For what? To find his family, or find out who this Charlotte person is?'

'I was thinking about Charlotte Willingham, but I guess you could do the same for his family too if you wanted to?'

'Hmm, all sounds a bit over the top and I am hoping my solicitor will be able to come up with something and deal with the matter and leave me well out of it. What do the rest of you think?' Kim looked around at them.

'Difficult really. I suppose you could,' replied Mia.

'Or you may get to meet this Charlotte person when the solicitor has tracked her down?' added Sophie.

'Not sure if there's any point finding more out about his family. It's not going to change anything now, unless there's something you're desperate to find out about Rupert, and will always wonder about?' said Jennifer.

Kim gave a big sigh. 'I don't know. Sometimes I think my head is going to explode there is so much to think about and sort out.' she rubbed her temples, trying to tease away the tension which was building up. 'What do you think Bella?'

Bella was surprised to be asked. As a newcomer to the group she felt hesitant about giving an opinion as she felt sure she had already over-stepped the mark with her ferreting around for information. 'I'm not sure,' she replied diplomatically, 'why don't you go with your gut feeling? That's usually a pretty good sign of what one should do.'

'Right,' said Kim decisively getting up, 'on that basis I've decided that today I've spent enough time thinking about it. I'm going to make a large jug of Pimms. You up for it?' There was a slight hesitation, as they knew how easy it was to down glasses of Pimms, which tasted so innocently like a soft drink, and not realise how imbibed you were becoming. 'Don't worry, I'll make it exceedingly weak, and bring an extra bottle of lemonade out and some nibbles to snack on. Besides, you can't abandon me just yet, it's only 5 o'clock!'

'I'll give you a hand.' offered Sophie, getting up and following her across the terrace to the back door.

The rest of the group lapsed into silence for a little while as they luxuriated in the late afternoon sun. A gentle breeze started to stir in the trees, making their leaves rustle like the grass skirt of a hula dancer.

'Do you think she's okay?' questioned Jennifer. 'She seems so upbeat, all things considered, despite the circumstances.'

'I was thinking the same thing,' added Cressa.

'Should we, or one or two of us, stay d'you think?' suggested Mia.

'Might be an idea. I can't - Henry and Emma are coming home for the weekend. Jack's picking them up from the station at 7 p.m. so I can't stay late,' replied Cressa, referring to her two children who were away at university.

'I can, I've got nothing planned.' volunteered Jennifer.

'Bit tricky for me too,' added Mia. 'Tess is coming to the end of her GCSEs, she's got her last one on Monday. Fred and I are taking her out for dinner and a movie, to try and get her to relax a bit. I've never known a child to work so hard for exams. Usually it seems to be more a case of dragging your child to the desk to revise - from what the other parents are saying - but Tess has been the total opposite.' she spoke proudly of her only child.

'Bella? Don't suppose you could help us out? Why don't you and I offer to take Kim out to dinner? There's a pub in the next village which serves excellent food. We won't get a table in the restaurant it'll be fully booked by now, but we could sit in the garden. Might be chilly later on, but it'll be glorious for a while.'

Bella felt flattered to be asked. 'Sure. I've got nothing on, it'd be nice and a good opportunity to start to discovering some of the local pubs.'

'Right, that's settled then.'

'What's settled?' asked Kim carrying a tray laden down with glasses, and a massive jug of Pimms stuffed full of cucumber, strawberries, mint and an assortment of other fruit.

'That you are coming out to dinner with me and Bella. Time we showed her what the local pubs are made of.'

'Tonight?'

'Yup. You haven't got anything on have you?' It hadn't crossed Jennifer's mind that Kim might have already made arrangements for the evening.

'Oh, er no, it'd be nice to get out of the house. What time?'

381

'Whenever we're ready. Half an hour will be enough for me to jump into the shower and change. I'll pick up Bella, and then come and collect you. At least you two can then have a drink.'

Sophie had been busy playing at being a waitress, pouring glasses of the sweet amber coloured liquid, and handing around the assortment of nibbles, which Kim had produced - baby crostini with an olive tapenade, strips of smoked salmon filled with cream cheese and chives, home-made honey roasted nuts.

Two hours later Bella was hopping out of the shower, frantically trying to get ready within half an hour - she had fifteen minutes left until Jennifer picked her up - and she still needed to dry her hair, do her make-up and get dressed. With the former and the latter completed she gave up on the idea of make up as Jennifer knocked on the door. But as a half hearted attempt she whisked a pale rose-pink lipstick across her lips and opened the door.

'Ready?'

'Just about,' she laughed, grabbing her bag and locking up. She still felt an all-over glow from all the exercise, and was convinced that her beige linen shift dress felt looser than it had done the previous week when she'd worn it. 'You look nice,' she commented to Jennifer, admiring the pastel coloured patterned dress, which accentuated every curve in her body. Bella felt a twinge of envy, and berated herself for it. Soon enough she would be back in shape she convinced herself, and she would treat herself to a brand new - non dowdy - wardrobe. She slipped into Jennifer's car beside her, and chatted lightly about nothing in particular on the way to Kim's house.

'Shall I hop out and get her?' she suggested as Jennifer pulled the car into the drive.

'Thanks.'

Bella hopped out and rang the bell. 'You ready?' she enquired as the door opened.

'Absolutely.' Kim seemed now to be radiating happiness, and Bella was puzzled as to how Kim's mood could change so quickly.

'You seem happier.'

Kim blushed scarlet. 'Oh. Well it's lovely to be going out. Gets a bit lonely, a bit maudlin, sitting in this big house all on my own.'

'I can imagine. So, what's the pub like that we're going to?'

'The Cow and Cart? The food's great, really good. Nothing fancy, but good, home-cooked food. Proper food, none of this haute cuisine stuff. I always think that if you want that kind of food you'll go to a high end restaurant rather than a pub. A pub is for pub food as far as I'm concerned.'

Bella clambered inelegantly into the backseat, feeling a tiny bit claustrophobic sitting in the back, with no direct access to a door. She distracted herself by gazing out at the countryside, as they whizzed down the winding lanes to the pub, which was quite literally in the middle of nowhere. Despite this the car park was packed, and it took some careful negotiating to squeeze the car into a tight spot by a hedge. So tight that Kim had to climb over the driver's seat to get out and Bella exited just as inelegantly as she had entered - she was relieved that there was no one else around to see.

'I'll go and get some drinks while you two go and prowl for a table,' said Kim. With their orders, she hurried off through the low door, which was the main entrance to the 16th century ancient brick, detached building. Bella could see through the low windows that it was packed inside, and most of whom she could see were tucking in to large plate-fuls of food, each table squeezed or manoeuvred round the quirkiness of the wonky shaped rooms, higgledy piggledy walls, low beams and ceilings and large fireplaces, which she could imagine would roar with flames from log fires in the winter.

'It's heaving!' commented Bella, as they walked around the side of the building into the beautifully kept gardens with expansive lawns, borders and trees providing much needed shade during hot, heady, summer days.

'Usually is. They must make an absolute fortune. In winter, when it's too cold to sit outside - though some brave souls do - you have to book a table about two weeks in advance if you want to eat. The bar is always crammed full with drinkers squeezed in like sardines. It's so nice that there is a smoking ban inside, years ago I'd never go into the bar because I'd choke as soon as I entered, but now it's heaven as far as I'm concerned.'

'I'm with you on that, it's made such a difference. Don't mind if people want to smoke, that's their choice, but as a non-smoker I don't want to inhale their smoke.'

All the time she was talking, Jennifer was scanning the packed tables in the garden, like a lion waiting to pounce, she was waiting for her prey to move. She tugged on Bel-la's arm and whispered surreptitiously. 'Over there, they're getting ready to go, let's sidle over.' Jennifer was aware that more people had arrived after them, and that if they didn't move quickly the table would be nabbed from right under their nose, unfortunately, the latest arrivals had seen the opportunity to nab a table too. Jennifer's subtle amble turned into a race to get there first. She weaved through the other tables as elegantly as she could, and got there moments before the others. She smiled politely at the rather startled current occupants. 'I don't want to chase you away, but I thought you looked as though you were about to leave?' she politely enquired.

The rotund, red-faced man laughed a deep booming laugh. 'Don't worry, we are going, it's always a challenge to get a table, looks like you made it in the nick of time!'

By this time, Bella had caught her up and gave what she hoped was a winning smile and thanked them profusely for the table, quickly sitting down as they were getting up so that there could be absolutely no doubt as to the new ownership of the table. Jennifer meanwhile, was smiling politely at the tall lanky male who had rather impolitely pushed past people in order to try to get to the table first. He scowled at her, and his girlfriend laid into him in a high pitched whining voice, complaining at his ineptitude for not getting there first.

Kim arrived with their drinks and the chalk board with that night's menu written on it. 'Fun getting the table, eh?' she whispered, for all in close proximity were now in no doubt as to who had not got the table.

'I feel almost sorry for him having to put up with that,' smirked Jennifer, 'but we were here first, there's no disputing that. Cheers!' she said picking up her glass of beautifully chilled Sauvignon Blanc – her only alcoholic drink of the evening - and chinked glasses with Kim and Bella who had opted to share a large jug of Pimms.

Life seemed good to Bella, basking in the evening sunshine, enjoying the company of new friends, in a beautiful rural setting, which - apart from the general hum of talk radiating from the other tables - was peaceful, no road noise, just the chattering of birds as they prepared to settle down for the evening, and the occasional bee who was out for the last drop of evening nectar. She virtually salivated at the menu, everything on it sounded delicious and the plates which were being brought out to surrounding tables made her tummy rumble in anticipation. She settled on cold poached salmon with salad – apparently the salads would be like none she'd ever come across before – along with baby new potatoes, opting to have a pudding instead of a starter as she knew she would not have room for three courses. Kim also chose the Salmon, and Jennifer chose the homemade haddock fish cakes.

They chatted whilst they waited for their order to arrive, which took some time as it was so busy and the food was all made to order. Kim seemed animated and happy and kept furtively glancing to the side of the building from around which Bella and Jennifer had walked earlier. Suddenly she jumped up.

'Oh look!' she cried. 'There's Seb! What a lovely surprise!' She waved at him and he strolled over.

Bella turned to look. A surprise? She was not so sure. He looked clean and fresh, and his face was bright and shining as he greeted Kim, they cautiously kissed each other on the cheek. He greeted Jennifer and Bella, kissing them both on the cheek too.

'What a lovely surprise!' reiterated Kim. 'Are you meeting someone?'

'No. I just thought I'd pop in for a drink. I saw Jen's car in the car park and thought I'd drop by and say hello.'

'Why don't you join us? We'd love it if you did, wouldn't we?' Kim looked expectantly at the other two, who smiled in agreement.

'Before I do, I'll get a drink. What can I get you?' He hurried off to get the drinks, a mineral water for Jennifer, and another large jug of Pimms for Bella and Kim. Bella couldn't remember the last time she'd drunk so much, and was beginning to feel light headed, particularly as her empty stomach was protesting ferociously for its food. As luck would have it, the food turned up and Bella tucked in as though she'd not eaten for a week. True to what she had been told, the food was excellent and the salads unusual and varied, not the run of the mill lettuce and tomato which was the standard offering in pubs.

Feeling slightly more sober as a result of the food hitting her stomach, Bella observed with interest the interaction between Seb and Kim - they were so easy together, as though they were two pieces of a jigsaw which fitted together perfectly - made for each other. She remembered what Mia had told her about their history together, and wondered how Kim could ever have chosen Rupert over Seb. Still, we all make mistakes, and it was apparent to Bella that Rupert had been Kim's. Bella wondered whether Kim regretted marrying Rupert? Did she regret breaking off her engagement to Seb? Sporadically Bella joined in the conversation, but felt sure that Jennifer was watching Kim and Seb as closely as she was. They seemed so wrapped up in one another and lapsed into periods of appearing not to notice that Jennifer and Bella were still present, only to remember with a jolt and then act cooley towards one another, as though hoping that neither Bella nor Jennifer had noticed how they were interacting. Having polished off a large bowl of creamy, homemade, strawberry ice cream, Bella felt replete, but slightly guilty that she'd eaten so much - so much for her diet!

Eventually at 11.30pm, she and Jennifer managed to get Kim into the car, who was on such a high that if Bella had not seen her with Seb she would have been convinced that Kim was popping mode enhancing pills or on the edge of some dreadful breakdown - the high before the plummeting low. They dropped Kim off, and she cheerily waved to them as she went inside. For a few minutes Bella and Jennifer sat in silence as they drove towards the village.

'Did you notice?' asked Jennifer.

'What?' Bella answered cautiously.

'Seb and Kim.'

'Yeah. You couldn't help but notice. Do you think Kim arranged to meet him at the pub? When we first suggested going out, she looked slightly disappointed. Do you think she had already arranged to see Seb?'

'Hmm, I wondered that. Bit quick after Rupert though.'

Bella remained tight lipped about what Mia had told her regarding Kim preparing to leave Rupert, sure that it was not generally known within the group, and she was not going to be the one to break a confidence. Instead she said 'Maybe they're just friends? They've known each other for years, he could be comforting her through this very difficult time.'

'Possibly. Not convinced though.'

Fortunately, they had just pulled up outside Bella's cottage and she felt relieved that she wouldn't feel obliged to be drawn into further discussions on the subject of Kim and Seb any further. 'Thanks ever so much for tonight. I've really enjoyed myself. See you soon.'

'Pleasure. We should do it again.'

'Absolutely! Bye.'

Bella snuggled down for the night, leaving her mind to assimilate the information whilst she slept peacefully.

# Chapter Ten

Bella's head throbbed when she woke up, and gradually she recalled how much she'd drunk. Although she hadn't been drunk, a steady stream of alcohol had processed its way through her system. - something it was unaccustomed to. Worst of all, she'd forgotten to drink water before bed, so she felt dehydrated and her mouth felt dry and disgusting. She struggled out of bed and into the bathroom and winced at her reflection, hair wild and knotted and skin looking sallow. Repeatedly she splashed handfuls of ice cold water onto her face, and patted it dry, waking her up enough to pull on her dressing gown and go downstairs to make, what she hoped would be, a restorative cup of coffee. Whilst waiting for the kettle to boil she glugged down a large glass of water, and prepared a couple of pieces of toast and marmalade. As the terrace at the back of the house was not overlooked, she went out in her dressing gown to eat her breakfast, the warm sunshine making her have to fight the soporific effect it was having on her. Reluctantly, at ten o'clock, she went upstairs and put on a pair of beige Bermuda shorts and a pale blue polo shirt. As she was dragging the brush through her hair for the final time, there was a knock on the door. Hurriedly she scooped her hair into a loose ponytail, and trotted downstairs to see who it was.

She smiled with pleasure when she saw it was Dave. 'Hi! Come in,' she welcomed. 'Coffee?'

'Love some please. Hope I'm not disturbing you?' He stooped under the doorway and followed her out to the kitchen, where she hurriedly tidied up her breakfast things, which she had left littered across the surfaces.

'Beautiful day,' he commented as she whizzed about tidying up and making the coffee.

'Certainly is.' She glanced up into his pale blue eyes and was once again struck by the kindness she saw reflected in them. 'Is this business or pleasure?' She didn't want to be presumptuous assuming that the visit wasn't for business, but she wanted to be sure, very much hoping that it was for pleasure.

'A mix really.' He saw a flutter of disappointment flick across her face, and was inwardly pleased. 'Mainly pleasure though.' He was even more delighted by the smile which came back to him. 'On the business front, we're still looking into the connection between Rupert and Kit. Once I can tell you anything, I will.'

She looked at him curiously, convinced that he had more information, but for whatever reason could not, or would not, tell her.

'That's the business over with. I know it's short notice, but I wondered if you're free for lunch tomorrow? Give me the opportunity to dazzle you with my culinary expertise?' he joked, but smiled hopefully.

'I'd love to! Nothing planned for tomorrow. What time?'

'Come whenever you like, come for coffee first, whatever suits you.'

'Okay. How far away do you live?'

'Not far, about ten minutes, in the village of Brookhurst.'

'How about 11.30 then? Church will be finished by 11 a.m., I'll come after that.'

'Perfect. Let me scribble down some directions and my address.'

She passed him a pad and pencil and watched the concentration on his face as he deftly drew a little map, wrote directions, address and telephone number. He could feel her gaze on him and glanced up; she blushed as though caught in the middle of something she shouldn't be doing.

'Here you are,' he said handing her the details.

'Thanks,' she tucked it safely under the fruit bowl so that it wouldn't blow away in the breeze. 'Let's have the coffee outside, it's glorious out there.'

They chatted about old times, happy times, when they were both still happily married, not dwelling on their very different reasons as to why it was no longer the case. Eventually Dave got up and bade Bella farewell until the next day. She closed the door behind him, and felt a rosy glow about her. Dreamily she munched her way through a salad sandwich, then went for a cycle ride - yet again determined to get fit and lose some more weight. She huffed and puffed her way through the country lanes and returned red-faced, and sweating profusely, her hair plastered to her head underneath her helmet. Thank goodness there's no one to see me in this state, she mused, as she pushed the bike into the garage and hurried inside to have a shower before someone did. The cool water splashed down onto her overheated body, gradually chilling her down. The endorphins had kicked in, and she felt on a high as she washed her hair, scrubbed her body, shaved her legs and primed herself in readiness for the lunch tomorrow. As she stepped out of the shower, she caught a glimpse of her body in the mirror, convincing herself that she had lost weight since this morning.

Wanting to get a little gift of some kind to take the next day, she gulped down yet another glass of water, picked up her purse and keys and strolled across the village green to the delicatessen, which was further along from the post office. The post office and delicatessen acted like the bread to the terrace of houses in between, which were like the jam. Despite having lived in the village for a few weeks, for one reason or another Bella had never made it in to the delicatessen. The windows looked enticing, and there was an old fashioned, dark green awning shadowing them, keeping the bright sun away from the delectable goodies on display.

Bella walked through the already open door onto oak floorboards - the store had a traditional feel but with a slight contemporary edge to it. She browsed through the unusual products which lined the walls and then inspected the glass fronted, chilled display cabinets. The woman behind the counter gave her a cheery hello and left her to it, something Bella appreciated - she was obviously not related to or of the same ilk as Sharon at the post office - and for which Bella felt relief. Having gone in just to buy a gift for Dave – a bottle of champagne, not original, but she felt it would suit the occasion, a celebration of friendship – she ended up buying several small pots of delicious looking salads, a few slices of Parma ham, a small portion of cooked lobster, and a small raspberry tart.

Whilst she was waiting for her purchases to be wrapped, she noticed that in the other half of the shop, behind a multitude of products, was a small coffee shop area where you could have a drink and order some of the offerings from the shop to eat. As she paid, she became aware of someone standing beside her and glanced to politely smile at whoever it was. Bella was surprised to see Florence, whom she'd not seen since Rupert's funeral.

'Hello! How are you?' she smiled, noting that, in her opinion, Florence didn't look well at all. She looked even thinner than before, her skin was grey and dull and her long, straight, golden blonde hair was lank and unkempt.

'I'm fine,' she replied quietly.

Bella rustled with her bags whilst Florence bought some ham and a pot of salad, curious to know why such a beautiful English rose - albeit currently obscured - should now look like one which had finished blossoming and needed dead-heading.

'I don't suppose,' Bella said, suddenly having an idea, 'you'd like to have a coffee with me? Here, or you could come up to the house?'

A haunted and panicked look flitted across Florence's face.

'Just a quick cup. If you've got time. I've not been in here before, I'm sure their coffee must be great, everything else looks it.' ploughed on Bella. The woman who had been serving them hovered discreetly in the background.

Reluctantly, realising that it would be tricky to get out of given Bella's persistence, Florence politely agreed and followed Bella over to a small, round, wooden table with two chairs.   There were a few other people enjoying a drink, and the young girl serving appeared almost immediately to take their order.   Must be a weekend job, thought Bella, as the girl could barely be sixteen or seventeen.

Bella chatted away whilst their coffees were being made.  It was only when their cappuccinos were in front of them that she looked steadily at Florence, who was doing her utmost to avoid eye contact. 'So, how are you, really?'

Florence smiled feebly, her green eyes looked sad, and the gold in them had lost their shine. 'I'm fine.'

'You look, um…' Bella sought for the right word, 'distracted, a little stressed, compared to when I met you at Sophie and Harry's party?'  I must sound really impudent, she thought, I hardly know the woman yet I'm quizzing her.

Florence stared at her for a moment, and then with an almost imperceptible shake of the head, she forced a smile onto her face. 'Oh, just busy, you know, work and that sort of thing.  How are you?  Are you settling in to the village alright?  Sorry I couldn't make it to the tennis yesterday, had to work, would have been such fun.   How is everyone?'

Hmm, thought Bella, odd that she's asking me, they're her friends.   Hasn't she been in contact with them? 'They're fine, everyone seemed on good form yesterday, even Kim, considering what she's going through.'   Did Florence just wince when I mentioned Kim's name?  She felt something go ping in her head.  Of course, how could she be so stupid?  Florence must have been one of the many who had had, or was having, an affair with Rupert! That would explain why she looked so awful, because she's mourning him herself.

395

'Good. It must be difficult,' she stuttered, tears welling up in her eyes.

Bella patted her hand. 'Difficult for a lot of people,' she replied with meaning.

Florence looked startled. 'I guess so,' she replied in a whisper.

Bella sipped her coffee and felt it wise to change the subject. 'So, how do you enjoy living here? You've been here about a year right?' Florence nodded. 'Where did you move from?'

She shrugged. 'It seems a long time ago now,' she replied wistfully.

Bella frowned. 'Really? Did you move away from family?'

Florence shook her head sadly. 'My parents died within six months of each other, two years ago. I have no family.'

'I'm sorry. I didn't mean to pry.' Bella felt guilty, she'd tried to move the conversation onto innoxious ground, and failed. Wracking her brains for something more light-hearted to discuss, she changed the subject again. 'What's the village fête like? Were you here for the last one?' The fête was a much talked about event, particularly in the post office, and would be taking place next month.

'It was fun last year. It was rather a traditional fête, seemed very popular.' She gulped down the remainder of her coffee and stood. 'Thanks for that. I'm sorry, but I really do have to go. Perhaps another time?'

'Sure. Thanks. Bye, take care.' Bella watched the waif-like figure disappear as fast as it could through the door. She felt unsettled by the meeting: was I too inquisitive, did I over-step the mark? Bella wasn't sure. She picked up her bags, paid for the coffee, and wandered thoughtfully through the late afternoon sunshine back to her cottage. Bella couldn't put her finger on it but there was something bugging her, she just couldn't work out what it was.

The next morning Bella spent an inordinately long period of time preparing herself before church, far longer than she normally would for a lunch with a friend. The previous evening had been spent rummaging through her wardrobe, in an attempt to find the perfect outfit for the lunch. She found it difficult to find the right balance – not too casual, not too formal – and finally settled on a cornflower blue cotton dress which was loose but with a touch of shape to it. She fiddled with the buttons which ran from top to bottom, should she leave one or two undone at the top? At the bottom? She pursed her lips and peered into the mirror, studying herself. Sighing, finally she decided she was being ridiculous and did all the buttons up - as it was a shirt-type dress the shape of the neckline came down in a V shape, she decided that if she exposed too much flesh Dave might get the wrong idea. Or was that what she wanted?

Carefully checking her make-up again, she slipped out of the house, and hurried up to the church, all her deliberations having made her later than usual. She slid into a pew just as the service was starting and, try as hard as she might, found she couldn't focus or concentrate properly, surreptitiously checking her watch every few minutes, eager to get away. With relief, and guilt, that the service was over she made polite conversation with a few of the congregation and made her getaway without staying for coffee. She hurried back to the house, trying not to run and make herself all hot and sweaty in the humid sultry morning.

Bella raced upstairs, went to the loo, swept her long, brown/blonde hair into a knot at the back, and secured it into place. Carefully she checked her make-up and reapplied her rose pink lipstick. Giving herself a final once-over in the full length mirror in the bedroom, and, satisfied with what she saw, she trotted downstairs, retrieved the perfectly chilled bottle of champagne out of the fridge along with the directions from underneath the fruit bowl. Though she'd read them a dozen times since yesterday, she still read them again to ensure she wouldn't get lost.

Slipping behind the wheel of her blue Golf, she eased the car out into the lane and turned left at the bottom, in the direction of Brookhurst. Cruising along the country lane with the windows open just a crack - so her hair wouldn't get spoilt - she glanced up in the direction of Fred and Mia's house as she whisked by the end of their drive. What would they think of her having lunch with Dave? They'd met him a few times at various parties she and Hugh had thrown, before Dave and Alison moved away. She wondered whether they would remember them both?

Brookhurst, like Monhurst, was a pretty little Kent village. It had the church, the pub, the post office cum shop and a tiny little bakers, but no green. She drove past the post office on the left and took the second left, into a small cul-de-sac of about six modestly sized, detached houses. She pulled up outside Number 4, and admired the pristine, postage-stamp sized piece of lawn in front of the house. There was no car on the drive, her heart sank, but hoped it was in the garage and he'd not been called out, realising that she'd forgotten to check her answer phone in her rush to get to his house.

The modest, modern, red brick house, built in the 1970s or 1980s she estimated, looked very neat and well cared for from the outside. The front door was central in the façade, and on either side was a window along with three windows on the first floor. As she walked up the path, the front door opened, and her fears that he'd been called out were allayed. He beamed at her and gave her a soft kiss on each cheek.

'You found it alright then?' She nodded, beaming back at him, feeling slightly off-kilter that she found him so attractive in his pale beige chinos and short sleeved pale blue shirt. 'Come in, let me show you around.' Still grasping the bottle of champagne, Bella followed him into a small sitting room, that - whilst tidy and neat - looked worn and tired; the small dining room looked unused, and the downstairs loo had an avocado suite which had gone out of fashion a long time ago. She followed him into the kitchen, which was bright and airy; there was a small table with room for two, and a dated, wooden, fitted kitchen, all spotlessly clean and tidy.

'Oh, here,' she said, suddenly remembering the champagne, 'I brought you this.'

He took it appreciatively. 'Thanks. It's been a while since I've had champagne! I'll put it into the fridge to keep cool and open it shortly.'

'Great,' she replied, feeling tongue-tied, like a schoolgirl on a first date.

'Let me show you the garden. Shall we have coffee out there or would you actually like to go straight to champagne?' he grinned.

'Coffee'd be lovely. I think one glass of champagne will be my limit as I'm driving.'

'Not that I want to encourage you to drink, but I think you could have a couple, along with lots of water, after all you're going to be here for a while?' he said hopefully.

She grinned back, and followed him into the garden, expecting it to be the usual microscopic size - of which modern houses tended to be allotted. Instead she was taken aback to see a large, colourful garden which disappeared off into the distance towards a little wooded area. 'Wow! I wasn't expecting this.' she cried.

He laughed. 'You mean, because of the size of the house?'

She blushed and stuttered. 'Oh, I didn't mean that, I just meant it's huge, it's beautiful.'

'Don't worry. Everyone has the same reaction. I did too when I first saw the house - it's what made me fall in love with it. The previous owner negotiated with the landowner who owns all the land at the back of these houses and purchased an acre from him. Half a dozen of the trees at the bottom belong to me then there's a fence. Apparently, he refused to sell any land to the other householders, just to the previous owner of this house. Needless to say all the neighbours are jealous.

She laughed. 'I'm not surprised. It's stunning. The lack of land is the only issue I have with modern houses, the gardens are normally so small that you can barely fit in a garden table and chairs.'

'I agree. Gardening has become one of my passions since Alison left. We used to just keep it as grass. Alison wanted a patio, grass and nothing else. It was hideously bland. Guess there's got to be some pluses to one's wife leaving!'

She smiled, not knowing whether he was joking or feeling wistful. 'It's certainly not bland, it's beautiful. You must spend hours weeding the borders.' They strolled slowly down the paths, which weaved in and around the borders and round the lawn.

'Oh, it's not too bad. If you keep on top of it, it doesn't take long at all. I usually pop out and potter around for half an hour each night or morning, and spend more time at the weekend, or whenever I have a day off. My next grand plan is to create a vegetable plot.' They arrived at the grassy area towards the end of the garden. 'I thought I'd create it here. The shed's nearby and the tap. It gets plenty of sunshine, and it's far enough away from the wooded bit to not be affected by it, in terms of shade and leaves fluttering down onto it in the autumn.'

'Sounds good. When are you going to start?'

'Later this summer. Missed my chance to grow things for this summer, but I might still have the opportunity to grow some vegetables over the winter if I get it done before summer ends, though I'm not sure, I'll try and get it ready before the autumn anyway.'

They chatted easily together, coffee turned into champagne, champagne into lunch and before Bella knew it 5pm had arrived. She was reluctant to leave, but keen not to outstay her welcome.

'I'd better be going,' she said, getting up out of the comfortable chair she'd been ensconced in for the afternoon.

'If you think so?' he replied, hopeful that she'd stay longer.

Bella hesitated, tempted to stay, but decided she'd best leave whilst the going was good. 'Thanks. It's been a lovely afternoon. I've really enjoyed myself and your cooking is great, those classes have certainly paid off!'

He grinned back at her. 'Glad you approve. Perhaps you'd let me dazzle you again sometime?'

'I'd like that, but maybe you should sample my cooking first - though don't go getting your hopes up!'

'But you're a super cook. I remember all the delicious dishes you'd cook for your parties. I always thought how lucky Hugh was to come home and have a tasty meal waiting for him every day, he often mentioned what you'd cooked him - being the food-lover that he was.'

Bella blushed deeply and muttered "thanks" as she hurried to the door.

'Thanks for coming Bella. I can't remember the last time I enjoyed myself so much.' He kissed her gently on the cheek, lingering for a moment longer than necessary.

Bella didn't think it was possible for her to blush much more, but she did. 'Thank you too. I've really enjoyed myself. See you soon.'

'I hope so,' he called as she got into her car, waiting by the door and waving until she was out of sight.

Once on the main road, she put the windows down to cool herself down. She was buzzing, on a total high, and not due to the champagne which had long gone through her system. It had been years since she'd felt like this, could it really be possible that she, Bella Sparkle, might find love again? Hugh had always been the love of her life, and no one could ever replace him, but she missed the companionship which came with a good, solid, loving relationship. She'd thought so many times that she would never be able to feel anything for another man, how could she possibly after loving Hugh so much? She'd never been able to understand how widowed wives or husbands could go on to have relationships and marry again, but now she had an inkling. However, balanced with the excitement was also the guilt - the sense that she was betraying Hugh, that somehow she was diluting her love for him and their relationship, that she might forget her love for him. In the space of a few minutes she went from high to low and back again. On impulse, as she approached Fred and Mia's house, she indicated right and drove up their drive, pleased to see that their cars were there.

She hopped out and knocked on the door. No reply. She trotted round the side of the house, calling out. She could hear the faint thump of rock music coming from upstairs, no doubt from Tess's room.

'Hello!' cried Mia who was sitting on the terrace. She put the pile of Sunday newspapers down and got up to greet her. 'It's good to see you. Fancy a drink?'

'Please. Cup of tea would be nice,' she whispered, having noticed that Fred was tilted back in his chair fast asleep, jaw drooping, mouth open. She waited until they were in the kitchen, before speaking again. 'Hope you don't mind, I was just passing and thought I'd pop in.'

'Don't be an idiot, of course I don't mind! You ought to know you can pop in anytime.' She looked suspiciously at her friend. 'Been out somewhere nice?'

Bella blushed the colour of a particularly ripe tomato. 'Oh, er, just out.'

'Come on Bella, you're as red as anything. What have you been up to? You've not been snooping have you?'

'No I have not!' she responded hotly, then giggling nervously.

'Come on, spill the beans, there's obviously something.'

'Well, I just had lunch with a friend.'

'Really?' Mia stared hard at her.

There was a prolonged silence as Bella decided what, or if, or how much, to tell Mia.

'I'm waiting.'

'Just lunch with Dave. You know. Inspector Ormandy, he trained with Hugh.'

'Of course! I knew I'd seen him somewhere before how on earth could I have forgotten! My brain must be going to mush, didn't you even mention something in the last few days about him training with Hugh? And?'

'I might have. And what?'

'You're determined to make this as painful as possible aren't you? Lunch, what about it?'

'He just invited me to lunch, to, you know - to catch up.' She glanced away, not wanting to look Mia directly in the eyes.

'Isn't he married? Didn't he have some ghastly wife, as I seem to recall.'

'Mia! She wasn't ghastly. Anyway she left him. They're divorced now.'

'Ah,' replied Mia with feeling.

I'm not getting into this, thought Bella, regretting having said anything to Mia. 'Have you had a nice weekend?'

'Yes, and you're not getting off that easily,' she retorted.

Bella ignored her comment. 'I saw Florence yesterday.'

'How is she? I called her last week and left a message but she's not phoned back, I really must try again.'

'Bumped into her in the deli in the village. She looked awful, I thought. Really thin and run down, depressed even, like something was weighing her down, worrying her.'

'Oh? I hope she's okay. I'll track her down this week.'

'I don't suppose...' Bella hesitated, 'she wasn't one of Rupert's women was she? I mean she looks like she's in mourning.'

'Florence? I don't think so. Not his type, not glamorous enough. I don't think they'd met before Sophie and Harry's party.'

'Mmm. She is pretty - I know she doesn't seem to dress very stylishly - not that I can talk! - and certainly doesn't do anything to show off her features, but she's got that English Rose look about her, and she's not likely to tell anyone if she's had, or was having, an affair with him.'

'I suppose. I guess anything is possible.'

At that moment a sleepy looking Fred appeared in the doorway. 'Hi Bella. Thought I heard voices.'

'Sorry Fred, hope I didn't wake you?'

'No, just resting my eyes for a bit,' he grinned.

'Do you know if Florence was having an affair with Rupert,' asked Mia bluntly whilst busily making a pot of tea.

Fred looked puzzled. 'Where did that come from?'

'Bella saw Florence yesterday, and said she was looking awful. Just wondered if you'd heard anything.'

He shook his head. 'Nope. Tried to steer well clear of Rupert's private life. He was playing with fire messing around the way he did. I'm surprised Kim put up with it for so long. Rupert was a great guy in many respects, but I think he was a total idiot when it came to women, and he seemed to be getting more reckless, more careless as the months went by.'

Bella pondered on this. So it could quite easily have been possible for Florence and Rupert to have been having an affair? Did anyone else know? Did Kim know?

'Perhaps she's got other worries on her mind. Just because she's looking depressed doesn't mean to say she was having an affair with Rupert,' commented Mia, flapping at Fred to come over and take the tray outside. 'Maybe she's having problems at work.'

Bella grabbed another chair and seat cushion, and pulled it over to where her friends had been sitting, and settled back with her cup of tea. 'Suppose.' she murmured thoughtfully.

'Enjoying village life Bella?' enquired Fred amiably.

'Well… it's not as quiet as I thought it would be!'

The conversation flowed easily and, despite Mia's attempts at trying to extricate further information about the lunch Bella had had with Dave, Bella managed to extract herself after an hour, without having revealed anything else.

# Chapter Eleven

In a frantic attempt to keeping improving her fitness levels, Bella spent the early part of the week cycling - a lot - and eagerly checking her answer phone and mobile for a message from Dave. The former was successful, but the latter was not so. She'd left a message on his mobile on Sunday night to thank him for a delightful day, and had heard nothing from him since, not even a text. It niggled away at her, worried that she'd scared him off in some way, and cross with herself for get carried away and allowing herself to start feeling emotions for another man.

By Wednesday there had still been no call from him. Every time the landline or her mobile rang she raced to pick it up in the hope that it would be him, and each time was disappointed. However, that afternoon she was off to Cressa's house. Cressa had phoned the previous day: the girls were going round for a catch up she'd said, and she wondered if Bella would like to join them? This at least perked her up. It was nice to be included, be welcomed and given the opportunity to develop new friendships. And to keep her occupied that morning, and in an attempt to get her mind off Dave again, she'd been for an early cycle, had breakfast and was now ready to go to the Farmers' Market.

This time Bella went prepared, armed with several bags stuffed into her shoulder bag which would make it easier for her to carry her goodies home. As usual it was crowded and Bella weaved her way in and out of people, making purchases at the stalls which took her fancy. In fact, she was again tempted to make a purchase from every stall but restrained herself, after her previous over-purchasing during her last visit she didn't want any food left over which might go to waste. She glanced at the clock, it was 10.20am, then looked at the queue which was again forming by the empty table, and smiled to herself. They knew he was coming and that their patience would pay off: Bread Man would make his entrance soon, though obviously he was late as usual as the Market started at 10am, but many stall holders were ready well before then.

Bella decided to have a cup of coffee, and somehow managed to balance the cup and saucer whilst carrying her bags and shoulder bag. She didn't recognise anyone sitting at the other tables, and felt a twinge of loneliness as she sat sipping her coffee. Bella observed the, what she assumed was, regular group of elderly people, who had pushed several tables together and marked their territory, as they had done previously. They were busy sharing out cakes which one of them had made, not, Bella noticed, purchased from the market which she felt was a little bit cheeky, but at least they were purchasing cups of coffee and tea and it looked as though a few of them had bought some produce from stall holders. They very much gave the impression that they were holding court, and Bella felt woe betide anyone who tried to mess with them - elderly they may be, but I bet they're not wallflowers, she thought. She mischievously imagined various scenarios of what would happen if someone sat at "their" table before they had arrived.

She was interrupted from her musings by a pleasant-faced, well-rounded woman in her fifties, who enquired whether it would be alright for her to join Bella at the table as the others were fully occupied. Bella smiled, happy to oblige and made polite but friendly conversation with her. It gave Bella a warm, fuzzy feeling, so many strangers being so friendly. Realizing that Bread Man had not only arrived but almost sold out, she made her excuses and hurried over to purchase a fresh loaf and a large white floury bap. Trotting happily back to the house, it was only as she opened the door and saw the phone that she thought about Dave. Determined not to check the answerphone - situated bizarrely in the unused dining room and of which she didn't feel was her place to move - nor her mobile, she hurried though to the kitchen, put away her purchases and made herself an early lunch of fresh smoked salmon pate inside the white flour bap with vibrant green rocket. She sunk her teeth into it and sighed with contentment at the delectable combination. Replete from this delight, she picked up the - as yet untouched - newspaper and did her best to concentrate on reading it, determined that she would not check the answerphone. She was not going to become emotionally reliant on any man again, she told herself fiercely, she'd coped somehow since Hugh had died, and that was not going to change.

Having managed to restrain herself from the temptation and get to 2pm, she briskly walked upstairs and changed into her pale blue dress. Bit of a mistake she thought as she did it up, as memories of lunch the previous Sunday came flooding back. Still, I am not going to let him, or anyone else, dominate my life. So with resolute determination she left the dress on, swept her hair up into a twirl, smoothed on some lip gloss and left the house for Cressa's.

In her car, Bella turned left at the green, and first right after a short distance into Coppice Lane, where the trees lined the road and branched over high above, creating the appearance of a leafy arch through which to drive. A short distance further on she turned left into their drive, noticing that, not too much farther down the lane, was where Rupert had died.

The house itself was beautiful, and Bella wondered if all of Fred and Mia's friends lived in such large, fabulous houses, which were most definitely not a true representation of the average property. She knew it had four bedrooms from earlier conversations, and that it was constructed of brick and tile hung under a Kent peg tile roof. There was a faded - slightly neglected air about the house - the sort of impression you get when you visit a stately home where there isn't enough money to maintain it properly. It looked neat, and the drive - and what she could see of the garden - was well manicured, but she supposed that it didn't cost much to maintain a garden if one did it oneself.

She rapped on the door using the cast iron door knocker and waited. Mia's car was already in the drive, as was Kim's ice blue Mercedes SLK. It was only then that Bella realised she could have given Jennifer a lift, annoyed she didn't think of it earlier.

'Hi Bella, come in,' welcomed Cressa upon opening the door, her tall willowy frame filling it.

She followed Cressa down a long dark corridor, past the staircase, surreptitiously glancing in through the door to the sitting room as they passed by. It, like the exterior of the house, looked as though it needed a bit of money spending on it, small bits of plaster had fallen off the wall and the sofa was frayed around the edges. Despite this, the house had a very warm, homely feel about it, one which suggested it was a happy home. They arrived in the dated kitchen, similar to the one that Dave had. There he was again popping into her head when she didn't want him to - she scowled inwardly to herself but outwardly smiled at Mia and Kim. The kitchen was spacious, with the requisite AGA - this time in a traditional green colour - located in the fireplace at one end of the room, making the room stiflingly hot on this warm summer's day, but there appeared to be no other form of cooking facility, so Bella assumed there was no alternative but to leave it on and swelter.

Cressa pulled the large jug of Pimms she had prepared earlier out of the fridge and placed it on a tray with some glasses.

'Come on, let's get out of here, it's too hot,' she grimaced, leading the way through an open doorway into the back garden. They sat on some wooden garden chairs which had seen better days, but were still usable, and the matching table wobbled slightly as Cressa placed the tray down onto it. 'Anyone want water?' she asked pouring four glasses of the amber liquid.

'Yes please,' replied Bella all too aware, from the other night, of the effect Pimms now had on her.

Cressa returned a few moments later with a jug of water and several glasses, followed by Jennifer, Sophie and baby Jemima. Bella wondered whether the baby ever stopped smiling, every time she saw her she had a big grin on her face.

411

'How's Jack?' enquired Mia.

Mmm, how is he, mused Bella. Wonder if she's tackled him about his behaviour?

'He's fine,' Cressa replied, sitting back and taking a big gulp of Pimms.

'Really?' added Sophie.

It was obvious to Bella that Cressa had vented to the others about Jack, and not just to her and Mia.

'Yes. I asked him out-right whether he was having an affair.'

'And?' urged Mia.

'At first he looked shocked, then he looked cross, and then he looked as though he was trying hard not to laugh. He said he'd absolutely not been having an affair, but when I asked him why he was being so secretive he refused to tell me. Said I'd just have to be patient, and all would become clear in the fullness of time. I mean, what's that all about?'

Sophie, Kim, Jennifer and Mia all glanced at one another as though they now knew something, Bella was convinced of it. Cressa hadn't picked up on this, but Bella was intrigued to find out what was going on.

'I'm sure if he says he's not having an affair then he's not. He's never lied to you before has he? No. So just trust him Cressa.' advised Kim and she of all people knew what it was like to be lied to and cheated on.

'I do believe him. I think if he were having an affair he would tell me if I asked him directly. I just want to know what he's up to! I've wracked my brains and I can't come up with anything.'

Sophie laughed. 'You're too much of a control freak Cressa. Just let him get on with things for a change.' If that had come from someone who didn't know her quite so well Cressa would have had reason to be furious at such a personal jibe, but she just laughed.

'I know, I know! I like everything to be perfect. Guess that's why the house irritates me so much. I want it to be all pristine and perfect. I want to spend some money on the house, do it up a bit, get some new furniture but Jack says no. I don't know why not, we've got a little bit saved now. It is really irritating.'

'Maybe he's just being cautious? After all, it wasn't so long ago that it looked as though you might lose this house.'

'Don't remind me. Thank goodness we managed to scratch around and find enough to hold onto it.'

Jack and Cressa's financial life had been full of ups and downs, more downs since the failed business deal with Rupert.

Jemima's cute baby giggle broke the contemplative silence the group had slipped in to. How could anyone be gloomy with that gorgeous girl grinning away?

'Any news yet?' asked Cressa, changing the subject.

'No.' Kim gave a long sigh. 'I've had the police poking around, they've wanted access to Rupert's bank accounts, business accounts and all that.

'Why?'

'Dunno. If it helps them find out who killed Rupert then they can snoop as much as they like. I just wish it would all be over. But that's me being rather naïve in hoping that the case will be solved instantly, done and dusted in a flash, so I can push it into the past.'

'Haven't they got any suspects in mind?' enquired Mia. 'I mean, surely they must have some kind of idea?'

Kim shrugged. 'If they have, they're not telling me.'

'Can't you ask your Inspector friend?' asked Jennifer, looking at Bella.

Bella shifted uncomfortably in her chair. 'I don't think that's really appropriate, he must be so busy with the case. Kim would have more chance of getting hold of him as she's the victim in all this - apart from Rupert obviously.' She could feel Mia's questioning gaze burning on the side of her face, and resolutely refused to look in her direction.

'Yeah. But as you've known him for so long he might push it along a bit more as a favour to you?'

'I don't think so. He's far too professional for that, and I'm sure he's doing everything he possibly can. I think he'd be insulted if I suggested otherwise.'

'Oh well, perhaps if you see him you could let us know if he tells you anything?' Jennifer gave her a beady look as she was keen to find out if there was a connection between Rupert and Kit.

'Sure. Anybody taking part in the village fête?' Bella not so subtly changed the subject.

'I've donated a couple of cases of Rupert's wine,' replied Kim.

'Think I've been roped in to help out on a stall,' added Jennifer.

'Gotta make some cakes,' said Cressa.

'Me too,' declared Mia.

'I hear from Florence that it's a good afternoon.'

'You've seen Florence?' asked Cressa, 'I've been trying to track her down for ages, she's not returning any of my calls.'

'Nor mine,' echoed Jennifer, Mia, Sophie and Kim.

'But why? Is there something wrong? How did she seem to you?' asked Kim.

Bella glanced at Mia who shook her head slightly. 'Perhaps a little tired? Not quite as bright and chirpy as she was at the party,' replied Bella diplomatically.

'Hmm. I think I might pop along and see her one evening. Once Harry's back from work he can look after Jemima,' said Sophie.

'Good idea. We don't all want to pounce on her though. Can you go tonight?' asked Jennifer.

'I'll try to.'


Out of habit, and not because she was thinking of Dave, Bella automatically checked her answer phone when she returned late afternoon. Still no messages and still no communication of any kind on her mobile. She sighed miserably and went to change into a pair of shorts and a t-shirt. She flung open the French doors in the sitting room and switched the television on, deciding to lose herself in an evening of rubbishy television after the 6 o'clock news. The sky had clouded over, and there was a heavy greyness in the air which matched her mood. The air was stifling and needed to be cleared and she felt sure that they would be in for a big storm that evening. After an hour she restlessly made herself a salad and rejected the open bottle of wine that was in the fridge, opting for a glass of water instead.

The thunder started to rumble in the distance, followed a little while later by the splosh, splosh, splosh of large drops of rain building up into a downpour. Reluctantly she closed the doors and turned the television up a bit louder in order to hear it over the rumbles and crashes crescendoing outside. She didn't hear the knocking on the door and let out a scream when there was a rap on the front window. It was Dave.

'You almost gave me a heart attack!' Bella cried, letting the bedraggled looking man in. She took his dripping coat and hung it over the banister.

'Sorry. I did knock several times but I suppose there's rather a lot of noise outside.'

'Come through,' she led him into the sitting room, 'would you like a drink?'

He hesitated. 'A cup of tea would be nice, thanks.'

Bella trotted off to make a pot of tea and returned a few minutes later with a couple of mugs of steaming liquid. She passed his to him then sat on a chair across from him, and waited for him to speak.

He looked sheepishly at her. 'I'm sorry I didn't return your call. I meant to, it's just that work has got in the way, and every time I thought I had a few minutes in which to phone you something came up, and I've been getting back really late.'

She felt slightly mollified by this explanation, but still miffed that he hadn't phoned or at least sent a text.

'I'm meant to be getting better at this work/life balance thing but not doing a very good job at the moment. Could we meet up this weekend?' he asked hopefully.

'What did you have in mind?' she replied noncommittally.

'If the weather is fine I thought maybe we could take the bikes up to Bedgebury Pinetum and have a cycle and a picnic?'

She couldn't stay irritated with him for long and smiled. 'That sounds like fun. There aren't too many steep hills are there?'

He laughed. 'No. Don't worry, there are a few slopes but nothing I'm sure you couldn't handle. Is Saturday okay?'

'That'd be lovely.'

'Okay. I'll pick you up about 10 o'clock. I've got a bike rack for the car and it'll easily take two bikes.'

She settled back into the armchair feeling more relaxed, and felt the warmth seeping through from her tea. She sipped it slowly and watched him. The slightly bedraggled look suited him, made him look vulnerable.

He smiled back at her. 'Anyway, as I said, I've been busy at work. I think you'll want to hear this.'

Her ears pricked up and she sat up alert. 'Really? What?'

'You were right. There's a definite link between Rupert and Kit. Unfortunately we haven't been able to find out precisely what it is, as Kit is in America at the moment and is not returning my calls. I've tried tracking him down to every place his office says he's going to be at, but mysteriously he never seems to be there when I phone at the precise time I've been told he is going to be there, and whenever I phone his mobile it either goes straight to voicemail or it rings and is then diverted.'

'Mmm, intriguing. So what have you got to go on?'

'This is confidential, but I trust you not to say anything to anyone. Not yet, not until I am ready.' He looked into her clear blue, beautiful eyes and awaited some kind of acknowledgement.

'Of course,' she murmured looking directly back at him.

417

'We've gone through Rupert's bank accounts and have discovered that regular payments have been made from one of his accounts into an account which is registered in Kit's name. Now, there could be a simple explanation for this but we can find no paperwork to clarify what, or why, this money has been transferred.'

Bella felt a frisson of excitement. Had she found out something relevant? Something which would assist the police in discovering Rupert's killer? 'How much are you talking about and how often?'

He hesitated again. 'Two or three times a year for the past two years. The latest one having been made six months ago, which would mean that, in theory, going on the previous pattern, another payment would have been due about a month ago.'

'And the amounts?' She held her breath in excitement, her heart beating furiously in her chest.

'That's the interesting part. About £50,000 each time.'

Bella let out a whistle. 'That's a lot. So how much has he paid in total? About £250,000?'

'Yes.'

'Wow! That's a huge sum of money. Could he afford that? And what on earth was it for?'

'That's what I need to speak to Kit about. And I think he knows it, but he can't avoid me for ever.'

'Does Kim know? Maybe she knows?'

He shook his head. 'I think if she were aware of these payments she would have confided in someone and it would have got round her close group of friends, but more than likely she would have told me as she is exceedingly keen to find out who is responsible for Rupert's death. Besides which she wouldn't have asked us to find out what the connection was between Rupert and Kit because she would already have known. Now, you are sure that at the party they were, on the face of it, introduced for the first time?'

'Absolutely. No doubt about it. Rupert had this strange look on his face but the impression I got from Kit was that these were first-time introductions, and I'm sure Mia would have told me if they'd met him before.'

'Okay. Until I've tracked Kit down and have more information, I'm not going to discuss this with Rupert's wife. With such large sums involved, it might just cause her more distress.'

'Sure. They have already asked me to ask you to hurry up with the case.'

He frowned at her.

'I told them that you are a professional and that you would be doing your utmost to solve this case.'

'Thanks. For a minute I thought you were implying I wasn't doing my job!'

'Of course not!'

'Good.' He took a long swallow of tea from his mug and felt himself finally starting to thaw out.

'Do you think it's blackmail?'

'I'm keeping an open mind, but it certainly is an option. It's unusual - and annoying - for there not to be any kind of paperwork or hint of a paper trail of some kind, no matter how minimal. The rest of his accounts, both business and personal, have all been meticulously kept. All the paperwork matches up, there is nothing missing, even down to the smallest of receipts. So, yes, it is definitely a possibility.'

Bella's mind tore through the numerous reasons why, she thought, Rupert could have been blackmailed. 'It must have been some pretty massive secret if it was blackmail. What on earth could it be?'

Not prepared to get into speculation, he rose reluctantly from the comfort of his chair. 'Thanks for the tea, I'd best be getting home.' He glanced at the clock - it was 9.30pm already. How quickly the time went when he was in her company. 'But please remember, not a word, not a hint, okay?'

'My lips are sealed. I promise.'

'Good,' he slipped on his still sodden coat and peered out of the door at the rain which was still rushing down in torrents. 'It's supposed to clear by Friday so it should be good for Saturday. I'll see you then.'

She smiled broadly at him. 'Looking forward to it. Take care.'

# Chapter Twelve

Bella awoke at 7 a.m. feeling lethargic and unrested. Her mind had been working overtime since Dave had left the previous evening. Curiosity was gnawing away at her and she was becoming illogically desperate to discover why Kit had been blackmailing Rupert. She had concluded that it had to be blackmail, what other possible explanation could there be? She lay there, too weary to get up but annoyingly unable to get back to sleep. With great effort she dragged herself out of bed half an hour later and, having soaked her face in an ice cold flannel, staggered downstairs to make an extra strong cup of coffee.

Rustling in the cupboards, she found an unopened packet of ground caffeinated coffee, and put a couple of scoops into her cafetière. She felt in need of all the help she could to get her body going this morning. Outside the sky was still grey, but the torrential rain had merged into a fine, misty drizzle which gently tickled the window panes. Bella sat at the kitchen table sipping her coffee, waiting for the buzz of caffeine to kick in. After a few minutes of flicking through the day before's paper, she could feel the surge as the potent liquid lit up her veins, as though somebody had suddenly flicked the 'on' switch and energised her whole being.

I wonder, mused Bella, making a start on her second cup: Sharon at the shop seems to know everything - fact or fiction - about so many people, and goings on, in the area, perhaps there's a tiny nugget of information she's forgotten about Rupert which could be teased out? Though the thought of being ensnared by Sharon was not one Bella relished, if it were a means to an end it would probably be worth it.

An hour later, and with the caffeine still working its magic on her, she hurried down to the post office underneath her blue spotty umbrella, and braced herself for what was to come. As someone who, in general, drank little caffeine - preferring decaffeinated - it had an incredible, mood-enhancing effect on her when she did finally succumb, so it was with relatively high spirits that she entered the shop. Relieved, she found that Sharon was on her own and that they would not be interrupted or overheard by inquisitive busybodies eager to spread more gossip.

'Good Morning Christabel,' smiled Sharon, 'how are you today? Bit wet still out there isn't it, but we need it - my tomatoes are suffering dreadfully, keep forgetting to water them and with not enough rain...'

Bella smiled politely and listened to Sharon witter on whilst she pretended to be looking at the magazines. Feeling that it would be mollifying to make a purchase, she picked up a copy of Kent Life and The Times and took them across to the counter to pay. Sharon continued on with her monologue, whilst Bella fished around in her purse for the correct change and gave, what she hoped was, a winning, friendly smile as she handed it over. As Sharon paused to catch her breath Bella swooped in, having re-hearsed a way to bring Rupert into the conversation in a not too conspicuous way.

'I'm hoping to buy some wine, Sharon, and thought I might go up to Rupert's wine place in Stream Lane. Do you know anything about it?'

'You should know, you mix with that lot,' retorted Sharon enviously.

'Well, yes, I'm newly acquainted with them, but I only met Rupert the once. As you seem to know everyone, and everything, about the area...' she trailed off, hoping flattery might get her somewhere, '...I thought you would be the most knowledgeable person to ask. You know, for an un-biased opinion,' she smiled conspiratorially at her. Sharon took the bait.

'Well, since you're asking, I wouldn't normally say, you know I don't like to gossip, too many of those in the vil-lage do.' Bella tried hard not to laugh at the irony of it. 'It's a bit pricey. He buys, or rather bought,' she corrected herself, 'fancy wines. Don't know why people want to spend twenty quid on a bottle of wine when you can get a very nice box of wine which lasts longer and costs a lot less.'

'Mmm,' murmured Bella. She thought boxes of wine were hideous but had to admit they'd come a long way in the past few years and were proving to be quite popular. Psychologically she couldn't get her head round drinking wine from a box, it made her think of packets of juice.

Perceiving this as approval and agreement, Sharon con-tinued, fluffing up with self importance. 'If you don't mind pricey though, it's supposed to be quite nice. Never set foot in there myself, wouldn't give him the satisfaction.

He was always a jumped-up, snobby, condescending man and that wife of his used to be lovely, why she married him I have no idea! Could only be for the money, why else? She was supposed to marry that lovely Seb, dumped him to go off and marry Rupert. It's beyond me.'

'Really?' Bella tried to act surprised and inwardly gritted her teeth. She loathed gossip - having been the subject of a lot of it when Hugh died - and was beginning to think that she'd made a mistake, that it had been an ill-considered idea to try to tease information out of Sharon.

'Oh yes. If there was a dodgy deal to be done, it would be done by Rupert, ripping people off left right and centre, just look at the prices of his wine! Says it all.' She stood there with her arms folded across her ample chest, with a self-righteous, smug look on her face.

Bella did her best to force a smile and felt it was futile to continue, she wasn't hearing anything of significance, and couldn't stand to listen to the gossipy, spiteful (whether Sharon meant to be or not), drivel spouting out of her mouth any more. 'Well, thanks for that. I might pop along and have a look at the wine, at least you have forewarned me that the wine is not going to be the cheapest. Bye.' She exited hastily and fumbled hurriedly with her umbrella, anxious to get it up and get away from the shop.

Without bothering to take off her coat, she slapped the magazine and paper onto the kitchen table and picked up her car keys. No time like the present, she thought. May as well visit the place now. She hopped into her car and took a right turn onto the village road off the green, shortly after she turned left and half a mile later right into Stream Lane. Another quarter of a mile further along, in the middle of nowhere, she came upon Rupert's wine shop. Aptly named Oast Wines, as the building itself turned out to be a beautifully converted triple kiln oast house. The cowls swung gently in the breeze which had sprung up, misting the drizzle into Bella as she got out of the car.

It was apparent that he had spent a fortune on the place. Everything about it screamed "money". The car park was pristine and there were beautifully filled terracotta pots, filled with a variety of fresh white blooms, welcomingly set by the entrance. I wonder how much local and/or passing trade it gets, mused Bella, after all it's not exactly on a busy through route. There surely could be no significant passing trade to talk of? You'd need to know where it was, and make a special trip. She noticed a couple of smart and relatively new vans parked to one side with "Oast Wines" imprinted in the logo each side. Perhaps a lot of its trade was done on the internet or by phone and then delivered?

Bella pushed the door open and heard a gentle ping from somewhere towards the back of the shop. She stood there in awe at what she saw. The area was enormous - two of the roundels and the adjoining barn sections were opened up to full height, running around at first floor level on each roundel was a galleried area with metal balustrade. On ground floor level Bella could see a huge quantity of stock, but whilst there was obviously a massive range of wines, it was not crammed to the rafters making it impossible to see the wine, nor was it overwhelming or intimidating. In fact it had a comforting, relaxed, welcoming air about it. Something that Bella had not expected.

'Hello. Can I help you at all?' asked a pleasant-looking woman in her thirties, who was dressed in jeans a white shirt and a dark green apron emblazoned with "Oast Wines" on it in gold.

'Oh, er, I think I'd just like to browse at the moment,' replied Bella.

'Of course, please do. If you need any help or advice, just let me know.' She gave Bella a friendly smile and went back to whatever she was working on at the computer.

Bella took a tentative step forward on the mellow oak stripped floor, there were discreet notices indicating which country and which area the wines came from, by far the largest section was dedicated to French wine, but as the whole shop was so huge there was an impressively enormous range from many different countries and regions - almost overwhelmingly so for someone such as Bella who was relatively ignorant about wine - and she was particularly pleased to see a decent sized section dedicated to English wine, which was a rapidly expanding market with a growth in award-winning wines.

Despite what Sharon had said, there was a broad variation in prices, the cheapest she could see was at £4.99 and the most expensive was £70. However, as she weaved her way around she saw a glass door with a sign that indicated that the more expensive wines were on the other side of it in a strictly managed, temperature-controlled environment. How much more expensive? £70 seemed like an awful lot for a bottle of wine to her. Intrigued, she turned the handle and walked through into the cool room, which was rather more dimly lit, presumably an attempt to create the perfect conditions in which to store the wine. She wandered around looking at the prices and whistled to herself. £70 turned out to be rather "cheap" compared to the prices in here, there were plenty of bottles at £1,000 and locked away behind a wrought iron gate were some selling for upwards of £2,500 - for a single bottle. These must be the wines that top London restaurants charged thousands and thousands of pounds for, often triple or more of the price they purchased them at, assumed Bella.

How on earth can anyone possibly pay so much for a bottle of wine? It cost more than the average monthly wage! If Rupert sold plenty of these, with a substantial mark-up, then it was no wonder he had been a multi-millionaire.

Despite their price, there was something very alluring about the wine; it reeked of luxury and extravagance, the likes of which she - and most of the general population - would never experience. As Bella finished looking round, she noticed a discreet security camera tucked up in the corner, inevitable, she concluded, as they would undoubtedly be a prime target for thieves.

She strolled out of the room and continued to wander around, selecting half a dozen bottles of wine, three red, three white. She was intrigued as to what taste difference there could possibly be in the wines. Did the price really match the quality? She therefore chose, in both red and white, a bottle at £4.99, one at £9.99 and one at £20.00.

Bella took her opportunity to - subtly she hoped - probe for information from the sales assistant behind the till, while the bottles were wrapped individually in tissue paper and then placed into a six bottle box with "Oast Wines" emblazoned on the side. Very slick, she thought. At most places you had to make do with a charged-for plastic bag or a redundant old box.

'Lovely place this. I've not been here before.'

'Thank you. I hope we will see you again. We regularly hold wine information evenings and tastings; if you are interested I could take a note of your details and contact you when we next hold an event?' She smiled encouragingly at Bella.

Oh, very smooth, thought Bella, get your details without you even realising it, and be on their mailing list for ever. In an attempt to keep the woman chatting, and to tease information out of her, she agreed. 'Thank you. That would be nice.' She peered at her name badge which was pinned to the top of her apron. It said "Libby".

'I'll just finish packing these for you, and then I'll take your details.'

'Thanks.' She watched as Libby taped up the box then deftly tapped into the computer and produced the bill. 'Have you any events coming up?'

A hint of sadness flickered across Libby's face, and her eyes welled up with tears behind her bright red-rimmed glasses. 'Er, no,' she croaked, then tried to clear her throat. 'Sorry.'

Bingo! Thought Bella. 'That's okay,' she paused hoping that Libby would expand on her response.

'I'm afraid the owner died recently, he was the expert and the owner of the business. We anticipate having some new events lined up for the autumn though.'

'Oh dear!' replied Bella feeling a fraud, 'how awful. That's very sad, was it unexpected?'

'Oh, it was,' Libby sniffed, doing her utmost to remain as professional as possible.

Guessing that Libby had been instructed not to go into any details, Bella tried a different tack. 'It would appear from the set-up here that he knew a lot about wine. I don't think I've ever seen such a huge variety of wines under one roof.'

Libby gave her a watery smile. 'Rupert definitely was an expert, he knew everything there was to know about wine, he was just so knowledgeable and a fantastic person to work for. He was so kind and caring.'

Bella tried to hide her surprise. Kind? Caring? From what she'd seen, though she admitted it wasn't that much, he'd been a horrible person, particularly to his wife. Unless of course Libby had benefited from a few extra 'perks' with the boss. A few after-hours sessions perhaps? 'Sounds like he was a good boss.'

'Oh he was. He was the best.' She looked dreamily into the distance.

'Do many people work here?'

'Oh, quite a few. Some in the office, others like me who work in the shop, the delivery drivers - quite a little family really. And Rupert always made sure that we were trained up properly. He didn't want anyone selling the wine who was ignorant of the products being sold, he took a lot of time and trouble over that. He was so kind, giving me extra tuition if I needed it.'

Yeah right, I know what sort of extra tuition that was. Bella immediately berated herself for such a thought. She smiled encouragingly at Libby.

'That's £69.96 please. I'll pop one of our wine lists on top of the box for you to read at your leisure, you can also see the stock online, the website address is at the bottom. And if you want any information about a specific wine - or the wines you have purchased - or have any queries, please do not hesitate to phone or email us, we're always happy to help.'

'Thanks,' replied Bella handing over her bank card. 'Rupert must have achieved a lot of qualifications to be so knowledgeable about wine?'

She shook her head. 'Oh, no, it was all self-taught. He spent several years travelling the world, picking grapes, working on vineyards and gaining first-hand experience.'

'Really?' she was surprised that Kim hadn't mentioned this when she'd seen the photo.

'Yes, he started off in France, went to Australia, New Zealand, California, Chile, Argentina and South Africa and probably more I imagine.'

'Wow! He did travel. I bet he had some tales to tell!'

'No. He was quite a private man, didn't like people asking questions about his past, he was very much a "living in the moment" sort of person. Shame, I'm sure he would have had some fascinating tales to tell.'

'I'm sure.' Well, there's further confirmation that he was in Australia, noted Bella.

'Let me take your details and I'll contact you when we next have an event coming up.'

Bella dutifully gave Libby her details, though by the time the autumn arrived, she'd be thinking of where to live next. The cottage was only rented for 6 months, but as the owners were away for a year there was possibly potential for a further 6 months, something Bella had initially discounted, not wanting to commit herself for such a long period of time, but her mind was slowly changing in that regard. Libby summoned a young man in his late teens, also wearing an Oast Wines apron, to carry the box out to her car, and Bella thanked her for her help.

When she got back home, she opened the front door, then returned to the car to carry the box in. The white wine she put straight into the fridge and the red she left on the side.

Intrigued by the fact that Libby knew that Rupert had travelled the world picking grapes and developing his knowledge of the wine business, but that Kim appeared not to have known, nor Jennifer either, she popped out to chat it over with Mia in the afternoon, as Mia knew about the photograph.

Bella recounted what Libby had said, and waited for Mia's response. She looked puzzled.

'Rupert never talked about his past. I'm surprised that Kim didn't know though, particularly if a member of Rupert's staff knew.'

'That's what I thought.'

'I guess she could have forgotten, grief can do funny things to the mind.'

'I suppose, but I'm not convinced.'

'But I don't think it's worth mentioning to Kim, she's still emotionally all over the place not surprisingly.'

Bella was impatient to tackle Kim, her sleuthing antennae on red alert. Perhaps, without realising it, Kim knew more than she thought she did?

'I'm sure it must be the stress that's made her forget. I mean, if she'd driven past a few minutes later she would have seen Rupert's accident,' muttered Mia absent mindedly.

Bella gave a start. 'What? What do you mean?'

Mia blushed. 'Bother. Fred made me promise not to tell anyone.'

'Mia! I can't believe it! Are you saying that you saw Kim drive past on the night of Rupert's death?'

Mia fiddled with a fold in her skirt.

431

'Mia?' said Bella sharply.

'I didn't. Fred did. We'd been out to dinner and come back quite early. I opened up the house and Fred walked back down to close the gate as he always does at night. He saw Kim drive past.'

'What time?'

'About 9.50 p.m.'

'And have you told the police?

She shook her head.

'Mia! I can't believe you'd hold information back.'

'Well, neither Fred nor I can possibly believe that Kim had anything to do with Rupert's death, she just wouldn't. I know she wouldn't.'

'Are you sure? Didn't you say she was planning on leaving Rupert?'

'Well, yes. But why would she bother to kill him if she were leaving him? And if she had wanted him dead, I'm sure she would have done it months ago.'

'You're going to have to tell the police. You know you are. Maybe she didn't kill Rupert, but alternatively, she may have seen something - or someone - and that titbit of information could help the police, even if it is to discount a person who may be under suspicion.'

Mia looked cross and upset. 'Just because your friend is leading the investigation, it doesn't mean you can tell me what to do, and don't you dare go sneaking to him!'

'Mia!' sometimes her friend exasperated her. 'It's got nothing to do with Dave being a friend. You know in your heart that you should have told the police, otherwise you wouldn't be reacting like this. You're cross with yourself and you're trying to deflect it onto me. I know it's hard, because Kim is a friend of yours, but don't you think it's important to catch the person who killed Rupert?'

Mia nodded miserably.

'I can't believe you and Fred kept this secret you are probably the most honest people I know.' A thought struck her as she looked at Mia, who was looking decidedly deflated. 'Which direction was she driving in?'

Mia looked furtively away.

'Well?'

'Towards Monhurst.'

So she could have done it, thought Bella. She was going in the right direction close to the time of the accident.

'Shall I call the police, or will you?'

Mia sighed. 'I will. But not until I have spoken to Fred, and then to Kim. See what she has to say for herself.'

'Mia, you know you can't do that, you'll be warning her, giving her a chance to work out her alibi.'

'I don't care. She's my friend and I know she didn't do it.'

'Okay. But I'm coming with you. I like Kim, she's a nice person, but I'm not as emotionally attached to her as you are. I can impartially observe her body language and listen to what she says and I WILL give my opinion to the police.'

Mia glowered at Bella even though she knew her friend was right.

'Let me phone Fred now, and then - but only then - we can go and see Kim.' Mia took herself off to another room and closed the door, precluding Bella from hearing their conversation. After a few minutes she reappeared, scowled at Bella, and tersely said, 'come on then if we're going.'

433

They took Bella's car and Mia sat sulkily throughout the journey. Bella deliberately drove down Coppice Lane and past where Rupert had died, slowing as they passed the exact spot, trying to make a point. When they arrived at the house Bella was relieved to see that Kim's blue Mercedes convertible was in the drive.

Mia stood and continued to glower at Bella as they waited on the doorstep for Kim to answer the door.

'Hi!' she said, looking surprised to see them. 'Come in, it's lovely to see you.'

I doubt you'll think that in a minute, thought Bella.

'Drink?' Out of politeness they suggested a cup of tea. Kim ushered them both out of the kitchen and into the sitting room while the kettle was boiling. It seemed gloomy and dark, matching the weather outside. She switched on a couple of lamps then returned to the kitchen to make the tea. Several minutes later she entered the sitting room, balancing three boiling mugs between her hands. 'Ow!' she yelped, putting them down quickly, 'knew I should have used a tray.' She settled herself down in a big comfy chair and tucked her bare feet under her, then frowned as she looked at Mia who, in return, was looking incredibly miserable.

'What's up? You don't look very happy.' Concern was etched over Kim's face.

Mia sighed, and scowled again at Bella who was waiting expectantly, eager to hear what Kim had to say for herself. She studiously ignored Mia and observed Kim who had a radiant glow about her. Interesting, mused Bella.

'Well, um…' Mia's voice trailed off.

'What is it Mia? You look awfully pale.' Mia was looking decidedly grey.

'It's a bit awkward really,' she paused and smiled feebly at Kim who smiled back and nodded encouragingly. 'It's, well,' she sighed, 'um, on the night that Rupert died, you told me, and I guess the police, that you were at home all evening,' she looked at Kim for confirmation.

Kim's smile wavered slightly, she leaned forward, picked her mug up and fiddled with it as a distraction. Bella noted every move, every change in her demeanour. Kim nodded and waited.

'It's just that Fred saw you drive past on the Monhurst Road at about 9.50 p.m. going in the direction of Monhurst.'

Fear flicked across Kim's face, but she held it together as she waited for Mia to continue.

'Why did you lie?'

There was an oppressive silence. Keenly Bella watched as Kim, obviously torn between sticking to her lie and telling the truth, wrestled with what to say. Could she really have done it? Was she actually responsible for Rupert's death? Bella held her breath in anticipation. Was she going to confess? She felt a bit like Miss Marple, maybe she was going to crack the case before the police.

Mia also sat waiting, miserable and fearing the real reason why Kim had lied to her - and to the police.

Eventually Kim spoke in a small, thin, defeated voice. 'It was the first thing that came to my head. I was in shock.'

'Okay. So what's the truth?'

Kim looked beseechingly at the two of them. 'I didn't want people to know,' she whispered.

Bella's body tensed in anticipation.

'Mia, you know what I was planning to do. To leave Rupert, I was leaving him for Seb.' She looked at Mia, then at Bella, expecting her to look shocked, and was surprised when she didn't.

'I told her that you were leaving Rupert,' offered Mia in reply to the unspoken question, 'the one thing you can usually do is trust Bella to keep a secret.' This confirmed what Bella had suspected, that Kim was leaving Rupert for Seb.

'So what was it that you didn't want people to know?' prompted Bella, eager to get the truth.

Kim sighed again. 'I didn't want anyone to know that I had been with Seb that night. I mean, how would it look if they knew that I had been having sex with my ex-fiancée on the night that my husband died?'

Put like that, Bella could see her point of view. Or was this just a clever ruse?

'No one would have believed that I didn't have anything to do with his death, and even if they did, they would have thought that I was some kind of dirty little slapper, someone who was as bad as - if not worse than - Rupert. And it wasn't like that. I love Seb, I always have done - I was a fool to be blinded by Rupert, to be swept off my feet. I've regretted it for so long. I thought I'd lost Seb forever. I never thought he could forgive me for what I did, for betraying him like that. I mean, how could he after what I'd done to him? But he did, and not only that, he still loves me and wants me, and it wasn't some kind of competition to get me away from Rupert, score one over on him. He loves me, truly, and for who I am, the real me.'

It all sounded so romantic to Bella, the sort of thing you'd read about in a magazine or trashy romance novel. But surely this could be even more of a motive for murder?

Now Kim gets all Rupert's money, whereas if she'd left him and divorced him she'd possibly only get a fraction of it.

'Did Rupert have any cause to suspect that you were planning on leaving him?' she asked.

Kim shook her head. 'No. I was very careful. Seb and I were meticulous in planning our meetings to ensure that no one would find out. The only person I had told was Mia.'

'And the only person I told was Bella. I've not even told Fred.'

'And I've not told anyone. Did you sign a prenup?' Bella inquired impertinently.

'Yes,' replied Kim not seeming offended. 'Rupert wanted to protect his businesses. I know what you're thinking. You're thinking I killed Rupert so that I could get all his money?'

Bella blushed. Mia rolled her eyes at her.

'I might have signed a prenup, but it was a very generous prenup. I'd get the house, which hasn't got a mortgage on it, and £50,000 a year for life whether I remarried or not.'

Bella whistled. Wow! That was generous. Rupert went up in her estimation.

Mia's mouth gaped open in shock too

'And even if the prenup had left me nothing, I wouldn't have cared. I love Seb for who he is, he may not be rich but he's an incredible person, completely amazing. Having money doesn't make you happy, I should know, I've had shed loads of the stuff to spend, courtesy of Rupert, but I've never been so unhappy in all my life. Sure, it means you never have to worry about where your next meal is coming from I don't deny that, and that is a huge privilege and one I have never ever taken foregranted. But a life with Seb means a life of love, a life of fulfilment, we'd have a small roof over our heads and enough food to eat. What more could we need?'

True, I guess, though Bella wasn't entirely convinced. It would not be easy moving from such a large house with copious amounts of money on tap, to a small place where careful budgeting would be inevitable. But she had no idea what sort of house Seb had and was being presumptuous in her assumptions. If the prenup held up they'd be set for life anyway.

Mia got up and went over to Kim and gave her a big hug. 'I'm sorry,' Mia whispered 'I had to ask. You understand why?' She pulled back to look into Kim's sad blue eyes.

'Yeah,' she replied hoarsely.

Bella shifted uncomfortably. Disquieted because she couldn't believe she'd got so carried away with her imagination that she could believe that Kim had killed her husband. Guilt crept all over her.

'I'm sorry too.'

Kim shrugged. 'I suppose I have to tell the police don't I?' She looked from Mia to Bella.

'I think so. What you tell them, no matter how small or irrelevant you feel the detail is, could help the investigation. Seb will also need to talk to them.'

'I feel so ashamed. So guilty.'

'Why?'

'There was I, full of the joys of life, having spent the most glorious evening with Seb, planning our future, and while I was doing that Rupert was dying, all alone in a country lane. I feel terrible, I must be such a bad person.'

'But you mustn't,' comforted Mia, 'how were you to know that this would happen? That he was going to die?'

Bella was tempted to tell Kim that Rupert had been trying to get Jennifer into bed that evening anyway, to make her feel better but Bella had promised Jennifer that she wouldn't tell anyone. It was up to the police, or Jennifer, to tell Kim.

'Do you think they'll believe me?' Kim looked beseechingly at them.

'Tell them exactly what you told us.' advised Mia.

Bella nodded. 'They're not idiots, somehow they'll discover whether you're telling the truth or not and it's better coming from you than them finding out some other way. I certainly believe you,' she added hastily in case Kim took umbrage at what she'd just said.

'I'll go and phone them now.' She went out of the room in search of the telephone number she'd been given. Shortly afterwards Mia and Bella could hear her talking on the telephone.

When Kim returned she said. 'They'll be round in a little while. I spoke to Sergeant Swart, she's going to come round along with Inspector Ormandy.'

Bella's heart fluttered when she heard his name and she tried not to blush.

'Would you like us to stay with you?' asked Mia. 'We don't mind, if it'll make it easier?'

'No. Thanks. I'd rather do it on my own. Don't worry, I'll tell them everything I've told you.' She twisted her fingers nervously on her lap.

'You sure?'

'Yup. Absolutely.'

'You do know you're doing the right thing don't you?'

'I guess so. Do you think they'll be able to keep this quiet?'

Bella shrugged. 'I don't know. I wouldn't have thought there'd be any need to tell anyone, unless it turns out to be a key piece of evidence in the case.'

Mia got up. 'We'd better leave you to it then. Call if you need anything. See you at tennis tomorrow?'

'Okay. See you tomorrow.' Kim returned Mia's huge hug of support, absorbing comfort from her friend.

'Bye,' said Bella meekly, feeling mean at having dragged all this up, even though, deep down, she knew it was the right thing to do.

'Bye Bella. See you tomorrow.'

The awkward silence dragged out between them as they got into the car. Bella pulled out into the lane and cleared her throat. 'Are you going to forgive me?'

'I suppose so. I know you're right, but why did it feel so horrible, so sneaky, so mean?'

'Because you wanted to protect your friend, you didn't want to contemplate that she might have had something to do with Rupert's death. I understand why you kept it quiet.'

'Sorry if I was horrible to you.'

'S'okay. I felt mean and guilty myself. You do know I wasn't doing it to impress Dave don't you? I was following my gut instinct.'

'Yes. Guess I'd better phone the police myself when we get back. They'll need a statement from both Fred and myself. Hope we won't be in trouble.'

'You'll be fine. Don't worry.' Secretly Bella was horrified. She hadn't thought about the ramifications for Mia and Fred, and prayed fervently that they wouldn't be in trouble for withholding information.

# Chapter Thirteen

Bella fretted and tossed and turned all night worrying about Mia, Fred and Kim. Had she done the right thing in forcing them into a corner so that there was no option for them but to tell the police? She could have just kept quiet, kept their secret, but would that have helped? Deep down Bella knew the answer, but it didn't make her feel any better. She spent the morning pottering around the house, half heartedly pushing the vacuum cleaner around, dusting, washing, ironing, keeping herself occupied in an attempt to keep her mind off the three of them. She had been looking forward to going to tennis that afternoon, but was now a tad apprehensive about the sort of reception she might receive from Kim, given that she should have spoken to the police by now.

With reluctance she changed into a pair of shorts and a t-shirt, smothered herself in sun cream as the sun was now beating down with a vengeance, as if wishing to make up for the previous couple of days of gloomy weather. At least the forecast was good for tomorrow, she smiled to herself at the prospect of the planned cycle and picnic.

As the tennis club was situated on the edge of the village in the direction of Sophie and Harry's house, and therefore not too far, Bella decided to get her bike out and cycle. Popping on her cycle helmet, Bella stuck her racquet into the rear side bag, with the handle protruding out of the top, and set off down the road. With the breeze in her face, the sun on her body and endorphins starting to kick in, Bella felt her spirits rise. There was definitely nothing better than an English summer when the sun was shining and the sky was clear and a vibrant blue she felt. There was a toot, toot of a horn as Jennifer drove past waving. Bella waved back, wobbling on her bike as she did so. She upped her speed and before too long she was bumping along the stony track to the cricket pitch and tennis club.

Red-faced with her exertion, she removed her helmet to cool down and took a long swig of water from the large bottle she'd remembered to top up at the last minute and slip into her bike bag.

Mia waved at her from a distance. 'Hi!' she called strolling over to her.

'Hi! How are you?' Bella peered anxiously at her friend.

'Fine.'

'How did it go?' she lowered her voice.

'It was okay.'

'And Fred?'

'Not impressed at first, more embarrassed that he'd suggested we omit say anything in the first place. The police were fine. In fact it was your friend Inspector Ormandy who called in, must have been about 8 o'clock, I suppose he was on his way home. Anyway, he was very understanding and he remembered who we were! I must say, he's got a jolly good memory.'

'Oh, great,' her heart fluttered again.

Mia grinned at her.

'What?' bleated Bella.

'Nothing. Just enjoying the look on your face when I mentioned him.'

Bella gave her friend a playful poke on the arm and turned to busy herself with locking her bike to the bike rack. 'Kim here yet?' she enquired whilst doing so, scanning the group that was gathering.

'Not yet.'

'Do you know how it went for her?' Bella's face darkened, her ridiculously over-active imagination again going into overdrive as she envisaged Kim locked up in a cell somewhere.

'No.' Mia looked equally concerned.

They were interrupted by Florence driving up in her old blue Honda CRV. There was a collective murmuring of pleasure at seeing her from the girls as they hurried over to Florence. They crowded round, eager to find out how she was. It must be nice to be missed so much, felt Bella standing slightly back from them. Florence looked as pale and thin as she had at the end of last week, but was putting on a brave face.

'Hi Florence,' greeted Bella, once Florence had extracted herself from her friends.

'Hi Bella. How are you?'

'I'm fine thanks,' she replied politely, 'how are you? Work still as manic?'

She nodded. 'Yeah.'

'Anyone know where Kim is?' called Sophie, who was trying to organise the matches.

Bella looked furtively at Mia. A general murmur of "no" responded to Sophie's enquiry.

'Oh well, sure she'll be here soon. I'll slot her in when she arrives.'

Mia, Sophie, Florence and Cressa were lined up to play their games first. Bella and Jennifer warmed up on the neighbouring court awaiting their turn in a doubles match. Half an hour later Jennifer called for a break.

'Phew! It's so hot!' she gasped, flopping down onto a bench in the shade and wiping the sweat from her forehead.

'Certainly is,' gasped Bella, offering her some of her water. Jennifer took it and eagerly gulped down some of the cool liquid.

'Any news on the photo yet?'

'Inspector Ormandy said he'd let Kim know when there was something to tell,' replied Bella guiltily, omitting - as promised - what else he'd told her.

'Fair enough. I'll be interested to see what they come up with. Oh! Here's Kim now. Hi! Thought you'd got lost,' she called out.

'Sorry I'm late. Had things to do.' She sat next to Bella who smiled at her, fervently hoping that Kim wasn't furious with her. Kim smiled back.

'I'll get some more water,' said Jennifer getting up and disappearing into the smartly-painted white club house.

'How did it go?' whispered Bella.

'Okay. Embarrassing, but I think they understood. Gave me a bit of a telling off about not being completely honest in the first place and how it could have had a detri-

445

mental effect on the investigation, but other than that they were fine. At least I wasn't dragged off to the police station and thrown into a cell!'

Relief flooded through Bella from head to toe. 'It was the right thing telling them. I'm sorry if I put you in an awkward position...'

Kim looked surprised. 'But you didn't! You didn't know.'

'No. But it was me who told Mia that the police ought to be informed.'

'It would have come out eventually, these things usually do,' replied Kim philosophically. 'Oh, there's Florence! It's good to see her out and about. Sophie didn't have any luck catching up with her the other night, and I think we've all left messages for her. I'm so glad she's been able to come.' She waved at her, Florence hesitated then gave a small wave back.

Jennifer returned with some more water and they chatted amiably until it was their turn to play. The afternoon passed swiftly and easily and, before she knew it, Bella was back home having supper and looking forward - with eager anticipation - to her day out the next day.


Bella awoke early and leapt enthusiastically out of bed, whipping the curtains back eagerly to see what the weather was doing. It matched her mood – the sun was bright, the sky was blue and there was not a cloud to be seen in the sky. Quickly she showered and got dressed, putting on the clothes that she had picked out the previous night. She couldn't wear anything glamorous - or particularly feminine - as they were cycling, so had opted for a freshly laundered pair of navy Bermuda-type shorts and a pale, sky blue, polo shirt. Her hair was swept back into a low ponytail, low enough to enable her to put the helmet on, and her make-up was simple, just a fresh a touch of concealer, mascara and a slick of lipstick.

She trotted downstairs to prepare breakfast, something more substantial than just a piece of toast, and glanced at the clock. It was only 7.30 a.m. - hours to go until he arrived. Flicking the kettle off, she decided to stroll down to the post office - which was open from 7 a.m. for newspapers - to pick one up to peruse over her breakfast.

She sat in the garden basking in the warmth of the early morning sunshine, and took her time munching through her large bowl of muesli with a chopped banana and yoghurt on top, followed by a slightly warmed croissant and a large cup of tea. Meticulously she read every page of the paper. When she finally allowed herself to glance at her watch she was surprised - and then panicked - to see that it was 9.30 a.m. already. Hurriedly she scooped up her breakfast things, along with the newspaper, and took them into the kitchen. All of a fluster, she raced upstairs, brushed her teeth, checked her hair, re-did her lipstick and put some cash, lipstick, handkerchief and keys into a small handbag about the size of a paperback book, small enough to comfortably fit inside her cycle bag. With the windows checked and closed, she quickly washed up her breakfast dishes and tweaked things impatiently in the kitchen as she waited for Dave to arrive. Spot on 10 a.m. there was a knock at the door.

Bella took a breath to calm herself and opened it with a broad smile on her face. 'Good morning!'

'And a very good morning it is too,' replied Dave beaming back at her, 'shall I get your bike onto the rack?'

'Thanks. I'm all ready. I'll just get the bike out and then I'll lock up.'

With her bike tightly secured next to his bike on his silver VW Passat Estate she sank down into the passenger seat next to him, and tried to contain the over-excited, hormonal-teenager-type feelings. They chatted easily as they sped along the leafy country lanes on the twenty five minute journey. When they pulled up into the stony car park there were few cars, but from what she had heard it would be rammed full of them later in the day. Dave got out, paid the parking charge and then set about unloading the bikes. Meanwhile Bella trotted off to find a loo as all the excitement was playing havoc with her bladder.

Hurrying back, she could see Dave in the distance, standing tall and looking rather gorgeous, she felt, in his khaki, knee-length, fitted shorts and moss green polo shirt. She watched as he clipped his helmet on and checked the bikes once again.

'I'll just put my helmet on and I'll be ready,' she said as she slipped her handbag into the bike bag. 'You won't go speeding off without me will you?! I've only just started cycling again and I'm not terribly fit.'

He smiled kindly at her. 'Of course I won't, we'll take it as slowly as you like. There's no rush we've got the whole day ahead of us and the picnic is all ready and waiting for us,' he patted the bulging bike bags attached to the back of his bike.

Unfortunately for Bella the start of the cycle route was uphill, it felt like it went on for ever, but she was determined not to whinge even though every part of her body

448

felt as though it was going to explode in agony. When they got to the top she stopped.

'Sorry,' she gasped, trying to catch her breath, 'just gotta stop for a few minutes. I thought you said there weren't any hills.'

Dave grinned. 'Well I suppose it depends what you call a hill. We can always walk up any more, we don't have to cycle at all if you don't want to, it's not meant to be tortuous!' He passed her a fresh bottle of water, then took a swig from his own.

Bella wiped away the sweat, which was trickling down from under her helmet, and gulped down the water greedily. She passed the half-empty bottle back to Dave.

'Come on, you'd better catch me!' she called mischievously as she cycled off, whilst he was still putting the bottles away.

'Oy! Wait for me!' It didn't take him long to catch her up and they cycled in silence for a while, enjoying the peace, beauty and tranquility of the forest. The diverse range of trees and foliage synthesising together in harmony, the birds singing happily in their beautiful environment, far away from any road. After half an hour they stopped by a small lake and, though it was only 11.30 a.m, Dave suggested that they picnic.

'Fine by me. It's a charming spot.' She laid her bike on the ground and gazed at the still, calm water.

'We should be alone for a while - give it another hour or so and there'll be hoards of people stopping for their picnics.'

'I'm not surprised. It's so beautiful here.' She turned back to see that he had laid out a large picnic rug and was busy unpacking plates, glasses, food and drink. She settled herself on the rug and watched as he worked, startled and unsettled at the feelings stirring within her.

'It looks like a banquet,' she murmured to him.

'I aim to please!' he smiled. 'Drink?' She nodded and he poured her a glass of chilled elderflower cordial. The sweet, aromatic, sparkling drink slipped down easily - it was like being in a dreamy tableau from another era, she felt.

Hungrily Bella ate the smoked salmon sandwiches, the mini quiches, the cherry tomatoes, the mixed salad, the French bread, and still had plenty of room for the fresh strawberries, raspberries and cream that he produced. Leaning back on her elbows, replete, she felt contented and happy. Conversation continued to flow easily and enjoyably between them. With the sun dancing on the lake, and a breeze gently brushing over them, everything seemed idyllic. They lapsed into a contented silence and Bella, now lying flat on her back gazing up at the sky, could feel herself drifting off. It was only when the excited screams of children racing past on their bicycles, competing with their parents to see who could go the fastest, which prevented her from falling into a deep sleep. Reluctantly she opened her eyes and saw Dave propped up on his side gazing down at her.

'You looked so peaceful.'

She smiled and sat up, pushing her desire to kiss him away at the same time. 'I felt it. This is just perfect.'

'Good,' he sat up too. 'Feel like anything else to eat? I've got chocolate brownies in here,' he patted the cool bag.

'Oh, I'd love to, but I think I'd pop if I had another morsel to eat at the moment! I'll definitely have one later though!'

'You ready to continue then?'

She nodded, pushed herself up and stretched, her body was definitely going to complain at having to get back onto the bike. Between them they quickly and efficiently packed the picnic things away.

'Just in time,' said Dave, nodding towards a group of about fifteen friends who were descending upon the area with their picnics.

Despite protestations from her body, the remainder of the cycle didn't seem nearly as hard for some reason. They'd spent so long by the lake that by the time they reached the end of the trail it was half past three.

'Fancy a cup of tea here?' he asked, nodding in the direction of the small café.

'What about a cup of tea and one of those brownies back at my house?' she replied.

'Perfect.' He deftly stowed everything away and put the bikes back up onto the rack. She settled herself into the car whilst Dave finished securing the bikes and a few minutes later they were on their way back to her house.

'I think you chose the right time for us to come,' she commented as they drove out. The car park was jam packed with cars and there were still more arriving. Some people were here to cycle, others were families going off to the spectacular wooden play area, and older children and adults going off to use the aerial walkway.

'Saturdays are always busy, but when the weather's as gorgeous as this it brings even more people out.'

They drove in a companionable silence until they got to the cottage. Dave got Bella's bike off the rack whilst she went and unlocked the house, putting the kettle on first before she opened up the back door and windows in the house to let the breeze flow through.

Dave settled himself in a comfy chair under the shade of the big, white umbrella and watched as Bella poured them each a cup of tea to accompany their chocolate brownies.

'Thank you. That was a lovely day,' she said passing him a mug.

'My absolute pleasure. I had a great time too. See, I'm not so bad at getting the work/life balance right!' he joked.

She laughed. 'Maybe. We'll see.' She hesitated, not sure how he'd react if she asked him a work related question, but her concern for Fred, Mia and Kim won out.

'You look worried.' he commented, having noticed the change in her demeanour.

She shrugged. 'I'm not. It's just…'

He nodded encouragingly.

'I hope you don't mind, but I just wanted to ask you about Fred, Mia and Kim.' She glanced nervously at him and noticed an almost imperceptible change as he sat more upright in his chair.

'Go on.'

'It's your day off and I feel awful about asking.'

'That's okay,' he replied gently.

'Fred, Mia and Kim aren't going to get into any trouble are they? You know, for withholding information and for Kim not being, well, entirely honest about her whereabouts on the night Rupert died.'

'Fred and Mia will be ok, although they should have been upfront at the beginning. As for Kim, well, she shouldn't have lied and it remains to be seen what will happen.'

'Oh, okay. It's just, I feel a little guilty as I was the one who pushed them into telling you.'

He looked surprised. 'Really? How long had you known?'

'Earlier that afternoon. As soon as Mia accidentally let it slip, I insisted she tell the police. She, in turn, was adamant that she see Kim first, though I advised her not to, but I did accompany her to Kim's.'

'And what did you observe when you were at Kim's house?'

'Well, I'm pretty sure she was telling the truth. I really don't think she was lying. She seemed genuinely shocked that she'd been found out and had no time to make up an alibi as good as the one she gave, and I can totally see why, with the shock and all that, she wasn't thinking straight and wanted to protect Seb too. As far as I could see there was nothing about her body language that made me in the least bit suspicious.'

He looked thoughtfully at her.

'You're not cross are you?'

He smiled. 'No. If it hadn't been for you we'd be none the wiser about it at the moment, and the more information we can gather about that night the better.'

'While we're on the subject of work, have you had any luck speaking to Kit?'

'Yes. I managed to finally get hold of him yesterday. According to him, he lent Rupert some money years ago and Rupert was just paying it back.'

'Yeah right. You don't believe that do you?'

'It is possible. But no, I don't believe him. At the moment we cannot prove otherwise. There's no paperwork, nothing, and nothing to suggest that there was anything improper going on either.'

'Did he provide any evidence at all regarding the loan? Anything to back it up?'

He shook his head. 'Nope. Nothing.'

'My gut feeling is that he was blackmailing Rupert over something, but over what I don't know.'

'I think you might be right, but I have no way of proving it. As Rupert is not here, unless we come across some documentation or other evidence to suggest that he was being blackmailed, then there is nothing we can do.'

Bella's curiosity had been nudged again. 'Did you find out whether it was him in the picture? Was he in Australia with Kit and if so, why the big pretence about not knowing one another? Did they know each other before Australia? Did they grow up together?'

'You should be a detective the amount of questions you ask!' he joked, 'and to answer your questions, no, they apparently didn't know each other before Australia, and no they didn't grow up together, though not too far apart: Rupert in Salisbury, Kit in Winchester. Yes he was in Australia and the reason for the big pretence was apparently because Rupert liked to keep the past in the past and didn't want questions being asked.'

She raised her eyebrows. 'Really? Why was that?'

'He wouldn't say, just said he was doing what Rupert had asked him to do.'

'Sounds dodgy to me. But what would be his motive for murder?' she pursed her lips together as her brain ticked away. 'Perhaps he wanted more money and Rupert refused to give it to him?'

'Maybe. But if he killed Rupert he was killing his golden goose and would definitely not get any more money from him nor from his estate when dead, as there was nothing to corroborate the fact that he was owed money by him.'

'Hmm. But perhaps in a fit of anger he drove off somewhere - maybe to calm down, I don't know - and, seeing Rupert, ran him off the road?'

'Anything is possible, but let's not leap to conclusions.'

'Did you find out anything else about him? What about his past?'

'Who? Kit's?' Bella nodded. 'Nothing really to tell, seems like he's kept his nose clean, hasn't got a record or anything. Parents are still alive, as is his sister, only traumatic event was his twin brother dying when they were younger. Apart from that nothing.'

'Oh, how sad! Poor Kit. Hang on, you just asked me if I meant Kit. Who else did you think I meant? Rupert?' Her eyes glistened with excitement. 'Have you found something out about him? What?'

'I think we've discussed quite enough work for today. I've told you all I can, but please remember to keep this to yourself. I'll be speaking to Kim about the picture in due course.'

Dave's mouth was firmly set. Bella knew there was something else, something about Rupert that he hadn't told her, or rather couldn't tell her, in which case it must be something really relevant to the case, she thought excitedly. But how am I going to find out?

'Here, how about a chocolate brownie?' He offered her the plate and, though frustrated that he wouldn't tell her anything else, she took one and bit into the soft, rich, chocolate brownie. It was melt-in-the-mouth divine.

'Where did you get these from?' she moaned in delight and took another mouthful, 'they are heavenly. So delicious.'

He finished his mouthful and had to admit they were rather good. 'I made them myself,' he replied proudly.

Her eyes opened wide. 'No! Really?'

'No need to look so shocked!' he laughed, 'they're not that difficult to make.'

'Don't be so modest. Anyone can make them, but not everyone can make them as divinely delicious as you have. A man of many talents,' she smiled coquettishly.

He blushed which made her smile as she didn't think anything would make him blush. 'You're too kind.'

'Mind if I have another one?' She couldn't resist. Forget the diet! She'd been cycling for what felt like all day, surely she deserved to have another one of these?

'Be my guest, think I'll join you, he couldn't remember the last time he had had such a pleasurable day. Secretly, he'd always been attracted to Bella, but had never made a move on her because she'd been married to one of his best friends, and certainly not whilst he himself had still been married. Maybe that was why he'd lost touch with Hugh? Maybe deep down, on another level, he'd realised what a temptation Bella was to him, and kept his distance to avoid such temptation. Had it really been such a good idea to lose touch with a good friend? He and Hugh had been so close, but the high hopes he'd had when he'd married Alison had soon diminished as he realised what a demanding, selfish female she was. Nothing was ever good enough for her, and all she did was nag. When the two of them moved away he thought a fresh start would do them both good, and he wouldn't be constantly reminded of how lucky Hugh was. How naïve - or stupid -he'd been, he reflected.

'You look lost in your thoughts? Penny for them?'

He looked lovingly at Bella's bright, open face. 'Just thinking about the past. About Hugh.' He searched her face for her reaction, not wanting to upset her, but eager to see her response. Her face clouded and he felt cross with himself for his stupidity (again) and tactlessness.

'Yeah. I often think about him.'

'Naturally, you were together so long.'

'Of course. He was such a big part of my life, he always was and always will be. It's been so difficult,' her eyes welled up with tears. Where was this coming from? She still missed him desperately, but it had been a while since the tears had sprung up quite so quickly. Was this guilt? Guilt at feeling so attracted to Dave even though she wasn't even sure if they were dating? Could she really move on or was she fooling herself?

'I can only imagine. It must have been,' he corrected himself, 'must be awful.' He was desperately sorry he'd brought Hugh's name up and could kick himself for spoiling what had been an otherwise perfect day. 'He was an incredible person. A really honourable man. You knew where you stood with him, and his total honesty and compassion were traits which appear not to be so prevalent these days.'

Just like you, reflected Bella, startled that the comparison had popped into her head. Companionably they sat in contemplative silence for a while. Eventually Dave made his excuses to leave - as far as he was concerned, he'd ruined the day. But if he had been able to read Bella's mind he would have known that that was the opposite to what she felt

'Thank you so much for a lovely day. I really hope we can do it again soon,' she said, feeling unusually shy.

'Really?' he replied hopefully, 'I'd like that. I'll phone you.'

She laughed. 'That's if you're not too busy at work!'

'Point taken.' He smiled back - perhaps he hadn't totally ruined the day after all. 'See you soon and I WILL phone.' He wanted to kiss her but didn't feel brave enough to risk it, instead he waved as he walked over to his car.

# Chapter Fourteen

Yet again Bella tossed and turned all night, the nugget of information Dave had given her subconsciously process-ing itself, jolting her into half-wakefulness at regular inter-vals throughout the night. Blearily she woke at 8 a.m. as the alarm shrilled at her, and though the temptation was to roll over and try to go back to sleep, she knew it wouldn't do her any good, in fact it would probably make her feel worse.

She dragged herself tiredly downstairs, pulling her thin white cotton dressing gown around her as she went, and switched the kettle on. What was it that was bothering her? There was something niggling at the back of her mind and she couldn't retrieve it, no matter how hard she tried. And what was it that Dave hadn't told her? She knew he was holding something back about Rupert, but what? And how could she find out? Yawning expansively, she made a cup of tea and filled a bowl with muesli. Sure-ly there was something she could do to find out?

Reflectively she took herself off to church. No divine intervention or inspiration came to her whilst there and, no matter how hard she delved into her mind, nothing came to her that afternoon. As the sky turned grey and the thunder began to rumble again in the distance, she withdrew inside and flopped onto a sofa, but not before she had switched the television on. She flicked from channel to channel and despite there being so many, no programme particularly appealed to her. Eventually she settled on the Antiques Roadshow and - like most people - watched it in the hope that there would be that one big find, the little old lady who turned up with something she'd kept a pot plant in believing it to be a worthless piece of crockery, and then finding it was some rare piece worth thousands of pounds. It was only as the credits rolled that Bella took note that it had been filmed in the precinct of Salisbury Cathedral.

'Oh course!' she cried, 'how stupid of me! If Rupert grew up in Salisbury then I might be able to find out something about him there. All I have to do is go to Salisbury - surely there must be some records somewhere? Maybe a local newspaper that he might have been in, giving a little titbit of information which can't be found on the internet, perhaps I could find out where he went to school? Possibly even track down an old school friend?'

Filled with renewed enthusiasm she got out her laptop and spent the next two hours researching Salisbury and tracking down a bed and breakfast she could stay in. She gave them a call and, yes, they had one room available from Monday for three nights. Bella booked it and hastily went upstairs to pack a small bag with enough to keep her going for four days if necessary. If it proved to be fruitless she could always come back after one night, but if not she might stay there a little longer. Her packing was interrupted by the phone ringing.

'Hello?'

'Hi Bella.' It was Mia. 'How are you?'

'Great thanks,' she replied, trying to keep the excitement out of her voice. If Mia knew what she was up to she might try and talk her out of it. 'How about you? Nice weekend?'

'Good thanks. What about you?' They chatted amiably for a while until Mia got to the point of why she'd phoned. 'Do you fancy a trip out somewhere this week? Tunbridge Wells, or down to Rye, or wherever you want really?

'I'd love to, when were you thinking?'

'Tuesday?'

Bella hesitated. 'Friday would be better. Thought I might have a few days away.'

'Oh? That's sudden isn't it?'

Bella searched desperately for a plausible explanation as to why she'd suddenly decided to go away. 'Totally,' she replied, 'surprised myself actually. I was just watching the Antiques Roadshow, this week it was in Salisbury. I've always fancied going there but never been. Got on the phone, booked a B&B and I'm off tomorrow for a few nights - might be one night, might be two or three. Of course I could get there and realise it was a big mistake,' she wittered on.

'Oh,' replied Mia puzzled, it seemed rather out of character for Bella to be so impulsive. 'Everything is all right isn't it?'

'Absolutely. Probably regret it in the morning, but it seems like a good idea at the moment.' She kept her fingers crossed.

'Well, have a lovely time won't you. So Friday for a day out then? That should be fine, I'm pretty sure that there's no tennis on this Friday because of the village fête, but I'll have done my bit the day before and I'm busy help-

461

ing out on the day itself. Shall I pick you up, say 10 o'clock?'

'Perfect. I'll look forward to it. See you then. Bye.'

'Bye.'

Bella felt a twinge of guilt at not having been completely honest with her friend. She pushed away the little niggling doubt which was starting to stir within her. Was she doing the right thing digging around?

Determined to get a good nights sleep and make up for the terrible one the previous night, Bella went to bed early and was relieved, and refreshed, to wake up at 7 o'clock and realise she had slept through. Washed, dressed and ready to go, she didn't bother leaving the house until 9 o'clock as she knew both the motorways, particularly the M25, would be so busy with rush hour traffic that it would be futile. She hoped that by the time she hit the motorways the traffic would be starting to calm down and clear, though knowing full well how hit and miss it was.

Bella topped up her car with fuel at the petrol station on the Monhurst Road and, armed with a bottle of water and some fruit to snack on in case she got stuck in traffic, she set off on her journey to Wiltshire. Unfortunately the M25 lived up to its reputation as being Europe's largest car park. As usual there had been an accident and, whilst that in itself had not particularly blocked the road - just a brief temporary closure of one lane - it was the rubberneckers slowing down to have a good look which added to the delay. Muttering a lot, Bella, who loathed sitting in traffic, drummed her fingers impatiently on the steering wheel as if by doing so the traffic would magically clear.

Three and a half hours later she eventually drove in to Salisbury, a trip that should have taken about two hours on a good run. She followed the instructions carefully to the Bed and Breakfast and prepared herself for the stereotypical, in her belief, type of person who ran those sorts of establishments, her preconceptions convincing her that it would be someone in their mid to late sixties, over-permed and coloured hair, lashings of make up, suffocating perfume and clothes that should only be worn by a girl in the first flushes of youth.

The house itself looked promising. It was old brick, double-fronted and neatly kept with not a net curtain in sight. It was down a quiet leafy road not far from the centre of Salisbury and had parking for several cars on the drive, she'd been informed that she was more than welcome to park on it. Bella took her bag out of the car and, though it was far too early for their normal check-in time, she had been reassured that it would not be a problem as the booking Bella had made covered a cancellation which had included the Sunday night and no one else had subsequently been booked into it for that night.

She rang the doorbell and waited. Eventually Bella could hear the tap, tap, tap of footsteps getting closer and braced herself.

'Ah, you must be Mrs Sparkle,' cried the woman welcomingly.

'Yes,' replied Bella, slightly taken aback as the woman greeting her was in her early forties and casually dressed in a pair of jeans and well cut white shirt, her red spirally curled hair was clasped casually to the nape of her neck by a simple, silver clip, and her feet were shod in a pair of blue espadrilles.

'Come in. Here, let me take your bag. Come through, I was just feeding the baby.'

'Oh, sorry. I didn't mean to interrupt.' Bella felt embarrassed now at having turned up so early.

'Don't worry. As I said on the phone, it's not a problem. Would you like a cup of tea?'

'Oh, thank you but no. I'll put my things in my room and then go into Salisbury if that's okay.'

'Sure?'

Bella nodded, looking at the rather cute baby – a boy she thought, but it was hard to tell – who was sitting in his high chair waving a spoon around and banging it on a bowl, the contents of which seemed to be all over his face and hair.

'Excuse Archie, he does like to try and feed himself, but he's not terribly good at it yet. Are you chicken?' she laughed, tickling him under the chin which made him laugh even more.

Bella's heart twanged with sadness. She had so wanted a baby. It wasn't Archie's fault that he was such a cutie, every baby seemed cute and, though she was okay most of the time, sometimes it hurt her heart more than she could bear. She could feel the tears prick at her eyes.

'You okay?' The women was looking at her concerned.

'Fine. He's so sweet, babies always make me go all soft. I'll leave you to it, you've got your hands full.'

'You're in the Spire Room, top of the stairs turn left. If there's anything you need please let me know. There's a sitting room for guests: it's the door at the bottom of the stairs, there's tea, coffee, milk, sugar and a kettle in there, help yourself.' She handed her the key.

'Thanks. See you later.' Bella walked to the stairs, picked her bag up - which was where the woman had left it - and climbed up two flights to the top of the house. She opened the door on the left and found that she was in a large, airy room in the roof of the house. The ceilings sloped and there was a double bed, dressing table, wardrobe and a comfy looking armchair. The walls themselves were pale yellow, and the bed linen was a sparkling, crisp white, the armchair co-ordinated with the theme in a white and soft yellow check. She peaked into the compact bathroom and found a small bath, basin and loo - all white, fresh and spotlessly clean. Bella sat on the bed to test the firmness of the mattress, convinced that it would sag heavily in the middle, but was pleasantly surprised to find that it was firm and even all over. Last but not least, she went to the dormer window and looked out. There was a spectacular view over to the top of the cathedral spire; no wonder it was called the Spire Room. Pleased with her accommodation, Bella freshened up, unpacked, and quietly slipped out of the front door to go and explore the city.

She wandered along in the hope that she was going in the right direction, following instinct and the mental map she'd worked out from looking out of her bedroom window towards the cathedral. Speeding up and after a brisk fifteen minutes walk, shops began to appear and eventually Bella arrived in the Market Square. Temporarily distracted by the shops, she wandered in and out of them, particularly enjoying the well-equipped kitchen shop but restraining herself from purchasing. She continued to stroll around, taking in the ancient architecture, and came upon the River Avon which meandered through the city. She stopped to watch the ducks with their ducklings, who were by now not so little and trying bravely to strike out on their own, much to the despair of the mother duck who kept having to swim round to rescue one or other of her offspring. Bella smiled as she observed them, she didn't know what it was about ducklings - or for that matter any baby bird or creature - but she found them irresistible and couldn't help but stop and watch, so sweet and adorable.

Her walk took her through the rest of the centre of Salisbury until she could see the cathedral looming large in the distance. The ancient arch opened up into a beautiful precinct. Stunning houses edged the lawns of the cathedral which looked majestic in its stature. Bella stood in awe looking up at the architecture which was even more stunning and beautiful in real life than in any picture or television programme she had seen. Not able to resist, she paid and went in to the breathtaking building. Slowly she strolled her way around the ancient building and, despite the number of tourists inside, she could feel a strong and overwhelming presence of God. For a while Bella sat and gazed around her, her thoughts drifting to Hugh and then to Dave, reflecting on the conflict she felt within herself. When she walked out of the cathedral, she felt a calmness and peace within her that lifted her spirits, something she had not felt for a very long time.

Reluctant to leave such an historic and inspiring place, Bella wandered through the gift shop and into the café, which was light and bright, the glass ceiling provided a magnificent view upwards to the exterior of the cathedral. The café itself was packed, and not just with tourists, there were a few mums bringing their children in for a drink after school and other people who were obviously local residents, at least from what Bella gathered as she overheard snippets of conversation. She purchased a pot of tea and a luscious looking, and very generous, slice of sponge cake which was filled with fresh cream and raspberries. Spying an elderly couple preparing to leave from a small table to one side of the café, Bella weaved her way across to it.

She tucked in to the cake which melted delightfully in her mouth. Bella almost moaned out loud, it tasted scrumptious. Having munched her way hungrily through half of it, she sat back to sip tea and deliberated on the fact that she had not done a single thing to help her in her quest to discover more about Rupert. But where to start? She really didn't have the faintest idea. In her rush to get to Salisbury Bella hadn't come up with a plan of how, or what, she was going to find out whatever it was she needed to know, even if there was anything to discover.

Perhaps the library, she pondered? Or maybe the local paper? Still, she was enjoying herself and Salisbury was a very beautiful place. Glancing at her watch, she realised that it was 5.30 p.m - too late she assumed for the library. But what to do? Go back and sit in her room all night? She strolled out of the cathedral precinct and eventually turned right, looking in the shop windows as she went, most of which were now closed. She came across the cinema which was still in an old building in the centre of the town. Decisively she checked to see what was on and bought a ticket for a romantic/comedy film starting in ten minutes time.

It was a light-hearted, non brain-taxing film and she enjoyed the fact that it took her mind off Rupert and everything else that was going on in her life. A couple of hours later she reappeared blinking in the glowing evening sunshine, her stomach rumbled, reminding her that it was well past its normal feeding time. As she'd noticed some restaurants around and off the Market Square Bella ambled back and settled on the pizza restaurant which was located directly on the square.

There was one tiny table left and Bella sat down, suddenly feeling very alone as she looked at all the couples engrossed in one another, and the groups of friends gathered together having a fun night out. She sighed miserably and ordered herself a glass of house white, garlic bread and a pizza with tomato, mozzarella, rocket and parmesan. Feeling conspicuous by her singleness, she fished around in her bag, found a leaflet on the cathedral and studiously read it from cover to cover several times throughout her meal. She ordered another glass of wine and felt herself relax and feel a little less lonely as it absorbed its way into her. Draining the last few drops, she paid quickly and hurried out, self-consciously feeling as though dozens of pairs of eyes were looking at her and judging her – sad woman, can't have any friends if she's eating alone, and such like.

It was half past nine by the time she got back to the B&B. Lights were blazing despite it still being light outside. She knocked on the door and the friendly woman opened it - she must remember to ask her name - Bella scolded to herself.

'Hello. Have you had a nice time?' she enquired letting Bella in through the front door. Bella could hear a couple of older children arguing in the distance. The woman grimaced. 'Sorry about that. Don't know what's got into them today, ever since they got back from school they've been bickering.'

'Poor you. Must be very wearing.'

The woman smiled and laughed. 'I've got used to it, but some days I feel like pulling my hair out! I've just put some fresh milk in there,' she indicated to the sitting room, 'or perhaps I could do you a hot chocolate or something?'

'Thanks. That's very kind of you but I think I might just go to bed, it's been a long day.'

'You shouldn't be disturbed up there. But let me know if they make too much noise for you! Breakfast is between eight and nine o'clock. Sleep well, see you in the morning.'

'Thanks. Good night.'

How on earth does she manage to stay smiling with all that racket going on? Two older children, a baby and a bed and breakfast to run - it was a tall order. Bella wondered whether her husband helped out. She was impressed, sure that there was no way she would be able to do everything that the woman juggled. Sadly there would be no chance of her ever being in that position, despite being a similar age to the woman who ran the B&B, Bella felt that at the age of forty-two - apart from the fact that she was not currently in a long-term relationship - her fertility would be diminishing by the month, making it unlikely that she would ever have one child, let alone three.

Sinking into a deeper gloom as each step took her up to her room, Bella felt isolated and completely alone. If she disappeared nobody would really care, she dwelled self-pityingly and morosely. All she saw around her in life were couples and families happily being together. In reality life wasn't like that, but tonight she had her rose-tinted spectacles on. Bella ran herself a deep bath and poured in some of the rose bath oil which was in a large bottle by the side of it. She sank into the steaming, bubbly, fragrant tub and lay there contemplating upon the negative aspects of her life, the peace and contentment she'd felt earlier in the cathedral having evaporated.    After half an hour she stepped out, feeling decidedly flushed and hot.  It had been a mistake filling the bath with such hot water on a warm evening, particularly considering that she was at the top of the house where all the day's heat was rising to.  She flung the bedroom window open and, making sure that the towel was wrapped tightly around her, she stuck her head out to cool down, a bit like a dog sticking its nose out of a car window.

She attempted to read but couldn't concentrate, then thought about phoning Mia or maybe Dave, but decided it was too late in the evening to do so.  Flicking the light off, she sank into the extremely comfortable bed and went straight to sleep.  However, two hours later she was wide awake wriggling and twisting, trying hard to go back to sleep, feeling sticky and hot as she shifted around trying to settle.  Finally, as a clear, gentle dawn started to break, she drifted off and was only woken by a slam of the front door.  A quick glance at her clock told her that it was half past eight.  Leaping out of bed she swiftly washed and dressed not wanting to miss breakfast, quickly tying her long hair up into a loose knot as she ran down the stairs, following the tantalising smell of cooking bacon.

Breakfast was served in the room on the opposite side of the hallway to the sitting room.  Four tables were occupied, with a fifth laid and waiting for her.  Bella's misconceptions about bed and breakfasts' took a further educational turn.  The tables were not occupied by geriatric pensioners noisily shovelling and slurping down their food, but instead there was an eclectic mix of people.  A young couple were gazing gooely into each others eyes.  A middle aged couple: both well rounded, with plates piled so high that it was obvious as to why they were the size they were. A lone gentleman, dressed in a smart business suit and an older American couple were pouring over their guidebooks to Salisbury and the surrounding area. All glanced in Bella's direction as she entered the room and gave her a cheery "hello". Bella smiled and reciprocated.

At that moment the owner, looking as fresh as a daisy, came hurrying back into the breakfast room. 'Good morning,' she said, 'sleep well?'

Bella nodded. Had she not had so much churning through her mind she was sure she would have slept beautifully, so it was therefore irrelevant even to hint at a bad night's sleep.

'What would you like for breakfast? There are cereals, yoghurt and fruit over there if you'd like to help yourself and juice too,' she indicated to a table that was prettily laid out and laden down with food, 'and I can do any sort of eggs you'd like, also there's bacon, sausage, mushrooms, beans, hash browns, tomatoes.'

'Oh thanks, it certainly smells delicious so, um, please may I have scrambled eggs, bacon and a few mushrooms, not too much, just a small plate, thanks.'

'Tea or coffee?'

'Tea please.'

'English Breakfast, Earl Grey, Darjeeling, Camomile, Peppermint, Green?'

Bella was impressed at the choice, she'd guessed - incorrectly - that it would be "builders" and no choice. 'Um, English Breakfast please.'

'Toast? White? Brown? Granary? Sourdough?'

Bella laughed. 'There's so much choice. I think white for a change please.' Sensible granary bread would have to wait for a few days. There was nothing quite so delicious as white toast lathered with butter, inspiring memories of childhood breakfasts, and for that very reason Bella tended to refrain from buying white bread because she knew she could eat the whole loaf in one go. The woman, whose name she could still not recall, though sure that she had been told it, trotted off to cook Bella's breakfast. Bella in turn got up and helped herself to a small bowl of muesli, a sprinkling of freshly sliced strawberries with a dollop of natural yoghurt on top, and a glass of freshly-squeezed orange juice. Sitting on the wide windowsill were a couple of newspapers, which Bella assumed were there to be read, so she picked up a copy of the Daily Mail and munched as she read. Her pot of tea arrived and a few minutes later a plate with a perfect quantity of scrambled eggs, crispy bacon and mushrooms. Surreptitiously squirting some ketchup onto her plate, she ate her breakfast heartily. The other guests started to drift away and soon she was left on her own. Her spirits had risen by merely being in the presence of other people, now she was starting to feel deflated and the fullness of her stomach made her remember, guiltily, the diet she had broken yet again.

The woman unobtrusively and efficiently cleared the tables around Bella and started putting away the food from the breakfast table. Bella poured herself another cup of tea and pondered upon her course of action for the day. Her thoughts were interrupted by the woman asking if she could clear her breakfast dishes away.

'Of course. Thank you, it was delicious. By the way, sorry, I can't remember your name?'

'Trisha, didn't I say when you arrived? Sorry about that, I'd lose my head if it wasn't screwed on properly! What have you got planned for today?'

'Oh, er, probably just do more sightseeing in Salisbury I would think,' Bella replied cautiously.

'Well, there's no rush, take your time over the rest of your tea, have a lovely day and I'll see you later. Archie's about ready for some more food,' she grinned as the wail of the infant could be heard to crescendo in the distance.

'Thanks. See you later.' Bella continued sipping her tea, feeling totally uninspired as to where she should start with her search for information. Popping upstairs to clean her teeth, she took her bag and car keys, checked the weather – brilliant blue skies and sunshine again – and quietly took herself downstairs and let herself out of the front door.

The sun felt warm and pleasant on her as she strolled back in to Salisbury again. This time resisting the temptations of the shops, she walked purposefully across the square to the library, which was housed in an unattractive, low-rise, relatively modern (compared to the prevalent ancient architecture) building. She pushed the door open and walked around in the hope that something would leap out at her and inspire. Of course it didn't so she went to the desk and whispered to the librarian that she needed some information.

'It's okay,' she replied 'you don't have to whisper,' dispelling the old tradition that you weren't allowed to make a noise of any kind, let alone breathe, in a library.

Bella blushed. 'Sorry.'

The middle-aged woman with short slightly greying hair, wearing a navy dress which looked as though it had gone out of fashion twenty years ago, smiled at her. 'Don't worry, you can talk at a normal volume here, that's all I was trying to say. Now what sort of information are you after?'

'I'm not sure really. Local news from about thirty years ago would be good, perhaps local papers?'

'Hmm, what sort of news? Anything in particular, or just general from about that time?'

'About one particular event.' She moved to one side, to allow a couple of young mums with their offspring to check their books out.

'What was that particular event? Oh hello Gladys, how are you?' She interrupted her conversation with Bella to greet, Bella assumed, her colleague who must have been the wrong side of sixty and walked with the higgledy gait of someone in dire need of a hip replacement. The woman was small and rotund, with tightly permed hair which had a faint orange tinge to it. Her lips were smothered in a bright orange lipstick which clashed beautifully with her orange and black patterned short-sleeved dress from which pro-truded chubby arms with loose-hanging flesh squeezing out around the edges of them.

Bella tried not to stare at the vision, who was talking ten to the dozen as she tucked her bag under the counter and straightened herself out ready for work.

'Hello?' Bella realised that the librarian was talking to her.

'Oh, sorry. What did you say?'

'I was just saying that Gladys here might be able to help you.'

Bella smiled. 'Really? That would be fantastic.'

'Tell me what you need to know and I'll see what I can do,' beamed Gladys at her.

'Okay. I'm trying to find out about someone called Rupert Ireton who lived here around thirty years ago. I believe that something happened, which might well have been in the local news, and I'm trying to find out what it was,' she finished and thought it sounded feeble.

'Thirty years? That's a long way back. Don't know how much we'd be able to find out. Have you tried the internet?'

Bella was amazed that this woman even knew what the internet was. 'Yes, but I didn't get anywhere.'

'I didn't live here thirty years ago. Moved to Salisbury twenty years ago otherwise I might have remembered.' She looked thoughtful. Bella stood patiently feeling any hope of finding something out slipping away from her.

'Tell you what though, that journalist might remember.'

'Which one?' asked the other librarian.

'Oh, you know. That chap who was in the papers a few years ago. Got some sort of recognition for all the work he'd done. What was his name?' she tapped her crinkled fingers on the surface of the desk.

'Don't remember anything.' commented the other one.

'Got it! Bert Burstow.'

'Who? Never heard of him.'

'Bert Burstow, you must have heard of him?!'

Bella watched as the two of them launched into a lengthy discussion as to whether or not the other librarian knew who Bert was. She was getting impatient now, it was taking for ever to get any information out of them and, additionally, they were being constantly interrupted by people borrowing and returning books.

'So, where could I find this Bert Burstow?' Bella eventually interrupted. The librarians both looked at her in surprise, again having forgotten that she was standing there.

'Well now, that I don't know,' replied Gladys.

Oh, for goodness sake, muttered Bella inwardly.

'But I think Daisy will know. You hold on here while I give her a call.' Gladys disappeared off to make a phone call, returning fifteen minutes later.

Instinct warned Bella that Gladys wouldn't be capable of making a short phone call, and she was right.

Gladys looked triumphant. She handed Bella a piece of paper. 'I knew Daisy would know. I thought to myself, if anyone will know, it will be Daisy, and I was right! That there is the address of where Bert is currently residing. I think you're more likely to get the information you want direct from him than spend hours trawling through microfiche of old newspapers.'

Bella clutched the piece of paper tightly between her fingers. 'Thank you so much for all your help. I really appreciate it,' she said with feeling.

'Pleasure dear. Good bye, and good luck.'

'Bye.' Bella hurried out of the library and read the scrawl on the paper. It gave the address of a nursing home. Leafy Lane Nursing Home to be precise. Uh oh, that means he's either very old, very ill or both. Her sudden high was not quite so high, fearing that Bert would not be able to remember what he had had for breakfast, let alone what happened thirty years ago. She felt in need of a caffeine fix and ordered herself a cappuccino from a local coffee shop, she sat outside on the pavement at the junction where the road curved away as it met the pedestrian area. She watched the hustle and bustle of people and cars as she sipped her coffee and hoped fervently that she would at least make some sort of progress with her information-gathering by the end of the day. Taking a last swig of coffee, she walked down the pedestrian area to the tourist office, which was housed in one of the many ancient stone buildings of Salisbury.

She waited patiently whilst those in the queue in front of her, tourists (both overseas and UK based), were dealt with until it was her turn. She asked for a local map, as she had forgotten to bring her road map of England, and for directions to the nursing home. On the off-chance, she enquired whether they had a telephone number for it. The helpful woman tapped away on her computer and swiftly produced the number which she scribbled onto a piece of paper for Bella. Thanking her, Bella left and blinked as she walked back out into the bright sunshine.

It occurred to Bella that they may have visiting hours at the nursing home or perhaps one could just turn up. Rather than having a wasted trip, she phoned and ascertained that, as the residents would be having their lunch in about half an hour and then most of them had a post lunch nap, it would be best if Bella postponed her visit until around 3 o'clock. So what to do until then? Impatient to get to the home and speak to Bert, she reluctantly admitted defeat and resolved to explore the city a little more.

Seeing a bookshop she wandered in, whiling some time away as she rifled her way through the vast selection of books. Inevitably if she walked into a bookshop she always came out with a book, it was impossible for a bookworm like herself to resist, but on this occasion she could not concentrate and the appeal of a freshly-printed, pristine book, did nothing for her. Turning left out of the shop, she ambled back up in the direction of the cathedral and walked the full perimeter of the precinct, endeavouring to engross herself in the historical atmosphere of the cathedral and the many buildings around it, but that did little to distract her. For the umpteenth time she checked her watch and groaned, it was still only half past twelve. Decisively she walked up to the cathedral café for some lunch and was taken aback to see such a long queue outside it. The food really must be good, she thought - the cake certainly had been the day before - and sure enough it was. Bella settled on the chicken, which was served with a creamy mushroom sauce and a selection of fresh vegetables. She added a sparkling mineral water to her tray and paid. The queue coming in was still just as long as when she had arrived, and the tables too were full. She hovered for a few moments until she saw a small table being vacated in the furthest corner, near the gift shop.

Lunch was as delicious as it looked and met expectation. Feeling her blood sugar levels restoring themselves, she felt some semblance of humour returning. Bella relaxed slightly and tuned into snippets of conversations floating around her, as always a fascinating insight into the lives of other people. Squashing her desire for a pudding, she left and strolled back to the B&B to collect her car. It was a good half an hour's walk at a slow pace to the house, so by the time she arrived it was approaching 1.45pm. Itching to get going she started her engine, having reviewed the directions and ignoring her satnav, set off. Eventually, despite several wrong turns, she arrived at the nursing home at 2.15pm - had she not gone wrong so many times she would have been even earlier. It was far too early to go in and she resigned herself to sitting in her car until it was almost 3 o'clock. Bella sank back in the seat and closed her eyes. A gentle breeze wafted in through the open window but the warmth of the sun beating through the windscreen sent her drifting off to sleep. With a jolt she woke up and looked around her, feeling disoriented and momentarily wondering where she was. She gave herself a moment to come to then glanced at her watch. It was 2.55pm. Putting the window up and grabbing her bag, she hopped out of the car and gave her loose beige linen dress a little shake to let the air circulate and refresh her.

The front door to the nursing home was open and there was a small reception area off to the right-hand side.

'Hello?' called Bella.

A girl in her late teens appeared from the office behind the reception desk. 'Can I help you?'

'Yes. I phoned earlier. I'd like to see Bert Burstow please.'

'Are you a relative?'

'No. Gladys at the library in Salisbury suggested I talk to him. If he's up to it,' she added.

'I think he's in the garden. Come with me, I'll show you.'

She led the way down the hall towards the back of the modern brick building. Bella had expected some dilapidated Edwardian building that was in desperate need of attention, but instead the nursing home had turned out to be brand new. The smell, however, was worse than Bella had expected. The aroma of overcooked mince, mixed with a musty disinfectant smell, combined with what Bella thought of as the stench of approaching death, made her shiver and she breathed through her mouth in an effort to keep her nostrils clear of the unpleasant odours. They continued past a room which had groups of chairs clustered together. Some of them were occupied by antique looking beings, a few chatting, some sleeping - it was everything that scared Bella about old age.

They stepped through some French doors and out onto a spacious flagstone terrace. A large expanse of neat lawn was edged by several highly colourful boarders.

'Nice gardens,' commented Bella.

'We have a full-time gardener - we believe that having somewhere pleasant to sit or to look at helps our residents and it certainly brightens the place up. We've even got a vegetable garden. Residents can go and help out if they feel up to it, and even though most of them can't do very much they seem to enjoy the fact that they have the option and benefit, both physically and mentally, from being outside in the fresh air.'

'Good idea.' Bella was impressed.

'There's Burt, over there,' the young woman pointed across the pristine lawn to a well established willow tree where there were half a dozen decrepit residents occupying chairs in the shade.

'Thanks.'

Bella strolled across the expansive lawn to the group of elderly people, who were clustered together, and braced herself for meeting Bert.

'Ooh, who have we got here?' warbled an elderly woman whose hair was so white that you could see the pinkness of her scalp shining through. She peered up through rheumy eyes at Bella. Bella smiled.

'Bert?' she asked questioningly at the only two men sitting with the group of four women.

'That's me. At least I can still remember my own name,' Bert chuckled. The others cackled with him as this was obviously some kind of "in" joke.

'That's more than can be said for old Violet over there,' added the other man, whose blue eyes had faded over time and were now ringed with white, hinting at a high cholesterol level. They all looked over at Violet who was a tall, willowy woman, younger than the group who were seated. She had a wispy dress on that floated around as she danced from side to side, her arms positioned, held by an imaginary partner, and deep in discourse with whoever was - or rather wasn't - there. Is this what it will come to, worried Bella. Will I be having conversations with imaginary people? Will the ageing process treat me cruelly? Will the younger generations show disregard and disrespect?

'So, you wanted me then?' asked Bert, snapping Bella out of her musings. Bert was shrivelled and shrunk, as though he'd been put into a washing machine at the wrong temperature. His skin was yellow and heavily wrinkled, and his teeth were obvious by their absence, other than three which were dotted about and such a dark, dirty, yellow colour that Bella could only conclude were a result of a lifetime of chain smoking. As if on queue, he let out a chesty, phlegmy cough which, in general, seemed to be symbolic of smokers, then spent a while wheezing whilst he recovered. The group looked at her expectantly, making her feel rather as though she were an exhibit in a zoo and she was today's entertainment.

'I went to the library this morning. I've been trying to get some information. Gladys there said that you used to work on the local paper. Quite a celebrity by all accounts, commended for all your work,' Bella felt flattery - much deserved by all accounts - would be a good softener to the conversation. Visibly she saw him grow a little taller, and his chest appeared to puff out in pride.

'Well, I don't want to blow my own trumpet but I am a bit of a legend in the journalistic world,' he grinned toothlessly.

'Oh, be off with you Bert! You were a local hack. It's not as though you were working on one of the big nationals,' piped up the white-haired old dear.

'Shows how much you know!' retorted Bert.

Bella stepped in quickly, fearing that the good-natured bickering would descend into a group event and she'd find it tricky to steer the conversation back in the direction she wished to take it. 'Anyway, she seemed to think that you would be able to help me.'

'Try me. I used to be able to remember everything, absolutely everything.'

'Pity you can't now! You're just like the rest of us. Go on, tell us what you had for breakfast,' goaded the blue-eyed man.

Bert folded his arms across his chest defensively. 'Shan't,' he replied like a truculent child.

Bella sighed. It was going to be a long afternoon. Persevering, she continued. 'It's about something that may or may not have happened thirty years ago.'

'So, if it didn't happen, how's he going to know whether it did happen and he's forgotten about it or whether it didn't happen and he can't remember that it didn't happen?' asked a petite woman who was sitting on the periphery of the group and had so far remained silent.

'Good point. How will he know?' added the white haired old dear.

'Just let the lady talk and then we will see,' snapped Bert. 'What's your name?'

'Bella,' she replied.

'I've got a granddaughter called Bella. By the way my name's Muriel,' introduced the white-haired, pink-scalped old dear holding out a gnarled arthritic hand for Bella to shake.

Bella took it gingerly, afraid to inflict any additional pain in the proffered hand, and felt the bones underneath the paper-thin skin.

Bert's interest had been stoked. 'Come on then Bella. Ask away.' He liked a challenge and he knew that even if he couldn't remember his friends would, sadly, not be able to remember Bella's visit by the morning.

'I'm trying to find out about someone called Rupert Ireton.'

'Why?' interrupted Muriel.

'Give it a rest Muriel, let her finish.' Bert rolled his eyes at Bella conspiratorially.

'He grew up in Salisbury, I believe, and something happened thirty years ago. I'm sure it did. I don't know what, but whatever it was it was bad enough for him not to have any kind of contact with his family afterwards.'

'Lots of people lose contact with their families,' murmured the blue-eyed man, who'd introduced himself as Jack whilst the others were arguing. He looked sadly at Bella and she felt a twang of pity for him. 'Like my family. Never come and visit. Lucky if they remember my birthday.'

There was a morose and reflective silence. Bella hesitated to interrupt but there seemed to be a growing number of reflective silences, she reasoned that they would have plenty of time for those after she'd left.

'He was fifteen when his family lost touch.'

'Oh poor love!' cried Muriel. 'Fancy being abandoned by your family. Poor little love. How cruel some people can be.'

'That's true enough.' There was a general nodding and murmuring at this.

Bella studied Bert who had remained silent. She willed his brain to work, for the cobwebs of old age to blow away and his mind to come back at full throttle. He pursed his lips then sucked the few teeth he had, shook his head and twisted his hands.

'It rings a bell, but I'll be blowed if I can remember why.'

'Why don't we all put our minds to it?' suggested Jack. 'Most of us were living in the area thirty years ago.' They nodded and gazed off in different directions. Bella couldn't be entirely sure whether they were thinking, or had actually gone to sleep with their eyes open. Each one of them must be at least eighty years old she thought, probably nearer ninety or more.

'That was the year before the Silver Jubilee year that was.'

'What was?'

'Thirty years ago, 1976. The year after was 1977, the Queen's Silver Jubilee.'

'Oh that were a good year it were. Do you remember the street parties? What fun we had, the children all dressed up, streets closed.'

'You got a real sense of community then, not like now where everyone is intent on looking after themselves and not giving a stuff about anyone else,' added Jack bitterly.

'Times have certainly changed. And not for the better, you mark my words,' added Dorothy.

Oh please, prayed Bella, please let them focus on Rupert and not have a reminisce about the good old days. But she was out of luck, the conversation wound its way through the seventies, then the eighties, then the nineties and into the twenty first century. She sat down on the grass, resigned to the fact that it could take all afternoon. Half an hour went by and cups of tea and some biscuits were brought out to them. Bella gratefully took the cup offered to her and sipped as she waited for the conversation to run its course, part of her fascinated by the tales they were telling.

'Didn't he do something bad?' Muriel suddenly piped up making the others halt their ruminations.

'I think you're right Muriel. There's definitely something.'

Bella sat up eagerly, hoping she was on the edge of a breakthrough.

'Something to do with a car as I remember.'

'Got it!' cried Bert triumphantly. Bella held her breath expectantly. 'He was the one who nicked his dad's car and went joyriding.'

So that was it, under-aged driving, stealing a car, no wonder he wanted to keep it quiet. But in this day and age would he really be vilified for such youthful stupidity?

'Pity it didn't stop at that though,' Bert shook his head sadly.

'What was it? What did he do?' urged Bella eagerly.

485

'He couldn't drive, thought he could like any cocky young teenager. Problem was he lost control, hit a child.'

'Oh no!' Bella's hand flew to her mouth. She had a horrible feeling in the pit of her stomach that there was worse to come.

'Poor child died. Rupert was locked up. Family moved away, never heard anything about them after that.'

Bella sat there stunned. Rupert had killed a child? And now he had been killed himself. There had to be a connection.

'What age was the child?' she asked.

'Ten. A boy. Tragic it was, tragic. Whole community was rocked to the core, and as for the child's parents well, I don't know how they coped, can one ever truly recover after the death of ones child?'

'Poor little lamb,' whispered Muriel, a tear running down her cheek.

Bella gulped back her tears as she remembered the devastation of her miscarriage. But to have given birth and loved and nurtured your child for ten years, then have him so cruelly ripped away from you... She couldn't bear to think about it, it made her heart ache so much she had to stop.

'That's so sad, so terrible,' she shook her head.

'Certainly was. Rupert didn't do it on purpose, it was a dreadful accident, but one that shouldn't have happened anyway,' continued Bert. 'Those were the types of stories I didn't like covering, particularly when they involved children.'

'What was the name of the little boy who died?' asked Bella quietly.

'Charles. Charles something, can't remember his surname.'

'Me neither,' added Jack. The rest of them sat in silence for a few minutes, reflecting and trying to remember, but they couldn't.

'Didn't he have a brother?' added Jack.

'No, it was a sister wasn't it?' said Muriel.

'Sorry I just can't remember,' Bert said apologetically.

Bella smiled and touched his hand. 'Thank you anyway. You have helped me a great deal.'

'Why did you want to know?' asked Dorothy.

'Rupert died in a car accident recently. Except that the police don't believe it was an accident. I wondered whether there was something in his past which might be connected to his death, tenuous though it may be.'

'Well I'm sorry to hear that. Despite what he'd done, it's tragic he's died too young, be it deliberately or otherwise.'

There were murmurs of "dreadful", "shocking" and the like. Bella seized the moment to leave.

'Thank you again, I must go now. It's been lovely to meet you all,' and she really meant it, the elderly seemed to be overlooked by society and yet they had a lifetime of experience and knowledge to offer and shouldn't be dismissed as so often happened.

She wandered reflectively back across the lawn, and turned to wave at them before she entered the house. In their own ways they waved back. She felt sad, not just about what she'd discovered but for all the residents there, this was no doubt where they were going to die. How depressing it must be to enter such a place with the knowledge that the next time you leave it will be by coffin. Bella sat for a moment in her car gathering her thoughts before driving back to the bed and breakfast. It was now five o'clock and she got ensnared in the rush hour traffic and, despite not getting lost this time, pulled into the B&B over half an hour later. What she really wanted now was to be at home surrounded by her own things. Funny how her rented cottage felt like home, despite there being few of her own possessions there. She knocked on the door and waited for Trisha to answer it.

'Hi,' her cheery face greeted Bella.

'Hello. I'm sorry Trisha but I'm going to check out now, I need to get home.'

Her face clouded. 'Is everything alright? Are you okay?'

'I'm fine, thank you. I just need to get back. I'm happy to pay for the nights I've booked, I know it's an inconvenience me departing early.'

'Nonsense, it's fine. Don't worry.'

Bella hesitated, feeling guilty at leaving her in the lurch. 'At least let me pay for tonight. It's so late in the day it's exceedingly unlikely you'll get anybody else to take the room for the night.'

'Well, alright then, thank you.'

They sorted out the payment and Bella nipped upstairs to pack her things. She bade farewell and popped her bag into the boot of her car. She felt she'd made the right decision and, despite driving home in very slow evening traffic which took her four hours, she felt her mood lift as she drove into Monhurst and parked outside her cottage. Dropping her bag in the hall she switched on the lights, feeling weary and mentally, physically and emotionally drained. Walking over to the answer phone she pressed the button and listened to two messages from Dave which made her smile, particularly at his second message where he made a joke of her paying him back for not returning her calls previously. It was half past ten, too late to phone and, as much as she wanted to talk to him, she was too tired and needed to get straight in her head what she'd say anyway. Without a doubt she was sure that Dave knew about Rupert's past, that must have been what he was withholding from her. She gulped down a couple of glasses of water to re-hydrate and munched on an apple as she ran a deep, bubbly bath. Throwing the apple core out of the window, she stepped into the bath and sighed as she sank down, feeling the tension in her muscles start to ebb away.

## Chapter Fifteen

Bella slept in late the next morning and the first thing she did upon getting downstairs was leave a message on Dave's answerphone. She pottered about and whiled away the day, not doing much physically, but allowing her mind to continue to process the information she had received yesterday, attempting to tease out what the connection could be. Who was Charles' brother or sister, assuming he had one? What was the surname? And was there a connection? Or was it completely irrelevant? What if Kit were the brother of Charles? That would make sense. Her heart raced as everything seemed - to her - to slot into place. What more of a reason could you need to blackmail someone? Out of guilt, as well as fear, Rupert would have paid up, she was sure of it. Surely Dave must know? What if Kit had changed his name?

Desperate to speak to Dave, she left another message on his answerphone asking him to call her as soon as possible. This must be the answer. She'd solved it! She was convinced of it. Maybe Rupert had finally refused to pay Kit any more money. Maybe Kit was asking for even larger sums of money. Maybe Kit needed the money urgently and in a fit of rage killed Rupert?!

The day dragged on as Bella waiting impatiently for the phone to ring. Perhaps I should phone him at work? She felt a bit uncomfortable at the prospect of doing so but told herself she was being ridiculous, surely Dave would want to know what she had discovered? If he already knows then so be it, but if he doesn't he will definitely want to know. Nervously she picked up the phone and dialled the station number, but it transpired that both Dave and his sergeant were out. She left a short message asking him to call, just saying that she thought she had some information relevant to the case. Her stomach was in knots and she found it impossible to eat anything. Why on earth couldn't he hurry up and phone? Surely he had his mobile with him and his colleagues could contact him? And why didn't she have his mobile number?

At eight o'clock there was a knock on the door. Who on earth is that, she thought crossly flinging the door open. It was Dave. Her demeanour changed and she hurried him inside.

'There was a message at the station saying you needed to speak to me urgently?'

'I've found the missing link!' she cried.

'Really?'

'I know who killed Rupert!' her face shone with excitement.

'You do?' he raised an eyebrow, feeling rather dubious at her assertion.

'It was Kit!' She eagerly looked for confirmation on his face.

'Kit?' He looked puzzled.

How dense could he be? He was supposed to be the detective! She sighed and led him into the sitting room.

'Yes, Kit.'

'But why do you think that?'

Triumphantly she told him her theory. 'So you see, he had the perfect motive for murder.'

Dave nodded sagely. 'I can see that.'

'But?'

'There is no evidence to suggest that Kit was responsible for Rupert's death.'

'But I've just given it to you!'

'What you've given me is a theory, a plausible one,' he hastily added in order to appease her.

'But it must be him. It all fits.'

'Not quite. Kit's twin brother was not called Charles, he's not changed his name, and the paint on Rupert's Range Rover does not match the paint on Kit's silver Porsche.'

Bella felt instantly deflated but defiant. She was convinced her theory and the connection was correct.

'However I think you may be right on some level.'

She looked up hopefully.

'I do believe that somehow Kit found out about Rupert's past, either by doing his own research or perhaps Rupert told him many years ago when they were picking grapes. I think that could be a possible explanation as to why and what he was blackmailing Rupert about. But I do not believe that he killed him.'

Bella had been so sure. She'd found out Rupert's secret and had been convinced that Kit killed him. She felt rather foolish and very embarrassed. How could she possibly have thought she could solve the case? And how insulting it must seem to Dave.

'I would appreciate it if you could not go around doing your own detective work. It's best if you leave it to us.'

That was her told. She flushed with embarrassment.

His face softened, and he went and sat next to her, putting his hands on hers. 'I don't want you getting hurt. You may unwittingly uncover something that whoever killed Rupert doesn't want coming out. I don't want anything happening to you.'

That freaked her out. Irrationally she worried that whoever killed Rupert had her in their sight, that she was their next target  How on earth would she now sleep at night?

'You don't think I could be being watched do you? Someone waiting until you've gone and then get me?' She shivered in fear.

'No, I don't. You'll be fine. But if you keep digging around you never know. I care about you and I don't want anything to happen to you.' He smiled at her and changed the subject. 'Are you going to the fête on Saturday?'

'Oh absolutely, particularly as it's going to be held right on my doorstep.' The fête was  always held on the village green which was right outside Bella's cottage.

'I'm working most of the day. How about we go to the evening barbecue together?'

'That would be nice. Why don't you come here about 7pm. Mia and Fred are going to park on the drive, so squeeze your car in behind theirs.

'Great. I'll look forward to seeing you then. Now remember, no digging about! Leave it to us, okay?'

She nodded, but knew that if some titbit of information came her way she wouldn't be able to resist. She bade him farewell and closed the door behind him. Her stomach was no longer crunched and churning but rumbled in hunger so she poached some salmon and made herself a salad.


The day of the fête dawned cloudy and ominous. Fortunately the marquees had been put up on Thursday so - despite the torrential rain on Friday - setting up for the event had been able to go ahead without any delay. Bella had enjoyed her trip to the ancient town of Rye with Mia the day before. The rain had kept a few of the tourists away but it was still heaving with them, and who could blame them? The cobbled winding streets and general ambiance of the town was very special, it was like nowhere else Bella had visited before and she made a resolution to go back once the peak summer season was over, and the town had recovered a bit from the onslaught of visitors.

She peered out of the back bedroom window looking for signs that the weather was going to clear up, but there were none. It was just typical, she thought, week after week of gorgeous weather and the one day it was really needed it did this. Perfect weather would attract more people and hence raise more money for the village so gloomy and wet weather would not have the desired effect. She pulled on a pair of jeans and slipped a thin red sweatshirt over her t-shirt, the first time in weeks she'd needed an extra layer. She hugged her morning cup of tea to her in an attempt to take the chill off. Perhaps if I go for a cycle it'll get me warmed up she contemplated? Peering out of the back door, dark grey clouds hung heavily but it hadn't started raining. She decided to risk it and scurried out. Half an hour later she was back - hot, panting and with rosy cheeks - as Bella put her bike away there was the pitter-patter of rain followed by a torrential downpour as she ran to the front door. She dried off and flicked the kettle on to make a cup of coffee. Feeling refreshed after her cycle, she settled down with the newspaper she'd picked up on the way back, and wrapped her hands around the steaming mug. The best thing she could do now was not to venture out, competitors had started to arrive with their entries for the various competitions taking place. They would be judged that morning, and the winner announced that afternoon during the fête. Bella knew that once the constant flow of traffic had temporarily ceased, it would just as soon start up again as the helpers arrived, and a little while later the massive, she hoped, invasion of visitors would start, cars would be parked everywhere, up the lanes, in the car parks, anywhere where there was a spare slot. Bella had been warned by Jennifer what to expect, it was the same every year, anyone who lived in the village was considerate but many of those visiting from the surrounding areas seemed not to care about where they parked, or what damage they caused. Fences had even been knocked down in previous years, but the organisers now put a strip of red and white striped tape outside each house in an attempt to prevent this. There would be worse this evening apparently. After the barbecue it would be likely that a select few, who had been drinking all day and all evening, would add unmentionables to the front gardens which would additionally have been littered with beer cans, bottles and other rubbish during the event.

About eleven o'clock Bella was interrupted by a knock on the door. It was Mia and Fred.

'Got time for a quick coffee before you hurry off to do your bit?'

'Love to but we can't. The cat threw up all over the kitchen just as we were leaving so we're behind schedule. See you later though.' They hurried off in separate directions to perform whatever allotted tasks they had been allocated.

Bella made herself another cup of coffee and sat in the window seat of the sitting room watching the frenetic activity that was going on in preparation for the grand opening at two o'clock. She saw Jennifer hurrying down the lane and waved; she waved back and came up the front path.

'Hi, how are you?' asked Bella opening the door.

'Fine thanks. How about you? Haven't seen you in what seems like ages.'

'Fine too thanks. Got time for a coffee? Just made one,' she raised her mug.

'Just a quick one. It's frantic out there.'

'I know I've been watching. It must take so much organising.'

'I understand that as soon as one fête is over they start planning the next. Thanks,' she said taking the mug from Bella and following her into the sitting room.

'I had to tell you,' Jennifer's eyes glistened excitedly, 'I saw Kim this morning. She had a visit from that Inspector - the one you know - yesterday, and guess what?'

Bella had a feeling she knew what was coming, but wasn't going to volunteer any information in case she made the wrong assumption and revealed something she wasn't supposed to. 'What?'

'The photograph. It was Kit. Rupert and Kit knew each other years ago!'

'Ah,' she replied.

'You don't seem very surprised?'

'I had a feeling it would turn out to be him. A gut feeling, you know.'

'Yeah. But what I want to know is why did they pretend not to know each other at Sophie and Harry's party? Weird, huh?'

'It does seem a little strange. Did Inspector Ormandy say anything else?' she enquired cautiously.

Jennifer pursed her lips. 'No. I think he asked Kim lots of questions but didn't give any explanation.'

'What sort of questions?' Bella's curiosity was peaked.

'Stuff like, what did Kim know of his family? Did she know anything about Rupert's life before he settled here? That sort of thing. Really just going over what they've already asked her.'

'Hmm.' What's he up to, thought Bella.

'Hmm, what? Do you know something?'

'I was just thinking that's all. Actually, are Sophie and Harry coming to the fête?'

'They're parking at my house. Don't know what time though. Why?'

'Well, I wonder if Ariadne has mentioned anything about Kit in passing to either Sophie or Harry, you know, about his past? What he was doing in Australia?'

'I don't know. Good point, I'll ask them. I wonder if Kim has mentioned the photo to them?'

'Don't think so. Think she was just going to keep it between you, me, her and Mia until she knew more.'

'Okay. Well I'll have a word and let you know. Intriguing isn't it?' she giggled. 'Best be off, thanks for the coffee, see you later.'

'Yes. Bye. Thanks for letting me know.'

What about Ariadne though? The thought suddenly struck Bella, she'd been so busy concentrating on Kit, that she'd dismissed Ariadne completely. What was her background? Bella knew she went to school with Sophie, but did Ariadne have any brothers? Could she be involved? Or did she know about the blackmail? In her head Bella heard Dave's voice reminding her not to dig about, but she banished it from her mind. She wasn't digging she was just enquiring, helping Kim, she justified to herself. Having convinced herself that she was doing the right thing, she made herself a sandwich then went to inspect her wardrobe, to make her choice for her night out with Dave. A further inspection of the weather revealed that blue sky was attempting to break through and the sun was starting to peek in and out from behind the clouds. She laid out another simple, pale blue, cotton dress with a tie waist; additionally she laid out a pair of navy linen trousers, long sleeved navy linen top and thin, pale pink cashmere cardigan, just in case the weather didn't warm up enough. Slipping into a casual, cream cotton skirt and a lime green polo top, she slid her feet into a pair of beige deck shoes and trotted downstairs. Bella opened her bag, retrieved some money from her purse, put it deep into one of her skirt pockets and picked her keys up - she was intrigued to see what the fête would be like and didn't want to miss the start.

The locals weren't wrong about the traffic, it was backed up in all directions and there was a lot of honking of horns going on. Volunteers in fluorescent jackets were waving people in the direction the flow of traffic should be going, the problem was being caused by those who thought they would take a short cut and nip in and park somewhere else, this in turn was causing problems with the traffic patiently waiting to get directed to a parking space.

In order to allow as many people as possible to witness the start of the fête, it was opened a few minutes late. Children ran around screaming with excitement and a local brass band played a mixture of popular and traditional tunes. The village green was packed with people, and more were arriving. Bella strolled round admiring the stalls. She'd expected stall after stall to be full of junk - cheap plastic stuff sold at ridiculous prices, but purchased by the vendor at a pittance, thus making a substantial profit. But she was wrong, every stall was different and of good quality. Additionally there was the traditional tombola, Punch and Judy, coconut shy, cake stall, guess the weight of the cake, guess how many smarties were in the jar, Splat the Rat and so on, as well as stalls selling local goods and produce. Handmade wooden items, pottery, honey, apple juice, jumpers, jams and preserves. Bella purchased a pot of lavender-scented honey, a bottle of apple juice and a couple of jars of jam. Living on the doorstep of the fête meant she could pop home, leave them inside the front door and then lock up again. She'd been advised to keep her windows and doors all locked, unfortunately it was inevitable in this day and age that there would be opportunists who would use this event for their own purpose i.e. petty theft and burglary.

Next Bella joined the stream of people heading into the marquees, which had just been opened up; the winning entries displaying a "first", "second" or "third" card beside them. She admired the multitude of floral displays, then moved on to the vegetable section. A great debate was going on as to whether the right decision had been made regarding the allocation of awards. Bella smiled - it was nice that, temporarily at least, people were only worrying about the results, rather than what was going on in the world in general. Next was the cake area, her mouth watered at the sight of them, such a waste not to be able to eat them she mused as she eyed up the delectable display in front of her. After the jam and chutney section was the last, and perhaps the sweetest, of the entries – the children's miniature gardens. It was obvious that some of the children had had a huge amount of assistance from one or other of their parents, as there was no way some of the perfectly produced gardens in the five and under category could possibly have been created by a five year old. It was blatantly apparent to anyone - except the parents involved  it would seem- and the judges were shrewd enough to award prizes appropriately, with the first, second and third prize going to the ones which basically looked like a pile of soil with a few twigs, and had inevitably been put together entirely by the child without parental assistance.

Her taste buds having been woken by the sight of the competition cakes, Bella wandered off in search of the tea tent. She knew there was one, as some of the group were making cakes for them. She bypassed the Pimms tent, preferring to wait until this evening before drinking alcohol, not wanting to be tipsy or drunk by the time Dave turned up. Patiently she queued and chose a large sponge cake stuffed with fresh cream and bursting with raspberries. People were sprawled on the grass eating which didn't appeal to Bella, fearing that damp grass on a cream skirt would leave an annoying stain. Instead, she noticed that there was a chair free at one table and went to enquire as to whether she could sit there. Settling herself down, she tucked into the cake. Before long the table was vacated and she was on her own and sat back to watch the maypole dancing the children from the village school were going to perform. Despite the real sense of community and togetherness, Bella felt a twinge of being an outsider, surprised that it bothered her so much as she had originally planned to stay for just 6 months.

'Mind if I join you?'

Bella turned and shielded her eyes against the sun. It was Florence. 'Please do. It's lovely to see you. How are you?'

Florence settled herself and placed her cup of tea and plate of chocolate cake on the rickety wooden table. 'I'm fine thanks. How about you?'

'Very well thanks. That cake looks delicious,' she observed as Florence took a mouthful, sorely tempted to buy a piece for herself.

Florence licked her lips. 'It is. Very moist and very chocolaty. Have you found much to keep you occupied?'

'Oh yes. I never seem to stop. There are so many places to visit round here and I've hardly got to any of them yet. I'm absolutely determined to get to Sissinghurst next week.'

'It is beautiful there, so tranquil and the gardens are magnificent. You know that it's closed on Wednesday and Thursday?'

'Thanks. I've got a leaflet on it. I think I'll go on Friday morning if the weather is good.'

'I'm sure you'll have a lovely time. What do you think of the fête then?'

They chatted amiably for a while and had refills of tea. Eventually Florence rose to go and Bella, feeling guilty about hogging a prized table and chair for so long, got up too, bade farewell to Florence and continued strolling around. She waved to Mia and Jennifer who were busy on a stall and paused to watch the children's running races. Deciding it was time for yet another cup of tea she ambled back to the tea tent and, despite the temptation, managed to resist having any more cake. As the afternoon drew on the crowds started to thin, another couple of hours and they would start to swell again as the evening crowd came in for the night's merriment. Feeling weary, Bella went over to an empty table and chairs, but before her bottom could hit the seat she was interrupted.

'Like to join us?'

Sophie and Harry were sitting on the next table with Jemima, giggling as usual and slapping her hands on the table, excited by the noise they made and eager to make the cups, saucers and plates rattle some more.

'Thanks, how are you all?' Bella made some cooing noises and faces at Jemima which made the little tot laugh even more enthusiastically. 'She's so sweet.'

Harry and Sophie glowed with parental pride. 'Thank you. We think she's pretty cute, but then we'd be a bit bi-ased,' laughed Harry.

'Are you enjoying the fête, Bella?' asked Sophie.

'I'm really impressed. Some of these fêtes can be dreadful, which makes me wonder why they're held, but this one is really nice. All villagey and with local produce and products too which is a nice touch.'

'Several years ago the fête was becoming a bit tacky, full of all the rubbish you're talking about. After a great deal of debate and deliberation, the committee eventually decided to take action, taking what was perceived at the time as a big risk. They decided that only local small businesses, or individuals, would be able to have a commercial stall, all of them being vetted and checked out prior to a stall being confirmed, and that no plastic or tacky mass-produced products not made in this country would be allowed at the fête. Of course there was an uproar, a lot of people thought the committee were mad to take the decision, fearing that it would be the demise of the village fête - particularly given that fêtes in general seemed to be dwindling, and visitor numbers decreasing, thereby not making them profitable or worth all the effort of organising them. Though the first year after the new policy change was not quite as successful as previous years, it has picked up every year since and now, it is far more popular and profitable than it has ever been, and has a real community spirit about it. I gather there's now a waiting list of craftspeople and local businesses wanting to have a stall here, I think it's become a good marketing tool for them,' said Harry.

'I agree with you, if we took more care to buy locally and to support our local businesses,  it would surely be good for them and us.  It seems to make sense to me,' commented Bella.

'Oh absolutely, we agree with you,' replied Sophie.

'Room for another?' asked Jennifer pulling up a chair. 'Has Bella told you?'

'Told us what?' they looked at Bella then Jennifer.

'About Kit?'

'What about him?'

'You know how at your party Kit was introduced to us all, because none of us had met him before?' They nodded. 'Well he knew Rupert many years ago.'

'Really? That's strange, why didn't they say?'

'Maybe they didn't recognise one another after such a long time?' suggested Sophie.

'Possibly, though I bet they did. But why did they hide it from us? Are you sure you didn't know anything?'

'No, definitely not. It was the first time Kit was introduced to us.'

'What made you think there was a connection?' asked Harry.

'Bella discovered a picture on the internet. It had what we thought was a younger version of Rupert and Kit so we took it and showed it to Kim, but she'd never seen it before and had no idea whether they had known each other or not. Kim then found a photograph of Rupert taken a few years ago which was the spitting image of one of the people in the photograph Bella found. So Kim then asked Bella to mention it to Inspector Ormandy, as Bella knew him from when he trained with her late husband.'

Harry and Sophie sat with open mouths whilst they listened, astounded at what had been going on and that they were blissfully unaware of.

'Why didn't you just ask Kit? I would have given you the number,' Sophie looked a little hurt.

'Oh Sophie, we didn't want to upset you. If it turned out that it wasn't Kit in the photo then the matter would have dropped. And Kim wanted to keep it quiet.'

'But how did you come across the photo Bella?'

Bella, who had been sitting feeling uncomfortable during the exchange, hesitated; she really didn't want them thinking she was a nosey old snoop.

'I suppose Rupert's death hit a chord with me. You know, reminded me of the death of my husband, and well, I don't know really,' she shrugged her shoulders. 'I was just fiddling around on the internet and this photo came up. I didn't know what to do. I didn't want to do anything behind Kim's back, and I hardly knew any of you and I definitely did not want to upset anyone. Anyway, I showed Jennifer and Jennifer didn't know anything and she suggested we show Kim and well, Jennifer's told you the rest.'

'I wish you'd come to me. I could have just asked Kit outright or asked Ariadne, she would know or if she didn't she would have asked. Could have saved Kim getting involved,' replied Sophie.

'Sorry,' said Bella meekly.

'Come on, don't be hard on Bella. Besides, if he didn't want anyone to know that they knew each other it's unlikely he'd have told you, isn't it?' said Jennifer logically.

'Maybe.'

'So what did the police say then?'

Jennifer reiterated what she'd told Bella that morning. Bella sat quietly, praying that they wouldn't ask any further questions. Questions she knew the answers too, but wasn't allowed to reveal.

'I'm going to phone Ariadne when I get home and find out what Kit has been playing at. Why on earth would she want him, as her part-time boyfriend and full-time agent, if he's not going to be honest with her?'

'I'd be careful Soph,' warned Harry, 'you don't know what you might be stirring up.'

Too right, thought Bella.

'I know, but she's a good friend and I've known her long enough.'

'I'd do the same for Mia,' added Bella, seizing the moment, 'I've known her for so long, since we were at school together.'

'Exactly!' replied Sophie looking pointedly at Harry.

'I expect you had fun with Ariadne when you were younger. Did she have any brothers or sisters? I bet they were jealous of the way she looked!'

Sophie laughed. 'She didn't always look so stunning. When we were at school, she was decidedly average, but always had a certain presence about her. But no, she didn't have any brothers or sisters, so there was no sibling rivalry.'

'I thought she had a brother?' queried Harry.

'She did, he died when he was young.'

She what?! Bella's ears pricked up.

'That's so sad. What happened?' asked Jennifer, echoing Bella's very thoughts.

'I don't know really. Wasn't something she or her family talked about and I didn't ask.'

At that moment Jemima let out a large belch and vomited all over Harry's knees. He mopped it up as best he could, but it had soaked through his shorts.

'Looks like we'd better go,' he rolled his eyes and stood up, strapping his daughter deftly into her pushchair.

'See you later?' asked Jennifer.

'No, worse luck. Couldn't get a babysitter, everyone seems to be busy coming to the barbecue.'

'You could bring her. You have before.'

'I know, but she's been a bit of a madam about bedtimes recently so we're trying to keep the continuity and get her back into a routine. I fear that if we bring her out tonight all our hard work over the last few weeks will have been wasted. Sorry.'

'That's a shame. I can't believe for one minute she'd be a little madam about anything!' Jennifer grinned and raised her eyebrows.

Sophie laughed. 'See you soon. Bye.'

'Don't forget to let us know what Ariadne says,' called Jennifer after her. 'Be interesting to see if she knows anything,' she muttered aside to Bella.

'Hmm,' replied Bella non-committally. 'Think I'll go too, see you later at the barbecue.'

'Bye, yup, see you later.'

Bella hurried home to scribble down the snippets of information whilst they were still fresh in her head. The fact that Ariadne had had a brother who had died before Sophie knew her meant that he must have been quite young when he died. Maybe Kit had inadvertently told her about his time with Rupert in Australia? Maybe she was in on the blackmail too? Maybe she deliberately brought Kit down to spook Rupert? Maybe she'd planned it all along, waiting for her revenge, biding her time? Bella was eager to tell Dave, but decided to sleep on it. After her humiliation on Wednesday night, she didn't feel she could bear another dose of it, besides it was his night off, they were going to have fun, and there would be no work-related talk.

So consumed was she at writing, from memory, everything down - from the day of Rupert's death to the present day - that when she had finished it was almost half past six. Panicking that she only had half an hour to get ready, she ran up the stairs, threw her clothes onto the bedroom floor and jumped into the shower to rinse off the stickiness that had crept up on her as the temperature had steadily risen during the afternoon. Quickly she towel-dried herself and slipped into the pale blue dress she'd laid out earlier, deciding to take the pale pink cashmere cardigan with her as well just in case it cooled down later on. Hair brushed up into a twirly knot at the back, tendrils whisping around her face, she admired the silhouette it gave her long slim neck; mascara and a touch of pale pink lip-gloss later and she was ready. Her pale pink toe nails peeked out from the toes of her wedge heeled suede soft pink shoes, so pale that they could almost be cream. Satisfied with what she saw, she took the empty miniature cream beaded shoulder bag downstairs and placed lip-gloss, keys, handkerchief and cash into it, just about managing to squeeze it all in.

Punctual as ever, Dave arrived spot on seven o'clock. Bella could smell wafts of hot barbecue charcoal coming over from the green as she opened the door to let him in. She led him through to the kitchen, where she silently admired the freshly washed and brushed man in front of her, his pale cream chinos crinkle free and pale blue casual long sleeved linen shirt freshly pressed. His citrus aftershave floated over to her and she breathed it in deeply, it mixed well with her lightly floral and citrus perfume.

'You look lovely,' he smiled, 'a picture of summer.'

She blushed. 'Thanks. You're looking pretty good yourself. Have you had a good day?'

'Not bad thanks. But tonight not a word of work, promise?'

She grinned sheepishly. 'Promise, though I can't guarantee that the others are not going to grill you.'

'Fair enough. I'll be polite but firm. This is definitely out of business hours. Shall we go?'

People were thronging onto the green, the tantalising smells from the barbecue stimulating their taste buds; they were edging closer and closer, eagerly awaiting the signal that the food was ready, rather like vultures waiting for their prey.

Bella and Dave weaved their way through the crowds to the bar, which had been set up in  what had been the competition marquees.  Dave waited patiently as people jostled one another trying to get the attention of the bar staff, eventually he managed to purchase a couple of large plastic beakers of Pimms and squeezed his way back through to the entrance of the marquee where Bella was waiting.  The sun was still strong and the evening was a perfect temperature.  Mosquitoes were starting to appear, juicy pickings for them this evening mused Bella.

'Here we are.  Got there at last.'  Dave handed her the drink.  'Cheers!'

'Cheers,' she responded, touching her plastic beaker against his.

They chatted comfortably as they wandered around through the milling crowds.  Food had started to be served, but there was such a mass of people queuing that they decided to wait for a while, instead nipping back to the emptying bar tent to replenish their drinks.  Eventually they joined the queue, Mia, Fred and Jennifer passing them with laden down plates.

'Want to join us?' asked Fred.

'Er, thanks.  See you in a bit.'  Bella wasn't sure whether Dave would want to sit with her friends or keep her all to himself.  'You don't mind do you?'

'Not at all. I naturally assumed we'd bump into your friends, besides it'll be nice to catch up with Mia and Fred, it's been a long time.'

Bella felt a mixture of relief and disappointment. Relief that he wasn't rejecting her friends, but illogical disappointment that he didn't want her all to himself. To her delight the evening turned out to be relaxed and great fun and, despite Jennifer trying to prise the odd piece of information out of Dave, there were no really awkward moments. Bella had thought that Kim might turn up but she didn't and Bella assumed she had opted for a quiet night with Seb. She hadn't dared ask Dave any more about them, working on the assumption that no news was good news, and additionally the fact that neither of them were currently residing in jail seemed a good indicator that they were both off the hook. Before she knew it the party was winding down and people were drifting off, Dave escorted her back to the house but only came in for a brief moment, his excuse being that it was so late he needed to get some sleep as he had to work again tomorrow, despite it being Sunday.

# Chapter Sixteen

Bella pottered around the house for the next few days, leaving her notes scattered on the kitchen table so that she could dip in and out of them, hopeful that at some point they would make more sense to her and that there would be a grand revelatory moment. She went out on her bike each day, which helped her mind mull through the sequence of events, but found no clarity. She was convinced that she was missing something, and this was added to by the niggling sense that there was a piece of information locked away in her brain that frustratingly she couldn't tease out. Bella went through the motions of everyday life, but was so distracted by Rupert's death that each day seemed to merge into the next. By Friday Bella decided that she had spent more than enough time on the case and needed to snap herself out of her current malaise, and, as the weather was bright and sunny, she kept her promise to herself and went to visit Sissinghurst Gardens and Castle.

Being a member of the National Trust, she waved towards her car sticker stuck next to her tax disc, to indicate that she was a member and therefore exempt from paying the car parking fee. The helpful volunteer gave her a map and information, and she went and parked her car in the car park which was filling rapidly, even though it was only eleven o'clock. Presenting her membership card in the ticket office resulted in a paper ticket being given to her, she showed this to the volunteer at the entrance to the castle and entered with great anticipation.

Bella wasn't disappointed. As she walked through the archway she was greeted by an expanse of lawn and an imposing tower with stunning views to the distance. Carefully she studied the map she'd been given, and decided to go clockwise round the gardens. The riot of colour was magnificent and she knew it must take many man hours to care for and nurture such beautiful gardens. Within the gardens she went into the library which was lined with fascinating books, and then walked through the Delos and into the White Garden which was exquisite in its array of white flowers and plants though sadly the beautiful canopy that had been covered in white roses was going over.

She was very taken with the wild flowers and grasses in the orchard, the bees buzzed happily and the white beehives made it look so quaint. Perfection, she sighed happily. Bella took the opportunity to sit for a while on one of the benches and to just enjoy and absorb the calmness and peace that the orchard gave her, despite the number of tourists milling around. Lost in her thoughts she didn't notice the person sit down next to her and it was only when she heard a quiet "hello" that she realised anyone was there at all.

'Oh! Hello!' she replied in surprise. It was Florence.

'Sorry, did I interrupt your thoughts? I'll go if you like?' She looked quizzically at Bella.

Bella felt irritated but she couldn't identify why, perhaps because she'd been enjoying the peace and tranquility, notwithstanding the visitors. 'No, that's fine,' she replied.

'It is beautiful here isn't it?'

'Magnificent. Mind you, I've only seen a fraction of the garden so far, it's amazing that it's so peaceful despite all the visitors.'

'I know. It's a great place to come and think.' They lapsed into a contemplative silence for a while, absorbing their surroundings.

'Charlotte!' Bella yelped out loud making Florence jump.

'What?'

Of course! She knew there was a nugget of information missing. What a fool she'd been! She'd been so fixated with trying to discover whether the boy who had died had had a brother or sister that she had blanked out the information about the name of the person who was mentioned in Rupert's will. Giving her brain the opportunity to drift and relax had released the piece of information she'd been trying to tease out all week.

'Charlotte Willingham. I forgot! How stupid of me.'

Florence was looking at her in a peculiar way, not surprisingly thought Bella, she probably thinks I've gone mad.

'Who?'

'Charlotte Willingham. She's the woman mentioned in Rupert's will.'

'His will?' she repeated faintly.

'Yes. But of course you weren't there at tennis, at Kim's house,' explained Bella, momentarily concerned that she'd let out a big secret, then relieved to remember that she hadn't as the others had been there too and Kim had been quite open about it. 'Yes, Rupert has left a chunk of his estate to a Charlotte Willingham. The only problem is no one knows who she is.'

'Really?'

'Mmm, yes. I think Kim's solicitor is on the case, but I don't know whether he's found her yet.'

'So why does it concern you?'

'Well it doesn't really. I just wish for Kim's sake the police would hurry up and find out who killed Rupert.'

Florence looked confused. 'I don't understand.'

As the photo was now public knowledge Bella explained what had been discovered, but kept everything else to herself.

'Oh. So you've been doing some detective work yourself?'

'Um, not really, no, er, maybe. I don't know, I suppose I was just trying to help,' Bella replied evasively.

'So why did you shout out this Charlotte person's name?'

'Something had been bugging me and then the name popped into my head.'

'So what are you going to do now?'

Bella frowned. 'Hmm, not sure. Probably do a search on the internet, I don't know why I didn't think of it before. Perhaps something will come up.' Her mind was running through the options. Charlotte Willingham must be the sister of Charles. She must be, and somehow I've got to be able to find out if they are related. Could Ariadne be Charlotte?

'I'm sure the solicitor would have thought of that. And besides these things are best left to the police.'

'True. But aren't you intrigued?' Bella looked at her curiously. Florence's eyes were flat and dull and she still looked exhausted, work must really be taking it's toll on her.

'Not particularly. I mean, you've no idea what the connection is between Rupert and this person?'

'You're right, but I'm sure it won't be long before the connection is made.'

'I feel like walking round the rest of the gardens,' said Florence changing the subject. 'Care to join me?'

'Why not.' Bella picked up her bag and they strolled companionably through the orchard to the herb garden admiring the moat walk as they past. Up the lime walk, round the cottage garden, through to the rose garden and across the tower lawn. Bella found the gardens, and their individuality, breathtaking. She wanted to take her time, but Florence seemed in a hurry; when she suggested going up the tower to admire the views Florence declined making Bella, out of politeness, miss out on something she'd been looking forward to. Still, it was a good reason to return soon. Hoards more people were arriving as they came out, it had been a wise move to come early.

'Fancy lunch?' suggested Bella, eager to try out the restaurant. She was never disappointed with a meal at a National Trust property. Each one created their own dishes, nothing fancy but good wholesome fare, and they used as much local produce as they could.

'How about lunch at my place? It looks as though it might be getting crowded in there.'

Bella looked doubtfully at the restaurant, from what she could see through the glass it seemed relatively quiet. But she was flattered to be invited to lunch and didn't want to be rude.

'That would be nice. Thanks. Whereabouts are you?'

'Not far from the village. Tell you what, why don't you follow me, it'd be easier than me giving you directions.'

'Okay.'

Bella dutifully followed Florence's blue Honda CRV along the Monhurst Road and off down a couple of country lanes. They then went down a narrow overgrown driveway which wound along the edge of a small wood, subsequently opening up into a clearing by a small, detached, tumbled-down looking cottage. Bella got out and could hear nothing but the birds singing, it was a truly isolated and tranquil spot.

'No noisy neighbours here then!' she joked as Florence unlocked the front door.

'No. Nice and quiet. Just how I like it. Come in.'

They walked into a tiny entrance hall. Bella noticed the peeling paint and unmistakable smell of damp. The stairs were uncarpeted and scruffy looking, which matched everything else in the house from what she could see.

'How did you find this place?' she asked politely, following Florence into a small dark kitchen which held units that had seen better days; there were doors hanging off, a drawer with no front to it and an ancient looking electric cooker standing in the corner.

'I contacted a few local farmers to see if they had any farm cottages they might want to sell. This one came up.'

'And do you enjoy living here?

'Oh yes,' she replied with the first bit of real enthusiasm Bella had seen in her.

As far as Bella was concerned this house was not fit for human habitation. She shivered, the warmth from outside was not penetrating inside and she wished Florence would unlock the back door and open a few windows to let the warm air flow through to ease the musty smell and dampness within.

'Have you got much garden?' she asked, hopeful that Florence would take her outside and show her.

'No.'

Oh well, that didn't work and what was up with Florence?

'You okay?'

'Fine. I've got some salad and some quiche, is that okay?'

'Lovely. Thanks. Can I do anything?'

'No you're fine there.'

Bella stood uselessly to one side of the kitchen. 'Mind if I sit?'

'Please do.' Florence suddenly smiled at her. 'Coffee? Tea? Something cold?'

'Coffee please.' She felt in need of warmth, her bare arms had goose bumps on them and her legs were following suit. 'You going to tennis later?' Tennis was being held later than usual; at four o'clock today.

'No,' Florence shook her head, 'I'm going to be busy.'

'That's a shame. Maybe next week then?'

Bella gratefully took the mug of instant coffee, which had been offered, and clung onto it as though it were a hot water bottle. She watched as Florence deftly cut and chopped tomatoes, cucumber, radishes, celery and lettuce for the salad, admiring the knife as it slid with such ease through each item, reminding Bella that she really ought to buy some decent kitchen knives.

When lunch was ready Florence sat across from Bella at the small, beaten, wobbly wooden table.

'Please. Help yourself,' offered Florence handing Bella a chipped white dinner plate.

'Thanks.' Bella scooped up some salad and a slice of homemade leek and potato quiche. 'This looks yummy,' she commented, referring to the quiche, 'do you like cooking?'

'When I have time, I'm usually so busy. But it's a lot cheaper to make food and you know precisely which ingredients have gone into it.'

'True. Half the time the stuff you buy at the supermarket is full of additives and preservatives. This quiche really is delicious,' she added.

Florence sat quietly eating her lunch. Bella wondered what was wrong, maybe she's regretting inviting me for lunch, she pondered.

'What made you decide to move to Kent?' Bella did her best to make polite conversation.

Florence shrugged. 'Fancied a change of scene and a job came up at the local surgery. Kent is a lovely county, a bit more built up than I thought it would be, but there are still some lovely pockets of rural countryside.'

'It's pretty here. I've settled in really well, which I wasn't expecting'

There was another awkward pause. Perhaps I should have stayed at Sissinghurst mused Bella, maybe I've unwittingly said something to upset her? They finished their meal in silence. By now Bella was desperate to make a quick exit, and get into some warm sunshine and fresh air, the house was feeling very oppressive.

'That was lovely. Thank you. Well, I'd best be off. I've got a few things that need to be done before tennis.' She rose to go. Florence leapt up.

'Oh, no, don't go yet. Have a cup of coffee or tea. Please.'

Bella felt a twinge of guilt and didn't want to be ungrateful. 'Okay, thanks, just a quick coffee then. Thanks.'

Florence cleared the plates into the sink and ran some hot water into it, washed the chopping board and knife up and left the plates to soak whilst the kettle boiled. Bella's eye was caught by a scrap of newspaper peaking out from a pile of post and papers, which was crammed onto one of the work surfaces. It was about Rupert. Why had Florence kept it? The house wasn't particularly tidy, but it looked carefully cut out, as though she'd specifically wanted to keep this article. Bella became more convinced it was because Florence had been having an affair with him and took it as confirmation that she had been. She dived in feet first.

'So... what did you think of Rupert?' she asked.

Florence spun round and eyed her suspiciously.

'Why do you ask that?'

'I just wondered. You must have seen him up at tennis. Did you get on with him?'

'I met him for the first time at Sophie and Harry's party, not before.'

Hmm, in denial and obviously been sneaking around with him, concluded Bella to herself. 'And what did you think of him then?'

'I thought he was an arrogant, self-centred, drunken idiot!' she snapped.

Oh dear, maybe he dumped her. 'I see. Er, could I use your loo please?'

'Upstairs, second on the left.'

Relieved to get away from Florence for a few minutes, Bella carefully negotiated the rickety stairs. Was that first or second door on the left she wondered when she got to the top of the stairs? She pushed the first door cautiously open and peaked in. Bella frowned, and walked in to what was definitely not the bathroom. The wall was plastered in newspaper cuttings, there was a decaying old garden table filled with scrapbooks. She opened one up quietly and peaked inside; the blood drained from her face. Every single newspaper article was about Charles Willingham's death - so that was his surname - detailing from when the accident happened, to the outcome of the court case. Bella tried to make sense of what she was seeing, alarm bells going off in her head at full volume. Despite her instinct to leg it down the stairs and out of the front door as quickly as possible, her legs wouldn't move. She picked up another scrapbook. This time it was filled with articles all about Rupert. Little snippets from over the years. It couldn't be? Bile rose in her throat and she turned to run. As she did so, she screamed as she saw Florence blocking her exit.

'Er... Sorry... I couldn't remember which door you'd said. I'll just pop to the loo now if I may?' She tried hard to steady her voice and hide her shaking hands.

'I don't think so.' Florence closed the door behind her.

They stood there in silence eyeing one another, each with a different motive.

'So, you've seen my collection?' said Florence eventually. Bella nodded nervously. 'Not bad eh? It's taken years, but it's been worth the wait.'

There was a weird look in Florence's eyes and Bella knew that the person in front of her had lost the plot a long time ago.  How could she not have seen it?  Florence seemed so normal.

'Why?' croaked Bella.

'Why have I got such a collection?  That's quite easy really.  I knew from the moment my brother was killed by that murderer that I'd get my revenge.  No one was going to take my brother away from me and not pay for it.'

'But your name's Florence, not Charlotte, and your surname is Petipas.'

Florence laughed.  'You're so stupid.  Petipas is my married name, and Florence is my middle name, first name is Charlotte.  You can imagine how surprised I was when you yelled out my name earlier!'

'Why use Florence?'

'I didn't want there to be any chance of anyone recognising my name and putting two and two together, I didn't know how much Rupert had told his wife or his friends about his past.  It was perfect and legal, continue with my married name and use my middle name.  Easy.'

What am I going to do, whimpered a terrified Bella to herself.  How can I get away?  She watched as Florence went over to a large, faded, colour photograph of a young boy of about ten.  She stroked it tenderly.

'Oh, Charlie,' she murmured, 'how I've missed you.'  Her head snapped round.  'I worshipped him, he was my everything.  I was only five when he died.  It shouldn't have been that way,' she snarled vehemently.

'Why don't we go down and have that cup of coffee you've made.  You can tell me all about him?  I'd like to hear about him.  Really, I would.  He sounds like a really super person, I would have loved to have had a brother like that,' she tried to smile in a sympathetic and encouraging way.

Florence stared at Bella, eyeing her up. 'Okay.'

'I need the loo first.'

'I'll wait.'

She followed Bella out of the room to the bathroom. Bella slipped in and closed the door, her heart hammering and her head swimming. She hurried to the window and flushed the loo to disguise any noise made in attempting to open it - hoping she could squeeze out and jump - but the window, swollen by damp, wouldn't budge. Frantically she pushed as hard as she could.

'Hurry up,' snapped Florence from the other side of the door.

'Coming,' called Bella, still frantically pushing and shoving the swollen wood, but it was no good, she concluded that it had to have been nailed shut. She washed her hands and took a deep breath, trying to calm herself down.

'Downstairs then,' ordered Florence, when Bella appeared.

'I'm a bit chilly, I'll just get my jumper from the car, and then you can tell me all about Charles,' Bella casually commented as she put her hand on the front door handle, turned and pulled. It was locked.

'Into the kitchen,' snapped Florence.

Maybe the back door will be open? How can I distract her? Bella thought frantically, as she sat as instructed at the table and grasped the mug proffered, tightly.

'So. Tell me Flor... Charlotte. What was Charles like?'

Florence's eyes softened as she spoke of her beloved brother, until she reached the part about his death, then a steely glaze came over them. Bella knew that it could only have been Florence who had killed Rupert. Somehow she had to get away from her.

'Perhaps you could show me some more photographs of him?'

Florence hurried into the next room and then upstairs, Bella seized the opportunity and leapt up, grabbing the back door handle. It too was locked, where was the key? Frenetically she searched, until she heard Florence coming back. She flung herself back into her chair, attempting to regain a calm composure, doing her utmost not to rile Florence. There seemed to be no way out. Patiently she looked at every photograph, attempting to make encouraging, friendly, noises.

'They're lovely. Do you have any more? What about photographs of you and him?'

Again, Florence disappeared upstairs, secure in the knowledge that there was no escape for Bella. Bella quickly grabbed her mobile and started to write a text. She got as far as "help" then heard Florence coming, she pressed send to the first number that came up, which happened to be Mia's. Unfortunately Bella was not quick enough and Florence saw it and snatched the phone off her.

'What were you doing?' she snarled.

'I was going to check with Mia to see if she needed a lift to tennis,' Bella lied.

'You won't need this!' Florence threw it onto the ground and stamped on it, the tiny silver phone shattered, shards flying across the floor of the kitchen. Bella gulped.

'I think I'd better be going.' Bella stood, randomly hoping that she might still get away.

Florence roughly shoved her back onto the chair.

'Oh, no you don't. You're not going anywhere,' she spat.

'But why?'

Florence smiled manically at her. It seemed to Bella that as every minute passed Florence spiralled further down into her delusions, losing a grasp of reality.

'If you go, you'll tell that Inspector boyfriend of yours. I've got away with it, and I'm not having you ruin it. If what you say about Rupert's will is correct, I shall walk away with a lot of blood money and will then disappear. No one will ever find me. But you could ruin it, and I can't let that happen. I've spent years planning this. Why do you think I moved here? Because I wanted to? No chance!' she spat, spittle flying out in all directions. 'I moved here because it was the next stage in my plan - get myself settled in, be a pillar of the community, and what better way than being a local nurse eh? I hated it, dealing with all those whingeing, moaning, sick people, but I knew the long-term goal would be worth it.'

Bella was starting to shake violently as her body went into shock. Florence meant to kill her, and her mind was so fuzzy with terror that she couldn't work out what to do, how to escape - desperately she tried, whilst Florence continued to rant and rave.

'The look on Rupert's face at Sophie and Harry's party made it all worthwhile. He knew. I hadn't spoken to him by then, but he knew who I was. I look so like Charles, there was no way he could not see the resemblance,' she grinned to herself enjoying the pleasure of the memory. 'It freaked him out, I could see that. It was so delectable, I could barely stop myself from moaning in ecstasy,' she licked her lips. 'It was so easy. I'd followed him for weeks, knew what he did, when he did it, and with whom he did it. He'd been following Kim for weeks, he knew she was having an affair with Seb and every time she went to see Seb, Rupert came back the same way, and he always stayed the same length of time outside Seb's house. All I had to do was time it to perfection. I knew he'd been drinking, which would make it so much easier. All I had to do was drive in the middle of the road, the look in his eyes when he realised, in that split second, what was happening, what was about to happen, was incredible, he knew he was going to die, justice was finally done for my darling Charles.'

What a freak! How insane! How could anybody be so evil? Terror coursed through Bella's veins. To plan something for so long, to be so obsessed, she wanted to throw up.

'But getting rid of me won't help. If you let me go, no one will be any the wiser, and you can disappear as you planned. I won't tell anyone,' Bella pleaded.

'Wouldn't you?'

'No. Honestly I wouldn't. Let me go now. They'll wonder where I am if I'm not at tennis. Mia's expecting me. Let me go and I promise I won't say anything,' she pleaded and looked beseechingly at Florence.

Florence seemed to consider this, then gazed contemptuously at her. 'You're like all the others. You won't keep your promise.'

'I will! Honestly I will. I'm good at keeping secrets. I know so many.'

'And what secrets might you have?'

'I know stuff about the case. I know how someone else can be framed for Rupert's murder.'

This sparked Florence's curiosity. 'Go on.'

'Kit was blackmailing Rupert. The police are suspicious, I'm sure he could be put in the frame,' Bella said eagerly, desperate to say anything which would get her away to safety.

'I need to think.' Florence paced up and down, rubbing her head, her knuckles white from the pressure, muttering to herself.

'It would work,' encouraged Bella.

'Shut up!' screamed Florence, 'I need to think.'

The minutes ticked by. Each minute feeling like an hour. Bella dared not move. Barely daring to breath as she waited to see if her plan would work. Florence continued with her pacing, becoming more and more agitated. Bella checked the clock, two hours had passed. Surely they would have missed her at tennis? She prayed fervently that somehow Mia had got her text and sounded the alarm. But why would she? And she had no idea of knowing where Bella actually was. Tick, tick, tick went the clock, Florence seemed lost in her own little world, talking incessantly to herself. Six o'clock came, then seven o'clock. Bella, by this time drenched in sweat from fear, became more and more desperate. Out of the corner of her eye she thought she saw some movement outside. She peered intently but could see nothing, she must have imagined it.

Explosively there was a crash. Bella screamed. Florence grabbed her and the knife on the draining board simultaneously, and forced the sharp blade against Bella's throat. Bella's heart pounded frenziedly, exploding in her chest cavity, she daren't move - one slip and that would be it, Florence had her in a vice-like grip.

'Police! Put down the knife.'

Though Bella couldn't see all around her, she could feel the presence of marksmen, poised and ready to shoot. Please God, not me. Please let me go, she prayed. Sweat poured off her in torrents and yet her body felt like ice.

'Put the knife down Florence. Let Bella go.' Dave's soothing voice was music to Bella's ears and her knees went weak with relief knowing that he was there, despite knowing that reasoning would not work with Florence. Sanity had left her a long time ago.

He continued to talk calmly, soothingly, quietly, persuasively, attempting to persuade Florence to voluntarily drop the knife and let Bella go. Bella's pulse raced more the tenser Florence's body got. Suddenly, and for some inexplicable reason, Florence shoved Bella forward. Bella stumbled and hit the kitchen wall, smacking her head against it. Behind her there was a thud. She turned and screamed. Florence had slit her throat and lay bleeding to death on the grubby kitchen floor. Bella threw up as she was bundled out of the room. All around her there was manic activity as paramedics and police swarmed into the building. But nothing could be done to save Florence. Bella was left sobbing, shaking, overwhelmed with shock in the arms of Sergeant Swart.

# Chapter Seventeen

Bella woke groggily the next day and sat up feeling bewildered and woozy in her bed. Next to her, in a chair, was Mia fast asleep with her mouth open and snoring gently. Bella smiled then frowned. What was she doing here? Her head was so muzzy, she shook it, trying to clear it, and quietly got out of bed and went to the bathroom. She splashed cold water on her face and then looked at the unrecognisable face peering back at her in the mirror. Hair greasy and wild, face pale, ink-dark circles under her eyes, a purple-black bruise on the side of her face, red welts at her throat. She screamed as she had a flashback of turning around and seeing Florence's body bleeding to death on the floor. Mia burst in through the door.

'You okay?' she asked breathlessly, her heart pounding as she recovered from being shocked awake by Bella's scream.

'Did it really happen?' Bella whispered.

'Come here.' Mia put her arm around Bella and guided her back to bed. 'Sit tight, I'll go and make a cup of tea, then we can talk.'

Bella sat there feeling shaken and nauseous, it was starting to come back to her. The whole nightmare in technicolour. Despite it being another scorchingly warm day outside, she shivered and tucked the duvet right up under her chin.

'Here. Take this.' Mia handed her a mug of tea and sat down in the chair clutching her own mug.

Bella gazed miserably into her steaming tea for a while.

'Did it really happen?' she asked again, even though she knew the answer.

'Yes. I'm afraid so.'

'And Florence? Did they save her?' Again she was sure she knew the answer.

Mia shook her head. 'No. She died quickly.'

'If the police hadn't turned up, she would have killed me. I tried everything I could to get her to let me go, I hoped I'd come up with a plan, but I think she was just using the time to work out what she would do with me, how to dispose of my body,' she shuddered.

Mia wiped tears from her eyes, it didn't bear thinking about. She couldn't imagine life without her best friend.

'How did the police find me?'

'I'm not sure. Inspector Ormandy turned up at the tennis club looking for Florence, he was on the way to her house when he remembered that she usually played tennis with us on a Friday. When he turned up, we were puzzling over your text. At first I didn't think much about it, but when you didn't turn up at tennis I started to worry. Anyway when he came looking for Florence I mentioned it to him. He shot off like a startled rabbit and said that if you turned up, I needed to contact him immediately. Well, we then all started to worry frantically, but we had to stay at the tennis club in case you arrived. Jennifer went back and knocked on your door and looked through the windows and went into the garden.  When she reported that you weren't there I really started to panic.  It seemed like an eternity sitting up at the club, none of us felt like playing tennis.  We waited until half past six then I phoned Inspector Ormandy and told him that you still hadn't arrived and you weren't at home.  He said he was fairly sure where you were and that we should all go home.  None of us wanted to disperse, so everyone came back to my place, checking your house again on the way.  I kept trying your mobile, but it would ring and then go to answerphone.'

'Florence saw me use it.  I didn't think the text had gone.  She threw it on the floor and stamped on it.'  Bella sipped the hot tea, not noticing the sweetness from the sugar Mia had spooned into it, as Mia continued.

'It was a couple of hours or so later that I had a phone call from Dave,' she reverted to using his first name, 'to say that you were safe but could I go to your house and stay with you overnight.  We were mystified by this, but the others went home - apart from Jennifer who dropped her car at her house and walked down to join me.  I let us in as I had the spare keys and switched a few lights on, we waited and waited, eventually a police car arrived with you in it and Sergeant Swart escorted you in.  They'd contacted the on-call doctor who arrived shortly afterwards and gave you something to help you sleep.'  A vague memory of this stirred in Bella's mind.  'The sergeant gave us an edited version of what had happened, we were absolutely stunned and horrified.  Anyway, they've had a policeman outside all night and Jennifer and I were told not to contact the others as Kim needed to be told what had happened.  Jennifer stayed for a while, then she left and I've been with you ever since.'

Bella tried to absorb what Mia was telling her. It sounded like a work of fiction, something you might read in a novel, not something that could happen in a small village in Kent. If she hadn't gone poking about trying to find out who had killed Rupert, this might never have happened and Florence might still be alive. She whispered this to Mia who shook her head.

'You don't know that Bella and, from what you said, it sounds as though Florence was incredibly mentally unstable and could easily have killed herself anyway. Besides, even if she hadn't, she would have spent a large part, of her life - if not the rest of it - in a mental institution or possibly prison. I suspect it's unlikely she would have been fit to go to trial.

'What a waste of a life. Waste of several lives. You don't consider, do you, what the consequences of your actions might be. I mean, when something happens, you would never imagine what the ripple effect might be, that the ripples could continue for years to come. Like a stone being skimmed on open water - which in this case was Charles' death - and the ripples kept spreading out for years, encompassing the lives of many other people: Charles's family - particularly Florence - Rupert's family, Rupert himself, Kim. It goes on. How do we know that what we do now won't result in tragedy in thirty years time?'

'You can't think like that Bella. Nobody knows what's ahead, that's life. You can't predict the future. Charles's death was a terrible and tragic accident. Rupert didn't mean to kill him, he was just a foolish young teenager who thought he was having some fun, but it all went horribly wrong, no one could have predicted what would happen.

What Florence did was different, it was planned, pre-meditated, she deliberately set out to kill Rupert.'

'Yes, I know that, but if Charles had not died, this wouldn't have happened.'

'Maybe not. Maybe his death triggered something within her, or maybe she was genetically disposed to be the way she was. Maybe she would have found a reason to kill someone else. It's all speculation, she's dead and we will never know.' Deliberately changing the subject, she said. 'Let me get you another cup of tea and some toast.'

'I don't feel hungry.'

'Maybe not, but you've got to eat. Dave will be here soon. You do know that you will have to give a statement at some point, don't you?' she said gently.

Bella nodded miserably and disappeared under the duvet to try to forget. When Mia arrived back with the tea and toast, Bella picked at a couple of pieces whilst Mia stood sternly over her, determined that Bella would eat at least a little of the toast, which she eventually did. Reluctantly, Bella got out of bed - quite happy to stay there for ever - and got dressed. A little while later Dave turned up. Mia made them some coffee and left them in the sitting room together.

'How are you?' he asked tenderly.

'Okay, I suppose. Though I can't get my last sight of Florence out of my head.'

'It should fade eventually, but you had a major trauma yesterday. I wanted you to go to hospital to be checked over, but you flatly refused.'

'Did I?' She couldn't remember.

'Oh yes. You left me in no doubt that you weren't going to go,' he smiled at her. He made her feel safe.

'How did you know it was Florence?'

'Eventually we tracked down a car body shop about forty miles away, where a blue car had been repaired and re-sprayed. The owner said the woman wanted it done in a hurry and she didn't mind paying extra for it to be done quickly, and she paid cash. The name was Charlotte Willingham. Anyway, with a bit of old-fashioned detective work, we discovered it was Florence yesterday afternoon. It was only when Mia told me about your text that alarm bells started ringing and I became concerned about your safety. I knew that you couldn't resist poking about, trying to find out what had happened to Rupert, and my gut feeling was that, somehow, you had discovered who Florence actually was. The rest you know really.'

'I was so relieved that you turned up. I knew she was intending to kill me. I tried to persuade her that Kit could be framed for Rupert's death, and for a little while I really thought that she was going to go for it, but as the hours passed my hopes dwindled. I'm sure she was just biding her time, trying to work out how to dispose of me.' Bella shuddered at the memory. 'I guess I'll have to make a statement?'

'Yes, you will. You told me everything last night but you were not in very good shape, not surprisingly. There's no rush, take a day or two to recuperate.'

She didn't remember telling him anything last night, but most of what happened after Florence killed herself was a blur.

He took her hand. 'I was so worried about you. I don't know what I would have done if anything had happened to you.' He kissed her hand tenderly.

She smiled wanly at him. 'I'm glad you don't have to find out.'

They sat in a companionable silence for a little while until Kim popped into Bella's head.

'I assume Kim knows?'

'Yes. I informed her last night.'

'How did she take it?'

'Shocked. Devastated. She's not just lost a husband, but a friend - or someone she believed to be a friend - too, a friend who had deliberately set out - and succeeded - to murder her husband. I'm sure she'll want to talk to you when you feel up to it. You're the one person who will be able to answer all her questions. I can only tell her the facts as I know them, whereas you were there, the only one who heard-first hand from Florence, her twisted perspective.'

'I guess so.'

'It will probably help to talk about what happened anyway. Bottling it up won't do you any good.'

'No, I suppose not.' The last thing Bella felt like doing at the moment was talking to Kim, or anyone else for that matter, but experience had taught her, from Hugh's death, that there would be a time and a place when it would feel right, and that it would indeed help her and probably Kim too.

# Chapter Eighteen

A week later and still Bella could not bring herself to go out of the house. The horror of what had happened was as vivid and fresh in her mind as if it had happened a few minutes ago. She knew that she was being irrational in fearing that something similar might happen to her again if she left the house, but there was also the element of fear about what people were saying about her, the fear that they were holding her personally responsible for Florence's death, that she was to blame. Despite Mia's insistence that everyone she came across saw Bella as a heroine and not the criminal, Bella did not feel reassured. In her head she knew she was being irrational and she knew that Mia wouldn't lie to her, but she couldn't shake the thoughts from her head. Mixed in with the jumble of emotions was also the fear that she might bump in to Kim, and with that she would have to go over again what had happened on that terrible day. By hiding herself away she didn't have to face reality or Kim.

Though the sun was out the warmth - which had most people in t-shirts and shorts - did not permeate into Bella, who was wrapped up in a thick fleece and still feeling chilled to the bone. She clutched her cup of coffee tightly to her in an effort to warm herself up and stared blankly at yesterday's newspaper which Mia had dropped off, along with a few supplies. The ring of the door bell made her start and she narrowly missed spilling burning coffee over her lap. She didn't move, hopeful that whoever it was would go away, but the bell rang persistently. Bella's heart started to race in panic, as again and again the bell rang. Eventually she got up and walked to the front door, slipping the security chain on before she opened it.

She peered round the edge of the door and saw the petite figure of Kim standing on her doorstep, her brow was wrinkled in concern.

'Bella, how are you? Are you alright?'

'Er, fine.'

'Can I come in?' she asked gently.

Bella sighed. The moment she had dreaded had arrived. Perhaps it would be better to get it over and done with. She closed the door and slipped the security chain off, reopening the door a moment later, fearful of what Kim might say to her, convinced that she would be angry with her.

Kim stepped in through the door and gathered Bella up tightly in her arms. Startled, Bella burst into tears. Kim smoothed Bella's long, unkempt, straggly hair away from her face, then hugged her again, pushing the front door closed behind her with a shove of her foot. They stood there as Bella cried and howled, as the tide of terror of that day flooded from her, as she finally let go and released the inner pain she'd repressed. As her sobs receded, Kim led her through to the kitchen and sat her down at the table, then busied herself making them both fresh coffee.

Bella dabbed at her sore face and blew her nose on some kitchen roll.

'Sorry,' she murmured.

'For what?' replied Kim without turning around.

'For doing that. It's you who's upset. You're the one who has lost your husband.'

Kim glanced over her shoulder and shook her head. 'I've had weeks to mourn Rupert, and part of me always will. We didn't have a perfect marriage, far from it, but I did love him for a long time. But you are the one who has gone through the most unimaginably horrific ordeal. I can't begin to truly comprehend how terrible it was for you, and in some way I feel responsible.'

Bella's jaw dropped open. 'You? Responsible? That's ridiculous!'

'No it's not. I was married to Rupert and it was his actions in his past that caused Florence to do this, so in a strange way. I feel like it was partly my fault.'

'Absolute rubbish!' cried Bella vehemently. 'There's no way that any of it has got anything to do with you. You're the victim in all this.'

'And so are you Bella. No one is blaming you for what happened.' Bella looked startled. 'Mia told me what you've been thinking, and there is not one person who thinks it's your fault that Florence killed herself. They have nothing but admiration for you, for what you did. How on earth could you have known that Florence would do that? I think that if she hadn't killed herself then, she would have done so at the next opportunity she had.'

Bella looked uncertainly at her.

'Really Bella. Everyone thinks you're a heroine. You helped solve Rupert's murder. You found out who was responsible, and for that I will be eternally grateful. I cannot imagine spending the rest of my life not knowing who had killed him. You've given me peace of mind.'

'But the police discovered who had killed him.'

'You got there first, and if it hadn't been for you looking in to things, then maybe they never would have. Here,' she handed her a mug of coffee, 'and Sharon at the shop sent these up for you.' Kim handed her a thick pile of glossy magazines and today's newspaper.

'Wow, thanks. That was kind of her.' Bella felt a flicker of warmth ignite inside her.

'And these are from the delicatessen, with their compliments.' Kim unpacked a brown paper carrier bag, which was packed full of delectable salads, a portion of cooked lobster, a crisp lemon tartlet, and a large box of organic dark chocolates.

'Gosh! I can't believe it, that's so sweet and kind.' Bella felt touched, and reassured, and also slightly foolish that she had thought they might all turn on her.

Kim placed the chilled food into the fridge, and suggested they go outside and sit in the garden. Bella carried the box of chocolates out and tore of the cellophane, her appetite suddenly showing a flicker of interest in food. She offered them to Kim, who took a moment to choose one filled with a dark chocolate mousse, while Bella chose one with a champagne truffle filling. They sat in companionable silence for a minute, before Kim cleared her throat nervously.

'Would you … Would it …?' her voice trailed off.

'Would I what?' Bella glanced at Kim and then comprehended what she was trying to say. 'Would I mind telling you what happened? Is that what you'd like to know?'

Kim nodded. 'If you don't mind. I really don't want to upset you any further than you have been, but it would be a such a help if you could tell me, not just of that dreadful afternoon, before that, when you found out the awful truth about what happened when Rupert was younger.'

'I don't think Rupert meant to kill that child. From what was said to me, I believe it was an accident. And it changed the course of his life for ever.'

'I agree. Rupert was many things, but he wasn't a cold-blooded murderer.'

Bella started to recount what she had done, and what had happened, the tears flowed not just from Bella but from Kim too. After she had finished, and Kim had asked all the questions she needed answers for, they sat in silence, each feeling a sense of peace coming over them. It was time to attempt to start to move on, no matter how hard it might be.

# Chapter Nineteen

Two weeks later Bella had started to get back a semblance of the routine into her life in Monhurst. She had been embarrassed, but flattered, by all the attention and praise she had received when she had eventually ventured out of the house. Even now, people were still complimenting and praising her about it. She had gone with the others to Florence's funeral. Despite what Florence had done it had seemed the right thing to do. She had no family, no other friends and, in her crazy mixed up head, they had been her friends. It had always been about Rupert.

Bella was determined to have a good evening on the Saturday night three weeks after Florence's death. Tonight was the surprise party for Cressa, organised by Jack to celebrate their twenty-second wedding anniversary. Bella had been invited, and also had the option to bring a plus-one, so she'd asked Dave. In fact, it was Kim who suggested she bring him, reassuring her that there would be no awkwardness, that, in fact, Bella would be doing her a favour as she was unofficially going to be there with Seb.

Bella spent quite some time getting herself ready. She'd even gone as far as having her hair highlighted and cut that morning and spent the afternoon painting nails and relaxing. Looking at herself in the long mirror, she admired the slimmer her, in the pale pink silk wrap dress she'd purchased. Ironically, Florence's death had put her off eating and she'd lost quite a few pounds in the preceding three weeks.

Prompt as ever, Dave knocked at the door and smiled appreciatively at her when she opened it, complimenting her on how beautiful she looked. She glowed in response and admired his chinos, beautifully cut navy jacket and blue and white, wide-stripped smart shirt, and spotted blue and red silk tie.

The party was in the village hall so they didn't have far to walk. The hall was packed with friends and family of the couple. It had been meticulously planned by Jack over the previous six months, hence the secrecy and the cause for Cressa's concern with regard to the bank account. How shocked she would be when she found out the real reason! Bella grinned to herself. The champagne was flowing and delectable little canapés were being passed round. Jack had certainly gone to town. This would be followed by a five course sit-down meal, and a jazz band for dancing afterwards.

'Sssh, they're coming,' squeaked Mia excitedly. Henry and Emma, their two children, hid well out of sight and someone switched the lights off.

'I thought we were going out to dinner,' moaned Cressa in the distance, 'why on earth do we have to check on the hall on the way? Why can't you do it tomorrow?'

'Surprise!' yelled everyone, as the lights were switched on again.

And, for once, Cressa was at a loss for words. She burst into tears and hugged Jack so tightly it didn't look as though she'd let go. It was only when she was tapped on the shoulder by her children that she turned and let out a howl of excitement and clung on to them, tears pouring down her cheeks in delight.

'I can't believe you've done this!'

'It's taken a while,' replied Jack bursting with pride at his success, 'not quite the affair you thought it was, eh?' he joked.

Cressa, poked him in the arm and hugged him again, smothering him with kisses.

It was enough to make you weep. Bella felt all mushy inside, she caught Dave's eye who was grinning at her, he subtly squeezed one of her fingers tightly, and for a while she forgot all that had happened, and felt blissfully happy.

*Out Now...*

*Dead Fit*

*Dead Fit unites, for the first time, Bella and Kitty as they strive to uncover the perpetrator responsible for the wave of deadly crime ricocheting through their respective Kent villages of Monhurst and Wynenden.*

*Can they do this before it's too late...?*

Instagram @emelliotoffical

**www.emelliot.com**

Printed in Great Britain
by Amazon